Pets Amore

Four Romantic Comedy Novellas

Amy R. Anguish
Linda Fulkerson
Heather Greer
Beth E. Westcott

Scrivenings
PRESS
Quench your thirst for story.
www.ScriveningsPress.com

Published by Scrivenings Press LLC
15 Lucky Lane
Morrilton, Arkansas 72110
https://ScriveningsPress.com

Printed in the United States of America

Paperback ISBN 978-1-64917-450-5

eBook ISBN 978-1-64917-451-2

Editors: Amy R. Anguish, Elena Hill, and Linda Fulkerson

Cover design by Linda Fulkerson - www.bookmarketinggraphics.com

Out-of-the-box
Valentines

A Novella
by
Amy R. Anguish

For my parents, who didn't make me wait until I moved out to get that hamster I wanted. Thanks for supporting my dreams, big and small!

CHAPTER ONE

Trey Jones would do just about anything for his sister. Standing here, hamster cage in hand, his hyped-up six-year-old nephew beside him, and a room full of heart-shaped balloons ahead, he might have reached his limit. Was it Valentine's Day?

Of course it was. He knew the date. The significance had slipped his mind, not having anyone to shower with gifts on the over-commercialized holiday.

"Uncle Trey, look." Rylan hopped from foot to foot. Trey placed his free hand on Rylan's shoulder.

"I see." Though, considering the insane amount of pink and red before him, he might not ever see straight again. Even the petite woman going from seat to seat, tying the balloons in place, wore bright pink overalls over a red shirt. Her hair was done in two braids and crowned with a headband with springy hearts bouncing on top.

"Ms. Winters." Rylan shouted, even though she couldn't be more than five feet away.

She sprang up, eyes wide, the balloon slipping through her fingers and bumping against the ceiling. "Rylan, you're back."

"Guess what." Rylan reached over and grabbed Houdini's travel cage from Trey's hand. "I brought my show-and-tell since I was sick last week."

Ms. Winter's eyes widened for a split second before she controlled her expression. But Trey had noticed. Apparently bringing a show-and-tell item on a day when it wasn't scheduled hadn't been in the plans. Of course not. She obviously had a whole day of Valentine's craziness prepared. Should he offer to take the pet back home for today?

"Wow, Rylan. Um, what is it?" Ms. Winters took a few steps closer and leaned forward to peer into the plastic box. Then she jerked back, hand to her heart. "Is that a … mouse?"

"No." Rylan giggled and lifted the box higher.

Ms. Winters inched back.

"It's my hamster, Houdini."

This time, there was no denying the expression of slight terror that raced across the teacher's face, followed by a big gulp. Her voice was barely audible as she said, "Oh."

"I apologize." Trey stepped forward, hiding part of the cage with his arm. "In the chaos of Julie having me pick up Rylan, I didn't realize he wasn't supposed to bring Houdini."

Ms. Winters's attention turned to him. "I haven't met you before. You're Rylan's dad?"

"Uncle." Trey held out a hand. "Trey Jones. Rylan's dad is still deployed. And his mom caught the nasty bug Rylan had last week."

Her grip loosened in his. "She's not coming today?"

"Only if you want her to bring the flu with her."

"Okay." She pressed her fingers to her forehead. "It's going to be okay."

"Was she supposed to come in today for something?" Trey frowned. Julie hadn't mentioned needing to be at school today. Just that everything Rylan needed was in his backpack.

"Julie is the room mom who signed up to help with the

Valentine's activities today." Ms. Winters offered a half smile. "But it'll be fine. I mean, I don't have a helper here most days. I can handle it today too."

Yet something in her voice suggested she was on the verge of panicking. Trey stifled a groan. How had he ended up in this predicament? It was his day off. He'd agreed to drop off his nephew, not spend the day herding five-year-olds. Never had he ever imagined offering to do something like that. Even when he was assigned to visit classrooms to talk about fire safety, he let the other firefighters do the talking.

So why was he standing here, contemplating giving up his day of rest to hang out in this wonderland of pink and hearts? For Rylan? No. He wasn't worried about his nephew. For this cute little woman, all bedecked in holiday splendor? Could he be a calming force in this tornado of changes he'd wrought on her carefully laid plans?

He could help her out. He was a firefighter—walked into fires and emergencies all the time. How much harder could this be?

"I'll stay." Trey shrugged. "I told Julie I'd be her today. If that includes being room mom, I guess that means I'm here to help you too."

Deep down inside, Kimberly knew men could do things as well as women. But the very title—room *mom*—indicated it was a job for a female. And she knew nothing about Rylan's uncle except that he brought a rodent on Valentine's Day.

A hamster.

Not a mouse. *Not* a mouse.

Maybe if she repeated that to herself a hundred—million—

times, her heart would quit having flashbacks to her preteen years when her brother Seth had a pet snake. One who liked to eat such creatures. And Seth had loved to torment her with them.

"Ms. Winters?" Rylan tugged on her fingers. "Where should I put Houdini?"

She blinked, took a deep breath, and then scanned the room. Which corner would be the least likely for her to notice during the day? She pointed toward the fish tank.

"Why don't you set his cage beside our aquarium?"

"Great idea." Rylan beamed a gap-toothed smile and bounded that way.

His uncle rubbed his hands together and scanned the room as if it held a bomb or something else just as dangerous. "Okay. I've obviously never been a room mom before. Can you quickly give me an idea of what you'll need me to do today?"

"Hi, Ms. Winters." Caroline held an enormous box in her hands, practically bending in half backward to hold it up. "I made Valentines for everyone in the class. Even you!"

"That's wonderful, Caroline." Kimberly gently touched the girl's shoulder. "Why don't you see if you can fit that big box in your cubby until it's time for that part of our day, okay?"

Once the excited girl had rushed across the room, Kimberly returned her attention to the man next to her, the one with very serious hazel eyes. "Guess we better do this quickly before everyone gets here."

He followed her to the desk and leaned over while she pulled her planner to the front. "Here's my plan for the day. We always have a schedule for Tuesdays, but since this one is a holiday, I incorporated the Valentine's theme in each of my lesson plans. I also had to shorten the lesson time, so we'll have time for our party at the end. It gets a bit crazy, but the kids soak it up."

She glanced his way to see if he was following her. His eyes were glazed.

He blinked. "I'm a firefighter. Lesson plans are a bit of a foreign language to me."

"Mostly, I need you as an extra set of hands. It gets a little wild on days like this, as I'm sure you can imagine. Everyone is excited, and they usually eat more sugar than normal. Having an extra adult to ... well ... put out fires, I guess, will be a big help."

"Putting out fires I can do." Trey lifted a brow. "Dealing with sugar-hyped kindergarteners?"

"I'm sure you'll do great." She glanced at her planner once more, running her finger over the morning schedule. "I guess we'll squeeze in Rylan's show-and-tell here. Right before they go to P.E."

"Sorry again about that." Trey ran a hand over his closely shorn hair. "I had no idea it wasn't actually show-and-tell day. Julie didn't have much energy or voice this morning."

"It's fine. One thing we kindergarten teachers know how to do is roll with the punches." She cut a glance in the direction of the hamster. Rolling with rodents was another thing completely. She muttered, "Despite how it might seem right now."

Deep breaths. She could not let herself break down over a pest no bigger than her palm—not in front of the students. Or their uncles. She tugged at the end of her braid, whispered a prayer that God would keep that hamster in his cage all day, and then straightened her back to greet four more students.

"Where can I help first?" Trey's gaze bounced all over the room as if he couldn't find a safe place for his focus to land.

"How about rescuing that balloon I lost earlier?" She pointed to the ceiling.

"I'm on it." He didn't even need to balance on a desktop to reach the end of the string, as she would've had to do. How nice was that? Maybe having a guy room mom wasn't such a bad thing after all.

"Ms. Winters, this is for you." Nolan handed her a small box.

9

She took it and knelt to his level before lifting the lid to find sparkly earrings, much longer than she would normally wear. "Wow, Nolan! Did you pick these out yourself?"

He nodded.

"Thank you so much." She squeezed his arm. "Go put your things in the cubby, okay? We're going to start soon."

As the rest of her twenty-five students filed in, all eager to share something with her or show off their treats for later, she soaked it in. This was what the holiday was supposed to be like. All about the children and their happiness.

Several boys congregated with Rylan around his uncle. If Trey was uncomfortable with the attention, he didn't show it outwardly. Maybe this day wouldn't be as bad as she'd feared, after all.

Kimberly clapped three times. "Macaroni and cheese."

The whole class replied, "Everybody freeze."

Trey lifted a brow, but there was no way he could deny how well it had worked. Every wiggly body in her classroom was still and facing her.

"Please take your seats. We've got some extra-fun lessons planned for today to celebrate Valentine's Day all day long. But we can only do extra-fun things if you're good listeners. Show me how great you're going to listen today."

Only a few whispers and giggles escaped as all the children sat at their desks. Morning announcements crackled over the speaker in the corner, and Kimberly gathered her conversation hearts. Time to sweeten up their math lesson.

"Why do you have chalk candy?" Trey's whisper in her ear caught her off guard, and several hearts fell to the ground.

She knelt to scoop them up and throw them away. "It's not made of chalk."

"Tastes like it."

"Well, lucky for you, you don't need to learn graphing, so you won't need to eat them."

"Sure about that?" One corner of his lips lifted into enough of a grin to cause a dimple to form. That was unexpected.

What had she been about to say? "Sure about you not needing to learn graphing? Or eating the candy?"

Trey chuckled, and the sound skittered all through her middle. What was going on with her?

He held out his hand so she could give him some of the candy too. "I meant the math, but I can see I'll have to be careful around you. You can hold your own."

"Have to be able to around all these kids."

The kids who now watched her and Trey in the otherwise quiet classroom. How long ago had the announcements finished? She needed to get her head on straight. Just because today was supposed to be a romantic holiday didn't mean she had to give in to the insanity of the rest of the world. She never had before, and not all records were meant to be broken.

Time to move back into teacher mode and pretend Trey was exactly like his sister Julie.

Except taller.

And with some stubble on his cheeks.

And shorter hair. And a deep voice that had a bit of a rumble to it.

Kimberly's imagination might not be strong enough for this task.

CHAPTER TWO

Ms. Winters spun around quickly and faced the students. "One, two, three. Eyes on me."

Trey started to roll his eyes but froze as the kids chanted in return, "One, two, eyes on you." And they did, for the most part, focus in her direction.

Did she have some sort of magical powers? First with the mac 'n cheese saying, and now this? Did Julie know these tricks to get Rylan's attention?

The only thing he regretted about her powers was that with him standing next to her, he was now also in the center of attention. All those little faces pointed straight at him. Maybe staying today wasn't such a good idea, after all. Flashbacks to every single time he'd had to be the center of attention in school sent a familiar wave of ice through his veins.

Not today. He should be past this all these years later.

"Okay, guys. What have we been learning in math lately?" Ms. Winters spoke, and Trey's breath eased up slightly. They weren't really looking at him—mostly.

A few little hands raised. She pointed to a tiny girl near the front with glasses that made her eyes look like an owl's. "Yes, Emory."

"Graphs and charts."

"Perfect." Ms. Winters beamed at the class while keeping her candy clutched to her side where it wasn't as visible. "Today, instead of using our cubes, we're going to make this a bit more festive." She lifted the pink bag for all to see.

The volume in the room increased by five hundred percent. How was that possible? But Ms. Winters quickly got things back under control with a few quick claps.

"Before we can do anything, I need you all to make me a promise." Her gaze roamed over the expanse of the pink wonderland known as her classroom. "You cannot eat these. They are for counting only. Do you understand me?"

"But Ms. Winters?" A boy near the back raised his hand. "Why are we using candy if we can't eat it?"

It was a fair question, though Trey debated the boy's usage of the term *candy* in this case. Conversation hearts were nasty—right up there with candy corn and those marshmallow rabbits. Still, he wondered the same thing. Did that mean he thought more on the level of a kindergartener?

"Because we're going to be having candy and cupcakes later during our party." Ms. Winters wiggled her fingers. "And this candy is for counting and drawing charts on your paper. Which means it could get dirty. No one wants to eat dirty candy."

A few *ews* sounded around the room.

Ms. Winters nodded. "Okay. Mr. Jones and I are going to give you each twenty hearts. I want you to sort them, and then we're going to fill in the graph on your math paper to show how many of each color you have. Go ahead and get out your crayons so you can be ready.

"Another reason to not eat the candy is because we're going to use it for our science lesson today."

Was the whole day going to revolve around candy? Trey's

fingers were already stickier than normal. How come he didn't remember doing anything like this when he was in elementary school? All they did was have a little party at the end of the day.

Of course, Trey's kindergarten teacher had been about eighty-five years old, with gray curls and orthopedic shoes. Or at least fifty. Old enough that one day, he'd accidentally called her "Grandma" instead of "Mrs. Carroway." Instead of using the conversation hearts for lessons, she'd given each child a box of them to take home and eat.

"Uncle Trey, isn't this the best day ever?" Rylan grinned up at him as Trey counted out twenty hearts onto the desk.

"The best." Trey winked and moved on to the owl-eyed girl. She grinned as big as Rylan had, and Trey couldn't help but smile in return. Yeah. Maybe this day wouldn't be so bad. So far, Ms. Winters had everything under control. Did she really even need him here?

"Alistair!" Ms. Winter's sharp voice broke into Trey's euphoria. "What did I tell you? No eating the candy."

"But I know what color I ate." The blond head ducked. "I can still color it on my chart."

"If I catch you eating any more, you'll have to use the blocks like normal. *Capice?*"

"Caposh." His little dejected reply sent a chuckle through Trey, which he quickly covered with a cough. Laughter probably wasn't good room mom protocol.

Ms. Winters met his gaze with a gleam in her eye, and he couldn't look away. Was he in trouble, or was she simply sharing the funny moment with him? "Did you get all your candy passed out?"

Trey blinked and glanced at all the nearby desks. "I think so."

"Is there anyone who didn't get their hearts?" Ms. Winters spun in a circle. "Great. I want to see some amazing charts. Who wants to help me make one on the board?" Her pink-clad little legs moved quickly toward the whiteboard, and she uncapped a marker.

And Trey couldn't tear his gaze away from her.

After math, Kimberly planned to transition straight into their messy science center. That way, the students could wash their hands before library time. She worked to keep her attention on the students and not keep glancing toward the firefighter, who was collecting the used candy from their desks.

With everyone gathered around the large table on the other side of the room, she set out four cups. "Okay, guys. Today, we're going to do an experiment and see how different liquids react to the candy. Who is excited?"

The children bounced on their toes, leaning over the edge of the table to get as close as possible. Kindergarten had its tough moments, but watching these little people be so excited to learn made it all worth it. As she pulled out the bottles of water, vinegar, soda, and juice, she was practically giddy herself.

"We're going to pour some of each of these liquids into a cup in a few minutes to see if the hearts will sink or float. Before we do that, I want you to pick a cup and put in the heart candy you chose to bring over here."

Several simply dropped their piece into the cup closest to them, but, of course, Malachi and Max, the twins, wanted the cups farthest from where they were standing. Trey placed a hand on each of their heads before they trampled little Emory. Kimberly shot him a grateful glance. Worth it to have him here today, if only for that one moment right there.

"Now, let's develop our theory. Raise your hand if you think the hearts will sink in the water." She marked the votes on a poster she'd prepped for this. "Now, who thinks they will float?" Repeating it for each liquid, she finished the graph. "Ready to see what will happen?"

Carefully, she poured the liquids about three-fourths of the way up the glasses. Of course, the only liquid the hearts floated in was the fizzy cola. She updated their chart with what had happened versus what they had predicted.

"Now, let's do one more thing. Let's add something else to the ones that didn't float and see if we can make it change."

"Yay," several kids shouted.

Pulling out a box of baking soda, she scooped a spoonful into the water. "Here, Paisley. You stir."

The little girl stirred, a bit of the liquid sloshing out. Nothing happened except the hearts spinning around and around.

Next, she added some to the juice and let Isaac stir. Again, no change.

She met Trey's eyes across the table, and he grinned. He'd probably done a volcano project in school, just as she had. She added the baking soda to the vinegar, and everyone gasped as the bubbles started automatically. Exactly the reaction she'd hoped for. No need to stir this one.

The homemade heart volcano continued erupting for over three minutes. Then she ushered the kids into a line at the handwashing stations to quickly scrub up and wait at the door for library time. So far, this day was going exactly as planned.

Her gaze landed on the hamster cage across the room, and she quickly looked away. Almost exactly.

CHAPTER THREE

After the exciting math and science lessons, Trey expected the kids to be wound up and rowdy, walking down the hall to the library. Especially as they passed other aides and helpers heading the opposite direction, arms full of flowers and ... were those cookies?

Instead, Ms. Winters told them to "put a bubble in their mouths and hold their hands behind their backs." Each student lined up diligently, cheeks puffed out, and fingers clasped behind them. Was she secretly a witch?

Safely under the supervision of the librarian, the kids settled in for a story before being allowed to pick a book to take home for a few days. Ms. Winters crooked a finger at Trey, and he followed her back toward the room.

"What now, oh, Fearless Leader?" Trey caught himself clasping his own hands behind his back and quickly freed them to swing at his sides again.

"Well, something tells me we have lots of goodies to sort through."

"Goodies?"

"Did you not see the cookie-grams and carnations being

delivered as we walked by?" Ms. Winters checked her smartwatch. "We have about fifteen minutes to get them all sorted."

"Cookie … grams." Trey blinked. Seriously, when did Valentine's Day become so complicated?

The table that had been full of science-experiment mess was now covered in flowers and little baggies of cookies. They had to sort all this in fifteen minutes? Ms. Winters quickly set to work, picking up a few items and turning them over where he could see the child's name.

"Different students or family members can order these through the PTO each year. They're delivered today, and we have to sort them and send them home with the right student. Since the boxes they brought will be full of cards after the party, I picked up some bags." She pointed to the cubbies and a canvas bag on top of each spot. "If you can help me get everything in the right bags, that would be so much help."

"Sure." He glanced at the bags again. "I assume all the kids' names are over there too."

"Yes, in alphabetical order … it's easier on me."

"Perfect." He stepped that way with a handful of cookies.

"Oh." She held up a slightly bent red flower. "And if you find any of these with my name on them, I have a vase standing ready over here."

He cocked his head. "That's so sweet. They buy you flowers?"

"The only flowers I get." She smiled, but it didn't quite meet her eyes like it had earlier when she was talking with her students.

"Your boyfriend doesn't send you flowers?" Why had he gone and asked something like that? Her love life was none of his business, though he had noticed her ring finger was bare. Not that it mattered. He was just helping out Julie … and in turn, Kimberly—Ms. Winters.

Must be all this pollen from the flowers. Scrambling his brain.

"No boyfriend." She set the poor flower in her vase and dusted her hands.

His heart danced a little jig, though he couldn't figure out why. Maybe the fumes from the vinegar earlier were affecting him somehow. Or could sugar creep into his veins through osmosis? Could he have a sugar high without actually eating any of it?

"You okay?" She brushed past him to slip some cookies in a bag.

"Yep. Sorry. Just zoned out for a moment." He shook his head and then continued searching for Charlie's bag. There. Charlie must be popular. Three cookies were addressed to him. Or was Charlie a her?

"I know this isn't how you wanted to spend your day." She slipped a couple flowers into another bag. "I really do appreciate your help."

"Not a problem." He scooped up a few more cookies. "Seriously. Think nothing of it."

She glanced at her watch again. "I'll need to go get the students in a few more minutes."

The pile was still pretty high. "I've got this. It's what I'm here for, right? What a room mom would do?"

Her lips tilted up more naturally this time. "Yes."

"Okay, then. You do what you need to do, and I'll continue sorting cookies and carnelians." Her giggle froze his hand, where he untangled the stems of several flowers. "What?"

"Carnations." She reached in and pulled a few flowers free so the others would come apart more easily. "These are carnations."

"Right." He passed one with her name on it to her. "Your favorite flower?"

She shook her head even while breathing in a sniff. "Roses

19

are my favorite. I guess I'm one of those girls. But carnations are cheaper and last much longer. So, I don't mind receiving a few for Valentine's Day each year. They brighten my desk and remind me my kids love me."

"How can they not?" The words slipped from his mouth before he could stop them.

She blinked at him for a second, seemingly frozen where she stood. Then, she spun, placed the flower in the vase, and pointed to the door. "I better go grab those kids before the librarian comes to find me."

As soon as the children saw Trey passing out the flowers and cookies, a switch flipped. Before, Kimberly had been able to maintain control. But now they were squealing and jumping around and spinning in circles, and the twins were even climbing on their desks to bat at the balloons.

Kimberly placed her hand on her head and said, "Hands on top."

Almost every wiggly body froze and put their hands on their head before replying, "Everybody stop."

"Malachi and Max, you too." Kimberly shot them her best teacher look, though she still wasn't sure she'd perfected it.

The boys scrambled down to the floor, snickering, but obediently put their hands on their heads.

"Thank you all for listening so well. I know it's super exciting today, especially seeing all those goodies to take home, but right now, we need to get through a few more lessons before we can get to the fun stuff." Kimberly motioned them into their seats. "Plus, if we can do our lessons quickly enough, Rylan has a special treat for us today since he missed show-and-tell on Friday."

Whispers ran through the room but quickly died as she tapped the board.

"It's time to practice our sight words. But today, we're going to do it like Valentine spies."

Trey tilted his head and studied her, but she tried to ignore him. She'd worked too long and hard on this exercise to let someone else's doubts ruin the fun. She pulled out a set of heart-shaped glasses with red lenses.

"These are our decoder glasses. I have pages that look like this," she lifted one with her other hand, "with secret messages hidden underneath the red squiggles. With these glasses, you can see which words are our sight words for this week and which are not. Look very closely. Underneath each squiggle blob is a set of lines. Below the ones that are sight words, I want you to write the sight word for me. Do it as neatly as you possibly can, and we'll count this for handwriting work too. Any questions?"

"What if there isn't a word under the red squiggles?" Grace shot her hand up as she asked the question instead of waiting to be called on. Something they'd been working on all year.

"There are words under every single red squiggle." Kimberly ought to know. She'd printed out the pages of words in green font, and then hand scribbled each and every single squiggle-blob over the words so that the kids would have to use the glasses to see them. She'd had to do several extras before she found the right combination of marker and printer ink. Seven, to be exact.

Before she could ask for his help, Trey took the stack of sight word papers from her to pass out. She blinked herself back into focus. Right. Glasses. Each child got a pair of the heart-shaped frames, and she couldn't help but smile as she looked out over the class with their red lenses and expressions of concentration.

"Hey! There are words," Rylan exclaimed and started writing *want* under the first red squiggle on his page.

A squeaking sound started behind her, and Kimberly spun around to find the source. The hamster raced in his little maroon wheel inside the plastic cage on the counter. Her heart sped up as if to keep time to the rodent's exercise.

Wait. Was the squeaking in time to the tune from *Jaws*? The beady little eyes of the creature stared straight at her as if to let her know he knew exactly what he was doing to her pulse.

"What's that?" Several kids asked, neglecting their tasks to look up.

Kimberly spun around and met the concerned gaze of Trey. *I'm fine. Nothing to see here. Just a crazy kindergarten teacher who can't move past the trauma of my brother hiding a mouse in my bed when I was thirteen. No big deal.*

Kimberly cleared her throat and tried to smile at the kids.

"That's Rylan's surprise for later. Right now, though, you need to focus on what you're supposed to be doing." Just like Kimberly needed to focus too. Though her focus was more on ignoring the creature behind her ... and the handsome man across the room. The one who seemed to be exactly where she needed him when she needed him. And was dealing with the chaos like a champ.

How was she supposed to ignore such perfection? Especially when he had asked about her having a boyfriend—and seemed happy with her reply.

No.

No boyfriends. This day was bad for relationships. A fact she'd proven more than once and didn't plan to prove again.

$\mathcal{M}$ s. Winters's magical sayings lost their potency as the day progressed. Not that Trey wasn't still impressed with her ability to keep twenty-five children in line on a super-exciting day. So much so, in fact, that he was tempted to try some of those sayings next time he was called to a fire.

Would "one, two, three, eyes on me" work on people in an emergency?

As the party neared, the wiggles and giggles increased among the students. Ms. Winters actually had to say "macaroni and cheese" three times at the end of centers before having everyone's attention so they could line up for lunch.

Wait. Trey looked at the clock. Why were they going to lunch at ten forty-five in the morning? Did it take them that long to get to the cafeteria?

"Did you say lunch?" Trey fell into step beside the teacher as she moved into the hallway.

"Yes. The school is small. Only so much space." She snapped behind her. "Malachi, back in line."

The boy hopped a little closer to where he was supposed to be.

"Anyway, they stagger cafeteria use. Kindergarten goes first. We always have a snack in the afternoon to tide us over due to the early lunchtime."

"But before eleven?"

"The kids don't seem to mind." She shrugged. "By the time we get to this part of the day, they're usually starving."

Thinking back on his growing years, Trey could believe it. For several years, he'd believed he'd never not be hungry. His mom probably had to take out a second mortgage just for groceries.

"Because you've been such a huge help today—on a day when you were supposed to be resting—" she touched his bicep as the kids filed past into the cafeteria either to the kitchen area or the tables, "I insist on treating you to lunch."

Trey leaned close. "Is it pizza day? That was the only day I wanted to buy school lunch growing up."

"Sadly, it is not." Ms. Winters faked a frown around the glimmer of humor wrinkling the skin around her eyes. "I think today is a chicken sandwich and fries with fruit cup and drink."

Trey grinned. "As long as there are fries."

"Pretty much every day. Isn't that a requirement?" She motioned him toward the kitchen.

They sat at a table close enough to the students that they could still help open juice pouches and fruit cups, but tall enough that their knees would fit. She bowed her head for a few moments, obviously blessing her food. Definitely made it less awkward when he did the same, finding himself thankful for this day … and surprising himself with a request to learn more about this woman.

Trey studied his tray—possibly one of the same ones used all the way back when he was a student here—and picked up some of his double helping of fries. A bit soggy, but not bad.

"I suppose I owe you more than that, really." Ms. Winters

motioned toward his lunch. "You've been a huge help when you didn't have to be."

"You don't owe me anything, Ms. Winters."

"Kimberly." Her pink lips turned up in a smile before she turned back to her chicken sandwich.

"Kimberly." He repeated before dragging a few more fries through his ketchup. It suited her. Bright and cheerful, friendly. Except when she happened to glance at Houdini. What was it about the hamster that threw her off her groove so much? Because it was obvious there was more to it than his unexpected arrival on a holiday.

"Ms. Winters, is our party right after this?" Rylan shoved his milk carton under her nose.

Trey reached over and gently took the carton from his nephew so Kimberly didn't have to breathe in the cardboard.

"Not yet, Rylan. First, Circle Time and your show-and-tell. Then, P.E. *Then*, the party." She ticked each activity off on her fingers. "Almost."

"Yippee!" Rylan jumped, sloshing a bit of the now-opened milk on the edge of the table. "Oops."

"Go finish your lunch so we can get to the rest of our day." Kimberly squeezed his nephew's shoulder, and she might as well have been squeezing his heart. She was so good with these kids, even when they were a bit wild or made mistakes.

"What?" She raised her brows, making him realize he was staring.

"Nothing. Just wondering how you do this every day." He took a big bite before he said anything else.

"It's easy when you fall in love with them."

The words ricocheted in his head. She was talking about her students, but could she fall in love with other people just as easily? One other person in particular?

Ridiculous thought. He'd only known her a handful of hours.

They'd hardly even had a chance to talk. How could he be thinking such things?

But it might be worth exploring, right? Would she be open to such an idea? Was there anything against teachers dating their students' uncles?

This day was headed downhill in a hurry. Kimberly tried to keep a neutral face as she shepherded her students to the Circle Time rug. But it was hard not to let the guilt overcome her.

She had used her *angry* voice coming back from lunch. She hated using her angry voice. Not only did it not really do any good, but it left her feeling separated from the kids. Because they all looked at her warily, as if she might explode again. Why, oh, why hadn't she counted to three—or three hundred—when Max and Malachi decided to try sword fighting with their leftover fries, only to spill poor Emory's milk and ruin the rest of Brooke's sandwich?

Even Trey was glancing at her sideways now. After all, he'd been bragging about how impressed he was with her ability to control the kids, and then *kablooey!*—she'd lost it. Not that she worried that much about what a student's uncle thought of her. But she wasn't proud of her actions right now. Time to try to smooth ruffled feathers and get through the rest of this day.

"Hands on top." She patted her head, knocking her bouncy hearts askew.

"Everybody stop," most of the kids replied.

"One more time." Kimberly straightened her headband and said, "One, two, three, eyes on me."

"One, two, eyes on you," all but one or two sat quietly and looked her way.

Probably as good as it was going to get at this point. Kimberly pulled her daily info board to right beside her and pointed to the slot marked "month." "Who can tell me today's date?"

Grace bounced on her knees, hand as high as she could stretch it in the air. "Valentine's Day!"

"Please wait to be called on, Grace." Kimberly smiled as she scolded the girl. "And that's the holiday today, but do you know what the *date* is?"

After another child gave the answer, Grace's hand shot back up. "Ms. Winters?"

"Yes, Grace?"

"I think Valentine's Day is the bestest holiday ever. My daddy gave my mommy a bunch of flowers this morning, and she kissed him on the lips!"

A variety of groans, giggles, and gagging noises worked through the group. Great. Now she would have to regain control all over.

I will not use my angry voice again.

I will not use my angry voice.

"Okay, okay." Kimberly tried the clapping rhythm, and most of the children calmed enough for her to talk to them. "What Grace said is very nice for mommies and daddies, but let's get our focus back to what we're doing now so we can have time for Rylan's show-and-tell, okay? Then P.E., then after that, we'll get to have our party."

"Ms. Winters?" Braxton raised his hand. "Do you have a Valentine? Did you get a bunch of flowers too?"

Kimberly took a deep breath in through her nostrils, trying to calm her speeding heart. She'd never had a Valentine. A fact she preferred not to dwell on and the reason she was trying to avoid any niggles of attraction toward her helper.

Most children thought the opposite sex was icky. Why couldn't Grace be like them? Why did she have to be so

27

obsessed with romance that the whole class followed her down this rabbit hole?

"Didn't you see all the flowers Ms. Winters received?" Trey's answer caught her off guard. Where was he going with this?

Several of the children looked around as if searching for a huge bouquet of roses.

"See?" Trey moved to right beside the vase on her desk, the one with all the carnations. "Ms. Winters has a bunch of Valentines. They sent her these beautiful flowers." Trey fingered one of the flowers.

"Did you send her one?" Max, of course.

Trey blinked. He wasn't used to the audacity of children's curiosity like she was.

"I did not. I didn't even know about these carnations before today. But she received so many already. She's having a great Valentine's Day. But you know what would make it an even better day? If you let her finish your lesson. I know Rylan is eager to share his show-and-tell with you."

Before Kimberly could shoot him a grateful expression, Grace's hand popped up again and again she didn't wait before asking, "If you had sent her flowers, would she give you a big kiss like my mommy gave my daddy?"

More giggles and gags.

Trey shot her a look she couldn't decipher. Was he mortified? Humiliated? Regretting every decision that led him to this exact moment of this day? Intrigued?

Where had that last one come from? That couldn't be right. Kimberly blinked herself back to the task at hand. Regaining control of this rampaging chaos.

"Grace, that's not appropriate." Kimberly's face burned. "Mr. Jones and I are not married or a mommy or daddy. And you're still not waiting until we call on you to ask questions. Do you need to be in the quiet corner for a few minutes?"

Grace ducked her head. "No, ma'am."

"Thank you." Kimberly tapped her board. "Let's go through these answers quickly so we can have time for Rylan's show-and-tell before P.E., okay?"

"But—" another student started.

"No. Unless it has to do with the weather or the time, we're not talking about it right now."

Or ever. Ever would be even better. Because how embarrassing had this all been? As if a handsome firefighter would even consider kissing someone like her. She wasn't exactly throwing off "Kiss me" vibes with these bouncy hearts on her head. Nor any other time.

Because she had sworn off romance on Valentine's Day for the rest of her life.

It didn't matter. All that mattered was making sure the kids had a great Valentine's Day. Then she could go home and stuff herself with all the chocolate they'd brought her. Soak in a tub and forget about hamsters and intriguing uncles and anything else that might fall into those categories.

Living for the chocolate.

CHAPTER FIVE

"*R*ylan's uncle is going to help him with his show-and-tell now. Everyone stay seated, please."

Kimberly hadn't actually asked Trey to help with this part, but she physically could not be near that creature. She stepped out of the circle and moved as far away as she thought she could without the children noticing.

If she weren't so responsible, she'd slip out the door. But no. She was a grownup woman, in charge of twenty-five little people. She could handle this. As long as she was on the other side of the room.

Trey lifted a brow but said nothing as he helped Rylan carry the cage over to the rug. Rylan wiggled something on top and lifted a flap. Wait.

"What are you doing?" Kimberly's voice came out way too high, but there was no way she could control it as her student reached his hand down into the cage.

"Don't worry, Ms. Winters. Houdini is super friendly." Rylan flashed her a grin and wrapped his fingers around the animal.

Kimberly's hand rested at her throat, where a lump had settled, making her wonder if she'd ever swallow again.

"Here, Ry. Why don't you let me hold him, just in case?" Trey caught the hamster before it could wiggle free. Because it had definitely been trying to wiggle free.

Kimberly stepped back another foot.

Breathe in, breathe out. Breathe in, breathe out. This is not a mouse. Nor being held by her brother. It was a hamster. A cute, little, innocent … beady-eyed … nose-twitching-as-if-it-could-sniff-out-her-lifelong-fear … rodent.

"Houdini is my hamster." Rylan proudly announced to his classmates. "We got him because the neighbor's hamster had baby hamsters and they offered one to me. All the others got eaten up by the mommy hamster."

"Maybe let's not tell that part." Trey stage whispered.

"Right." Rylan nodded seriously. "Houdini lives in a bigger cage in my room with long tubes that stretch out of it so he can run around and slide. And two wheels. Sometimes they're really noisy when I sleep at night, but Mommy says he can't live in her room. This is only his travel cage. It's much smaller. And he has a plastic ball I can put him in, and he rolls all over the house. But then mommy complains about his poop everywhere."

Giggles burst from the group. Rylan was quite the storyteller. If only the story he was telling were one Kimberly could appreciate. Instead, the face of the beast was giving her serious flashback trauma.

"Do you want to pet him?" Rylan asked before either adult could stop him.

Of course, almost every hand went up, and several kids were already jumping to their feet to scoot closer. Trey looked her way as if silently to ask permission. Kimberly swallowed and gave a half nod.

"Macaroni and cheese." But her voice was barely a squeak.

Trey's voice sounded much louder. "Macaroni and cheese."

"Everybody freeze." And they did.

"If you want to pet Houdini, you have to sit on your bottom

and be very still. If you get too wild, he'll bite me, and then we'll have to put him back in his cage." Trey's fingers never wavered from their grip on the animal, despite the words that sent shivers down Kimberly's spine. How could he be so calm with such a risk in hand? Literally.

But everyone did as he asked, and he carefully stepped through all the bodies, letting them all have a turn to pet the tiny head between his pink ears. Kimberly rammed her hands into her pockets to keep anyone from noticing her fingers trembling. Had he been through everyone now? Two more.

Rylan started her way. "You want to pet him, Ms. Winters?"

"I don't think we have time, bud." Trey caught the little boy before he could get any closer to her. "Isn't it time for P.E.?"

"Yes." Kimberly straightened. "Everyone, line up while Rylan puts Houdini back in his cage. And make sure you thank him for sharing his pet with you today. I know that was an unexpected treat."

Trey's lips quirked up at her statement as if he could hear the emphasis she'd so carefully avoided on the *unexpected* part of it. He waited while Rylan fiddled with the cage a few more moments but never took his eyes off her standing next to the door. Now what was running through his head? Would he tease her for her irrational fear? Did he think she was a silly nincompoop?

"Are we going now, Ms. Winters?" Alistair tugged on her sleeve.

"Yes. Yes, we are. Bubbles in your mouth, everyone."

And for good measure, maybe she should keep one in her own mouth the rest of the day.

"You want to talk about it?" Trey looked up from where he'd been cleaning up the last traces of the science projects.

Kimberly glanced his way and then headed to the cubbies. "About what we need to do next before the kids get back from P.E.?"

"Not what I meant, and you know it."

The perky, well-organized, together woman from earlier in the day had disappeared somewhere along the way. Because of the hamster? Or Trey's presence?

"Well, we need to move all these fancy boxes from their cubbies to their desks. That way, when they get back, they can pass out all their cards." She held up a shoebox decorated with so many stickers, Trey could barely make out the name on the side. "The names are on the desks, as well as the cubbies, so it's just a matter of matching."

"Kimberly." He caught her elbow as she moved past him.

She stilled. Was she regretting allowing him to use her first name? Or was it something else?

"I'll help with this if you'll start talking about what happened earlier. Looked like some pretty major trauma running through your head."

"What makes you so qualified for me to spill my guts?" Kimberly tugged her arm free. "Are you a shrink as well as a firefighter?"

"No." He ran his fingers through his short hair. "But I am the chaplain."

"You are?"

Was it so hard to believe? He needed to do a better job of wearing that title as much as the other. Of shining his light, so to speak.

"I am." He turned and moved to grab a few boxes, noting the names before searching for them among the desks. Maybe if he didn't focus on her, she'd be more comfortable letting him in.

"My brother had a snake."

Well, that wasn't what Trey was expecting. And how did a snake have anything to do with a hamster freaking her out? He stayed quiet, delivering boxes and waiting for her timing.

"Of course, the snake had to eat. And what do snakes eat?" She stopped and looked him dead in the eye. "Mice."

"Right." Things started to click into place.

"Except my brother thought it was hilarious how much I didn't like the mice. He had to work a job at the pet store to be able to afford them. And he could have fed the ..." she shuddered "snake something else. But he thought it was funny to watch the mice try to get away."

Everything within Trey itched to reach for her, but would she let him?

"Needless to say, he also enjoyed terrorizing me with the mice before he fed his pet. I found one in my bed—"

That was it.

"The little feet, scurrying up my leg—"

"I'm so sorry." His words were pointless. Empty. But what else could he do?

"I know in my head there's nothing the same about Rylan's hamster and those mice, but—" she motioned toward the cage. "They look so ... similar."

Her eyes widened, her skin going pale, and he followed the direction of her gaze. What was she looking at? He moved closer to the counter. What?

The door on top of the cage stood open.

CHAPTER SIX

rey had never seen a person move so fast. One moment, Kimberly was standing on the floor, Valentine's box in hand. The next, she was standing on the nearest chair, frantically searching the ground.

"Oh, no. Oh, no. He's escaped. Where is he? Do you think he's on the floor somewhere?" Kimberly spun around and squealed. "What if he got out the door? He could be anywhere in the whole school!"

"He might not even be out. Maybe we just left the cage open on accident." Trey tried to maintain a calm voice to offset the rising panic dancing on the tiny chair behind him. "See?" He pushed the bedding around a bit, but no tan and white fur showed up hidden in any of the corners as he hoped. So much for that theory.

"Is he in there?" Kimberly's voice was barely a whisper.

Trey slowly turned her way, hands out as if she were a wild horse. An analogy rather fitting, considering how wide her eyes were right now, but probably not appropriate. Or appreciated.

"Deep breath. We'll find him."

She squeaked and started looking down again, holding the bottoms of her overalls up as if they were a fancy skirt. "Where could he be? Wait. Can hamsters climb? Mice can climb straight up walls. Can hamsters? Oh. Of course they can. I mean, he would've had to climb to get out of his cage. And they have all those tubes they climb around in—"

She jumped up on top of the nearest desk, her breaths quick and rapid between the words spewing out of her mouth faster than a vinegar volcano.

Of all the things to name a hamster, why did Julie have to pick Houdini? And why did the stupid rodent have to live up to that name? Today of all days?

"When do the kids need to be back from P.E.?" Trey glanced at the clock. How long had they been gone? He couldn't even remember.

"Um. Ten minutes." She now fanned her face, gulping air, eyes watering. "What are we going to do? I can't let them back in here with the hamster on the loose. I can't even—" She flapped her hands toward the floor.

"Calm down. It's going to be okay." He moved a step closer to her, just in case. That desk didn't look so sturdy.

"Right." She squeezed her eyes shut. "It's just a hamster." Gulp. "Just a furry little creature smaller than my foot. If all else fails, I can just step on him." Extra-large gulp. "No. I'm wearing the wrong shoes."

Trey chomped down on the inside of his cheek to contain the chuckle that threatened to burst forth. Now was not the time. Not at all.

"Rylan's going to be so upset. What if we never find him? I'll have to come back to school tomorrow and wonder where he is. He could be anywhere. Always lurking around another corner. Waiting. Just like those mice—"

Her shriek alerted him to her fall not a moment too soon. He stepped in, arms braced, and let his knees bounce on the impact. Her wide eyes met his as he snugged her closer to his chest.

He dipped his head where their eyes were level. "One, two, three, eyes on me."

"One, two," she hiccupped, "eyes on you."

Maybe her phrases would work in an emergency.

"I doubt that hamster made it very far. I *will* find him." He refused to let her look away. "But I need you to pull it together. You've done great today. Amazing. I could never do this, but you make it look like a breeze. That being said, your students are going to be back in here in a few minutes, ready to party. And if you're having a panic attack, they're going to join right in."

She nodded. "I know."

"Okay, deep breath in." He counted to three. "And out."

A few more and she wasn't quite as stiff nor panting so heavily. Who knew his EMT training would come in handy in a kindergarten classroom? Not something he'd ever expected, for sure.

"I don't see Houdini anywhere. Will you be okay if I set you down now?"

"Oh!" She stiffened in his arms, but he didn't think from panic this time. "I am so sorry. Please ..."

He gently lowered her to the floor, though her feet still tiptoed a bit. "Okay. Now, go ahead and work on those last few boxes. I'm going to search the perimeter."

As if this were a fire and he needed to make sure everyone was out. This was that important. Not only for his nephew but also for this poor traumatized woman who never should've had to put up with this today or any day.

She visibly swallowed but slowly leaned down and picked up the box she'd dropped earlier to set on the desk. "I can do this."

"You can. I promise, on my honor as a firefighter and your room mom of the day, I will not let that hamster near you." He raised his hand in a scout salute.

Her lips twitched as if holding back a smile. A great sign. He steered her toward the cubbies and the last few boxes while he pulled his phone out to use the flashlight and explore various corners and crevices around the room. No sign of Houdini. And it was time for the students to come back.

What was she doing? Kimberly placed the last Valentine's box on the last desk and surveyed the room. In two minutes, she'd have to fetch her students for the party. But if she let herself leave this room, would she be able to convince herself to come back in?

On the other hand, it would be a relief to get away from the man now checking every square inch of her cabinets. The one who had caught and held her like she weighed no more than a couple pounds when she knew exactly how many sacks of sugar she equaled according to the scale that morning. Way more than one.

How embarrassing to have him see her like that. To have been so weak in front of him. What was it about this day that made her a complete ninny in front of attractive men? Or was she a ninny all the time and just too stubborn to admit it?

"I meant to set out the hearts for our game during the party, but ..." She motioned to the clock as she edged toward the door.

"Where are they? I can try and set them out while watching for any movement." Trey continued to scan the room even as he moved her way. This guy was too good to be true.

"Here." She passed him a box full of laminated hearts. "They need to be in a big square, preferably taped to the floor. Maybe on the Circle Time rug?"

"Sure. And the tape is?"

"Desk drawer, top right." She hovered in the doorway for one more second. "Thanks so much."

"Hey." His hand caught her elbow before she could achieve complete freedom.

She faced him slowly, trying to hold her chin up and pretend ten minutes before never happened.

"None of this is your fault. And I don't think any less of you for it, either." There he went again, holding her gaze captive with his hazel eyes. "It's all going to work out. Would you be comfortable if I said a quick prayer?"

She blinked, but nodded.

"Father God, thank you for how well this day has gone up to this point. Please help us locate Houdini and get him back where he belongs. Calm our spirits and help us through the rest of the day. In Jesus' name …"

"Amen." She licked her lips and whispered, "Thanks."

No time to analyze how much more attractive that made him. Or remind herself that she wasn't supposed to go there.

"Oh, Ms. Winters." Mrs. Montgomery appeared at her side. "We're here for the party. Is it time?"

"Almost." Kimberly forced a smile for Grace's mom—the kisser—who was accompanied by the twins' mom, Mrs. Harding. "I'm about to grab the kids from P.E. This is Mr. Jones, Rylan's uncle. He's helping us today too. I'm sure he can fill you in on what's going on and put you to work getting things ready."

Trey nodded slowly, then motioned with the hearts. "Want to help me get this game set up?"

"Isn't that so sweet? I'll just put down these cupcakes." Mrs. Montgomery gushed her way into the room, exclaiming over every little thing.

Kimberly caught Trey's eyes and hoped he understood her thoughts. These moms needed to understand that an animal might scurry across their toes any second. Or that a little boy might be very upset in the near future.

Poor Rylan. Kimberly scanned the edges of the hallway as she walked quickly toward the gym. With Rylan's dad deployed and his mom sick, this day needed to be the best it could be. But he would be heartbroken when he found his pet missing.

The students eagerly waited in line at the gym door. Coach Stiles saluted her as if to wish her luck harnessing the excited energy radiating from each bouncing body in line. Whatever game they'd played during P.E. hadn't been enough to wear them out. Okay.

"Bubbles in your mouths." She pointed to her lips and then motioned them forward toward the classroom.

A few giggles and whispers broke free as they walked the hallway, but the party sounds coming from other rooms assured her they weren't disturbing any of the other classes. Still, she moved them as quickly as possible.

Closing in on her room, she slowed. Had Trey found the hamster? Was all well within her little world once more, or would she have to keep her guard up the rest of the day? How would they handle telling Rylan?

She stopped right outside her door, eliciting groans from the students who wanted to rush right into the party.

"Hands on top."

"Everybody stop." The reply sounded much more depressing than it had that morning.

"I need everyone to listen before we go in our room. We are going to start our party, but only if you can follow instructions. Can everyone do that?"

Each head nodded.

She drew in a deep breath. "All right then. Everyone calmly *walk* to your desk and stand beside it, please."

A few of the students' walks looked more like speed walks, but no one was run over, and everyone soon stood at attention, though a few hands fiddled with balloon strings or the decorations on their boxes. Kimberly's gaze strayed to Trey, and he gave a minuscule shake of his head. She sighed.

He was still the hero of the day, but now what? Go on as if nothing had changed and deal with Rylan at the end? Tell him now? What was the best way to handle this? And how could she function like a normal human being knowing that thing might be around here and run out at any moment?

CHAPTER SEVEN

"*T*he first thing we need to do is pass out Valentines," Kimberly announced.

Cheers erupted, and several kids bounced up and down while a couple more took off for their cubbies.

"Uh, uh, uh, uh." Kimberly stopped the children. "We're going to do this in an orderly fashion."

Groans, but the children returned to standing beside their desks.

"Thank you. Some of you have your cards stashed inside your boxes, and others have them in your cubbies. Raise your hand if you need to get them from your cubby."

A little over half.

"Okay, these back two rows may walk *calmly* to your cubby and grab your cards." Once all were back in their spots, she let the others go. It was still a little wild, but not nearly as crazy as it could have been.

"Thank you for listening." Kimberly moved to the far corner of the desks. "Here's how we're going to do this. I want each one of you to walk down the row you are on, putting those cards in the boxes. We're going to match the names on your cards to the names on the boxes. If you need help remembering who sits there, just ask one of the grownups, and we can help you. Now, watch me so you can see which way to go."

She walked from the left end to the right on the row she was on, then the right end to the left on the next. "See what I'm doing? We're going to do opposite directions on each row, okay?"

Several children looked confused, so Kimberly explained further.

"When you get to the end of the row you're on, you're going to go the opposite direction on the next row. Like this." She got to the very front row. "Then, when you get to the end, you'll calmly walk all the way back to the back row. Got it?"

There were still a few befuddled expressions, but most of them were too excited to care. Time to get this party started, whether they understood or not.

"Grownups, why don't you come over to help direct traffic?" Kimberly smiled, then turned back to her students. "Okay, guys, let's pass out our Valentines."

Some of the students had an easier time than others. A couple of them dropped all their cards on the floor trying to get one out. Thankfully Trey and the moms were there to help as Kimberly tried to keep things moving. Which included keeping students from pushing past each other when they thought the person in front was taking too long.

Great practice for someday when they had to stand in line at the DMV. Scary thought. Kimberly shuddered at the idea of some of these kids driving in ten years.

Twenty minutes later, after only a few mishaps and a ton of glances at the ground to see if any nefarious scurrying was happening, the boxes were filled. On to the next part of the party. She ushered the students over to the hearts Trey had taped neatly in a big square. Seriously, did he use a yardstick or something? His lines were so straight. Hers would've been blob-like.

"Are you all ready to play a game?"

Shouts and laughter assured her this was a great idea.

"Great. This is sort of like musical chairs, except we're going to be aiming for a certain color each round. I have this spinner." She held up the cardboard circle with five different shades of pink, purple, and red. "This time, when the music stops, if you're on a … dark pink, then you'll be out. But listen, no pushing, okay? Everyone goes the same speed. Got your feet on a heart?"

She pushed play on her phone's music app, letting the Beatles croon about love being all you need. It wasn't all she needed, but it would be nice to have. All things being equal.

Stopping the tunes, she watched the kids freeze in place, several of them groaning. The other adults helped make sure those students moved off the area, and she spun again. Red.

A few more rounds, and all but a few children were out. They spread them out so they all stood on a different color. This time she told them whoever stopped on purple would win.

She pushed play on a jazzy Michael Bublé song that spelled out *love*. This type of music always made her toes tap, but she locked her hips in place lest they begin to shimmy with the kids. No need to show all her tricks. Spinning on top of the desk earlier had been embarrassing enough.

Closing her eyes, she played it a few more seconds before hitting "stop." Little Emory jumped up and down, her feet sliding on the purple heart. Good for her.

"Okay, one more game." Kimberly motioned them to spread out. "How about freeze dance?"

Unanimous approval sounded around the group.

"Wait. I hafta do something first." Rylan stepped over to Trey and started unzipping the pocket on his pants. "Houdini doesn't like it when I dance with him in my pocket."

Out popped a little tan and white head with beady eyes. Kimberly almost fell over. She met Trey's gaze and couldn't decide if she wanted to laugh or cry.

Of all the places Trey had expected to find Houdini, Rylan's pocket was not one of them. He pulled the little boy over to the hamster cage and made sure he locked the creature inside this time. How had he snuck out the poor pet in the first place? Had Trey been staring at Rylan's teacher instead of paying enough attention to his nephew?

Maybe it was a good thing there wasn't any video footage.

"Rylan, why was Houdini in your pocket?" Trey knelt in front of his nephew, who wanted nothing more than to go join his friends dancing to "Love Potion No. 9."

"I wanted to show him to Coach Stiles." Rylan shrugged as if there were nothing wrong with what he'd done.

"What if he had escaped from your pocket? What if you forgot to zip it up, or he dashed away before you could catch him?" Trey pulled Rylan's attention back to him and away from the dancers. "Can you imagine how bad that would be? We might not find him again if he got lost in that great big gymnasium."

"But he didn't." Rylan's little forehead wrinkled. "And he rides in my pocket all the time at home. He knows ezzactly what to do."

"I'm sure he does, but he's not used to being in school. This is all new to him and much bigger than your house." Not to mention the fact that if Julie found out Rylan was carrying the rodent around like that at home, it wouldn't happen there, either. But that was a problem for another time.

Rylan's eyes started to tear up. "Are you mad at me?"

"No." Trey tousled the dark brown hair. "No, I'm not mad at you."

Was Kimberly? Rylan's little trick had given her quite the scare earlier. But a glance in her direction showed her focused on catching kids who didn't freeze when the music stopped.

"Go dance, and we'll talk about this more later, okay?"

Rylan didn't wait for a second invitation. He jumped in right as the Beatles started singing "She Loves You." She sure was rocking the classics today, but the kids didn't seem to mind. Neither did Trey, honestly. Some songs never grew old.

He checked the cage door one more time, assured it was locked tight. The prodigal hamster greedily slurped from his water bottle, probably due for a long nap after all the excitement of the afternoon. Poor Houdini might never be the same.

Two songs later, the dancing game wound up, and Kimberly sent everyone to their desks for cupcakes and juice pouches. The day was almost over. Had seven hours passed so quickly? At the beginning of the day, he'd wondered how he'd ever make it through. Now he hoped to find an excuse to linger.

"Would you mind helping tie balloons to backpacks?" Kimberly's hand at his elbow jerked him from thoughts of her to … awareness. Had he really known her only less than a day?

"Of course." He joined the other adults as they transferred the balloons to the backpack straps, stuffed as many of the goodies into the backpacks as they were able, and bagged up the rest for transport.

A bell rang, loud and crisp.

"Bus riders, line up at the door."

The day was over. But Trey wasn't ready.

CHAPTER EIGHT

Kimberly propped her hands on her hips. "Max and Malachi, you're not bus riders today. Your mom is here."

"We want to ride the bus." Malachi shrugged.

"Fine by me." Mrs. Harding tugged her purse on her shoulder. "That's forty-five more minutes of peace and quiet. But I will take these." She snatched the Valentine's boxes from the boys' hands. "See ya at home, boys."

Kimberly smothered her giggle. If she were the boys' mother, she might do the same thing. The bell rang again, and she sent the bus riders out into the line of other bus riders streaming down the hallway. Several other faculty and staff were out there to make sure all got where they were going.

"Okay, car riders. You ready?" She glanced around. Only about seven today. "Let's line up."

The balloons tied to their backpacks bounced as they skipped into line, giggling and clutching their goodies to their chests.

Trey hung back with Rylan. "Anything I can do before I go?"

"Oh. Um …" She glanced around at the room, slightly less

festive than it had been this morning. "Don't worry about it. You were a huge help today. Thanks again."

The bell for car riders trilled through the hallways.

"Thank you," Kimberly called over her shoulder as she shepherded her remaining students down the hallway toward the pickup lines.

It felt wrong, leaving Trey standing there. As if she didn't actually appreciate everything he'd helped with today. Including that crazy hamster. She'd probably still be standing on a desk if it weren't for him talking her down ... and catching her. Her bottom twinged as if feeling the bump that would've happened had she hit the floor instead of his strong arms.

Maybe she could get his information from Julie and send him a thank-you note. It still didn't seem enough. But what else could she do? She had to get these children out the door.

The cold February air reminded her she hadn't grabbed a coat. She rubbed her hands up and down her arms while making sure the children were under the supervision of Coach Stiles and Mrs. Banberry.

As the other two grownups took over, Kimberly speed-walked back inside. Brr. This day had thrown her for a loop. She never forgot her coat for car line.

Now, another hour or two of cleanup and prep for tomorrow. Then she could take her own goodies home and kick her feet up with a dinner of cookies and a rom-com. Another Valentine's Day in the books.

Inside her doorway, she froze. Trey straightened from where he'd been picking up their musical hearts. He slowly wadded up the piece of tape in his fingers and set the purple heart on the stack on her desk, his eyes searching hers, though for what, she had no idea. He was still here?

"Look at this one, Uncle Trey!" Rylan held up a Valentine from inside his box. Apparently, he was sorting them while Trey worked because there were piles of candy and cards around him in an order that made sense only to a six-year-old.

"That's a cool one, Ry." Trey bent over and pulled up another heart.

"You're still here." Kimberly finally convinced her feet to walk again and moved to help him with the last few hearts.

"I couldn't leave this whole mess to you." He motioned around the room.

Honestly, it wasn't in that bad of a shape. A few smears of chocolate frosting on some desks, one lone forgotten balloon hugging the corner of the ceiling, the limited leftover goodies sitting on the table, not taken home by the moms. But other than that, the room looked tired.

"You didn't have to." She reached for the heart in his hand, and their fingertips brushed.

"It was my pleasure." He might as well have said, "As you wish." The effect was just as romantic.

Romantic? Ridiculous. He was just a nice guy. A nice handsome firefighter, who happened to be good with kids, able to calm her down during a freakout session, and was now staring at her like she had lost her mind.

Oh. She pulled the heart away from him, disconnecting from that weird zingy feeling she got when they accidentally touched. She was tired. That's all.

"Well, I appreciate it."

Together, they finished cleaning up the party mess. Rylan helped by eating one of the last cupcakes and taking the leftover balloon. Houdini helped by sleeping quietly in his cage, where Kimberly didn't have to worry about him.

Trey dusted his hands together and looked around. "Anything else?"

Disappointment settled in Kimberly's belly. She honestly couldn't think of another thing he could do. "I think that's it."

His lips pursed to one side, and he gave a stiff nod. "Guess we better get out of your hair then."

She pinched her lips together to keep from begging him to stay. Why should he? He'd already gone above and beyond what a typical room mom would do. There was no more reason to keep him here.

"You know …" Trey stepped closer. This was a risk, but if it paid off, it would be worth it. "We never did finish our conversation earlier."

One of Kimberly's brows rose. "Our conversation?"

"The one where I let you know I am a chaplain, and you were finally explaining …" he glanced back to where Rylan still sat, looking through his Valentines. "your reaction to certain animals."

"Pretty sure I told you enough for you to figure it out." Her eyes narrowed.

"True." He cocked his head. "But if you wanted to talk about it more, I'd be willing to treat you to dinner. I've been told I'm a good listener."

"Dinner." Was this persistent repetition a good sign or a bad one?

"Tonight?"

"On Valentine's Day? Are you crazy? Every restaurant in town is going to be packed with couples on dates." She tugged at the end of one of her braids. "I've been told it's absolute chaos to go out on Valentine's Day."

"You've been told? Not experienced yourself? None of your boyfriends took you to dinner for Valentine's Day?" Trey frowned. That couldn't be right.

She turned to her desk and fiddled with a stack of papers at the edge. "I've never had a relationship make it to Valentine's Day. They always ended right before."

Trey blinked. Idiots. What had they been thinking, letting someone like her go instead of spoiling her like crazy? And obviously not caring what it did to her self-esteem on this day that should be all things romance.

He moved so he was right in front of her and gently covered her hands with his. "Then it's time we fixed that."

Her head jerked up. "What?"

"I know we only met this morning—though it feels like this day was a lot longer than that—but I'd really like to treat you to dinner tonight. To get to know you more. Without twenty-five kids around us."

"Just to have me talk about my brother's snake and his stupid pranks?" Her forehead crinkled as if she couldn't quite understand.

"No." He squeezed her fingers. "Because I really like you."

She glanced Rylan's way, but his nephew was now showing his favorite cards to Houdini, who waddled around in his cage. Something Trey probably needed to get back to Julie's house as soon as possible before Kimberly realized the creature was awake. But not until he had an answer.

"Kimberly Winters, I'm asking you on a Valentine's date. Will you let me treat you to dinner tonight?"

A small giggle escaped her, and she pulled her hand free to cover her mouth for a second. "Only if you can find a place to eat that's not already completely booked up. I'd much rather stay home by myself than face a mob of gooey-eyed couples."

A chuckle released some of the pressure that had built up inside him while he waited for her answer. "Same. But that gives me an idea. I've picked up a few recipes over the years at the station. How about I cook for you?"

"You can cook?"

"I can."

Still, she hesitated. "I don't know. I mean, we barely know each other. That seems ..."

"I'd offer to take you on a picnic, but it's a bit chilly. February in Tennessee is like that."

Her pretty pink lips turned up again. "It is."

"Listen, I'm living in the garage apartment at Julie's right now. I transferred here a few months ago when Dylan deployed so I could help her out. So we'd be within shouting distance of Julie. Does that make it better?"

She pulled the edge of her lip between her teeth for a few more seconds. "You're sure you want to do this?"

"I'm seriously standing here about to beg you. Because after spending all day together, I can't seem to accept that I have to leave and have no idea when I'll see you again."

Her cheeks turned almost as bright pink as her overalls. "Okay."

"Yeah?" His feet itched to jump up and down like some of the kids had earlier when they got excited.

"Yeah."

They worked out the details, and then he slowly inched away from her to gather up Rylan and all his things. She'd agreed to a date. Tonight.

At his apartment—which needed a good cleaning.

Did he even have any groceries?

He moved a little faster. Now that she was coming, he had to make sure this wasn't going to be a one-time thing.

CHAPTER NINE

Rylan burst through the door of his house. "Mom! Mom!"

Trey cringed. Hopefully, Julie hadn't been sleeping. But no. She shuffled into the kitchen, a box of tissues under her arm. Though her nose was red, her eyes were brighter than they had been that morning.

"You guys are later than I expected." Julie's hoarse voice was barely above a whisper.

"Uncle Trey helped Ms. Winters clean up."

"Oh!" Julie's hand slapped her mouth. "I totally forgot I was supposed to be helping her today. Did she have enough moms there?"

"A few showed up for the party." Trey shrugged.

"It was the best day ever." Rylan bounced on his toes as he shoved several Valentines at his mom. "Uncle Trey stayed the whole day. And I got to show everyone Houdini. And I got cookies."

Julie's attention jerked from Rylan to Trey. "You stayed the whole day?"

"I promised you I would do whatever you needed me to do

today." Trey ran a hand over the back of his neck. "You were supposed to be room mom, so I stayed and helped instead."

"And Houdini." Julie's attention jerked back to Rylan. "Why did Houdini go to school today? It's not show-and-tell on a Tuesday."

"But I didn't get to go on show-and-tell day. So, I brought him today." Rylan grinned as if nothing were wrong.

"Oh, Ry." Julie ruffled his hair. "That's not the way it works, bud. I wish I'd been more coherent this morning."

"It all worked out." Trey set the cage on the table. "Kimberly … rolled with it."

Julie fixed him with a stare. "Kimberly, huh?"

Trey glanced at his watch. "Look at the time. We are running late, aren't we? Well, you guys have a great—"

"Freeze." Julie's mom voice was almost as good as their mom's. Not fair. She didn't even have to put "macaroni and cheese" before it.

Trey spun and lifted a brow. Leaned against the edge of the counter. Slipped and knocked his elbow against the marble top. Propped his fist under his chin as if he meant to do it in the first place. Totally natural. Not guilty at all.

Nothing to be guilty about. So why did guilt nibble at the edge of his spirit? Because of that horrid stare Julie was shooting at him, as if she could pierce all the way through to his brain. He had to stay strong.

"Spill it." Julie's hoarse voice gave her command a gangster feel. Did she plan to torture him if he didn't comply?

"Uncle Trey is making dinner for Ms. Winters." Rylan sang the words even as he dumped his party loot on the kitchen table. The ratfink.

"Oh, is he?" Julie motioned Trey to follow her into the other room. "I didn't realize you knew Ms. Winters."

"I didn't." Trey scuffed his toe on the floor, feeling very

much like a child being reprimanded though he'd done nothing wrong. "We met this morning."

"And you asked her to dinner?"

"I got to know her enough during the day, I'd like to know her more. So, I invited her to dinner." He shrugged. "No big deal. Nothing in the handbook saying a student's uncle can't date his teacher, right?"

"No." Julie grinned. "It just caught me off guard. It's been a while since you were open to the idea of seeing anyone."

"Yeah, well." Trey ducked his head. "I guess after losing a third girlfriend who 'can't handle the pressure' of dating a firefighter, I figured there wasn't any point. But something tells me Kimberly can handle it."

Julie nodded slowly. "Firefighters do act a lot like kindergarteners."

Trey mock laughed. "Julie has the jokes this afternoon."

"Couldn't resist." She blew her nose and then grinned again. "I'm happy for you, but I have another question."

"Yeah?" What now?

"You're having her over to your place?"

He cringed. "I gotta go. It's a mess."

"Trey." Julie stopped him once more.

"Hmm?" His attention was elsewhere as he contemplated everything he needed to do before Kimberly arrived.

"These flowers?" Julie pointed to the bouquet Dylan had sent her that morning. "Take the pink ones. Extra vases over the dryer."

"I'm not taking your flowers, Jules. No way."

"I don't like the pink ones. Dylan always forgets. I like all the others, so just take the pink ones." She winked at him and then shooed him on his way. He rushed through, plucking the pink flowers from the red, pink, and purple bouquet, ramming them into a vase with a little water, and headed out the door and up to his apartment.

Where to start? He needed to clean, for sure. But ... hmm. A glance at the clock showed dinner needed to be started soon too. Okay, time to think fast. Start the meal and clean while it cooked. He could do this.

Just like cooking for his crew. Except not. At all.

Kimberly was much prettier than any of the guys. But she'd probably not overlook his slovenliness like they would, either. Right.

Why had he thought this last-minute cooking-at-home idea was a good one? He'd be completely stressed out by the time she got here. Not a great mood to start a first date in.

Releasing a breath, he shook himself, then straightened. One thing at a time. He could do this.

He dug out ingredients. Cook, then clean. And maybe put on a fresh shirt.

A quick sniff of his armpits verified. Definitely a clean shirt.

Kimberly stared at herself in the mirror. This was all wrong. She'd traded her pink overalls for her little black dress, but was it too much? And her hair. The braids earlier had been cute, but now it left her tresses kinky—more in an eighties-wannabe style than beachy waves like she'd hoped. No time to straighten it now. Lesson prep for the next day had taken longer than normal.

Maybe because her thoughts kept roaming to a certain male room mom. The one she was supposed to be meeting in twenty minutes.

Gah.

Deftly, she parted her hair, grabbed a scarf, and started working it into the hair with loose twists on each side and then tying it all up into a sort of chignon at the bottom. Not the best hairstyle she'd ever concocted, but better than nothing. Pinterest tutorials for the win.

She examined herself in the full-length mirror, smoothing out the skirt that hit right at her knees. Was it too much? She was only going to his apartment. Over a garage.

But it was Valentine's Day.

Heading out to the kitchen, she grabbed her keys and purse, then stopped. "I can't."

Her fingers wrapped around the keys so tightly they began to cut into her palm. What was she doing? She wasn't the type to date a parent—or uncle, as the case may be. She didn't accept dinner dates from guys she'd met only seven hours before. Or *any* guys in the last few years. Had Cupid somehow snuck into her classroom earlier and shot her? She patted her chest. No hole.

"What are you doing?" Beth stood in the garage doorway, watching Kimberly pace back and forth. "Where are you going?"

"Nowhere. This was a mistake. I—"

Her roommate stepped over to her and grasped Kimberly's shoulders, forcing her to stop. "Breathe in, breathe out."

Kimberly sucked in several lungfuls of air.

"Good." Beth nodded. "Now, from the beginning. What's going on?"

Kimberly quickly summed up all that had happened that day at school involving Trey. Well, not all. The instance where she fell off the desk into his arms didn't need to go further than the two people who were there to witness it. So humiliating.

"Argh. I can't go." Kimberly started to grab her hair and then remembered her fancy do. "This was probably just a pity invite. He knew I'd had a crazy day and decided to do something nice for the off-kilter kindergarten teacher."

"Girl, are you kidding? Did you look in the mirror?" Beth motioned to her outfit. "You're sort of a hottie."

"I didn't look like this earlier. I had bouncy hearts on top of my head all day." Kimberly wrinkled her nose.

"Which means he saw the beauty through your silly holiday outfits. Not to mention no one offers to make dinner for a near stranger just because they had a rough day."

"See? We don't even know each other. Not a good idea."

"Do you know Julie?"

Kimberly opened her mouth to deny it but couldn't. "Yes."

"And you trust her, right?"

She sighed. "Yes."

"This is her brother. Surely, she wouldn't have sent someone you couldn't trust to your class today. Or let her son ride with him to school." Beth gave Kimberly a slight shake. "And the only way to get past not knowing each other is to spend time getting to know each other."

Kimberly stuck her tongue out at Beth. "Why are you so insistent on me going on this date?"

"It's good for you. You've had an unhealthy obsession against Valentine's dates and dating in general since that last idiot dumped you. It's time to move on and see that there *are* good guys out there." Beth waved toward the calendar. "This one not only didn't try to avoid Valentine's Day—he invited you for a date on it."

"I'm not sure I'm in a date-worthy mood, though. It's been a really long day, and you know how contentious I can be when I'm tired." Kimberly's excuses were sounding more and more pathetic.

Beth merely raised a brow.

Kimberly crossed her arms and narrowed her eyes. "You just don't want to watch rom-coms all evening, do you?"

"I mean, that's definitely a perk." Beth battled her eyelashes a few times while twirling a strand of her brown hair. "You're my favorite roomie ever, but sometimes you get a little carried away with those."

"Don't touch my ice cream." Kimberly poked Beth in the nose before wrapping her in a hug. "I'm going."

"Good girl."

"But not because of what you said." Kimberly spun her keys on her finger. "Because there's nothing good to eat here, and I didn't get gussied up to go to the grocery store."

"Whatever it takes." Beth pushed her through the garage door and closed it behind her.

Okay. No big deal. She'd spent the whole day with him. What was another hour or two?

Julie's driveway gravel crunched under her tires as Kimberly pulled in a few minutes later. Lights shined through the windows of the house and the garage apartment. Movement from the curtains indicated Julie knew she was there. At least that meant Julie must know about the date.

Kimberly carefully maneuvered the wooden stairs up to Trey's place. Deep breath in. And she knocked.

CHAPTER TEN

The knock came at the same second the timer dinged. Trey didn't want Kimberly left waiting, but he also didn't want to serve her burned garlic bread. He rushed to the oven, jerked it open, and grabbed the tray. *Hot!*

The tray crashed against the oven door as he dropped it.

One piece of bread hit the floor.

This time, he grabbed a mitt, set the pan on the counter, and kicked the oven door closed. Trey flailed his hands back and forth, trying to get the sting out. Smart move—grabbing a four-hundred-degree piece of metal.

He raced to the door and opened it as she was lifting her hand to knock again.

Kimberly jerked back and then slowly lowered her arm, looking very unsure. And—wow! His gaze followed her from the top of her head—minus the bouncy hearts—past her red pea coat and to the tips of her bright pink heels. Wow. His button-down and jeans felt underwhelming.

She shifted her weight, looking down. He was staring. And his mouth was hanging open.

"I shouldn't have come." Kimberly spun on her feet and

would've started down the stairs if he hadn't reached out to catch her.

He winced as his tender fingers wrapped around her arm. "Wait."

"I should've known better. You didn't really mean for me to come, and now I've shocked you by actually showing up." Her words spilled from her lips about a mile a minute. "I don't know why I thought this was a good idea. I mean, after everything today—"

Pressing his hand gently over her mouth, he shook his head. "Kimberly."

She blinked a few times, her eyes suspiciously moist. Oh, no. Women afraid of hamsters he could handle, but women crying— no way. Time to get this situation under control.

"I *did* mean for you to come. I would've answered sooner, but the oven timer went off the same time you knocked and I didn't want the bread to burn. I was in such a hurry that I made a rookie mistake and grabbed the pan without a mitt."

Her gasp whispered against said hand, but he didn't mind.

"And then, when I opened the door, I didn't recognize you for a second. I mean, you aren't wearing your overalls or your headband." He winked, and her answering giggle relieved some of the nervousness cha-cha-ing through his spine. He lifted his hand from her mouth, and she smiled sheepishly.

"I left the headband in my car, if you really need it to recognize me."

Another quick glance at her fancy hairdo, and he shook his head. "I think it would clash with this scarf thing you've got going on."

They stood there grinning at each other for another minute until she full-body shivered. Right. He was a lousy host. It was thirty degrees outside, and here they were, lingering on the porch instead of going inside where it was warm. Julie would never let him hear the end of it.

"Come on in. Everything is ready." He closed the cold out behind them and then helped her slip off her coat.

Wow again.

The black dress skimmed over her body in a way that made him want to stare at her all night. Good thing she was his date, and it wouldn't be terribly awkward for him to do so. That sounded wrong on so many levels. He needed to get out of his head.

"Let me get the drinks poured, and we can eat." He motioned across the open living space to where his table was set up with the flowers and one lone candle he'd unearthed when grabbing the vase from his sister's house. Some strange scented thing like ocean breeze or winter evening or something that really didn't tell a person a thing about what it actually smelled like.

"Tea or water or soda?"

"Tea, please." Her fingertips grazed over the petals of the pink flowers before her nose dipped to breathe in their scent.

Score another point for Julie. Not that he'd admit it to her. No. He wasn't one to kiss and tell.

Not that there would be kissing.

Although he wouldn't complain if there was.

But it wasn't a requirement.

He'd have to wait and see how the night went. See if that might be something they'd both want to try before she went home later. But that was for later. Now was for dinner. And to have dinner, they needed drinks. Right. *Focus, Trey.*

"You okay?" Kimberly's question helped pull him back into the here and now.

"Yep. Just seeing you with those flowers made me think of earlier. That little girl, what was her name? Faith? Hope? And how she was talking about her parents."

"Grace." Kimberly's cheeks pinked. "I never know what's going to come out of that child's mouth."

"Well, good thing she's not here then. Otherwise, she'd

expect you to plant one on me." And there he went, thinking about the very thing he'd told himself to not think about.

Could this get more humiliating? First, she'd tried to run away when he'd finally opened the door. Then, he'd been staring at her as if maybe she wore the wrong thing. Finally, the kiss comment. Oh, that Grace Montgomery. She needed a good talking to.

The aroma of something garlicky wafted her way a moment before Trey set down a pan of what looked like cheese-covered pasta with tomato sauce. Then, the garlic bread. And a salad. Her tummy rumbled in appreciation.

"You made all this?"

"Don't be too impressed. I've learned a few things working at the firehouse, but I only have about four dishes up my sleeve. Anything else is beyond me." He pulled out her chair and motioned for her to sit. "Still, the guys seem to appreciate this meal more than some others we have."

"It smells wonderful." She'd have to remember not to eat too much. This dress got snug in the waistband if she ate too big a helping. But Italian was her favorite.

"May I pray over it?" He held out his hand.

Gently she slid her fingers over his, wincing for him as she grazed his burns. But he barely reacted before bowing his head.

"Father God, thank you for today and for allowing us to make this new acquaintance. Thank you that we found Houdini safe and sound, that the kids all had a great day, and that we can now spend time getting to know one another. Bless us as we explore the possibilities and help us to keep You in the center of everything. Bless this food to our bodies. In Jesus's name. Amen."

"Amen," she murmured.

She blinked. He really did want to explore possibilities. After all, a person didn't just throw those things into a prayer if he wasn't serious about them. A few more doubts and misgivings slipped away as he dished up a huge helping of the pasta.

"That's more a firefighter helping than one for me." She smiled as he set it in front of her.

"I'm so used to feeding men, I sometimes forget the rest of the world eats more reasonably. I can take some back, if you want." He started to reach for her plate, but she waved him off. She could handle a slightly tight dress for a little while.

"What's it like being a firefighter?" She took a bite and barely held back a moan. Was that pepper flakes? "Besides cooking for men?"

"Oh, ya know." He chewed for a minute. "Lots of rescuing kittens and getting called to help Mr. Lezinski up when he drives his lawnmower too close to the edge of his hill and tips it over. Mrs. L. keeps trying to hire their neighbor boy to mow for them, but her husband won't allow it. Says it's his only time he doesn't have to listen to her."

Kimberly smiled. She knew the Lezinskis. The older couple were at church every time the doors were open and sweet as could be. Mrs. Lezinski could definitely talk a person's ear off.

"Every now and then, there's a fire. Or at least a fire alarm going off, whether there's a legitimate reason for it or not. We still have to go check things out. Time at the station is a lot of cards and basketball and grilling. And bad jokes."

At that, she guffawed. "Mark Winters must still be there."

Trey joined her laughter. "Oh, yeah. His jokes are the worst! Mostly potty humor. But we all love him enough to put up with it."

"I know. He's my cousin."

Trey blinked. "No way."

"Way. My dad's brother's son." Kimberly swiped her bread through some sauce on her plate. "He's always been that way."

After a few more minutes of chatting about the life of a firefighter, Trey threw the conversation back on her. "What about you? I saw some of what it's like to be a kindergarten teacher today. But it's not always like that. What's the life of a kindergarten teacher like?"

Kimberly pushed the last bit of salad to the side. "It's a lot like today. Lots of trying to make learning fun and interesting enough to keep the kids' attention. Lesson plans and researching new ideas at night. That's actually one of the reasons my past relationships ended. They couldn't understand why I still had to work on things at night. Why didn't I finish my work during the school day? It's not like school hours were the same as a 'real' job." Her voice took on a bitter note, but she couldn't help it.

"You're kidding." Trey leaned back in his seat and laid his hands on his flat stomach. "I guess working a job that has me on several days in a row and then off again makes me more understanding that work hours aren't always the same across the board."

"Right? And then, when I wanted to work ahead on the next school year during the summer, they complained because wasn't I off for three months? Um, no. I love doing different decorations each year. Especially if I end up having the sibling of a child I've taught before. And who wants to stare at the same posters year after year? Do you want to stare at the same things for seven years?" She tucked her napkin under her plate. "Just because I'm on break from teaching doesn't mean I'm not thinking ahead."

"As you should be." Trey's words warmed her heart. Finally, a man who seemed to get her. It almost seemed too good to be true.

"Speaking of thinking ahead, we normally have a special guest each month. Sometimes a doctor or dentist or a librarian. But we also love to have police officers and firefighters. And we haven't had a firefighter yet." Kimberly glanced up from her plate.

Trey remained silent, an unreadable expression on his face. Was he paler than he had been?

"I thought, maybe since you'd already come today, and the kids knew you, you know, that it might be fun ... well, to have you come back and speak to us about being a firefighter." Her words rambled on while his face grew stonier with each word.

What was wrong?

"I don't speak to groups." Trey pushed away from the table and moved into his tiny kitchen.

"I just figured, you know, since you already knew the kids and they knew you ..." She was repeating herself. Kimberly rose and followed him, stopping at the counter's edge. "You spent all day with us today. Spoke to the children several times."

"Not the same." Trey reached in the freezer and pulled out a container of fancy ice cream. "Dessert?"

Kimberly shook her head. "I don't understand. The kids would absolutely love it."

"There's nothing to understand." Trey turned his back to her. "Speaking to groups of people, kids or otherwise, is not what I do. I rescue people. I don't get up in front of them and talk. Other crew members do that."

Why was he being so stubborn? Kimberly wanted to stamp her foot and growl, just like her students did when they didn't get their way. She wasn't asking for anything fancy. Simply talking to the kids as he had several times earlier that day. There had to be a reason behind his refusal. What could it be?

"Will you talk to me about it?" She propped her fists on her hips. "You were the one insisting I talk to you earlier about why I don't like hamsters. Isn't what's good for the goose good for the gander?"

"This is nothing like that." He spun around, hands splayed out. "Yours is from a past trauma, and you needed to work

through it in order to get control of yourself earlier. Mine is …"
He turned his head away, his jaw clenching. "It's just the way I
am. Mark can come talk to your class. Or my friend Jeff."

"I don't want Mark or Jeff." Kimberly blinked. "The kids
already know you. That would make it more comfortable for
them to ask questions. Plus, it would give you an excuse to
come…" she trailed off before finishing her statement. To come
see her.

"I'm sorry I can't give you a better answer." Trey shrugged.
"But I can't change who I am. And it's really rotten of you to
expect me to."

"I'm not expecting you to change. I know how it feels to
have someone want that. All those other guys I dated wanted me
to change. Didn't deem me worthy of a Valentine's date. Never
would've come to my class to help with anything. I figured this
was just like the way you helped today."

"Except you want to make *me* the show-and-tell instead of
Houdini."

"No." Kimberly bit her lip for a second. "Sort of, but not
really."

"Yes, really. Why are you being so stubborn about this?"

"Why are you?" Suddenly, the long day caught up with her,
weighing down her limbs and mind. She'd had to deal with
craziness for almost twelve hours now. She didn't want to deal
with more.

Kimberly spun on her heel, marched across the room, and
grabbed her coat.

"You're leaving?" Trey followed.

"It's been a long day. I have another long day tomorrow. The
kids will be coming down off their Valentine's sugar high. If you
want to talk more another time, let me know. But I can't do this
anymore tonight." She pulled a button through its hole and
opened the door.

"Kimberly."

"Thanks for dinner." She moved down the stairs before he could stop her again, the biting cold a relief to her hot cheeks.

Had his refusal been worth getting all worked up? Not to the point she'd allowed it. But he was just being so ... so ... argh! She cranked her engine and pulled out of the driveway.

She'd probably regret leaving like this later, but right now, she couldn't. Maybe Cupid had missed after all. Because she couldn't see a future with someone not only so set in his ways, but also who wouldn't even talk about it. That's all she wanted.

For him to give her the same courtesy he expected her to give him. Was that too much to ask?

She pulled into her garage a few minutes later. Ugh. She'd forgotten her flowers.

Probably better that way.

Maybe she'd believe it tomorrow.

CHAPTER ELEVEN

"*I* wish you'd get up and do something. It's been weeks. Stop moping." Jeff smacked Trey on the back of the head in the fire station lounge.

"What?" Trey rubbed the crown of his head. "What are you talking about?"

"You know what." Jeff folded his huge arms over his big belly and fixed Trey with a stare. "Ever since Valentine's Day, when you took Rylan to school and met his pretty teacher, you've been walking around here like a gloomy Gus. And you only cook that baked tortellini. Nothing else."

"It's what I'm in the mood for." Trey scowled. "You've never complained when I made it before."

"That's before I had to eat it three times in two weeks." Jeff slid down on the chair across from him. "If you like the girl that much, go do something about it."

"It's not that easy." Trey ran a hand over his face. "She got upset with me because I won't come speak to her class about being a firefighter."

"That's ridiculous." Jeff shook his head.

"Right? I never speak to anyone publicly. Why should I start now?"

"I mean that you won't do it, you idiot." Jeff tossed an old candy wrapper at him. "I've never understood what holds you back. You're not shy any other time."

Before Trey could come up with a comeback, Mark walked in. "Hey guys, I just heard this great joke. What does a shark—"

"Not now, Mark," Trey and Jeff said at the same time.

"Well, I never." Mark turned up his nose. "What's got y'all's undies in a twist?"

Trey shot a glare Mark's way.

Mark narrowed his eyes. "Is this still about my cousin?"

Ugh. Trey had forgotten Mark was related to Kimberly. And there went the zing. The little ache that ran through him every time her name crossed his mind. He'd only known her for a day. Not long enough for him to hurt this much two weeks later.

"You know we're scheduled to visit her class next week." Mark sat down beside Trey and draped an arm across his shoulders. "What we need, fellas, is a plan."

Trey shoved Mark's arm off. "*We* don't need anything."

"Oh, yes." Mark returned his arm, this time a bit tighter around Trey's neck. "We do. Because if we have to eat tortellini bake one more time this month, the whole station is going to rebel. We've got to get you out of this funk. And seems the only way to do that is to make you talk to Kimberly."

"You can't *make* me do anything." Trey squirmed against Mark's ever-tightening grip.

Mark looked at Jeff. Jeff lifted a brow and gave a slight nod.

"Guys." Trey jerked but couldn't get free. "Come on, guys. I don't mess around with your love life."

"That's because we're smart enough to not have one." Jeff flicked a rubber band at him before rubbing his hands together. "What you need is a grand gesture."

"Grand ... gesture?" Trey stilled. "What does that even mean?"

"According to my sister, it's when the hero in all the movies does something ... grand ... to show his undying devotion for the woman and make all right in their relationship again. Usually, after he's done something stupid to push her away."

"Why is it always the guy who does something stupid?" Trey stiffened.

Jeff and Mark both looked at him. Yeah, okay. So, guys didn't always think before acting. But still.

"Didn't you say she wanted you to come speak to the kids? We have the perfect opportunity next week. Sounds like God is lining things up for you, brother." Jeff moved his fingers as if to show each point on a timeline. "We'll put you in full gear so she can't see who you are, the two of us go in with you to introduce you, and then you lift your helmet and kiss her senseless."

"That's the worst plan I've ever heard." Trey finally wiggled free from Mark's arm. "First, me in full gear could scare the kids. Second, there is no way I'm kissing her in front of her class. Some of those kids already have some shady ideas about kissing. And most importantly, I'm not going."

"Oh, you're going." Mark held his arm up as if threatening to strangle him again. "Why wouldn't you? Why would you want to stay unhappy?"

"She doesn't want to see me." Trey focused out the window instead of on his friends. "She thinks I'm stubborn."

"You *are* stubborn." Jeff tossed a pencil at him this time. Where was he getting this stuff?

"Yeah, well, so is she." Trey hopped up and started pacing.

"What keeps you from speaking to groups? I know you never have before, but I've never understood why."

"I *can't*." Trey sliced his hands through the air. "All the way back to middle school, if I had to get up in front of a group, I'd freeze. Just stand there, unable to speak. Barely even to breathe. As if I were caught in a force field or something."

"So, how did you survive a whole day of helping Kimberly?" Mark frowned.

"She did the talking and stuff. I just helped." Trey ran a hand through his hair. It was longer than his fingers—time to chop it off again.

"You never had to say *anything* to the kids?" Jeff scratched his chin.

"No." Trey stilled. "I mean, except for when I helped Rylan with his hamster. But he did most of the talking."

The other two waited.

"Okay, and there was that time that a little girl was asking if Kimberly would kiss me if I gave her flowers."

The guys hooted and fell back, guffawing.

"Yeah, yeah. Very funny. I reminded her that we didn't really know each other, and we went on with our day."

"Was it hard to answer the girl?" Jeff asked between his remaining chuckles.

Trey frowned and thought back. It hadn't been, had it? "No."

"So, if she had asked you if you rescued kittens as a firefighter, would that be hard for you to answer?"

Trey narrowed his eyes. "Probably not."

Mark stood up and shoved Trey's shoulder. "You know what you need to do."

Three weeks.

It had been three weeks since Valentine's Day. Kimberly had all the supplies ready to make leprechaun traps next week and had located her Kelly-green pants and her shirt with the rainbow-striped sleeves. But first, she had to get through the firefighters coming today.

She didn't expect a certain firefighter to come, of course. Not only because he had promised her he wouldn't, but also because Rylan wasn't acting any more excited than normal. Wouldn't he be more excited if his uncle were going to come back? Kimberly would be.

No. She scolded herself. She wasn't going to act that way over someone who hadn't even contacted her since he made her Valentine's Day the most amazing one she'd had in forever— until it wasn't. She hadn't asked Julie about him. Hadn't requested his number. It was as if it had never happened.

Except she remembered every single moment with too much clarity for that to be true.

"Finish up your math sheets, guys." Kimberly scanned the desks around her to see how many blanks were left. Not many. "Once you're done, turn your page in and then move to the Circle Time rug. Remember to squeeze in close, because the other class is going to come join us too."

She flipped the end of her ponytail over her shoulder and ran a hand down the side of her bright red pants. Firefighters actually wore a dark blue most of the time, but the red had seemed more appropriate today. Mrs. Sanders's class came in quietly and joined her kiddos on the floor, whispers and giggles skittering around as friends greeted each other.

"Ms. Winters." Mark stood at the doorway, grinning at her like the goofball he was. "Are you ready for us?"

She peeked behind him but couldn't tell who else was there. Didn't matter. Because the one she'd hoped for wouldn't come.

"Ms. Winters?" Mrs. Sanders touched her shoulder, and Kimberly realized she hadn't answered her cousin.

She quickly clapped her hands and attained the silence needed. "Class, we're in for a treat today. Some of our local firefighters are here to talk to us about fire safety and what they do at the fire station. But you need to make sure you stay really quiet so everyone can hear, okay?"

She waved Mark in, and he sauntered over, another fireman by his side.

"Hey kids. I'm Officer Winters, and this is Officer Parks."

Before Mark could say another word, Grace's hand was in the air and she was asking a question, "Officer Winters? Our teacher's name is Ms. Winters! Are you her husband?"

Mark snickered. "I'm her cousin. Isn't that neat? How cool is it that Ms. Winters has a cousin who fights fires?"

"Whoa!" several of the boys replied. Great. That would only egg Mark on further.

"Okay. First things first, Officer Parks and I want to go over some fire safety rules. Then, we have a special treat for you. We're going to show you what it looks like when a firefighter puts on all the clothing and gear we have to wear when we go to a fire. So, I need you to listen really closely so we can make sure you hear everything, okay?"

The two officers tag-teamed, going through the stop-drop-and-roll bit, talking about dialing 9-1-1, and having a safe place to go if a fire happened in their home. They allowed the kids to ask some questions. Then they exchanged a look Kimberly couldn't quite interpret before turning to her and Mrs. Sanders.

"It's a gorgeous day, and we brought the truck." Officer Parks pointed toward the front of the building. "Want to go outside for the rest of this?"

Fortunately, it was a day when the kids would be okay without jackets. One of the first pretty days they'd had this year. Kimberly and Mrs. Sanders agreed and lined everyone up to follow the officers out to where the truck sat in the fire lane. Probably the only vehicle ever to get away with parking there when there wasn't an emergency.

Another officer stood next to the truck, full gear on, including a mask that shielded his face from sight. Some of the kids slowed down when they saw him, but she shepherded everyone where they could see as well as possible. Mark clapped a hand on the decked-out man's shoulder and pointed to everyone around.

"Okay, kids. This is what we look like when we come to a fire. We wear these really thick clothes to protect our skin. Gloves to protect our hands. A helmet to keep our heads safe if anything falls." Mark knocked on the helmet until the man under it shoved him off. "And the mask helps us breathe when the air is smoky. I'm going to have Officer Jones turn on his oxygen so you can hear what it sounds like, okay?"

Jones?

Kimberly's gaze flitted once more to the decked-out fireman, but the way the sun was shining, she couldn't make out any features. And with all that gear, it was hard to know how big or small he really was. The clicks and hisses of his breathing apparatus had several children backing up a few steps.

"See? He's not scary, is he?" Mark asked. "He wears all this to keep him safe so he can help you if your house is on fire. If you see someone like this, you don't run away. You yell so he can find you better, okay? Say, 'Over here!' or 'Help!'"

The kids all practiced while the officers gave them the thumbs-up.

"Okay, who wants to give Officer Jones a high five?"

Even though she couldn't see through his mask, Kimberly could swear he gave her cousin a glare. *Could* it be Trey? Surely not. He told her he didn't do this. *Wouldn't* do it. She was probably just imagining things.

"Everyone give a round of applause for Officer Jones. We're going to let him take off the outer gear now so he can cool off, okay? Who wants to see inside the truck?" Officer Parks opened the door, and they helped the kids climb in one side and then out the other before lining back up on the sidewalk.

Though she should've been helping monitor her students,

Kimberly couldn't tear her focus away from the officer removing his helmet. And then, his face mask. Her heart pounded as he turned back her way, slipping the heavy jacket from his shoulders. Trey.

She would *not* react.

She wouldn't show surprise or curiosity or interest or yearning. Definitely not that last one. Maybe if she didn't show the emotions, she wouldn't feel them. She waited a second. Yeah, no. That didn't work.

Once he'd stepped out of the work boots and into a pair of tennis shoes, he moved her way. She braced herself, unsure what might be coming. Was he still upset with her? Had she guilted him into coming today?

"You were right."

She blinked. "What?"

"It wasn't hard being in front of the kids because I'd already been around them all before. I'm sorry I doubted you." He reached like he was going to take her hand, but then pulled back again.

She shook her head. "I owe you an apology."

He lifted a brow. "Because I ended up having to stand out here in that hot outfit for like half an hour while Mark did who-knows-what inside before bringing y'all out here?"

She snickered. "No. Because I shouldn't have pushed. I don't even know why I did, except it felt like you weren't listening to me, and after a whole day of having little people not listening to me, it's hard when I felt like a big person wouldn't either. Or maybe I was just overly tired. Regardless, I shouldn't have made such an issue of it. Not everyone is cut out to be in front of a crowd."

"Thank you for that." He glanced over his shoulder where the line was still moving through the truck. "Obviously, now is not the time to talk things all the way out, but I'd love to try again."

She nibbled the corner of her bottom lip before agreeing. "I'd like that too."

"Yeah?" He stepped closer.

"Yeah." Her smile had to be stretching across her whole face. She couldn't help it.

"Uncle Trey!" Rylan slammed into Trey's legs, knocking him into Kimberly. His arm wrapped around her waist as he steadied them both.

Too bad they were standing on the sidewalk in front of the school, surrounded by a horde of kids. But the look in Trey's eyes promised they'd find a time sooner rather than later to talk away from this chaos. Maybe even end the evening without an argument.

And that was even better than a Valentine's date.

EPILOGUE

Valentine's Day the next year

Trey stood in the doorway, watching a cute little woman attaching balloons to the desks. How had this classroom been so scary the year before? This year, the shirt under her pink overalls was purple instead of red. And her hair was in a ponytail with a great big heart-covered bow. It never ceased to amaze him how many holiday outfits she owned. He'd teased her about being related to Ms. Frizzle and requested a trip on the Magic School Bus on their next field trip.

She finally glanced up and blinked. School didn't start for another half an hour, and he'd had to bribe the secretary with chocolate to let him in. But it was worth it to see her beautiful face for a few moments before they both had to work.

"Trey. What are you doing here?"

"I wanted to be proactive this year and bring you flowers before anyone else could. I know you'll get tons of carnations later, but maybe these will go okay with them." He pulled a bouquet from behind his back, full of red and pink and white roses. Good thing she'd told him her favorite flower last year.

"Trey." She tenderly took the flowers and buried her nose in them for a minute.

"Too bad Grace isn't in your class again this year. She would've egged us on to follow her parents' example. Told you to plant a big ol' kiss—"

But then she did just that. No Grace required.

"Maybe Grace's parents had the right idea." Trey smiled, unwilling to let Kimberly go yet.

"Maybe so." She smiled back. "And bonus points for not bringing a hamster this year."

"Aww, come on. That turned out okay. Not many people can say God used a runaway hamster to bring them together."

"Mm. I guess so."

"So, it was a bit of an out-of-the-box Valentine's Day ..."

Kimberly groaned. "You've been spending too much time with Mark."

"I had another Valentine's box for you, but if you're not interested ..." Trey lifted a brow.

She narrowed her eyes and backed up a step to look him over. "Well, I can guarantee it's not another hamster, unless you're hiding him in your pocket."

"Nope. No hamster in my pocket." He reached into it and pulled out the black velvet box. "Just this."

Her flowers crashed to the floor as both her hands covered her mouth. "Trey!"

He got down on one knee. "Kimberly Winters, you made Valentine's Day the best I ever had last year. I want to spend every Valentine's Day with you for the rest of our lives. Will you marry me?"

She nodded, and he slid the diamond on her finger.

"Did she say *yes*?" A loud whisper came from the hallway.

Trey chuckled, only an inch away from kissing her again.

"Hush. Uncle Trey will tell you when you can come in," Julie's voice replied.

"But I want to know if she's going to be my aunt." Rylan's voice whined.

"Come on in, you two." Trey stepped to Kimberly's side and picked up what was left of her bouquet.

Rylan rushed over and grabbed Kimberly around the waist, looking up at her with pleading eyes. "Well, are ya? Are you going to be my aunt?"

Kimberly tousled his hair. "I am."

"Yippee! I get an Aunt Winters!" Rylan did a little happy dance.

"She won't be Ms. Winters after we get married." Trey knelt in front of Rylan. "She'll be Mrs. Jones."

Rylan frowned. "But that's weird. We won't remember it after calling her Ms. Winters for so long."

"Well, you could just call me Aunt Kimberly."

"Kimberly? Your name is Kimberly?" Rylan put both hands on his cheeks. "I thought it was Miss."

The adults all laughed.

"I'll get this crazy out of your life." Julie waved at Trey and Kimberly. "But remember, you two, school starts in fifteen minutes."

"Anything else I can help with before the bell?" Trey looked around the room, noting slightly different decorations.

"Don't suppose you want to be room mom again?" Kimberly winked.

"Can't today. My shift starts at nine."

"All right, then. Guess I'll see you in a few days when you're off again?"

"You better believe it." He kissed her once more. "Don't have too much fun without me."

"Never."

He tugged at the end of her ponytail and walked from the happy pink-and-red environment she'd created back to the mostly grey-and-black station. Strange how things had changed in the last year. All for the good.

Though it was hard to choose which Valentine's Day was his favorite. This one or last year. Maybe they could just aim to have a better one each and every year. Sounded like a great goal to him.

ABOUT AMY R. ANGUISH

Amy R Anguish grew up a preacher's kid, and in spite of having lived in seven different states that are all south of the Mason-Dixon line, she is not a football fan. Currently, she resides in Tennessee with her husband, daughter, son, and usually a bossy cat or two. Amy has an English degree from Freed-Hardeman University that she intends to use to glorify God, and she wants her stories to show that while Christians face real struggles, it can still work out for good.

No Butts About It

A Novella
by
Linda Fulkerson

To my husband.
Words can't express how grateful I am
that God gave us to each other.

CHAPTER ONE

"*No* worries, Phil. I've got this." Charles Franklin Sterling III tucked his phone under his chin, twisted his key in the lock, and hip-bumped the door to his midtown Little Rock loft. "I'll find you the best property available."

A diminutive middle-aged woman met him at the door and made a slicing gesture across her throat. Her eyes cut toward the oversized, numberless wall clock, then shifted back and bore into his.

"Uh, I gotta go. I'll keep you posted." He set his phone and briefcase on the brushed metal entryway table and placed his hands on the woman's shoulders. "Hello, Rosa. Something smells delicious. What is it?"

She shrugged out of his touch. "It's cold, that's what it is. *And* it's seven-thirty. I'm supposed to get off at six."

Charles felt his face crumple like a scolded child. "I'll compensate you for the extra time." He reached to retrieve his money clip, but Rosa swatted away his hand.

"It's not about *compensation*." She practically spit out the word. "You're a parent now. You have responsibilities." His housekeeper's accent thickened with each word, indicating the growing level of her irritation.

He sucked in a deep breath and whooshed it out. Two long strides brought him to the fireplace. Charles picked up a framed photograph from the mantle and glared at a young man's smiling face—a face identical to his, were it not for his brother's perpetual grin. He returned the photo with more force than necessary. "I didn't sign on for this!"

"Neither did *she*." Rosa nodded toward the guest bedroom. "Besides, she's been waiting to ask you something."

As if on cue, the door opened. A young girl emerged, clutching a book to her chest. Her tear-glazed brown eyes gazed up at Charles. "Unc—I mean, Papa Charles, would you please read my book to me?" She unwound one of her hands from the book and swiped the moisture from her eyes.

The child held out a bright yellow volume. Its cover bore an illustration of a dancing baby goat. In bright red script, the word "*Cabrito*" arced above the goat.

Charles spun to face Rosa, who was gathering her jacket and purse. "But I thought *cabrito* meant—"

The warning shot from Rosa's eyes cut him off. "Although some are only aware of its culinary connotation, the word technically translates as 'goatling' or kid."

"Where'd she get it?"

Rosa shrugged. "I bought it for her."

He traced his finger over the author's name. "B. L. Barlow. Never heard of him."

"The series is quite popular—fun stories about the antics of farm animals." Slipping her purse strap over her shoulder, Rosa bent down and placed a kiss on the little girl's cheek. "I'll see you tomorrow, *mijita*. Be good for your new papa." Turning toward Charles, she punched a finger into his chest. "And *you* be good to her." With that, she headed out the door, leaving him alone with his niece-turned-daughter.

He flipped to the back of the book and read the short nondescript author bio and a list of additional titles in the series: *Andie the Wonder Dog, Thomas the Tame Turkey, Rocky the Raucous Rooster*, and, coming soon, *The Day of the Duck*. Seemed harmless enough. Charles hadn't considered this aspect of parenting—screening literature for age-appropriateness for his soon-to-be-five-year-old niece. Er ... daughter. *Daughter.* Even though it had barely been a month, he doubted he'd ever get used to that word.

"All right, Hannah." He moved to the sofa and patted the place next to him. "I'll read to you. Then we can warm up whatever deliciousness Rosa cooked for us."

She clambered onto the overstuffed cushion. Charles gazed into her hesitant eyes and bit back a lecture on ladylike movements. Should he send her to boarding school? He could wield multi-million-dollar deals in a single bound, but parenting? And a girl, no less? For the first time in his life, inadequacy overwhelmed him. He squirmed in his seat.

His ponderings were interrupted when Hannah unceremoniously plopped onto his lap. "Oof!"

Yep. Definitely boarding school.

A smile beamed across her face as she flung open the book. "Papa Charles?" Her voice was tentative, eyes wistful. Then, she suddenly blurted, "I want a goat."

Blossom Clarke pressed her back against a large oak tree. Sweat trickled between her shoulder blades. She forced herself not to wriggle. How could January temps be seventeen degrees one day and nearly seventy just a few days later? Arkansas weather. Gotta love it. She snuck a glance over her right shoulder, hoping her stalker wouldn't see her. Did keen bird vision apply to roosters?

Probably.

She focused on her goal—the barnyard gate. Movement from the left caught her attention. She leaned back until the furrowed bark scratched her arms. Glancing down, she noticed a patch of poison ivy that survived the recent cold snap coiling around her ankles. That was the least of her concerns. She sucked in a deep breath and took off.

A rustling of brush sounded behind her. By the time she reached the gate, she was at a dead sprint. She grasped the fork latch and flung it upward just as a flash of gray and white fluttered past, wings flapping like a flag in high winds. How could something so awkward-looking run so fast?

Before Blossom could swing open the gate, talons sank into her left calf. She shrieked. Her poor leg had barely healed from the last attack. She jerked her foot in a futile attempt to dislodge the beast and lost her balance. Flailing her arms to steady herself, she grasped at the nearest object—the gate.

The ruckus caught the attention of most of the barnyard residents, and an assortment of animals rushed toward her, probably hoping for a handout. Penelope, one of the Pygmy does, pushed past the crowd and bumped the gate, knocking it just beyond the reach of Blossom's outstretched hand. The momentum swung her into an over-the-goat cartwheel. She flopped into the midst of a mudpuddle. Swiping a glob of mud from her mouth, she muttered, "That's it. We're having rooster and dumplings for supper."

A fuzzy white face filled her vision as Blossom propped up on an elbow and eased onto her knees. Andromeda. "Thanks for coming to my rescue, girl." She tousled the fur of her Great Pyrenees.

Blossom looped her right-hand fingers through the chain-link fence and pulled herself up. Thankfully, the rooster had fled the scene.

The big dog bumped her head against Blossom's hand.

"Oh, you need petting?" Blossom laughed, knelt, and gave her farm's guardian a good ear scratching. "Let's get you some breakfast, shall we?"

She wove her way through the crowd of beggars, grabbed a red plastic bucket from a shelf, and filled it with a large scoop of kibble. Andromeda gripped the container in her teeth and marched off. Blossom laughed as she watched the dog plod away, the faded coffee label fluttering with each step.

Penelope nibbled on the cuff of Blossom's overall shorts, demanding attention.

"You think you're next, huh?" She rubbed the white star between the goat's horns. "Well then, let's get everyone fed."

CHAPTER TWO

wenty minutes later, Blossom returned to the farmhouse. She kicked off her shoes in the mudroom and toweled the sludge from her face and hair. After washing her hands in the small sink, she traipsed into the main part of the house, nearly running into Grams.

Her grandmother's eyes swept her up and down. "What happened to you?"

"Tripped over a goat."

"I hate it when that happens." Grams laughed, deepening the lines of her sun-browned face. "Penelope?"

"Of course."

"Good thing the weather is warm today or you'd catch your death of cold."

Blossom grinned but quickly sobered at the word *death*. Nodding toward the back door, she asked, "What were you doing out there?"

Grams shrugged. "Put the mail on your workstation."

"You could have put it on the kitchen counter or on my desk in the office like we usually do."

"Yes. But you have to go in there again sometime."

Blossom shook her head, dropping a few mud remnants onto the floor. "Not yet."

Her grandmother pulled her into a hug then stepped back, her warm eyes gazing at Blossom's face. "I miss him too. But avoiding the studio won't bring him back." She rubbed a smudge from Blossom's cheek. "Besides, you got an important letter."

"The permit application?"

"I didn't open it, but there's a letter from the city, yes."

She pushed past Grams and eased out the back. Blossom hesitated before grasping the studio doorknob. Sucking in a deep breath, she pushed open the door and flipped on the light switch. A trio of LED lamps brightened the space, illuminating over two decades of memories. The chair where her father had read countless books to her. The John Deere coffee cup, filled with an assortment of well-worn colored pencils. The now-empty pegboard, once brimming with his favorite hats. When had Grams removed them? She shook her head. A fog of sorrow clouded her thoughts as she moped across the room and ran her hand across a wooden stool. She jerked back her hand. Like the middle bowl of porridge—too cold.

Blossom lingered over the lightbox and stared at the cover sketch of her next book. A pair of Muscovy ducks bobbed heads toward each other as a handful of ducklings clustered close by. She half-expected to hear Dad's booming laugh fill the small space. She shuddered. Turning her back on the reminders of her father's absence, she snatched the letter from her desk and rushed from the room, slamming the door behind her. When she reached the main house, she leaned against the wall and caught her breath.

Grams sidled up to her, placing her hand on Blossom's shoulder.

She buried her face into her grandmother's waiting embrace and sobbed. "I hate her."

Grams held her at arm's length. "Hate is a strong word." Her voice was soft but mingled with caution.

"I should have told him he didn't have to go." She wiped her nose on her sleeve, ignoring the handkerchief Grams had pulled from her jeans pocket.

"He *chose* to go. Rehashing it won't bring him back. Or her, either. We can only do what needs to be done."

So matter of fact. The sudden realization hit her that not only had Blossom lost her father, Grams had lost her son. Her only child. Time to suck it up and, as her father said after her mother died, "Treasure the memories, but keep living life." If he could do it, so could she.

Or *could* she?

She cleared her throat. "Time to see what the city permitting office has to say." Blossom slid her thumbnail across the envelope's flap and pulled out the letter. She scanned the legalese mumbo-jumbo, looked up at Grams, and smiled. "It gives instructions on how to apply for a permit online. I'll need to gather the requested information and complete the form, but it looks like the G.O.A.T. Goat Rescue is one step closer to fruition." She smiled at the name. Hopefully, the soon-to-be rescue center would live up to its name and be the *Greatest of all Time*.

"You know he'd be proud of you."

Blossom sniveled as she nodded. "We can't bring him back, but we *can* make his dream a reality."

Mental images of prancing Pygmies playing with a brown-eyed little girl invaded Charles's thoughts while he punched at his keyboard. He sighed and sipped his coffee. So far, the morning was proving to be unproductive. A rap on his office door window returned Charles from his reverie to reality.

"You look deep in thought." Geoffrey, his assistant, pushed his glasses farther up his nose. "Here's something else for you to think about." He waved a manila folder.

Charles set his mug on the desk. "Phil's official request?"

"Yes. And it's a doozy. Minimum sixty acres, preferably eighty. Utilities available on site. Waterfront. At least seventy percent cleared. Close, if not in the city limits."

Charles took the folder and skimmed the list. "And, of course, I promised him I'd take care of it."

"Good luck!" Geoffrey stepped toward the door.

"Hey, Geoff—"

The young man spun around. A shock of wavy red hair fell in front of his face. He brushed it away with the back of his hand. "Yes, Mr. Sterling?"

"What do you know about goats?"

"Goats?"

"I'm, er, considering purchasing a pet for Hannah. She wants a goat."

"I'm not trying to tell you how to run your life, Mr. S., but there are a lot of good reasons why people get little girls kittens. I mean, even though puppies are popular, they take up a lot of time. But a goat?" He pushed back his unruly locks. "I wouldn't even know where to start."

"Then learn." Charles closed the folder. "In two hours, I have a break in my schedule. By that time, I expect to know as much as possible about the care and upkeep of goats, including where to acquire one."

"Again, not trying to overstep, but just because the kid wants a goat doesn't mean—"

"She already lost her parents. A pet seems like a simple request."

"A pet, yes, but a goat? A goat's a farm animal. It probably requires special accommodations, and—"

"And you have one hour and fifty-six minutes to find out the particulars."

Geoffrey's jaw dropped.

"Don't just stand there with a dumb look on your face. You have a lot of work to do. I will see you at two o'clock sharp."

CHAPTER THREE

*B*lossom rummaged through her father's file cabinet, searching for the property description. The permit people sure had a lot of nosy questions. She was thankful he'd done much of the preliminary work to transform their goat sanctuary into an official rescue site. Grams's voice filtered through the closed door.

"Do you have an appointment, sir?"

Her gatekeeper voice. Blossom smiled.

A moment later, Grams knocked and opened the door a smidgeon. "A man's here asking about buying a goat."

"Wonder how he found out about us. We're not technically open yet."

Grams glanced over her shoulder. "He looks important."

"Think he's from the permit place?" Blossom stood and headed into the hallway. A man wearing a pinstriped suit, complete with matching hat, stood just inside the front door.

He removed his hat and gave a slight bow. "Good morning, Ms.—"

"It's *Miss*. Miss Clarke, with an *E*. Blossom Lane Clarke." Who wore hats nowadays, anyway? She glanced down at her overall shorts, still smattered with mud after the Penelope incident. *I should have showered and changed.* But she and Grams weren't accustomed to company.

"Pleased to meet you, Miss Clarke with an *E*."

"Thanks." *I think.* She motioned for him to follow her into the office and pointed to a chair across from her desk. "And you are?" Blossom moved to her side of the desk and sat. She shuffled some papers, attempting to cover the information she'd been working on.

"Charles Franklin Sterling the Third."

"Wow. That's a mouthful. So, you go by Charlie? Chuck?"

He cleared his throat. "No, I go by Charles."

"Well, that's about as stuffy as an attic in August." Grams had often said her bluntness would get her into trouble someday. She hoped today wouldn't be that day. "How can I help you?"

"I've come to purchase a goat."

"Um, look, Mr., er ... Charles. This isn't a pet store. We're an adoption center for rescued animals." *Or we* will *be, officially, once we get the proper permit.*

"It was my understanding that your establishment is a registered breeder of the National Pygmy Goat Association. Would that not mean you have goats available?"

"How did—never mind." Blossom looked Mr. Sterling in the eye and immediately wished she hadn't. His eyes were gorgeous. Deep brown. Well-tanned skin, not weather-worn like Grams. And his hands—strong, yet ... manicured? *Ew.* "Yes, but we don't sell goats to just anybody. Certain criteria must be met before one can purchase a goat."

"Such as?"

His voice. Smooth, yet powerful. Commanding, like he was used to getting his way. She needed to get this guy out of her office. Now. "Um, okay ..." Why was she stammering? He was just a city guy, likely trying to fulfill some childhood fantasy about being a cool country boy—peanuts in his Coke, and all. It probably wasn't his fault his parents raised him to be a concrete dweller.

"First of all, goats are notorious escape artists. What type of fencing do you have? You do have acreage, correct? Space for a goat to run and jump and play? And proper shelter? Next, goats are herd animals. They don't adjust well when they're alone."

"I was hoping we could come to some sort of arrangement on the care and upkeep of the animal."

"Arrangement?" How could such a smooth-as-silk voice transform from intriguing to irritating so quickly? "What type of arrangement did you have in mind?"

"I would buy the goat and pay you to maintain it."

"Maintain it? Sir, we are breeders, not boarders. And I suppose you'd want some sort of visitation rights agreement as well?" She did a poor job of hiding the sarcasm behind her question.

"Yes."

This guy was serious. Blossom stood. Before she could collect her thoughts and give him a piece of them, the office door flung open. A small Hispanic woman marched in, holding the hand of a young girl—the spitting image of Mr. Charles Franklin Sterling, the Third.

"There you are!" the woman said, accusation seething from her voice.

The tanning-bed bronze tone drained from his face. "Rosa. What are you—"

"What am *I* doing here? The real question is, what are *you* doing here? It's Thursday. My day off. Remember?"

Blossom knew she shouldn't be as amused as she was,

watching Mr. Calm, Cool, and Collected getting the what-for from a woman half his size. But she ignored her twinge of conscience, leaned against her desk, and settled in. A show like this needed popcorn.

Charles glanced at his watch. Probably a Rolex, if she were guessing. But then, Blossom had never seen a Rolex before. "My apologies. But that doesn't answer the question. How did you know I was here? And why is Hannah with you?"

Hannah. A beautiful name for a beautiful child. Blossom noticed the two adults who were supposedly her keepers were speaking as though she weren't in the room, listening to every word.

"When you didn't pick her up, the preschool called me. I called your office, and—"

"Geoffrey."

"Yes, Geoffrey. After he absolutely refused to pick her up, I hurried over there and got her." She tousled Hannah's hair. "*¡Ay, pobrecita!*"

He forgot his daughter? Blossom slid off the desk. "Look, Mr. Sterling—"

"So, are you ready to show me the goats, Miss Clarke? Now that Hannah is here, she can pick out the one she wants."

CHAPTER FOUR

"*O*f all the pompous, presumptuous, puffed up—"

Grams wiped her hands on a dishtowel. "You forgot dashing, debonair, dressed to the nines."

Blossom huffed. "At least he's practical. Drives a 4Runner instead of some fancy-schmancy rich car."

"Have you priced those things lately?"

Blossom plopped onto a barstool at the kitchen counter. "I still can't believe his arrogance. Assuming I would just mosey out to the barnyard and let him have his pick of the stock."

"Which is exactly what you did, if I recall."

"Only because he had his daughter with him. What was I supposed to do?"

Grams sat beside her and poured them both a glass of iced tea. "Did you get the boarding agreement details lined out?"

Blossom blew out another breath. "Yes." She spun her stool around to face Grams. "But only because that adorable little girl was with him. How could he have left her at school? It's like she never crossed his mind."

"She crossed his mind enough for him to drive out here and go goat shopping."

"I guess."

"And he agreed to do his part in co-parenting the kid?" A smirk formed at the edges of her mouth.

Sometimes, Grams's sense of humor grated on Blossom's nerves. "We are not *co-parenting.*" She squeezed the lemon wedge into her glass and swirled the tea with a long-handled spoon. "If I ever have a child—"

"You will."

Blossom laughed out loud. "Yeah, right." She looked at her hands and ran her thumbnail inside her index finger, removing a stubborn bit of grime that had withstood several hand washings.

"I thought Mr. Sterling was rather handsome."

"Humph. You're always telling me, 'Pretty is as pretty does.' Wouldn't that go for handsome as well? Besides, he's a father. Probably has a wife somewhere. Hopefully, he hasn't forgotten about her too."

"I didn't see a ring. Of course, that doesn't always mean anything." The oven timer beeped, and Grams got up to remove a sheet of peanut butter cookies. "Cookie?"

Blossom shook her head. "Maybe later. Thanks."

"So, when's he coming to uphold his part of the bargain?"

"He said he'd stop by in the morning before he goes to his office."

"So, he'll be fighting traffic twice—coming out here and then heading back downtown. Bless his heart."

"Don't you go blessing his heart!" She stood and tossed the lemon into the garbage. "Because you're not changing my mind about him. Handsome or not, ring or no ring, Mr. Sterling *forgot* his daughter. He might be a successful businessman, but in my mind, he's a loser."

"So, let me get this straight." Geoffrey padded across the carpet toward the espresso machine. "You want me to do some legwork on Phil's request because you have to goat-sit?"

"I don't think goat-sit is the correct term here since I technically own the goat."

"But she's keeping it for you? The farm girl?"

Farm girl. That wasn't the image Charles conjured when he thought of Blossom, which he had done more than he cared to admit. Her carefree spirit. Her genuine love of her animals and nature. The way her pigtails flopped as she bounced around, playing with the goats. Bounced. How long had it been since he'd bounced? Had he *ever*? She was everything he wasn't. And perhaps everything he should be.

"Earth to Charles?"

He jerked his head toward Geoffrey's voice. "Sorry. Yes. The 'farm girl' is allowing me to keep the goat on her property as long as I help take care of it."

"And what do you know about taking care of a goat?" Geoffrey scoffed. "I'm the one who did all the research."

Charles stood and grabbed his hat from the rack.

"What about compensation? Will I get a commission on this deal?"

"I've always done my best to take good care of you financially, Geoffrey. This situation will be no different, I'm sure. You find Phil the perfect property, and I'll make sure you get a nice bonus."

Charles stepped through his office door, suddenly wondering what it would be like to live a carefree existence, much like Blossom. The name suited her. Too bad he didn't.

CHAPTER FIVE

*W*ithin a few minutes of Charles's arrival at the
rescue center the next morning, Blossom led him
to a large, fenced area with a few goats meandering about. At
that point, she stopped and studied him. "Hmm."

"What? What's wrong?" He'd worn jeans and a T-shirt, just
as she had on. He figured this was the most practical attire he
owned for whatever lay in store for him today.

"What size shoes do you wear?"

Ah. The leather loafers. He noticed she was wearing boots
today, but these shoes were the best he could do on short notice.
"These will be fine. They're comfortable. And old. It's okay if
they get dirty."

"You sure? They look expensive."

They were. Very. "It's fine. Really."

She shrugged. "Suit yourself." A pensive expression crossed
her face. "Since it's your first day, we'll do a tour." She was
probably thinking, *And because you're not wearing proper
footwear.* Pointing to a mid-sized shelter enclosed by a pen, she
said, "Let's start with the intake area."

Before they reached the area she'd indicated, Charles noticed something sneaking up behind them. He spun and pointed to a black-and-white rooster. "What is *that?*"

Her expression did a one-eighty, transforming from borderline bored to high. alert. "That is Stu, a Dominicker rooster"

"Stu?"

"Short for stupid or, probably one day, Stew Pot. Take your pick."

Stu did a quick touch-and-go jump on the back of Blossom's legs. The rooster circled around and lowered his head, keeping his gaze directly in her eyes. He flapped his wings and did a mock charge.

She let out a squeal and grabbed Charles's hand. "Shoo! Get away!" She nudged Stu with the toe of her boot, but the beast didn't budge.

"You heard her. Go on, now." The bird cocked his head sideways and shifted his glare to Charles. He suppressed a laugh because he realized Blossom's fear of the small creature was real.

Stu puffed up his feathers, then turned and skittered away in a gawky gait.

Perhaps just realizing she was still holding his hand, she dropped her grasp as though a hot potato had been tossed toward her. Her hand in his had felt so natural. And now, missed.

What was I thinking? Blossom couldn't believe she'd grabbed Charles's hand without considering the man had a wife and child. Warmth still tingled her palm where it had rested in his only moments ago. "Is Hannah coming to see her goat this afternoon? Has she thought of a name yet?"

"I asked Rosa to drop her off here after school, and I'll meet them. She is so excited. But I'm not yet sure about the name. It's not like it will come when she calls it, though."

Blossom gave him a hard look. "They can learn their names and recognize people they've bonded with."

"I had no idea."

"You'll learn. And so will your daughter." Blossom cringed inwardly at the word. *Daughter* meant *wife*. She had to keep reminding herself. This man was *married*.

A young woman drove by on a golf cart. "That's Lauren, one of the vet techs, who stops by regularly to check on our menagerie." Blossom waved.

Charles followed suit and lifted his hand slightly, scanning the area. She observed as he took in the expanse of the operation.

"This is a large property."

"Um-hmm. Nearly seventy acres. About ten of those along the Little Maumelle River are wooded, but my father had most of the place cleared, leaving enough trees to keep the natural beauty." Her voice caught at the thought of her father's dream, now so close to coming true—without him.

Charles yelped and jumped back, swatting at something behind him.

"What's wro—?" Blossom stopped short as she spotted the culprit, thankful Stu hadn't returned. "Penelope. Mind your manners. We have a guest, and you'd better get used to him. He'll be a frequent visitor."

As if she understood, the goat stepped away from where she'd been nibbling on Charles's back pocket.

"She seems very friendly."

"Penelope doesn't know she's a goat." Blossom laughed. "She acts more like a puppy, but, of course, she has a lot of native goat tendencies."

"To be honest, I don't know much about goats."

"They don't really eat tin cans, you know," she began. "They will eat the labels, though, so old wives' tales claim goats eat the cans as well. They're actually pretty smart. And mostly docile." Resisting the urge to grab his hand again, she motioned toward the gate. "Here's the intake area. This is the first stop when a new rescue arrives. You've already seen the registered goat area. We keep the rescues separate for obvious reasons."

"I'd never considered goats being animals that needed rescuing. What would bring one to your facility?"

"Pretty much any animal that is abused or neglected needs a rescue facility. There are even donkey rescue centers." She pushed a stray hair from her face. "But to answer your question, some of our residents have come here because a child started a 4-H project but later went off to college. Millie over there," she pointed to a brown-speckled goat, "arrived when her former owners said she was harassing their blind horse. What they didn't say, or perhaps didn't know, was that she was pregnant with triplets."

"Surprise, huh?" He chuckled, and the sound warmed her heart.

Stop it! "Yeah. Big time." Pointing to the intake center, Blossom explained the process. The vet tech on duty collected as much information about the new arrival as possible. Approximate age. Health issues. Papers, if it was registered. Then, the hooves were trimmed, shots administered, and the goat was given a general once-over. Once the initial examination was finished, the animal would be placed in quarantine for a short time. "That's the hard part. As I mentioned earlier, goats don't like to be alone. Right, Penelope?" She scratched between her tagalong's horns.

"How many goats do you have now?"

"Eighteen. We've applied for a permit to keep livestock within the city limits. But until that is approved, we need to limit things until we become official." She formed air quotes as she said the last word. "As long as no one complains, we'll be fine until the permit is approved. Then we can open to the public. Since our property borders the river on one side and is otherwise bounded by the wildlife refuge, we don't really have any neighbors to bother." She paused, realizing she was over-sharing. "Well, I've been babbling. Let's hop in a golf cart, and while I drive you around the property, you can tell me about yourself. What line of work are you in?"

He slid into the passenger side while she started the cart. "I'm a real estate consultant."

"I've never heard of such a thing. What exactly does a real estate consultant do?"

Charles grabbed the seat handle as Blossom took a curve a bit too fast.

"Sorry." She grinned.

"Most of my clients are commercial developers. They come up with a concept that includes the exact kind of property needed for the project. The specs are sent to my company, and we search for the perfect place for them to buy."

She waved her hand around the area. "I hope you can make your clients as happy with their new properties as I am with mine. This place has been in our family for decades. This, Mr. Sterling, *is* the perfect place."

He smiled. "Yes, it is."

CHAPTER SIX

The next day, Charles arrived early, clad in work clothes and muck boots. The tour was over. Time to get down and dirty. It was a bit chilly, and he shivered as hurried through the gate leading to the main building. Blossom was pouring coffee when he opened the door.

She gave him a quick once-over. "Well, look who went shopping." She handed him a steaming mug.

"Thanks. And yes, I decided I'd better get some proper working attire." He placed a hand on her arm. "By the way, thanks for spending so much time with Hannah yesterday. I'm sure you had a lot to do, but she was thrilled."

"It was truly my pleasure. She is an adorable child."

"Thank you."

"So, what made you decide to get her a goat?"

He chuckled. "Rosa got her a book titled *Cabrito*. It's her favorite book." Blossom's face paled. He hoped she wasn't feeling ill.

"I think the pet she picked out will be perfect. He's very sweet."

"The goat is fixed? Neutered?"

She gave a small laugh, and her face glowed. "Yes. He is a wether. A neutered male. They make excellent pets."

"Great. What's on the agenda today?"

"You in a hurry to get done so you can head back to your office?"

Charles shook his head. "I have a capable assistant working on some projects for me there. Today, I'm all yours." He felt his face redden. "I mean, I'm ready to earn my keep. Or my goat's keep."

She cackled out loud. "Maybe you should stop while you're behind."

"Good idea."

"I think today we'll go visit your little girl's goat and let him get to know you better."

After a five-minute golf cart ride, they disembarked in front of one of the small shelters that dotted the property. A young man led Hannah's goat on a leash. "Thanks, Parker." After he left, Blossom glanced up at Charles. "He's one of about a dozen volunteers who work here. They help with leash training, grooming, mucking stalls—things you'll be doing." She winked.

"I can't wait." He laughed.

She knelt down and scratched the goat's chin. Looking up at Charles, she asked, "Has Hannah come up with a name for him yet?"

Guilt twinged his conscience. He'd gone back to the office after leaving the farm and arrived home after Hannah's bedtime. The scowl he received from Rosa still stung. "Um, no. Not yet. I'll talk with Hannah tonight." Maybe he'd buy her another book in that animal series she liked and read it to her.

A bump against his leg jolted him from his thoughts. A white mound of fluff nudged his hand. At least it wasn't Penelope, the nibbling goat or Stu, the crazed rooster.

"This is Andromeda, the Great Warrior Princess. Our farm's guardian. She wants you to pet her."

Charles suddenly wished he'd spent more time at his grandparents' farm and less time in the house playing video games. "Well, hello there." He patted the dog's head.

"Scratch behind her ears. She likes that."

As he complied, a high-pitched chirping interrupted. Charles followed the sound and saw a duckling twirling around, continuing its frantic cries. Andromeda bent over the baby duck. She opened her jowls and enclosed the yapping duckling's head in her mouth.

"She's eating the duck! Stop her!"

Blossom laid a hand on his arm. "Wait. And watch." She pointed at a mother duck, followed closely by several babies.

The massive dog plodded three long strides and plopped the duckling in front of its mother as if to say, 'Here's your kid. Keep up with it.' A moment later, she returned to Charles's side, nudging him for another ear scratch.

"That was amazing. I was certain she was going to eat it."

"She does that anytime one of the babies gets left behind. I think the chirping annoys her." Blossom laughed. "She's pretty awesome."

He snuck a side glance at the dog's owner. Speaking of pretty and awesome ... He scolded himself for letting his thoughts stray. He was here to help Hannah cope with losing her parents. The child had asked for one thing. A goat. Not exactly a simple request. But doable.

If he could stay focused.

Later that evening, Charles drove past the manicured landscaping edging the driveway of his father's country club home. When his father requested a 'meeting,' Rosa had agreed to stay late and watch Hannah. Shouldn't be too hard, since Charles had tucked the child in before leaving. Rosa could read and relax until he returned.

He circled his SUV around the fountain and parked near the entrance. Normally, a valet would rush to park the vehicle for him, but his father said the servants had been dismissed for the evening.

"Knock, knock!" He let himself in the entryway, wondering why he had been summoned.

To the right of the double grand staircase, he heard his father's voice bellow, "Come on in, son."

As Charles entered the sitting area, Frank Sterling clapped his hand on his son's shoulder. "Glad you could make time to visit your old man."

The lyrics from Harry Chapin's "Cat's in the Cradle" cruised through Charles's conscience. One of the hazards of listening to oldies music. "Of course, Dad. Always glad to visit you." He resisted the urge to touch his nose to check for any sudden growth.

"So, how are things in the ... what exactly do you call your industry?"

"I'm a real estate consultant. I research properties for clients based on their specifications."

"Ah. I was wondering how you were putting that law degree to work."

Charles bristled at the unspoken accusation. "Not everyone is cut out to be an attorney like William." Nothing had changed. No matter how hard he worked, he'd never reach the top of the pedestal his now-deceased brother had climbed.

"Easy, now. No need to get defensive. I didn't ask you over to compare your accomplishments with Bill's."

Bill. His brother even got a nickname. And so did his father. Instead of Charles Franklin Sterling the Second, his dad went by Frank. Yet, here he was, stuck with Charles. *About as stuffy as an attic in August.* Blossom was right.

"Then why did you ask me to come?" he asked. May as well cut to the chase.

"Well, it does concern Bill. Or rather, Elise."

"Elise? If you're wondering how things are going with Hannah—"

"No. Nothing like that. I'm sure you're adjusting well to being a parent. Besides, you have Rosa to help. Although I'd love to see my granddaughter again soon."

Good to know his dad trusted a family employee more than his own son. "Hannah seems to be doing well, considering ..." His heart pinched. Despite his differences with Dad, at least he still had a living parent. And Mom had only been gone a few years. What must it be like being orphaned at such a young age? He cleared the lump of emotions from his throat. "So, Elise?"

"Her sister, Kara, actually. I know this whole tragedy has been hard on all of us, but Kara seems to be taking it exceptionally hard. She was very close to Elise."

He'd never considered how the accident had affected others. Was he that self-centered? "How can I help? Perhaps I can reach out and set up a play date with Hannah."

"I'm sure she'd love that. But she needs a friend, Charles. Elise was her— how do youngsters say it now?"

"Bestie? BFF?"

"Yes. Bestie. That's what she said. She misses her bestie. I think Kara needs someone to hang out with."

"You mean like shopping or chit-chatting at the coffee shop?" The only person near Kara's age who came to mind was Geoffrey. He couldn't do that to the poor girl. Or, perhaps Blossom. Like those two had anything in common. He shook his head. "I can't think of anyone off the top of my head who may be able to fill that void."

"I was thinking *you* could," his father said in a deadpan voice.

"Me?" He was already a surrogate father to Elise's daughter. Now his dad thought he should babysit her younger sister as well?

"You're only a few years older than her. Now that she's finished her master's, she's been looking for a job. I believe Elise was helping her with job search prep."

"But, Dad—"

Frank shook his head. "No buts about it. You'd be perfect. In fact, the church Valentine's Day banquet is coming up soon. You could take her again, like you did last year."

"Last year, I asked her as a favor to Elise so she could hang out with her 'bestie' at the banquet."

His father waved in a dismissive gesture. "True, but I'm sure you still had a good time. She is quite lovely."

Lovely. The word struck him like one of Cupid's arrows as he realized another young woman who pegged the lovely meter.

"Charles?"

"Um, sorry. I was just—"

"Wait. I recognize that look. You're already smitten with someone. I had no idea, or, of course, I would have never suggested taking Kara." His father rocked back and forth on his heels. "So, can you tell me about your little lady? I'd thought you were a confirmed bachelor." The older man winked.

"I am," he answered a bit too abruptly, but his father's interest in his non-existent love life caught him off guard. "I have neither the time nor the inclination to begin a relationship." He needed to check that nose again. If he kept this up, Pinocchio would have nothing on him.

"But there is someone ... I can see it in your eyes. Indulge an old romantic and tell me."

Old romantic? His father? "I ... um," Charles stammered. "She—she runs a rescue operation in the west part of town. Not too far from Pinnacle Mountain."

"What kind of rescue operation?

Charles sucked in a deep breath. "Goats."

"A *goat* farmer?" His father's look of astonishment said it all.

He knew it. He'd just added to the already vast arsenal of criticism material. "Look, Dad," he began.

Frank held up a hand. "Hear me out, son." He motioned to the opposing sofas near the fireplace. "Let's sit."

The sweet fragrance of cherry wood filled the room as the fire crackled. Charles watched the embers float upward, disappearing in the chimney. If only his worries could float away so easily.

After they'd settled across from each other, his father continued, "I'm well aware that you think I favored your brother over you, and perhaps I did. But have you ever wondered why?"

"Because he was a lawyer, like you. And quite successful. Would've probably wound up becoming a judge. Like you."

"Successful. Yes, I suppose he was successful by the world's standard. But his true success lay in his compassion for others. He preferred the term 'counselor' to attorney. He'd often say, 'Everyone who enters my office has a problem. And it's my job to help them resolve whatever issues they're facing.'" His father leaned back against the headrest, looking deep in thought. He then moved forward, leaning his elbows on his knees. "Compassion. *That's* what made me proud of him."

Charles swallowed hard. "I always thought—"

"That you needed to win no matter what the cost. Well, son, sometimes that cost isn't worth it. You're nearly thirty, and what have you got to show for it? A fancy loft condo? A comfortable vehicle? Designer suits? Do those things make you happy? I'm afraid you've confused legacy with luxury. One lasts. The other is fleeting."

His dad stood and walked to the coffee bar. After filling two mugs, he returned and handed one to Charles. "Now, tell me about your friend. Because the thought of her brought a look to your face I thought I'd never see—an expression that tells me you're thinking of someone else instead of just yourself or your career. And *that* is something I want to know more about."

CHAPTER SEVEN

*B*lossom shut the studio door behind her, frustrated with her story's lack of progress. The due date to turn in *The Day of the Duck* to her agent was fast approaching. She doubted she'd ever have a manuscript worthy of the cover her father had illustrated. She sucked in a long breath and blew it out.

And once she got the story down, she'd have to find an illustrator to match the style Dad had used in the previous books. Or have her publisher find someone. She shuddered at the thought. Nope. *She* would recruit her father's replacement. *When* she was ready. Her agent had already negotiated that point for her. She couldn't have just anyone finish her father's work.

Grams passed her in the hallway. "Been writing?"

"Yeah, a little. Guess it's time to search for an illustrator. I've been dreading that."

"I can imagine you have." A master at changing the subject, Grams asked, "How's the new hand working out?" She gave Blossom one of her lopsided smirks.

"He's fine." Blossom felt a blush creep up her neck and face. "I mean, just fine. He's just fine."

"Um-hmm. I knew he was fine the first day he stopped by." She winked.

"I'm actually impressed at how hard he's trying. I mean, this has to be as far from his normal as possible, yet he does whatever is asked of him without complaint. He held Claudia still so Parker could milk her. And then he actually gave Penelope her annual shots. Of course, Penelope is pretty patient."

"Got to start him out easy."

"Yeah, whatever."

After pondering the conversation with his father, Charles realized his feelings for Blossom had blossomed enough to be noticeable. He decided to end this—whatever *this* was—before he got in any deeper. With his demanding career and now a child to raise, he certainly didn't have time to develop a relationship. This self-talk was crazy! Blossom had given him no indication she was even attracted to him, so why had he allowed her to take up residence in his heart and mind?

That would all stop today. He'd return ownership of the goat to the rescue center and take Hannah to a pet adoption place where she could pick out a kitten. All little girls liked kittens, right?

As Charles pulled into the drive of G.O.A.T. Goat Rescue, he could almost feel the stress leave his body. Serenity. That's what this place produced. He exited his SUV and breathed in a lungful of clean air. Although the cityscape could be seen across the river, the hectic chaos seemed a thousand miles away. Peace.

"Tommy, no!" Blossom's voice tore through the calm, followed closely by a loud shrill.

A moment later, the only turkey Charles had seen outside a

grocery store freezer bin trotted toward him like a bowling ball barreling down a lane. Who knew something so big and awkward could move so quickly? The bird halted within a few feet and puffed out its feathers.

"Stand still. Don't move, and don't make a sound."

Easy for her to say. Charles held his breath, remaining close to the 4Runner, while Tommy strutted and gobbled.

Blossom walked up to the turkey and patted him on the head. "He's usually quite tame, but turkeys are territorial. He'll have to get used to you coming around." She held out some sort of treat and bade the bird follow her, which it did as if it were a puppy.

She stopped long enough to glance over her shoulder, pigtails flipping to the front as her head moved. "Coming?"

Charles followed at what he hoped was a safe distance. "I thought you raised goats. But I've seen a chicken, ducks, and now this—" His voice cracked.

She shooed Tommy into a pen and shut the gate. "We do. But we also raise some heritage-breed turkeys and other critters who need a home. Tom is a Narragansett." Her tone flowed like honey, as though witnessing a near-turkey attack was the most normal event on the planet.

Giving a nod toward the turkey, he asked, "Can he fly?"

Blossom tossed another treat toward Tom. "He can fly, but he's usually content to roost in a tree and watch."

Like a stalker.

She almost skipped along the left side of Tommy's pen and gave Charles a mischievous smile. "Let's go check on your adopted goat."

Charles hesitated for a few seconds, staring at his nemesis. Big mistake. The turkey took that moment to prove indeed he *could* fly. Looking more bungling than one of those Airbus Beluga planes, the bird bobbled to the top of the fence and hopped down, landing within inches of Charles's feet.

He turned and ran to catch up with Blossom, yowling like a

little girl as he felt sharp talons digging into his backside. Charles spun in a circle, hoping to disengage the bird from his body.

"Don't turn your back toward him!" Blossom warned.

Good to know. Would've been better had she shared that info about four seconds earlier. Flailing in a flurry of feathers, Charles finally shook off the beast and hurtled himself through the door of a nearby outbuilding. He slammed the door shut and leaned against it, his chest heaving as he fought to catch his breath.

A moment later, the knob turned, and he moved to let Blossom enter.

"Thanks for coming to my resc—"

"You have no right to be in here!" Her attack was as sudden and unexpected as the turkey's. "This is a private space." She quickly moved between him and the rest of the room, blocking his view.

He hadn't yet noticed where he was, but her odd behavior piqued his curiosity. "What's so secret about this building?" He leaned his head to peek over her shoulder. An art studio? Placing his hands gently on her shoulders, he eased her out of his way and studied the pages littering the top of a lightbox. He spun to face her. "You're an artist?"

Blossom brushed away a tear. "This is none of your business!" She shuffled the sheets in an attempt to hide them from his view.

"*The Day of the Duck*? That's the next book in the series Hannah is reading. She loves those books! She'll be thrilled to know you're the illustrator. Is it coming out soon? She's been asking about it."

Blossom pushed him toward the door. "I am *not* the illustrator, and it is *not* coming out soon." Tears spilled down her cheeks, and she sank to the floor, leaning against the wall. "It's *never* coming out."

He slid to the floor beside her. His first instinct was to hold her, but he hesitated. He'd already upset her. Uncertain what to do, he brushed a tear from her cheek. "Hey, I didn't know this place was off-limits when I ducked in here to escape from that crazed turkey. I'm sorry I upset you. I'll pretend I never saw those drawings."

Blossom sniveled for a few minutes, then stood and reached for a paper towel. After wiping her face and nose, she looked at him intently. "My father," she stopped to subdue a sob. "This is his studio. That is his work."

She walked slowly to the workstation and picked up one of the sketches, then clutched it to her chest. "I miss him so much."

Charles met her across the room. "I'm so sorry. How long has it been since ..."

"A month. It still doesn't seem real." She placed her father's drawings on top of the lightbox.

He pulled her into a hug and let her sob gently on his shoulder. "That's about when my brother—" He stopped. This wasn't about him or his family. She was mourning her father.

"When your brother what?"

"I'm sorry. You were sharing about your father, and—"

"You lost your brother?"

He nodded.

"He must have been young. How?"

"Drunk driver." He shook his head. "And your dad? If I may ask."

"Small plane crash. With his new wife."

"I'm so sorry. Bill's wife was also killed. Such a waste. And poor Hannah—"

"Wait—Hannah is your niece? She was just orphaned?"

"Yeah. Well, daughter now. Elise and Bill ... in their wills ... I still have to formally adopt her, but I thought I'd give her some time to adjust first."

"That's a huge responsibility. And an honor. I mean, they

must have trusted you greatly to arrange for you to raise her should anything happen to them."

He hadn't thought about it that way. "She's such a sweet girl. I just want the best for her. Thus, the goat." Gazing into her eyes, he wished he could remove the pain from her heart. He brushed her tear-dampened cheek with his thumb. The act of brushing away a tear—so innocent—quickly transformed into a caress. His thumb moved to trace her lips, and before he realized what he was doing, he shifted his thumb and covered her lips with his.

She snuggled against him, molding her mouth to his. After a few glorious seconds, reality struck. He'd come here to renege on the goat deal. Instead of stopping *this*, he'd made it worse.

He pushed back. "I'm so sorry." His voice came out in a husky gasp.

Her eyes flashed with nearly as much pain as they'd displayed at the thought of her father's death. "Sorry about what? For kissing me?"

The words struck like a slap, and for a moment, he wasn't sure she hadn't hit him. He stepped back, hands still on her shoulders. "You were vulnerable. I just wanted to comfort you."

"You want to comfort me?" That grin peeked through. "Then kiss me again!" She grabbed his cheeks and moved his face toward her until their lips met.

CHAPTER EIGHT

*C*harles was whistling when he entered his house at 5:42 p.m.

"You're early. Or at least, on time." Rosa gave him a side-eye. "And whistling? Who are you, and what'd you do with my grumpy boy?"

"I'm blessed. And I'm sorry for taking you for granted all these years. Why don't you take the day off tomorrow?"

Rosa swatted at him with a dishrag. "I plan to. It's Thursday."

He laughed. "And where is Hannah? I have a present for her." He opened the bag enough to let Rosa peek inside.

"Oh, you got the dog book! She'll be thrilled." Rosa turned to stir a simmering pot. "Go read it to her now. I'll keep supper warm." She shooed him into the great room.

A moment later, Hannah was snuggled against his chest. He'd never dreamed of holding a child on his lap. Now, *his* child. Perhaps one day, the Good Lord would see fit to give him a mother for Hannah. He hadn't prayed in far too long. Now would be a good time to start. He prayed for a good woman to help him raise this precious little girl as he opened the book to page one.

"I love the crinkling sound of a new book opening. Don't you, Papa Charles?"

"I hadn't thought of it before, but yes, it is a nice sound. Let's see what Andie the Wonder Dog has to say."

"You're silly." She swatted his hand. "Dogs don't talk."

A few pages into the story, Andie had already helped an abandoned baby goat keep warm through the night while its mother did who-knew-what. He turned another page and saw a drawing of a little duckling *cheep-cheeping*. The next page showed Andie the Wonder Dog picking up the baby duck with her mouth. He slammed the book shut and read the cover. B. L. Barlow.

"Papa Charles, what's wrong?" Hannah's large eyes sought his.

He flipped back to the page where he'd stopped. Sure enough, the dog plopped the duckling in front of its mother. Was this a common occurrence on farms? What did B. L. stand for? What had Miss Clarke with an *E* said her full name was? Blossom … he thought for a moment. Blossom Lane.

B. L.?

Surely not. If she had authored this book series, she would have told him while they were in the studio. Right? But if she wasn't the author or the illustrator, just what role did she have in producing these books? And why was she so secretive about the studio?

Charles arrived at the G.O.A.T. Goat Rescue center a few minutes early. Andromeda was the first one to greet him, followed closely behind by Penelope. He noted that the two were practically inseparable, almost as if the dog were the goat's mother.

Blossom followed the pair toward Charles. "Good morning." Her bright smile erased his mind of all wandering thoughts. Today, he would spend the entire morning with this beautiful woman, and he planned to enjoy every moment of it. "Good morning to you too." He reached down to scratch the dog's ears and give the goat a chin-scratching. "These two seem to have a special bond."

Blossom hesitated before responding. "Yeah. Our warrior princess here adopted Penelope at birth."

"Adopted? Was her mother ill?"

Blossom shook her head. "Not exactly. Miss P was born early on a March morning. It was bitterly cold. We'd been watching, knowing the doe would kid soon. I didn't think it was time yet, but Penelope had other plans, didn't you, girl?" She knelt down and nuzzled the Pygmy, nose to nose.

"When Grams and I came out to make the rounds, we could tell the doe had given birth, but there was no sign of the baby. I was frantic." She stood, and Penelope pogo-stick-hopped over to the dog.

"I can imagine so," Charles said.

"After searching everywhere imaginable, I heard a muffled bleat. Andromeda was lying on the ground in her usual spot." She pointed to the area where the dog and goat both were resting. "But after a few minutes, I realized the bleating was coming from there. I rushed over, and Andie, er—Andromeda— had the baby snuggled in her underbelly, keeping her warm."

"Wow." That was *exactly* what happened in the book he'd read to Hannah last night. He paused, wondering if he should express his suspicions. Her expression gave him no clue about her thoughts, so he dared to speak up. "I don't want to stir up any emotions, but I'm guessing the author your father illustrated for must have witnessed some of the antics of your animals. Did Mr.

Barlow visit the farm frequently? Or did your father share stories with him?"

"I ... um ..."

A look of such uncertainty spread across her face that he held up a hand to stop her pain. "Hey, I'm sorry. I know your loss is fresh. Please forgive me. Finish your story."

"Okay." She nodded, looking relieved. "The doe rejected Penelope. Wouldn't nurse her. We had to bottle feed." She paused, looking thoughtful. "I'm not sure exactly why the doe refused her kid. It's rare, but it happens. I'm grateful her adoptive mother stepped in. Miss P is such a hoot. I can't imagine life here without her."

As if on cue, Penelope leaped along, twisting and side-kicking until she landed in front of Blossom. She nibbled on the edge of her jacket, gently head-butting Blossom's hand. "You are *so* spoiled, little girl!"

The next morning, Blossom wadded up a page and tossed it into her office's trashcan—for the fourteenth time. Ugh! As hard as it had been for her to focus on the story after her father died, daydreaming about kissing Charles again made writing even harder. Would he kiss her again?

She shook the memory from her mind, forcing her thoughts back to what had inspired this story. One of the Muscovy hens had escaped. The duck seemed to have a mind of her own. The bird waddled into the woods adjoining the wildlife refuge, head-bobbing all the way. The not-so-simple feat of netting and returning the duck had turned into an all-day affair. She laughed at the memory.

Glancing at her watch, she realized Charles would be here

any minute. Her conscience twinged at the unkind thoughts she'd had about him and the words she'd spoken to Grams. No wonder he forgot Hannah that day. In the studio, he mentioned giving his niece-turned-daughter time to adjust, but he was also still adjusting.

She snuck a quick peek at her reflection in the wall mirror and hurried out the door. His SUV was already parked near the rescue center entrance.

The gate to Penelope's pen was unlatched. But there was no sign of her. Or Charles. The strap used for securing the gate was hanging from its hook instead of through the fence. Odd.

She called out, "Charles?" After waiting a moment for an answer, she yelled, "Penelope?" No response. Not that she expected the goat to reply, but if Miss P thought a treat was possible, she'd come running.

Glancing around, Blossom noticed some goat berries near the edge of the woods. *Uh-oh.* Hopefully, today wouldn't be a repeat of *The Day of the Duck*. Perhaps Charles had taken her for a walk. Why would he do that without asking? He wouldn't. And a quick once-over of her empty pen revealed the leash, hanging in its regular place.

Blossom moved quickly toward the pile of droppings. Not exactly breadcrumbs, but maybe she could Hansel and Gretel herself in the right direction. She noticed a bush with a couple of broken twigs. Good thing she'd helped her cousin achieve his Boy Scout Search and Rescue merit badge when they were teenagers.

She'd complained to Grams about the cold rain they had two days ago, but because of it, she spied a boot print in the soft soil. She could almost guess what happened. Charles had brought Hannah by after supper the night before to play with her pet and give him a good brushing. Blossom smiled as she recalled the pure joy on the child's face as she interacted with the young goat.

And, as with every visit, Hannah requested to play with Penelope. The child was smitten with Miss P and would've adopted her, but Blossom wouldn't allow it. She wasn't for sale. When Grams hollered that Blossom had a call on the house phone, she'd left them, with Charles assuring her he'd secure the place before he and Hannah left.

If only she'd remembered to show him how to fasten the extra strap on the gate to keep Penelope locked in place. She should have been named Houdini. Charles must have noticed her open pen when he arrived. What if he couldn't find Penelope? What if Blossom couldn't find *him*? She did her best to brush aside the what-ifs and worries and focus on the search strategy and tactics she'd helped her cousin study.

She was thankful that Charles and the little escape artist weren't concerned with stealth because their path was easy to pick up. Unequipped with any specialized listening devices, Blossom used what she had—her ears—and stopped frequently to listen for sounds of distress or cries for help. After a few pauses to listen for movement, she finally heard something— Penelope bleating and Charles pleading.

"Come on, Miss P. You need to cooperate."

Blossom could hear him grunting. What had he and Penelope gotten themselves into?

"Stop butting me! I can't help you if you hurt me."

Still working her way through the undergrowth, Blossom suppressed a giggle. It didn't sound as if they were in too much distress.

"Now, listen," boomed Charles's voice. "I need to get you untangled and back to your pen before Blossom discovers we're gone."

"Too late." Blossom pushed aside a large bush and emerged into the clearing where Charles was negotiating with Penelope.

"What?" He spun to face her.

CHAPTER NINE

"*H*old her still. The harness is slipping." Blossom's voice came across more demanding than she'd intended. "Um ... please?" she added.

Charles straddled the goat while Blossom lathered her face and neck. "*Ew!* What is that smell?"

Blossom shrugged. "Who knows? Normally, goats are pretty clean animals, in spite of their reputation." She dipped a rag in a bucket of clean water and wiped away the soapy mess.

Penelope wriggled and bleated, conveying her annoyance to the humans. After the rinse, Blossom tossed a towel to Charles. She could tell he was watching her actions and doing his best to mimic them. "Today, you can cross off 'goat bathing' from your bucket list."

He laughed. Within a few seconds, his expression turned pensive. He stopped drying Penelope and draped his towel over the barn stall's partition. "Speaking of bucket lists, I recently added something special to mine."

"Oh?" Blossom removed the harness and patted Penelope on her back. "Good girl. You can go but stay in the barn until you're fully dry. It's chilly out."

Charles nearly doubled over with laughter. "Do you think she understood that?"

Blossom shrugged. "She may not understand all the words, but she's pretty intuitive." She wiped her hands on a towel and hung it next to the one Charles had used. Glancing down at her soppy clothes, she said, "What a mess! Now I need a shower." She laughed. "But first, what's this bucket list item you need to cross off?"

He hemmed and hawed for a few seconds. "I'd like to take you on a date. A *real* date."

Despite the chilly air and her damp clothes, Blossom felt a blush warming her face and neck. "What did you have in mind?"

"Someplace nice. With a fancy dinner and fun entertainment."

"Sounds interesting." If flirting class had been a graduation requirement, she would have flunked school, but something inside her nudged her to try. She moved a step toward him. "Are you thinking about a specific place?"

"Um ..." He cleared his throat. Perhaps he was as bad at this as she was. The thought put her at ease. "There's a Valentine's Day banquet at church—"

"Church?" The warmth from her blush evaporated so quickly, she almost shivered.

He gently touched her forearm. "Hey, I get it. Church isn't everyone's deal. But this is just a banquet. Not a worship service. They'll have a band. Good food. It's always a fun time."

Her heart halted. "You've been before? With whom?" *What a stupid question.* She'd known him what—three weeks? Of course, the man had a life before Blossom.

Now it was his turn to blush. She chastised herself. "I'm sorry. I had no right—"

"No, it's okay. I rarely date because my work keeps me so busy. But last year, my sister-in-law asked me to take her sister."

"And?"

"And she was in the midst of finishing her master's degree in art, and I was swamped with client work. Neither of us was ready to focus on a relationship ..."

Whatever he'd been about to say remained unsaid. "Look, I'm sorry. It's none of my business."

"It's fine. Really. It was a one-and-done date. But the banquet was fun. I'd love for you to go."

What was holding her back? *Charles?* No. He was fun. Gorgeous. Helped her relax. Definitely not him. *Valentine's Day?* Kind of a big deal for a first date ... but no. *Church?* She really didn't have enough experience there to form an opinion. So ... *God?* Bingo! Where had *He* been when her dad's plane nose-dived into a mountain? "I'll ... I'll, um, have to think about it."

"I tell you what," he began, tipping up her chin with his finger, "I'll take Hannah as my backup date, but I'd love to have you join us." He slipped a postcard from his jacket pocket and handed it to her. "This invitation has all the banquet details. If you decide to come, just show up. No pressure. But I'll be there, no matter what." With that, he placed a sweet kiss on her forehead and moved back a step. "Go take your shower. I'll go clean up and get to work. And if it's okay, I'd like to bring Hannah to visit Fred this evening."

"Fred?"

"Yep. That's his name."

"I like it." She smiled. "Um, sure. Bring her by." She waved the postcard as she spun toward the exit. "And thanks for the invite."

"Ugh! He's a church guy! Why didn't I see that coming?"

"Lots of people go to church. It's not the end of the world, honey." Grams stirred whatever wondermous-smelling something she'd concocted and turned off the burner. She patted a barstool at the kitchen counter. "Coffee?"

To Grams, every situation could be fixed by sipping a cup of coffee. Why hadn't a smidgeon of that laid-back manner trickled down the gene pool into Blossom's DNA?

She plopped onto the seat and huffed out a sigh. "Sure. Thanks." A few seconds later, she cradled the mug in her hands, soaking up the warmth. "I wish coffee could fix everything."

"What's broken?"

Seriously? The word landed in her mind so hard, she thought she'd said it out loud. "The church guy thing—remember?"

That smirky smile crept across Grams's lips. "Your dad was a 'church guy.' And you didn't have a problem with it."

"Only the past few years. After he married *her*."

Grams spun her stool to face Blossom. "Let's talk about her. What is it you hate about her so much? The fact that she made your father happy? The fact that she shared her faith with him? That fact that—"

"Enough!" Blossom stood so quickly, she sloshed her coffee. As she bent to wipe the tiled floor, tears splashed from her eyes and mingled with the dark brown liquid. She plopped to the floor and sat cross-legged. After a moment, she gazed into Grams's eyes. Her father had often said Blossom had her grandmother's eyes. Now, looking into their depths, she could see herself. Same eye color. Same hair, minus the gray, streaked through the once-blonde waves. Same spunk. Grams was right, of course. Would she be as wise as this woman when she reached her age?

"I'm sorry, Grams," Blossom said, her voice barely above a whisper.

The older woman joined her on the floor and wrapped her arms around Blossom's shoulders. "You feel as though she stole him from you, right? Is that why you hate her?"

Blossom nodded slowly. Her father had been so busy lately,

wrapped up in his new wife's career, helping her build her platform as a motivational speaker. Using his talents to help her, while his illustrations for *The Day of the Duck* remained unfinished, untouched.

His final words to her swam through her mind. 'I'll only be gone a few days, kiddo. I know you've been focused on transforming the farm into a rescue, but carve out some time to finish your manuscript so I'll know what to draw.' Then, he'd kissed the top of her head and followed Maureen out to the waiting cab.

So I'll know what to draw. It wasn't his fault the book was unfinished. And it wasn't Maureen's. It was hers. She'd never finished the story. Why?

"What's rolling around in that head of yours, Blossom-girl?"

"He couldn't finish the illustrations because I never finished the story."

"And you didn't continue writing it because?"

She sucked in a deep breath. "I suppose because I was angry. Jealous of Maureen." A tear trickled down her cheek. "I wish now that I'd tried to get to know her. But now, it's too late."

Grams gazed into her eyes. "It's not too late. In fact, you have more than all the time in the world—you have *eternity.*" She brushed away a tear from her granddaughter's cheek. "I thought I'd done my best to help your father raise you after your mother passed away at such a young age. Curse cancer." She paused, her expression somber. "But I failed you in the most important thing."

"Grams, you haven't failed at anything. I'm so blessed to have been raised by you."

"I taught you all the things you need to be a strong, successful woman on this earth. But I've been remiss about sharing with you the good part—the best part." She stood and refilled their mugs. "Let me tell you the story about two sisters named Mary and Martha and their good friend Jesus ..."

Grams's voice sang through the house. "Blossom, there's a gentleman here to see you."

Charles? A kaleidoscope of butterflies twirled in her stomach. She glanced at her fitness watch. He would be at his office now. Her giddiness instantly evaporated. She made her way to the entryway, wondering who could be there. Surely the city permit department didn't make house calls.

Grams was making small talk with a middle-aged man. Balding, and not tall enough for his girth, the man's smile pegged the Cheshire Cat meter as she approached.

"Ah, Miss Clarke. So good to meet you." Over-eagerness oozed from his voice and the quickness with which he extended his hand in greeting.

Caution lights flashed in her mind as Blossom took his clammy palm in hers. She resisted the urge to jerk back her hand. "Thank you. And you are?"

Thankfully, the man retracted his hand. "Where are my manners? Phil Fairfax. I'm a client of your friend, Charles Sterling."

She opted against the standard 'Pleased to meet you' reply and took the direct approach. "How may I help you, Mr. Fairfax?" She hoped she hadn't sounded rude, considering this man was a client of Charles.

"A woman who wastes no time on frivolities. I like that." He cleared his throat and inched farther into the house. "I've come to submit an offer on your property."

"What?" No amount of finishing school training could have prevented the shock of his statement nor the bluntness of her response. She gathered her bearings and spoke again, "I beg your pardon, Mr. Fairfax, but my property isn't for sale."

He raised an eyebrow. "When Charles first spoke of this place—"

The ringing of her phone cut off his thought. Charles. She silenced it. How dare he send a client to her home. To buy her property? "You were saying?"

"My development plans require a waterfront property with no less than sixty acres, mostly cleared. As you are aware, this place," he made a sweeping gesture, "is perfect."

"I agree this place is perfect, but *not* for development."

"You haven't even heard my offer yet. I know the value of a good property, and I'm willing to make selling worth your while." He glanced around, obviously noting their modest home. "Enough to transform your meager existence into one of opulence."

Her thoughts were spinning. Why would Charles do this to her? He knew how much this place meant to her. And developing the goat rescue for her father. Had the whole thing been a ruse? Getting a goat for Hannah. The kiss. Working side by side on the farm. Had he been checking out the property for his buddy Phil? She was going to be sick.

"Are you well, Miss Clarke? You look a little peaked."

"Mr. Fairfax, I'm not changing my mind about selling the property, no matter what the price. Good day." She moved toward the door.

He clasped his hand around her forearm, and she wrenched out of his grasp. "Let go of me!"

Grams rounded the corner in an instant. "You heard her. She's not selling the place. Now leave and don't come back!"

"It's a shame you won't budge. You could have negotiated a hefty sum for your place, but now, you'll get nothing once it's condemned and auctioned on the courthouse steps."

Blossom gasped. "What are you talking about?"

"You're blatantly in violation of the code for raising farm animals within the city limits."

"We've applied for a permit," Grams interjected.

"Ah, yes. The permit." He withdrew an official-looking document from his breast pocket. "I'm afraid it's been denied." Fairfax held the page closer and squinted. "And, unfortunately, it seems as though you have just seven days to remove all the animals from the property, or they will be impounded."

He dropped the page on the floor and turned to let himself out. "Good day, Miss Clarke."

CHAPTER TEN

$\mathcal{T}$ he creak of his office door caught Charles by surprise. He jerked his head up from the client file he'd been reviewing. Geoffrey sauntered across the room.

"You didn't knock," Charles said quietly, pushing back the urge to quiz his assistant about the purpose of his unannounced intrusion.

Geoffrey waved a small square of paper. "I've finished your little assignment."

"Assignment? Oh, for Phil? What'd you find?"

Geoffrey slapped the sticky note on the desk.

Charles read the address on the note and stifled a gasp. "That's the address of the G.O.A.T. Goat Rescue."

"Yep. Looks like Farm Girl will be relocating soon."

"You spoke to her?" He didn't add, *Without telling me?*

"No, but Phil's heading that way right now. Wants to see the place in person." He glanced at his watch. "In fact, he's probably already there."

Charles stood and slammed his fists on the desk, sloshing coffee onto the open file. "You were supposed to research properties and report to me. You know the procedure. We don't notify clients until we know the property is cleared for sale."

"Well, it will be soon. Seems like she's been operating without the proper permit for keeping livestock within the city limits. She'll be shut down as soon as Phil's lawyer files an injunction."

"That property has been in her family for years." Charles pushed past his assistant and grabbed his hat. "You know what, Geoffrey? You're fired."

"I figured you'd go that route instead of thanking me, which is why I collected an advance on the finder's fee from Phil." The young man smirked and patted his breast pocket. "Unless she has a ton of money for a top-notch lawyer, Phil's got this in the bag."

Charles stormed out the door and yanked his phone from his pocket. He punched in Blossom's number. No answer. Phil must have already arrived.

The second Blossom heard Fairfax's car leave the driveway, she ran out the back door and through the gate. She plopped on the ground, leaning against her favorite large oak tree. Penelope bounced over to her and nibbled at her sleeve.

Blossom reached around the Pygmy's neck and tried to hug her, but the goat wriggled free and hopped off. A moment later, Andromeda was at her side. The dog nuzzled against her. Blossom buried her face in the thick fur, sobbing.

She pulled away and stared into the sympathetic eyes. "Why did Charles do that? And what am I going to do with *you*? With all of you?" She did an eye sweep of the pens full of goats, ducks, chickens, and turkeys. Tom's gobble sounded above her muffled sniffles.

Seven days. Where could she find a property with adequate fencing and shelter for these innocent creatures in just one week?

"Okay, God," she whispered, still hugged against her wonder dog, "here's Your chance to show off. I'm begging You to help me find a solution. Or a way to fight this. Please, do Your thing!"

The whole prayer deal was new to her, but she hoped her heavenly Father knew her words came from the heart.

Charles barely threw the SUV into Park before he flung open the door and jumped out. He saw her, slumped against the old oak, hugging her faithful dog. When he shut the door to his SUV, the sound alerted her to his arrival. She stood.

"Get out!" She pointed back toward his rig.

"Blossom, wait. It wasn't me."

She stormed toward him. "*Your* company shared info with *your* client. Sure sounds like it *was* you!" She wiped her nose on her sleeve. "If you'll excuse me, I have a lot of work to do. I have one week to rehome nearly forty animals." She pushed past him.

"I can fix it!"

She spun around. "Haven't you done enough already? Besides, in spite of what you and your client think, I'm not destitute. I can afford an attorney—someone who probably truly *can* fix this. Or at least buy me some time."

He reached out to touch her, but she spun out of his reach.

"Don't touch me! Why are you still here? I told you to leave. I don't ever want to see you again!" She spun away and ran toward the house.

Charles sucked in a deep breath and held it. He gazed upward and mouthed a prayer to the One he knew really *could* fix the situation. Before he finished praying, the solution came to him, and he closed out the petition with praise. "Thank You!"

CHAPTER ELEVEN

*A*s Blossom grasped the bookstore door and pulled it open, she replayed her words over again in her mind. *I don't ever want to see you again!* Lying was a bad way to start off her new-found relationship with God, but when she spouted those words yesterday afternoon, her lie was true. She'd spent the better part of the night convincing herself she meant those words. First, lying to Charles. Then, lying to herself. And now, she didn't know what to believe.

Okay, God, I'm gonna need Your help with this one. Please keep my thoughts focused on the present because right now, I've got a job to do.

She forced herself forward and sat in the chair reserved for the bookstore's story time presenter. Blossom read the first few pages, then peered over the book's top edge at the group of little faces, each one engaged in the story as she read. Looking back at the book, her heart warmed at the amazing illustrations her father had created, which brought the story to life. She continued reading, "So, Andie the wonder dog—"

"I've met her," interrupted one little voice, a voice Blossom recognized.

She looked up to see Hannah, standing at the edge of the story circle, clinging to Rosa's hand. "Sorry we're late," Rosa mouthed.

"It's fine. Please have a seat." She motioned to an empty space on the brightly colored carpet squares of the bookstore's children's area. "We are nearly finished with the story."

At the book's conclusion, the children clapped and disbursed to find their respective adults. The store manager greeted Blossom. "Thanks so much for filling in at the last minute. It's hard to plan author events during flu season."

"It was my pleasure. And it's best to not have someone around the children who feels ill, just in case." She caught Rosa and Hannah weaving through the throng, presumably to speak to her. Had Charles sent them? Pretty low of him to send his niece-daughter to this event. "Excuse me," she muttered to the manager. "I need to get going."

"Of course."

Blossom moved to the edge of the sitting area but paused when she heard Hannah's small voice. "Mr. Book Store Man?" She noticed Rosa in a protective stance, resting a gentle hand on the child's shoulder.

Her heart pinched. Such a precious child. Good thing she had Rosa. Too bad her uncle-turned-father was a scoundrel.

The manager knelt at eye level with Hannah. "Oh, hello. You're the little girl who said you'd met Andie the Wonder Dog. Right?"

Hannah nodded. "She's Miss Blossom's dog."

"So, you know the author?"

Blossom felt a twinge of guilt, spying on their conversation from behind a bookshelf.

Hannah's face contorted into a confused look. "What's an author?"

"An author is a person who writes stories for books."

"Oh. Is Miss Blossom the story maker for this book?" She held up a copy of *Thomas the Tame Turkey*.

"Why, yes. She wrote that whole series."

"Not the *whole* series," Hannah contended. "It's missing *The Day of the Duck*."

"Aren't you a smart little girl? Yes, that book isn't done yet."

"Why not?"

"Peter, no!" A frantic mother pushed past Blossom, nearly toppling her, as she rushed to grab her preschooler, who was ripping pages from a book. "What are you doing?" the exasperated woman shrieked.

"I don't like him!"

"Why don't you like him?"

"He is mean!"

The mother calmly looked the child in the eye. "If someone is mean, that doesn't give us the right to be mean in return. We need to be kind, even to mean people. Ripping out the pages won't fix the mean person—it just hurts the book. It's not the book's fault the character is mean. And it hurts Mommy, too, because now I have to pay for a book you ruined." She took the boy by the hand and led him to the counter.

Even to mean people. Blossom sucked in a deep breath and held it. *Even when someone rips out your heart, just like the boy ripped out those pages, Lord?* Although she was new to praying, she figured the guilt niggling in her conscience was an affirmative response.

And it wasn't Hannah's fault that Charles was mean. Or manipulative. Or whatever he was. She glanced around but couldn't see Rosa or the girl anywhere. They must have left.

Blossom tossed and turned before she finally gave up on sleep. She trudged to her office and flipped open her laptop. She had an email from the bookstore manager. He explained that a young girl had asked about her, and while he didn't feel comfortable giving out her email address, he agreed to convey a message from the child. Attached to his message was a scan of a note from Hannah, likely written with Rosa's help.

Dear Miss Blossom,

The bookstore man told me you were sad about your daddy dying and that he was your book draw-er. My daddy died, too, but God gave me Papa Charles to be my daddy now. Please ask God to give you a new daddy so you can finish the duck book. If you need another book draw-er, you should talk to my aunt Kara. She is a great draw-er. Papa Charles can give you her phone number. I will be praying for you not to be sad anymore so you can make more books.

Sincerely,
Hannah Sterling

Aunt Kara. Charles's dead sister-in-law's sister. The young woman he took to the last Valentine's Day banquet. Could she be trusted? Because her brother-in-law certainly couldn't.

CHAPTER TWELVE

The next afternoon, Blossom sat at her desk, rubbing her sleep-deprived eyes. She crossed off the umpteenth name from the list of lawyers she'd researched. Apparently, less than a week wasn't sufficient time for the lawyerly types to do their lawyering. Ugh! Her goat rescue center was doomed.

Voices from the entryway trickled into her office. Grams and —it couldn't be. Surely Charles knew better than to return after she'd banished him from her life. For good.

She listened carefully. No. Not Charles. Similar ... but something was different. Curiosity forced her into the foyer. The man speaking to Grams had Charles's features and mannerisms, however, gray framed the edges of his hair. He was a tad taller and, if possible, even more distinguished-looking.

"Oh, here she is now," Grams said to the visitor.

The man bowed slightly. "It's a pleasure to meet you, Miss Clarke. Please pardon my intrusion into your day, but I have something of utmost importance to give you." Before she could respond, he held out a signed legal document.

Blossom glanced at the paper. Somewhere in the midst of the

legal mumbo-jumbo, she read the words 'stay' and 'injunction.'
"I'm not sure I understand, sir."

"My apologies. I should have explained. This is a stay
against the injunction filed previously by Philip Fairfax and the
city inspector. Unless the plaintiffs drop their case, it will likely
go to court, but in the meantime, you may keep your animals on
the premises, and no further action will be needed on your part."

"But ... how? I haven't even hired an attorney yet. Who—"

Grams pointed to the signature. *The Honorable Franklin
Sterling.* "Blossom, Judge Sterling is Charles's father."

Heat rose within her. So, in an attempt to ease her fury,
Charles had run to his daddy. "Thank you for your time, Your
Honor, but I can't accept this."

"I don't follow. What can't you accept?" the judge asked.

"Charles butting into my business. It was his client who
started it. If he hadn't blabbed about my property—"

Judge Sterling held up a hand to halt her. "Charles said you
were strong-willed." Laugh lines formed around his mouth as he
smiled broadly. "There is nothing to accept or reject. This
document has been filed and is effective immediately. As to your
accusation about Charles butting into your business, he told me
you kicked him off the property without allowing him to
explain."

"Explain what? That he blabbed to a client about how
perfectly my property met the man's needs? Mr. Fairfax
explained the truth in no uncertain terms."

"Did he now? I believe after three decades in my position, I
know a bit about discerning what is truth." The judge's voice
held a condescending tone. "Yet, you took the word of a stranger
—a person you'd just met—over someone you've been working
alongside for weeks? Someone who you obviously care about
and who cares deeply about you?"

"H-he cares deeply about me?" Not tears again. She forced
herself to hold them back.

"I believe you know the answer to that. But to confirm your suspicions, my son has spent the better part of the day working to resolve any harm he inadvertently did to you and your operation. He fired his assistant—the one who disclosed confidential information. The young man is efficient, although he's a bit of a loose cannon."

"He fired his assistant?"

"If you have further questions on that matter, I'm afraid you'll need to discuss them with Charles." The judge glanced at his watch. "I have to go now. I have a dinner date tonight with my granddaughter. It's Valentine's Day."

Blossom turned to Grams. Her nod confirmed it. "Oh, my."

"Are you all right, Miss Clarke?"

She nodded. "It's just that—Oh, never mind. You go and have a good time." She paused for a moment and added softly, "Thank you." The tears she'd been forcing back broke through.

CHAPTER THIRTEEN

harles stood in front of a mirror and draped his bow tie around his neck. He positioned one side to be longer than the other. Crossing the longer side over the short side, he moved the end beneath the shorter side, flipped it over, and tightened it. After shaping the shorter side, he wrapped the long edge around and pulled it through, forming a knot. He attempted to shape the tie, but after a few tries, he undid the strip of fabric and started over.

What was wrong with him? He couldn't even count the times he'd worn a tuxedo during his career, and tonight, he suddenly couldn't even tie a bow tie? He plopped onto his bed and put his head in his hands. He'd totally botched the entire situation with Blossom and, at this point, couldn't think of anything he could do to fix it.

Blast! Why had he asked Geoffrey to research buying a goat? He should have done it himself. Assigning the task to his assistant had been an impulse request. So unlike him. He'd been so excited about getting Hannah the pet she wanted. And, after he met Blossom, about her fulfilling her dream. How her face lit up whenever she talked about her plans for the rescue center.

G.O.A.T. Charles chuckled at the playful name she'd chosen. But now, he'd never get to see the goat rescue again. Or the goat he'd bought for Hannah. *Or Blossom.*

He wondered how his dad's meeting with her had gone. Dad hadn't called him, but then, he hadn't expected him to. Charles could talk to Dad during the banquet, but he knew his father's long-standing rule about not discussing business at social events. He would have to wait.

A rap at his door brought him out of his thoughts. "Come in."

Rosa ushered Hannah through the doorway. She was wearing a pink satin dress with a sparkly waistband separating the embroidered lace overlaid skirt from the simple bodice. A huge pink bow on the back wrapped up the look. Rosa had arranged her hair in an age-appropriate updo.

Charles whistled and knelt before her. "You look absolutely gorgeous!"

Hannah wrapped her little arms around his neck. "Thank you, Papa Charles."

When he stood, Rosa gave him an up-and-down exam. "You're not ready?" She lifted an eyebrow.

"Well, um—" he stammered and held up the tie, dangling the culprit over his fingers.

She moved to his sitting area and patted a chair. Standing behind the seat, she motioned toward the tie. "Give it to me and sit."

Within a few minutes, Charles was sporting a perfectly tied bow tie and slipping his arms through his jacket. "Thanks, Rosa."

As soon as he'd spoken his gratitude, the intercom buzzed. "Your car is here, sir."

Dad had insisted on sending a limo. After all, he wanted the date the two men were sharing to arrive in style.

Charles looked down at Hannah. "You ready?"

She answered with a shy grin.

"Great. Valentine's banquet, here we come!"

Thirty minutes later, Charles's father was pulling out a chair for their date. Hannah beamed. Not many children were in attendance, but she didn't seem to mind. Charles picked up a program from his place setting and scanned the evening's agenda. The festivities would start at 6:30 p.m. He glanced at his watch. Six twenty-seven. The empty chair to his left mocked him. Blossom wasn't coming.

Less than two minutes passed when he heard a quiet voice say, "Excuse me. Is this seat taken?"

Charles was instantly on his feet. As he pulled back the chair, his eyes met hers, and his breath caught in his throat. The farm girl in pigtails and overalls was cute, but this woman before him in a wine-colored off-the-shoulder fitted gown was absolutely stunning.

"Y-you are beautiful," he whispered in her ear.

Her blush matched her dress. "We need to talk."

CHAPTER FOURTEEN

*P*robably not the best response to the best compliment she'd ever received from a man, but Blossom was still sorting out the events of the past couple of days. She smiled and complimented Hannah's dress, greeted Judge Sterling, and made small talk with another couple seated at their table. Etiquette behaviors Grams had taught her but that Blossom had rarely used, preferring stables to social events.

The warm breath in her ear from Charles's greeting had raised goosebumps on her skin. How could a man she was so angry with stir up such feelings inside her?

Focus. She scolded herself. The guests at this event didn't come to witness drama. After the invocation, servers placed salads in front of each attendee. Blossom twirled a tomato on her fork and dipped it in Ranch dressing. She risked a glance at Charles. He was looking at her. Of course.

She leaned over and whispered, "Your dad said you fired your assistant. What's up with that?" She bit into the tomato, spewing a smattering of seeds. As she dabbed her chin with the cloth napkin, she noticed Charles fighting not to choke on the mouthful of tea he'd just taken in.

After he finally managed to swallow, he said, "He betrayed me—and hurt you in the process." He leaned back and sighed. "You know, I just need to make an entire career change. This line of work doesn't bring me the joy it once did." He looked as though he wanted to say more but stopped.

Fair enough. "What would you do?" She realized he wasn't broke by any stretch, but she imagined it took a hefty amount of income to support the lifestyle he was accustomed to.

He smiled. Probably amused at her concern for his future. "I have a realtor's license and a law degree. I'll get by." He winked.

Judge Sterling looked over Hannah's head and gave them the stink-eye.

"What's his problem?" Blossom pushed a tomato aside and speared an olive. Less juice.

Charles finished off his salad and pushed the plate aside. "He has a rule about mixing business with pleasure."

The word *pleasure* hardly described her current situation. Awkward social setting with a man she's just as soon dual as date. Was this a date? Probably. Since that's the word he'd used when he invited her. Ugh.

The delectable tenderloin entrée was served without incident. Midway through dessert and coffee, Hannah climbed onto Charles's lap. "Did you get my letter?"

Blossom noticed Charles's expression. He obviously wasn't privy to his daughter's correspondence. "Yes, I did. And thank you for praying for me."

The child nodded. "Of course. We're supposed to pray all the time, but sometimes, I run out of things to say. Then, when the bookstore man told me how sad you were, I got a new thing to pray about."

Her sweet innocence warmed Blossom's heart. "Happy to help." She smiled.

"So, did you call my aunt Kara?"

"Excuse me?" Charles asked, shock in his tone.

Hannah spun to face him. "Papa Charles, can't you see we're having girl talk?"

He held up a hand in mock defense. "Pardon my intrusion. Carry on, ladies."

Blossom laughed out loud. "Not yet, but I plan to do that soon. I need to get her number from your papa."

Hannah wriggled her small hand into Charles's breast pocket and retrieved his phone. "I'll get it for you."

"Now, just a minute, young lady. What have we learned about asking permission?" He gently removed the phone from her hand. "And why does Miss Blossom need your aunt's number?"

"How else can we women conspire against you?" The teasing tone emerged before Blossom remembered she was mad at him, but the smile she received in return made her *faux pas* worth it.

"Her daddy died. He was her book draw-er. Now she needs a book draw-er so she can finish the duck book," Hannah blurted.

"Finish the duck book? Wait, what? *You're* B.L. Barlow? *Busted. "I ... uh—"*

"I'd suspected, but I figured you would have told me after we ..." He made a dismissive gesture. "Oh, never mind." A thousand emotions crossed his face at once, but confusion, surprise, anger, and—was that betrayal?—topped the list.

Before she could respond, Blossom's phone rang, echoing throughout the venue's formal banquet hall.

Grams. Embarrassed, she clicked to silence the call but knew Grams wouldn't interrupt unless something serious had happened. She moved the device to her ear and whispered, "Hello?"

"Honey, I'm so sorry to bother you during your special dinner, but we have an emergency here at the rescue center." Panic laced her grandmother's normally calm tone.

"What's wrong?" She was already gathering her purse.

"It's Penelope," Grams said, voice trembling. "She's been kidnapped!"

"I'm so sorry, but I have to go." Without an explanation, Blossom rushed out of the banquet hall. Charles handed Hannah to his father. "I'm going after her."

"Do you know what happened?"

Charles shrugged. "She got a call from her grandmother. Something must have happened at the rescue center."

"Papa Charles? What's wrong? Is Miss Blossom okay? What about our date?"

He leaned down and touched her cheek. "I'm sorry, baby girl, but I need to go help Miss Blossom. Grandpa Frank will have to take over for me tonight, but I'll make it up to you." The disappointment on her face made his heart clench.

He straightened and was about to turn when Hannah asked, "Can Miss Blossom be my new mama?"

Charles planted a kiss on the top of her head and grinned. "I certainly hope so." He paused for a moment and added, "Something else for you to pray for."

He rushed to the parking lot in time to see the taillights of her four-wheel-drive pickup spin out onto the road. He was on foot. Normally, he would call Geoffrey, but that ship had sailed. He pulled out his phone and was about to download one of those ride-hailing apps when the limo pulled around.

Nigel hopped out and rushed to open the rear door. "Your father called me," he explained. "I'll come back for him after I drop you off."

"Thanks, Nigel." Charles settled into the rear seat. determined to ignore his irritation that Blossom had never shared with him about her side hustle. Lots of people published books these days. He could tell her real passion was caring for the animals and working to fulfill her father's dream. The more time he spent with her, the more he admired her for that.

Why was he angry? What she did for fun in her spare time was her business. He had no claims on her. Besides, he hoped she'd keep writing her little stories because Hannah loved them.

Charles wasn't sure what he expected to find when he arrived at Blossom's place but certainly didn't expect to see Geoffrey's Corvette parked haphazardly near the gate.

What was *he* doing there? *Did she abandon me for another date?* What could she possibly see in Geoffrey? Had they met while he was researching goats? Another thought crossed his mind—what could she possibly see in *him*—someone as stuffy as an attic in August?

"It's okay, Nigel, I've got it," he said as his father's driver moved to exit his seat.

Charles sprung from the vehicle and yelled, "Thanks!" Then, he rushed toward the gate. It stood slightly ajar. Odd. Grams and Blossom were sticklers for keeping that gate secured. He knew from experience. The memory normally would have brought a chuckle, but he sensed something was terribly wrong inside the compound.

A commotion ahead prompted him to run faster.

"I'll do whatever you want, but please don't hurt her!"

Blossom. He'd never heard such panic in her voice. Was someone hurting her grandmother? When he rounded the side of the studio, he skidded to a halt. Geoffrey was straddling Penelope. He grasped one of her horns with one hand, and in his other hand, he held a knife. Grams was brandishing a shotgun, and Blossom stood at her flank. The moonlight glinted off the knife's blade and reflected in Geoffrey's crazed eyes. Was he on something?

"I already told you, old lady. Put the gun down. Even if you shoot me, I will slice this goat's throat on my way down."

He hadn't noticed Charles's arrival. None of them had. Yet. But by the time he developed a plan, his advantage of the element of surprise would be long gone, because he had no clue what to do. If he'd only known the situation, he would have called the police.

"Geoffrey!" The word escaped before Charles could think what to say next. But his concern about the terror in Blossom's voice had forced him to act. He couldn't just stand there and do nothing.

In a split second, Geoffrey's expression transformed from unhinged to outraged. "You!" His former assistant's tone said it all. This situation wasn't about Penelope or Blossom—it was about him.

"I got here as fast as I could, Geoffrey. What can I do to fix this?" He motioned his hand between Penelope and Blossom and Grams.

"Nothing! I'm going to stick this goat right now."

"That'll just land you in jail. The animal cruelty activists will go nuts, and you'll never get out." Charles was winging it, but he noticed Geoffrey loosening his grip on the goat.

Penelope bleated. The fear in her voice was heart-wrenching. Blossom looked as though she'd lunge for her pet any second. Charles eased up to her and placed his hand on her forearm. She remained motionless. For the moment.

"That goat didn't hurt you, Geoffrey. I did."

"Yeah, but hurting the goat will hurt her." Using the knife as a pointer, he motioned toward Blossom. "And *that* will hurt you!"

"What is it you want? Money?"

"Did you know Fairfax reneged on his agreement? Stopped payment on that check? I'd already spent some of it. Now, I'm overdrawn." Visible anger welled up from within him.

"I can cover it. But not if you're in jail." He glanced toward Grams. "Or the morgue."

"How? You closed your business. Now you'll be as broke as I am."

"You what?" Blossom interjected.

Charles nodded and gave her a we'll-talk-later look. "Yes, but I'm still good for it. How much?"

A maniacal laugh escaped from Geoffrey's lips. "You're offering a *carte blanche* deal for a goat? You're crazier than I thought!"

"How much?"

A pensive look passed over Geoffrey's face. "Two million."

Charles uttered a low whistle. "That's a big number, Geoff."

A commotion in the tree branch hovering above Geoffrey distracted him, and before he could spin around, Tom flopped from his perch and was on the would-be kidnapper with a combined attack of talons and pecking. Geoff loosened his grip on Penelope, and she turned and butted his kneecap with all her might, then rushed to Blossom's side.

Blossom knelt to nuzzle the goat.

The forgotten knife clattered to the ground as Geoffrey used both hands to protect his face and head. Tom's attack was relentless.

Charles ran toward the brawl, retrieved the knife, then backed away. Blossom gave a long, loud whistle, and Tom instantly stopped clawing and pecking. For a moment, an eerie quiet enveloped the scene.

A medley of sirens pierced the silence, and a moment later, two police cruisers and an ambulance pulled up to the fence.

Grams, who had set down her shotgun, waved her cell phone slightly and gave a sheepish grin. "While everyone was focused on the fight, I figured it was time to call for backup," she laughed.

"What set him off like that?" Charles asked.

"You whistled." Blossom's expression showed she was torn between laughing out loud or crying. She scratched Penelope's ears. The tears won.

"Well, you might have to consider changing the title of Thomas the Tame Turkey," he said, attempting to lighten her mood.

The smile displayed said a thousand words without speaking one. He put his arm around her waist and snugged her against him. When she didn't flinch or push him away, hope welled within him.

Several police officers emerged from their vehicles as Geoffrey stumbled while attempting to stand.

"These people are crazy, officers! They sicced their turkey on me. It would have killed me had you not shown up."

The officer who appeared to be in charge looked skeptical. "That's not what the 9-1-1 caller described." He looked back and forth between them. "I'm going to need someone to tell me what really happened here."

Blossom gave Charles a tentative smile, then stepped forward, out of his embrace. "Thank you for coming, officer. I believe the footage from our security camera will give you all the information you need. But in the meantime, this man," she pointed toward Geoffrey, "threatened an innocent animal with a knife." She nodded toward the knife Charles now held.

While everyone's attention was on Blossom and Charles, Geoffrey took off in the nearby woods. A moment later, his howling echoed throughout the property, and he reemerged, followed closely behind by Stu, the rooster.

"Officers, as you can see, these animals are dangerous. This woman has applied for a permit to keep them within the city limits. When you file your report, please ensure the proper authorities have access to it as they make a decision on her request."

Blossom huffed a heavy sigh. "He's right, you know," she said to no one in particular.

"Right about what?" Charles asked.

"Although the surveillance tapes will prove Geoffrey's guilt about threatening Penelope, they will also prove that at least some of the animals here can be dangerous." She nodded toward Stu, who continued to peck at Geoffrey's heels while the police officers escorted him to one of their vehicles. "I'll never be able to get that permit."

"Aren't you going to call him off like you did, Tom?"

"Not on your life," Blossom laughed. "I'm terrified of that rooster! I hope they lock him up too." She looked thoughtful for a moment, then said, "You know, Stu has his own book, only the rooster's name is Rocky."

He laughed. "I think it's sweet that you write those little animal stories."

CHAPTER SIXTEEN

$\mathcal{T}$he next morning, Grams refilled coffee mugs as Charles and Blossom sat at the kitchen counter.

Blossom yawned. The late night at the police station was catching up with her. "Pretty sure I'll need a nap later." She stifled another yawn. "Only the curiosity about your proposed solution got me out of bed at this hour." She glanced at her fitness watch. Nearly nine-thirty. Not as early as she thought. But still ...

"I don't know why I didn't think of this sooner," Charles began, "but when you said last night that you'd never get a permit, I started thinking." He took a sip from his mug. "I know of a place just outside the city limits that could accommodate all the animals. It would need some fencing and shelters built, but there's even a house big enough for you and Grams and, well, a lot of people. It's a big house."

"Whose place?"

He paused for a moment. "Um, well, technically, it's mine."

"What?" Blossom almost spewed her coffee.

"It was my brother's house. Hannah's home. I didn't move out there because it was inconvenient to drive into downtown from there. But the house is empty, and there's plenty of acreage."

"You moved that little girl from her home in the country to a city loft apartment?" Grams pierced him with an accusatory look. "No child needs to be cooped up like that." She obviously believed his actions borderlined on being criminal.

He held up his hands in defense. "Guilty. And Rosa has already lectured me enough for both of you, even though it's just now sinking in." He took in a deep breath. "I'm afraid I didn't see the value of raising a child in the country ... until I met you two and started working with all the animals. I was selfish."

Blossom looked toward Grams, who gave her a slight nod. "Your suggestion might actually complement the plan Grams and I discussed last night." Now, she nodded to her grandmother.

"As Blossom has mentioned, this property has been in our family for generations, but we've come to the conclusion that it's likely not feasible to use it for developing the rescue center. As long as it remains within the city limits, complying with codes and regulations would be a constant battle. Last night, or rather, in the wee hours this morning, we agreed to let the property go and search for somewhere near the city but not within the limits."

"Let it go? Surely you don't intend to sell it to Phil."

Blossom shook her head. "That vulture? After the way he treated us? Never. I don't wish to see a bunch of high-dollar high rises ruining this land. However, I am fine with allowing the wildlife refuge we border to annex it. That would hopefully preserve the place for people to enjoy for generations."

Charles smiled. "That sounds like a perfect idea. And you're right. It goes well with the suggestion of you moving to Hannah's home."

"*If* we do that, and that's a big if," Blossom began, "I wouldn't feel right living there without a lease agreement. I don't want to mooch off of anyone. What's the fair market value for renting your property?"

He paused before answering. "Well, I—"

"You're in real estate," she cut in. "Give me a ballpark figure."

"Fair market value? A property like that ... fifty-two acres and a five-bedroom home ... I can't ask you to pay that. It would be quite expensive." He stood to refresh his coffee. "Anyone else need a refill?"

"Don't go changing the subject on me. That's Grams's tactic." She laughed. "I need a figure. How much?"

"Blossom, look. I don't need the money. I've set back a lot of my earnings. Plus, I've decided to combine my law credentials with my real estate experience and resume my brother's practice. He was an estate-planning attorney. I need a change. His clients need to be taken care of."

"That sounds like the perfect career path for you. But I seriously can't move into your house without paying what's fair." She punched some words into her phone's search engine app. After a few minutes, she looked up. "Eight thousand a month? Does that sound about right?"

"Sure, but seriously—"

"Young man," Grams butted in, "I heard you mention last night how sweet it was that Blossom 'writes those little animal stories.' And it is sweet. But are you aware how many copies her books have sold?"

He stared blankly between the two women. "Um, to be honest, I have no idea."

"I thought so." Grams put on her smug face. "A bit shy of five million."

His eyes widened. "And you get what, a dollar a book?"

"Just over two, actually." She grinned. "You're not the only one who has put money back. *Now*, will you let me lease your property?"

Charles laughed. "My dad called you a farm girl." Well, so had Geoffrey, but he didn't want to bring thoughts of him back into the conversation.

"Well, I kind of *am* a farm girl. Sounds better than 'goat herder,' which I've also been called." Blossom winked, then paused in thought for a moment. "So, if we did move out there, where would you live? In the same house?"

"There's a house behind the main house. Rosa had been living there until I got her an apartment near the condo. If she's agreeable, I could live there, and you four could move into the main house."

"So, you'd be living in the *outhouse*?" Blossom laughed a little too hard at her joke attempt.

"For now." The look he gave her was one filled with hope.

And promise.

EPILOGUE

Eight months later

"Come on, Papa Charles, we're going to miss it!" Hannah tugged on Charles's hand, pulling him through the crowd gathered outside their home, while his father hurried to keep up.

Charles glanced around at the growing mob of children and their accompanying adults. Grams was right. Having the book signing in conjunction with the newly licensed G.O.A.T. Goat Rescue Center's grand opening was a great idea. The children would be thrilled to meet the real-life animals that inspired Blossom's stories.

Blossom and Kara stood behind a table stacked with books. Grams hovered nearby, writing each child's name on a sticky note and ensuring the spelling was correct before handing the note to Blossom and Kara to sign inside the front cover. The process looked well-practiced. Rosa manned the snack table with help from Lauren, and Parker sat near the book-signing table, holding onto the leashes of Fred and Penelope.

While Blossom bent to hear a small child's question, Kara

spotted Charles and Hannah. She waved them to the front. Using a mic set up to perform the public reading, Kara announced to the crowd, "Please pardon us for a moment, but my brother-in-law, his father, and my niece have just arrived. Could you please allow them through so they may join us at the table? Thank you so much."

Charles was proud of his sister-in-law's sweet demeanor, and the mass of people moved aside as quickly and efficiently as the Red Sea parting. When he reached Blossom, he planted a gentle kiss on her cheek. A few *oohs* and *aahs* filtered through the crowd. She blushed.

He picked up Hannah and perched her atop one of the unused chairs between the author and illustrator. She grinned at Blossom. "I'm glad you called my aunt Kara. I told you she was a good book draw-er."

"And you were right! I'm so glad you told me about her." The two women smiled.

Charles flipped open one of the books. His first view of the finished product. Pride beamed through him as he stood next to Blossom. "What story do you plan to write next?"

She stared at him. Authors probably didn't discuss their upcoming projects on release day of the newest book, did they? He had no idea. But he *did* have an idea of what he hoped her next book would include.

"Miss Clarke," he knelt on his right knee and pulled a small velvet box from his breast pocket. "I want to be part of your next story."

A collective gasp echoed through the group. Phones were yanked out of pockets and purses as the onlookers captured the moment.

"Will you marry me?"

A chorus of swoony-sounding *awws* swept through the room. Blossom stood, frozen in place. Then, her mischievous grin replaced the blank look. She bent close and said, "Are you asking me just so you can move into the main house?"

"Don't try to change the subject." He winked. "I'm asking you because I love you. So, will you? Marry me?"

Her grin transformed into a huge smile. She hesitated as she looked around the gathering as if just realizing dozens of witnesses were sharing this moment. Blossom gazed into Charles's eyes, and Penelope nudged against her, gently butting her leg. "Yes, but—"

He stood and silenced her protest with a kiss as he slipped the ring on her left hand. "Let's get married. No buts about it."

ABOUT THE AUTHOR

Linda Fulkerson began her writing career as a copyeditor and typesetter at a small-town weekly newspaper. She has since been published in several magazines and newspapers, including a two-year stint as a sportswriter, and is the author of two novels, four novellas, and several nonfiction books. In 2020, she purchased Mantle Rock Publishing's backlist and founded Scrivenings Press LLC.

She and her husband, Don, live on a ten-acre plot in central Arkansas. They have five adult children (including their goddaughter) and thirteen grandchildren, two of whom are married. Linda enjoys photography, RV travel, and spoiling her two dachshunds.

Pegboards, Parrots & Pickup Lines

A Novella
by
Heather Greer

CHAPTER ONE

"*H*ooks. Hooks. Where are the—shouldn't a hardware store have a better organizational system?" Charlotte Herring's frustrated huff lifted auburn strands from her forehead.

She brushed her wayward bangs back into place with her fingers. Not that it would help. The tweed newsboy cap she'd taken off upon entering the store had seen to that. Cute caps looked great and might even cut the effects of a chilly January breeze, but they did nothing for hairstyles.

Enough with her hair. Time was a precious commodity. Finding the hooks she needed for her shop's pegboard walls was a necessity. Finding them quickly was imperative. There was too much to do to waste minutes fussing with her unruly locks.

"Can I help you find something?"

Critical words poised on her tongue for entry into the conversation. Poor, unfortunate soul probably wouldn't know what to do with her. Fiery redhead wasn't just another stereotype. God needed to sand down that rough spot, but today was not the day.

She whipped around. Her sharp words tumbled from her

tongue back down her throat in surprise as she gazed into the palest blue eyes she'd ever seen. Any woman would kill for the thick, dark lashes framing the man's eyes. They would turn any amateur painter's work into a masterpiece worthy of the Louvre.

His patient smile drew Charlotte's attention from the magnetic pull of his gaze, breaking the spell. Her mind churned in an effort to return to a functional state.

"Pegs." She shook her head. "Hooks. I mean, I have pegboards. I need hooks and shelves." Wow. The intelligence rolled right off her. Where was a hole when you needed to crawl in and hide?

The man's grin widened. Light scruff highlighted and increased its appeal. It was unnecessary help. Boyish charm radiated off him.

"You're two aisles too far." The man led her back the direction she'd come. "Here you go. Let me or Ellie, up front, know if we can help with anything else."

"Thank you." Charlotte remembered her manners as her guide walked away. Giving her attention to the items she sought, Charlotte perused shelf after shelf of perfectly displayed pegboards, shelves, baskets, and hooks.

Never had she been so thankful to lose complete control of her mind and mouth. How embarrassing it would have been to chastise the man on the store's lack of organization only to find it was her own frenzied pace keeping her from what she needed. Being tongue-tied was bad enough, but at least her silence could be taken as social awkwardness and not full-blown rudeness.

Charlotte loaded her basket with all the accessories she needed and made her way to the cash register. Relief warred with something akin to disappointment when a petite blonde teenager, if looks weren't deceiving, waited to check her out.

Not disappointment. Couldn't be. Charlotte didn't even know the man. The girl—was it Ellie?—totaled her purchase. Charlotte bumped her card against the reader, snagged the bag from the salesperson, and nodded goodbye on her way out.

She mulled over her to-do list as she tossed her bags in the back seat of her Niro. A quick press of the start button, and the hybrid engine quietly whirred to life, lighting the clock on the radio panel. Charlotte pulled from the curb, releasing an exasperated sigh. She should've gone to the post office first, then the hardware store, two doors from her own shop, on her return.

If push came to shove, her pegboard accessories could've waited. Her mailing could not. After wasting so much time searching for what was right in front of her, what if her vendor arrived at the antique shop before she did?

She pressed the pedal a little closer to the floorboard. Being new in town was difficult enough. Being labeled incompetent and unprofessional wouldn't help. Brookview was her chance to leave behind the demons of her past, even if they tried to sneak a ride in her moving boxes.

"No." She spoke aloud to the empty car. "Eric, get outta my head."

This store wasn't going to fail, no matter what he'd said. He'd convinced her to scrap her dreams. They wouldn't be enough to live on, and she didn't need them since she had him. If she'd adopt his dreams as her own, they'd succeed. And they had, at least in business. But the cost had been exorbitant.

Never again. It was time to be true to the dreams God placed in her heart. Charlotte had to stay rooted in the here and now if Living in the Past Antiques and Vintage Collectibles was going to prove him wrong. Great-auntie Annie had given her the opportunity. Charlotte wasn't going to squander it.

Tyson Abbott scanned the aisle of peg boards and accessories as he strode past. The flustered woman with the red hair and hazel eyes was gone. Not a surprise. She'd seemed in a rush. Probably why she'd already passed the aisle she needed when he found her.

"Did the red-headed woman find everything she needed?" Tyson joined Ellie behind the long counter.

"Yep." The girl finished a text and dropped her phone into her pocket.

"You didn't recognize her, did you?"

Ellie's ponytail swung back and forth with her headshake. "Nope."

Hmm. A tourist? Historic Brookview enjoyed their share of tourists. They rarely frequented the hardware shop and didn't buy pegboard accessories when they did. The quaint little boutiques and gift shops were more their speed.

No. Locals made up his customer base, usually when something broke in their own shops. Whether they wanted to DIY their project or hire him, Ty's Hardware was their answer.

"Must be new in town."

Ellie's shoulder dropped as quickly as it raised. "Sure."

Their customer apparently didn't make as much an impression on his employee as she had on him. She was out of sight, out of mind. If only he could push aside thoughts of long red hair and worried green eyes as effortlessly.

CHAPTER TWO

$\mathcal{T}$yson exited the hardware store as his mother climbed from the cab of his truck. She'd parked two doors down where Auntie Annie's Sweet Shoppe now sported a new sign and purpose. Though brand new, the Living in the Past Antiques and Vintage Collectibles sign had a weathered look fitting the store's theme.

"I sure hope Annie's great-niece knows what she's doing." Fiona Abbott shook her head as she met Tyson at the truck bed. "Can't believe she nixed the candy store to start an antique store. Sweets are a sure thing. Antiques? Maybe not."

"You don't seem to mind much." Tyson eyed the boxes in the truck bed before hefting out the largest. A grunt escaped as the weight of his cargo hit him. "What in the world is in here, Mom? Bricks?"

Fiona rolled her eyes and tossed the end of her scarf around her neck. "Don't be silly. Those are the old books from Dad's collection."

"What?" Tyson dropped the box back onto the open tailgate. "You're selling Dad's collections? Why?"

His mother looked at him like he was an injured puppy. "It's time, Ty. Your dad's been gone five years. None of us is interested in these things. They should go to someone who'll love them as much as he did."

"But …"

"But you already took the items you wanted. So did your sister. Unless you want to come dust them each week, it's time to pass them on. Don't you agree?"

Tyson didn't answer. It *was* time. But why did it feel like purging Dad from every part of his life? He eyed the empty shop between the hardware store and the new antique place. He and Dad always planned to expand the shop, offer woodworking classes and simple weekend projects for kids to draw in the tourist crowd. Things were lean when his livelihood relied solely on the patronage of the Brookview residents.

The *For Sale* sign in the window provided hope that maybe his dad wasn't completely erased from his life. If the offer Tyson put in on the storefront was accepted, he'd be able to fulfill their dream, secure his store's future—his future. *Lord, let it be.* The prayer slipped from his heart even if it didn't pass his lips.

Tyson sighed and hefted the box from the tailgate once more.

"Lead the way." It was an answer without an answer. But it was the only honest one Tyson could give. He followed his mom to the candy shop. No, the new antique shop.

He frowned. New and antique didn't coexist in his mind. This shop would always be a candy shop. Growing up, every time he opened the doors, he stepped into Wonka's chocolate factory. Everything was bright and colorful and fun.

This time as he entered, the sharp scent of fresh paint hit Tyson, and his stomach dropped. Every trace of his childhood memories was gone. The wild colors and shapes adorning the walls had disappeared under cool shades of blue. Two shades, to be exact. A light blue and a deep navy. Trim, once gleaming white against a rainbow of color, was now warm oak. Row after row of candy tubs with their scoops in pockets on the side had vanished. The space was now partitioned into booths, complete with pegboard walls.

The candy shop he loved was gone. Soon, the possessions his dad loved would be too. Mom had talked about it several times over the last few months. But it didn't remove the sting of knowing those memories would belong to someone new, and he was helping it happen.

"Hello." The greeting came from his right. "Mrs. Abbott? It's nice to meet you."

Tyson turned in tandem with his mom toward the woman's voice. The pegboard woman from the hardware store emerged from an office. Of course. He should have known the moment he'd spied those walls. Pegboard Woman was new. The antique shop was new.

He should have put two and two together at his store. He'd surmised she was new in town. But for whatever reason, he'd not made the logical jump to realizing she was the woman responsible for closing Auntie Annie's. The person erasing a successful anchor shop in Brookview since before the Main Street renewal program turned the town into the popular tourist spot it was today.

"Tyson, dear, you still with us?" His mom's voice yanked him from his internal monologue as effectively as a childhood tug on his ear.

What had he missed? An introduction, apparently. Balancing the heavy box on one arm, he smiled and held out his hand. "Hello. I'm Tyson."

"Your mother said as much while you were busy wool-gathering. But I'm pleased to meet you anyway." Pegboard Woman giggled and briefly shook his hand before allowing him to shift the box's weight back to both arms.

Tyson tasted a retort to her judgment about his wool-gathering, but he held it in. What kind of person their age— because if appearances could be believed, Pegboard Woman was around his thirty-two years—used words like wool-gathering anyway? He wouldn't go there, having already earned one social strike for zoning out of the conversation, but he needed to say something.

"Looks, uh," he paused as he glanced around again, "different in here."

The corners of her hazel eyes crinkled when he struggled for the right word. Her welcoming smile faltered. Apparently, his choice wasn't as satisfactory as he thought.

"Oh." She glanced at the walls and displays, many of which were still bare while others were a jumbled mess. "Well, I loved Auntie Annie's Sweet Shop as much as the next person, but the set-up wasn't conducive to selling antiques and vintage collectibles." Her chin raised. "Booths work much better when dealing with consignment. It may seem empty now, but vendors have only just started filling their spots."

He'd frustrated her. He could understand why she might feel slighted, but it wasn't his intent. Her hard work shined in all the changes. A frown from his mother confirmed he'd earned strike two. Could this meeting get any worse?

Mom laid a gentle hand on Pegboard Woman's forearm. Man, he should've been listening during introductions so he could start using her real name.

"Of course, your décor isn't going to stay the same." Mom shot him the look from his childhood that brooked no argument. Thankfully, the woman couldn't see it with the way she turned her head. Mom's censure gave way to a friendly smile as she turned back to Annie's great-niece. "Candy and antiques are worlds apart. What you've done is inviting, lovely. Customers will love it."

The tightness around Pegboard Woman's eyes eased. Her lips relaxed into a smile, even if a bit tentative. "I've reserved a double booth for you, as requested. I understand your contract is not an ongoing arrangement, correct?"

Wishing he could slip outside, Tyson shifted his weight to one side. It would be a breach of manners to leave Mom or Pegboard Woman to carry the rest of the boxes. Now knowing what the other boxes held, they'd only be slightly lighter than the one he currently hefted. Tyson was appalled his mom had loaded them into his truck she'd borrowed the night before. Of course, he hadn't known what was in them when she'd asked for his vehicle.

He did now. So, he dutifully followed the pair as they discussed the specifics of his mother's rental on their way to her space. It was his only hope of avoiding strike three. He couldn't stand earning that final strike.

"I've put a small table in the middle and shelves on two of the edge panels. I picked up some hooks for the pegboards at the hardware shop yesterday, too, if you need any of those." She glanced his way.

Her smile was shy, though he couldn't figure out what could be embarrassing about visiting the hardware shop. She hadn't done or said anything wrong. Of course, if it meant seeing the light blush fill her cheeks, Tyson wouldn't rush to alleviate her concern.

"The hardware shop?" Mom placed a hand on her chest. "Tyson's store? It's a wonder you didn't meet him."

"We did. Briefly." She turned away, busying herself with a shelf against the wall. "He showed me the pegboard accessories. Do you need any?"

Mom tapped her lip with her finger and took in the arrangement. "I think I might. Some of my pictures would look nice if they're hung instead of propped."

"I'll go get a handful and your paperwork to sign. You don't have to wait, though. Feel free to start moving things in." Pegboard Woman made her way back to her office.

Tyson's eyes were as incredible as she remembered. Tyson. He had a name, other than the silly nonsense she'd been calling him. Westley, because he had "eyes like the sea after a storm." She shouldn't have been calling him anything. Getting the store up and running was her first—her only—priority. Fielding calls from concerned citizens about the change from candy to antiques was eating up enough of her days. There wasn't time for anything else.

Only her mind didn't get the memo. All day yesterday and through this morning, she'd dealt with the disgruntled residents of Brookview. But in between the complaints? Her mind meandered down a path ending with those unforgettable eyes more often than she cared to admit. She'd thought herself daydreaming again when she found him standing there with a box of whatever Mrs. Abbott was placing in her space. And then, when he caught her staring, she could have melted right into the floor. She had more control than the situation suggested. She was a professional adult, not a starry-eyed teenager.

Charlotte shook her head in an effort to dislodge her wayward thoughts. She opened her file cabinet and pulled Mrs. Abbott's folder from the drawer. Snatching a pen and a few hooks off her desk, she sucked in a steadying breath and lifted her head before marching from her office. She had a job to do, and she would do it well. If only she could ignore Westley—no, Tyson—with his captivating eyes.

CHAPTER THREE

harlotte chewed her bottom lip. Tessa Borrows, no, it was Tessa White now, gave every inch of Living in the Past a thorough inspection. As a local and her closest childhood friend from the summers she stayed with great-aunt Annie, Tessa's opinion carried weight like no one else's could. After Tyson's critical eye the day before, doubt had gnawed at Charlotte's confidence.

Tessa reached the back wall, spun on the toe of her fashionable ankle bootie, and spread her arms wide. Almost as wide as her smile.

"It's gorgeous in here." She strode to the front of the store. "I'm serious, Charlie. You've done an amazing job."

Charlotte tried to see her work through her friend's eyes. "You sure? The pegboard walls don't detract from the vintage feel?"

"Stripping the walls back to the original brick for each stall's base is perfect. The unfinished oak shelves match the shelving on the pegboard. Along with the Edison-style lighting, you gave it the perfect feel."

"Is it too cluttered?" The space was large for a candy store, but as an antique store, it could have used more room. Too bad Auntie Annie hadn't expanded into the store next door. Of course, at the time, it hadn't been available.

Tessa shook her head, bouncing the messy blonde bun on top of it. "Nope. You did a great job with a small space. I can't tell you the number of antique shops I've visited that are almost too cramped to find anything. Though yours isn't the biggest I've seen, your requirement for the vendors to keep their areas organized helps a lot."

"Great. I need everything to be perfect if I'm going to win over the good citizens of Brookview."

Tessa grimaced. "Still getting calls?"

"Daily." Charlotte groaned. "People can't believe I'd do away with a tourist favorite like a candy shop in favor of selling, and I quote, 'old junk.' Apparently, I'm going to single-handedly kill the tourism trade in town."

Tessa laughed. "Not a chance. Tourists like antiques too. It's just that Annie's place catered to the children who visited with their parents. She was always hosting special events to draw people in. They don't want to lose the family-friendly feel. Besides, before it was Auntie Annie's, it was still a sweet shop. That's a lot of candy-selling years. It'll take a bit to win people over."

"I love jellybeans and lollipops as much as the next person, but selling them is not me."

"It doesn't have to be. Your great-aunt would want you to make the shop your own. Chase your own dreams."

"I just hope my own dreams pay the bills."

Tessa scanned the booths one more time. "Looks like they're supporting you at least a little. Otherwise, you wouldn't have vendors. Right?"

Charlotte sighed. "Very little and only those who think they can make a few bucks. I'm thankful for them, but they won't sustain my business." She grabbed her purse from under the counter. "I need a few things from the hardware store. Want to come?"

"Sounds magical." Tessa rolled her eyes and looped her arm through Charlotte's. "Lead the way."

With the hardware store only two doors down, even if the supplies weren't small enough to carry, her car wasn't needed. She preferred walking anyway. Working a few extra steps into her day was always her first choice.

A bell jingled as she pulled the door open. The teenager who rang up her previous purchase smiled and waved from behind the counter.

"Good morning. Can I help you find anything?"

Charlotte shook her head. "No. Thank you."

Tessa followed as Charlotte veered in the direction of the pegboard supplies. Her current vendors had claimed all the previously purchased pegboard accessories, and there were still a few sellers scheduled to set up their booths before the grand opening event on Saturday.

Forty-eight hours until judgment day. Charlotte sucked in a deep breath. Thinking such things didn't do anyone any good. In two days, her dream store would open. Whether Brookview believed it or not, her store was something to be excited about.

"Tessa," Charlotte turned from the display to face her friend. "Can you ask if they have any of those cute, shaped bulbs for my Edison fixtures? I'm short a few. Plain ones aren't the same."

Tessa saluted. "Aye-aye, boss."

When she scampered away to the front counter, Charlotte returned to her selection. No need to be the one to ask when Ellie and not Tyson would be behind the counter. Though, she really shouldn't care one way or the other.

"Hey, Tyson." Tessa greeted him as she stepped up to the counter. "Charlie wants to know if you have any Edison-fixture-styled bulbs in stock."

Tessa hitched her thumb over her shoulder toward one of the aisles. Tyson could just make out the top of a redhead at the end of the row. Pegboard Woman. It had to be. So, she had a name. Charlie. Different, for sure. But it fit her.

Tyson nodded toward the back wall. "I've got a couple boxes. If she needs more, I'll order them. The only reason I stocked them in the first place was their popularity for patios and stuff. But I've not sold many."

"A couple boxes will do for now, but you might want to restock." She started toward the display but kept talking. "It may be a while, but Charlie will need replacements eventually."

"Got it. Thanks."

While there was plenty to do in his office, Tyson remained behind the counter. He'd sent Ellie to take out the trash at the perfect time. Too soon, the teen returned. Desperate to stay behind the counter but not needing two people up front, Tyson grabbed a couple bills from the drawer.

"Here. Can you head to The Bean Counter and grab us both something?"

When Ellie took the money and exited without a word, Tyson was glad afternoon coffee runs were a regular occurrence. He didn't want questions. Just coffee. Being the one to ring up the purchases of the beautiful redhead picking out peg board pieces had nothing to do with it.

Tyson busied himself dusting the counter and straightening the register displays while Tessa and Charlie perused. With no interruptions, his tasks went quickly, leaving him in a quandary.

He could stand behind the counter and wait. Would he appear awkward or overly eager to speak with her? Possibly. What else could he do? Tyson scanned the shelves under the register. A bottle of window cleaner and a rag caught his eye. Perfect. The front door was only a few steps from the counter. When was the last time he'd cleaned the front door, anyway?

The top pane was finished by the time the girls stepped up with their purchases. Tyson stowed the cleaning supplies on their shelf. Picking up the first box of lightbulbs, he aimed the scanning gun at the UPC.

"Did you ladies find everything you needed today?" Tyson included Tessa in his glance but let it come to rest on Charlie before picking up the next item.

Charlie's smile was only the expected polite response, but it was still beautiful. "Yes. Thank you."

"Tessa let me know I need to order more of these special bulbs. Do you know how many fixtures you have? So I can figure out how many to buy."

Her wide eyes resembled every high school student's when the teacher announced a pop quiz over material they had yet to read. Tyson flashed her a reassuring grin.

"It's no biggie." He finished scanning the last item and snapped open a plastic bag. "I'll stop by and count them. I don't want to have an abundance, but I'd like to stock enough to cover it if you have multiples go out at the same time."

"Oh, no. Please don't. I mean, you don't need to take the trouble." Charlie's words tumbled over her lips like water over a waterfall. "Really. However many you have on hand, I'll make it work. Don't worry about me."

"Happy to do it. We take care of each other in Brookview." He pushed the filled bag across the counter with a smile. "Eighty-three fifty-nine, please."

Charlie plucked a card from her purse and tapped it on the reader. In moments, she'd entered her PIN, and the receipt printed. Tyson tore it from the machine.

"Here you go." He handed her the slip of paper. "Have a great day, Charlie."

Her lips and brows lowered simultaneously. "Uh, you too. Thanks."

Tyson's attention followed Charlie and Tessa out of the store and down the sidewalk until the front windowpane turned into cold, hard brick, cutting off the view. He'd clearly upset or confused her. But what was offensive about telling someone to have a good day? It was polite.

Tyson smacked himself in the forehead. He called her by the wrong name. He'd been so sure Tessa called her Charlie. He must have misheard. Charlie was expected for boys more than girls. Carly, maybe, or perhaps, something else entirely.

He would correct his error and find out her name when he stopped by her place to count the light fixtures. He meant what he said about the people in town taking care of one another. And it would provide the perfect opportunity for Tyson to apologize to the woman he couldn't seem to get out of his head.

CHAPTER FOUR

*H*ow could he have forgotten today was the grand opening of Living in the Past Antiques and Vintage Collectibles? Tyson sidestepped as a woman pushing a stroller suddenly swerved into the aisle, keeping pudgy toddler fingers away from the breakables displayed in the booth.

"Sorry," the chagrined woman muttered.

Tyson shrugged and offered a placating smile. "No problem."

But there was a problem. He'd tried counting those light fixtures three times and lost count every single time due to the volume of people browsing the aisles. All the whispered complaints he'd heard around town didn't seem to matter, at least not on opening day.

"They could be gathering ammunition for later, I guess." A quick scan of the customers around him confirmed no one heard Tyson's whispered concern. Good. He wasn't inclined to stir up trouble for the store's adorable owner.

He wove his way to the front of the store, where the woman in question rang up purchases for a steady line of customers. The chit-chat while they waited was occasionally interrupted by a squawk coming from the beautiful gray parrot caged in the corner behind the counter. The bird was new. Of course, the whole enterprise was new, so he shouldn't be surprised.

Tyson knew it would be neighborly to tell her he'd stopped by, but he didn't dare break her focus. She was busy enough without an unnecessary interruption. He wouldn't explore why having her know he'd been there appealed to him.

He'd stop in again closer to closing. He could easily slide in the information then. It would even provide a bit of small talk to break the ice.

A small display caught his eye at the far end of the counter. *Looking to downsize your collectibles? Short-term and ongoing booth space rentals available now. Call to schedule your appointment.* Connected at the base of the plastic display frame was a smaller container filled with business cards.

Tyson snatched one. *Living in the Past Antiques and Vintage Collectibles. Charlotte Herring, Owner.* Charlotte. Tyson smiled as he strode out of the store. He hadn't heard incorrectly. Tessa did call her Charlie. Based on her reaction to his use of it, Charlie must be a nickname reserved for her closest friends.

Silence greeted Tyson when he entered the antique shop. Strange. He could've sworn there was a bell earlier. He grinned. Had Charlotte tired of the jingling and removed it? Every shopkeeper in town wanted the same kind of problem.

Though one customer stood by the front counter, Charlotte was nowhere to be found. Tyson checked the time. Five minutes until six. Just short of closing. Even on the weekends, the shops in historic Brookview tended to close at what folks considered a decent time. Family came first, and it couldn't if family didn't make it home until bedtime.

Either Charlotte was close by, or she was the most careless woman he'd ever met. Even in a safe place like Brookview, one didn't leave the front of the store unattended without a good reason. And really, there wasn't a reason good enough in his mind.

Not wanting to disturb the customer, he wandered the booths. In the few seconds it took for Charlotte to reappear behind the counter, he'd found a box of vintage comic books. Some of his childhood favorites were housed inside. He flipped through cover after colorful cover, barely registering when the customer left. Even then, he didn't return to his intended task. Would Charlotte set a couple of the comics aside for him to purchase Monday, maybe during his lunch hour when he could bring his wallet back with him?

A high-pitched wolf whistle erupted behind him.

"Can I get your number?"

Comics dropped, forgotten, into the bin as his head jerked up at the feminine voice. What in the world? Charlotte didn't seem the sort to resort to brazen attempts at gaining a man's attention, but then, what did he really know about her?

Tyson swung her direction. Her eyes, rounded to the size of two small planets, stared at him, brimming with as much shock as he experienced. The horror reflected in them was almost tangible. Her already creamy complexion paled to sickly white, except for bright red splotches on her cheeks. Her mouth hung slack as if she couldn't believe what she'd just done. That made two of them.

"Excuse me?" Tyson tried to keep the objection to her bold flirtation out of his voice.

"It wasn't …" Her head barely shook. "I didn't … I mean, it wasn't me."

Tyson scanned the store before looking back at her. His disbelief challenged her with a raise of his eyebrows.

Her headshake was more pronounced this time. "No. I mean it. It wasn't me. It was Jack."

This time, he couldn't hide his doubt. "Jack? I distinctly heard a woman's voice, and you're the only woman here. In fact, you're the only other person besides me."

Her hand waved frantically in front of her. "No. It wasn't me. It was Jack." Her hand stopped waving and pointed to the cage directly behind her. "Cracker Jack, actually."

The parrot he'd noticed on his first trip toddled from one clawed foot to the other without a care in the world. Not to mention, without making a sound.

"That parrot just asked for my number?"

She nodded.

Tyson eyed the bird. Cracker Jack tilted his head, giving Tyson a once-over as well. Then, he straightened his head and chirped. Not spoke. Chirped. Like a bird.

Charlotte huffed. "He really does speak." She paused as if the bird would answer. When it didn't, her shoulders dropped. "I mean it. He does. Watch this."

Charlotte gave the bird her full attention, stepping up to the side of the cage. "Are you a good boy, Cracker Jack? Good boy?"

Claws shifted on the perch. The black beak opened, and the bird's chest puffed as if filling his lungs.

Tyson waited.

Charlotte grinned in triumph.

A loud squawk filled the silence.

Charlotte glared at the animal. "Stupid bird."

"You didn't have to whistle at me to get my attention." Tyson moved to the counter.

Charlotte's jaw tensed, and she glared at the parrot again. "I didn't."

"I mean it." Tyson smirked. "No grand flirtatious gestures

were necessary. If you wanted it, all you needed was to ask for my number."

"Can I get your number?"

Tyson straightened. Charlotte's lips hadn't moved. She hadn't even opened her mouth to retort. The parrot's beak, however, stretched open with a yawn right after uttering the inquiry.

The corner of Charlotte's lip tucked between her teeth. Tyson could imagine an *I told you so* fighting for release. Her color had returned to normal, but the heat creeping up Tyson's neck assured him his humiliation was written on his face.

She'd not been flirting with him. His confidence drained into a puddle at his feet. Was there any way to salvage this situation? Nothing sprang to mind. Humiliation warred with the knowledge he must have sounded like an arrogant jerk. He definitely sounded like one to himself.

Light danced in Charlotte's eyes. Her lips curved into a too-innocent smile. She snagged a card from her display and slid it across the counter. A pink manicured nail tapped the small rectangle as if his attention wasn't already drawn there.

"I didn't ask for your number. But here's mine. I wouldn't object if you think you might want to use it sometime."

Tyson jerked his head up. Was she joking? Standing there with an adorable smile, one finger still resting on the card, and just a hint of doubt showing in her eyes, she must be serious. Charlotte wanted him to call her? Even after making a fool of himself?

Something about a gift horse and its mouth skittered through his mind. He reached out. Doubt slowed his movements. Still, she didn't snatch the card away and laugh. That was a good sign. Right?

The tips of his fingers barely brushed hers as he slid the card the rest of the way across the counter and into his front jacket pocket. Could the slightest touch be enough to cause a spark? It sure felt like a spark.

"You can count on it." If it wouldn't draw more attention to his current lack of brain function, Tyson would palm his face. *You can count on it.* Was he twelve? He needed to leave, fast. Before he could do any more damage and find his calling privileges revoked. "I've got to go. But I'll call soon."

"Sure." Uncertainty furrowed her brow. "I look forward to it. Talk to you later."

He waved and hurried from the store. Plucking the card from his pocket, he transferred it to the security of his wallet. All Tyson needed was to add failure to call due to card loss to his list of infractions and embarrassments. It came to mind he had yet to apologize for the misuse of her nickname. Though, since she said he could call, he might have already been forgiven. But an apology wasn't the only reason he'd visited the antique store.

He still didn't know how many Edison bulbs he needed to order. This time, Tyson didn't refrain from the facepalm.

CHAPTER FIVE

*C*harlotte slammed down the deposit bag on her desk, upending a cup of pens, pencils, and assorted office supplies. A growl emanated from her throat.

"Perfect." She righted the container and unceremoniously dropped the writing implements back into their place. "Could this day be any worse?"

"Worse?"

Charlotte slapped a hand to her chest as she spun around, knocking the cup she'd just filled to the floor. She stifled the scream, trying to escape as she realized Tessa stood in the open doorway. "Didn't anyone ever tell you not to sneak up on people?"

Tessa jerked a thumb over her shoulder. "Your front door was open. But seeing as you closed forty-five minutes ago, I went ahead and locked it for you."

"Thanks." Charlotte couldn't help her tone sounding less than grateful. "I can't believe I forgot to close it."

Tessa shrugged and scooped the cup from the floor before kneeling to clean up the mess. "It happens. But even in a town as safe as Brookview, I wouldn't let it happen often. You never know. Now, what's this about having a bad day? Every time I stopped by, the place was packed. Usually, business in a place of business is considered a good thing."

"It is." Charlotte pushed a stray curl behind her ear before joining Tessa in the cleanup. "I don't know why I said it. I mean, they're pencils, right? Pick them up. Problem solved."

Tessa dropped onto her rear and folded her legs in front of her. "Mm-hmm."

"What?"

"Oh, I don't know." Tessa rolled her eyes. "Maybe I just find it odd when dropped office supplies take your day from roaring success to *could this get any worse*. Why don't you tell me what's really got you all twisted up?'

Charlotte snatched the refilled cup from her friend and stood in a move more graceful than she would have imagined possible, at least for her. Crossing behind the desk, she set the cup back in place before scooting it an inch or two farther from the edge.

"It's nothing."

"This can't-do attitude is not nothing."

Tessa stood and snagged Charlotte's purse from its wall hook. Before Charlotte could prepare for it, the bag flew toward her. She snatched the airborne accessory mid-flight and plopped it on the desk in front of her.

"Hey. I could have something breakable in there."

One brow rose impossibly high. "You don't, or you wouldn't have plunked it on the desk. Now, come on. We're going to Mitch's Diner for milkshakes. Then, you're going to spill the tea —not literally, please."

"Fine." Charlotte grabbed her purse and slipped into her coat. "It's not like I have a choice. You're not going to leave me alone until I agree anyway."

Charlotte followed Tessa out of the office and through the store, pausing only to make sure she locked the door this time.

Tessa choked on the sip of milkshake she'd just taken. An odd assortment of laughs and coughs erupted as she tried and failed to contain herself. Charlotte eyed her from across the table, smiling, much less laughing, nowhere near her list of things to do.

"Really?" Charlotte pursed her lips. "Are you about done?"

Tessa wiped moisture from her cheek. "I need to borrow your bird."

"It wasn't funny."

"It kind of was."

"No. It was not. It was humiliating."

Tessa stifled another giggle and stirred the straw in her strawberry milkshake. "I can see where you might find it a bit embarrassing."

"You think?"

This time the giggle escaped. "But you explained everything, right? No harm. No foul."

"Yes, foul." Charlotte plucked the cherry from her milkshake and dropped it on the pile of napkins at the end of the table. "The bird was not the end of my humiliation."

"You can't have done anything actually horrific. I know you too well to believe it." Tessa snagged the cherry, pulled it from its stem, and popped it in her mouth.

"I gave him my business card."

"Charlotte, your business cards are available for everyone. You're making this bigger than it needs to be."

Charlotte lifted a hand to stop her friend. "I told him I didn't ask for his number, but he could have mine and use it any time."

Tessa's mouth hung slack. Her eyes wide. A slow smile spread across her face.

"It's not funny."

Tessa clamped her lips shut to no avail. If her eyes didn't betray her desire to laugh, the snort that escaped did. Charlotte slapped her arm.

"Stop it." Charlotte dropped her head to the table. "What am I going to do?"

"What?"

Charlotte lifted herself from the table only enough to make herself heard. "What am I going to do?"

Tessa's hand pushed against the crown of her head. "You're going to sit up like a normal human being. Really. This isn't as horrible as you think."

"I don't think you understand the ramifications of my rash behavior." Charlotte held up a finger. "One. I don't do stuff like this. I'm an under-the-radar kind of girl when it comes to men. Two." She held up the next finger. "I'm new in town. And it's a small town. It's bad enough people think my antique store is out to destroy the atmosphere my great-aunt helped create. I can't have them think I'm here to chase men or something."

"You're being ridiculous."

Charlotte tilted her head and silenced her friend with a look. She held up a third finger. "This is a small town. I'm going to run into this guy. Even if I buy everything online to avoid the hardware store, I'm going to see him around."

"Charlie …"

She ignored Tessa's tone, which, along with her expression, begged her to stop. "Sure, I gave him my number. Told him to call."

"Charlie, I really think—"

Charlotte cut off her friend with a raise of her hand. "I'm not being dramatic. You don't understand."

"Please, Charlotte—"

Charlotte shook her head, ignoring the use of her full name. "This is so much worse than my silly bird. What if I gave this guy my number, and he never called? Like, what if he's got zero interest in me, and I just threw myself at him?"

"Then again, what if he *is* interested?"

Charlotte jumped at the masculine voice. Tessa's shoulders dropped. Her eyes were filled with apology along with a very clear *I tried to warn you.* Fighting back her body's sudden urge to make her milkshake reappear, Charlotte shifted to give her a clear view of the man at the end of their table.

Tyson stood there, grinning like an idiot. A beautiful, charming idiot waiting for her answer. Too bad Charlotte's mind could only manage one word with a myriad of synonyms. Run. Flee. Escape. She'd read a million stories where the character wished they could melt into a puddle of humiliation on the floor, and Charlotte had never wanted the occurrence to be possible more than at this moment.

As Charlotte sat mute in her embarrassment, Tyson's smile widened. He leaned down until he was face to face with her.

"For the record, I was definitely going to call."

CHAPTER SIX

While Tessa slipped from the booth in his peripheral, Tyson didn't take his eyes off Charlotte. The blush in her cheeks made the green in her eyes sparkle. The effect was charming.

"Well," Tessa broke the spell. "I've got to get going. I'll see you later, Charlie."

Tyson glanced in her direction and received a nod and encouraging smile.

"Tyson."

Though he hadn't been invited, Tyson slid into the empty booth bench. A waitress made her way to the table. Tyson gave his attention to her only long enough to greet her and order a Coke before returning to Charlotte, who watched him, caution in her eyes and pink still tinging her cheeks. Her attention dropped to the table as their gazes connected. When she refused to look anywhere but the cup in front of her, Tyson struggled to find a way to ease her embarrassment, despite how adorable flustered looked on her.

"I didn't mean to eavesdrop." He held up two fingers, side by side, when she looked up. "Scouts honor."

Charlotte's gaze dropped to the table again. "You were a boy scout?"

The flick of a glance.

Tyson frowned. "No, actually. I mean, my dad and I camped a lot. He taught me about fishing, hiking, camping. Even worked in subtle lessons on being a godly man in the middle of building fires and baiting hooks. But no. Never a scout. I guess I just said it 'cause that's the thing people say."

"Sounds like maybe you learned more of the important stuff from him than you would have through scouting." A shrug punctuated her thought as the last vestiges of embarrassment drained away.

"I never gave it much thought, but it's true." He licked his lips. Did he dare? He needed to, but her embarrassment might return. "While we're talking about true things. I meant it."

Her eyes narrowed slightly. Tyson could almost see the wheels turning in her head, trying to follow the subject change. No choice now but to dive into the deep end. He held her gaze.

"I was going to call you."

She sucked in a quick breath.

He smiled, hoping to put her at ease. "You captured my attention the first time I saw you. Then, every time we met, I managed to mess up. After coming across like a lost cause so often, I was surprised you wanted me to call."

Charlotte leaned against the back of the booth. Her eyes searched his. Was she weighing the honesty in his words? Her mouth opened, closed, and opened again. No sound escaped.

"What?"

Charlotte shook her head. "You can't be serious."

"What?"

Her hands momentarily framed her cheeks before she aimed them at him, palms up and fingers splayed. "You. I can't think of one awkward thing you've done."

"Um, I kind of insulted you about your store's decor. I mean, not intentionally. I didn't mean it as a negative. It caught me off guard. But still. I did it, and I'm sorry."

Her frown took on a glare-like quality, though Tyson was certain she wasn't mad. He might as well continue.

"And I accused you of using a cheesy pickup line on me. Not to mention the wolf whistle."

Charlotte's eyes slid shut as she groaned. "Which wouldn't have happened if it weren't for Cracker Jack. So, I think that one rests firmly in my column."

"Fine. I guess we'll have to call it a draw." Tyson extended his hand across the table.

Charlotte's brow furrowed as she stared at his hand and then at him. "You mean, like, we're equally in need of some classes on social grace?"

"Exactly." Tyson wiggled his outstretched hand, waiting. "Are you going to leave me hanging here?"

Charlotte's smile was tentative and sweet. Was there a look that wouldn't cause his pulse to quicken? As she slid her hand into his, he kept the gesture nonchalant. He longed to brush his thumb against her skin to see if it was as soft as it looked.

Tyson cleared his throat. "But in lieu of classes, since I doubt they'd help at this stage of the game, how about we try something else? I'll forget your parrot. You'll forget I insulted your decorating skills. We'll each pretend the other is the picture of social grace and normalcy and get to know one another instead. Work for you?"

"Sounds perfect. I could use another friend in town besides Tessa. After a while, she's going to get tired of being my sole support system."

"I don't think you'll have any problems making friends."

"Sure." Her gaze fell to the tabletop.

"I mean it. With Tessa as your friend, it won't matter if you're shy. She'll introduce you to everyone."

"I'm not shy."

Tyson fiddled with the straw in his drink. He'd spoken without thinking. In their few interactions, Charlotte didn't appear introverted. Though he doubted she'd ever been quite as bold before, he had the card with her number in his pocket, proving the opposite. But if she wasn't shy, what was the problem? Did he miss something?

"If you're a people person, then making friends is easy."

She faced the window bordering one side of their booth. Her shoulders lifted long and high before dropping back down. "Not when everyone thinks you're ruining their town."

He couldn't have heard her mumbled statement correctly. "Ruining the town?"

She turned to him, her lips quirked to one side in a that's-the-way-it-is smirk.

"You can't really believe people think you're ruining the town. Right?"

"Forget I said anything."

If he believed Charlotte really wanted him to ignore her statement, he would. The resignation accompanying her words told a different story. Charlotte was hurting, and she wanted someone to see it. To see her.

A couple of months. Charlotte had been in town only a handful of weeks, and she apparently already felt the town was firmly against her. Tyson's chest ached with the realization. Brookview was an almost idyllic town where everyone was a neighbor, and the designation meant something.

His own complicity crushed his chest.

"I'm sorry." He held up a hand to stall her interruption. "I mean it. I don't know what others have done to make you feel less than accepted. But I do know, accident or not, my attitude didn't help. I loved the candy store, and I have great memories of it and of your great-aunt. But your antique store deserves a chance. In the few minutes I was there, I'll admit, I was impressed. Was even reminded of my childhood by a few things."

Her smile seemed forced. "I'm glad."

"But?"

She blinked as if the gesture would transmit her feelings. Tyson didn't want to push. He opted for silence.

"But you're one person." Charlotte held up a single digit. "If the town doesn't get behind the store, I don't know how long it will survive. And I don't have a clue how to change their minds."

"How do you know they aren't supporting it?" A queasiness in his stomach warned he might not want the answer. These were his friends. But a reasonable solution could only be found if they looked at the situation truthfully. How well did he know Charlotte? She could be a sensitive person, taking remarks personally that were unintended as slights against her against her or the store.

Charlotte slowly inhaled a deep breath. "Do you know how many comments I've heard regarding the new setup? You might not have meant yours, but others weren't so polite in their displeasure. One lady tried to smooth over her dislike by telling me she was only surprised how easily a coat of paint could take a space from warm to cold, as if there was nothing wrong with that. She said my store was *cold*."

Tyson winced. He could only imagine which woman uttered those words. While the people of Brookview might be like family, being close carried both good and bad connotations. Every family had one or two headstrong aunts, unafraid to speak their minds, no matter how tactlessly.

"First, I'm not defending her." Tyson held his hands up in surrender. "But let me play devil's advocate here. The change is drastic. The store was bright and energetic. Now, there's less playfulness, and blue does reside on the cool side of the color spectrum."

"So, my shop is boring. Clinical." Charlotte groaned. "Great."

"Those aren't my words. Blue is cooler. It's also calm, steady, classic. Like antiques. If you want pops of color, blue coordinates easily. Remember, the person who wants a birthday cake ice cream cone with sprinkles one day may enjoy the less flashy butter pecan the next."

"Butter pecan?" One brow rose. "I guess it's better than a dentist's office. At least people enjoy ice cream. Maybe they'll enjoy the store too."

"How could they not?"

CHAPTER SEVEN

*"B*utter pecan? Who buys that?" Tessa complained, pulling the carton from Charlotte's freezer.

Charlotte smiled just as she'd done when she picked the flavor from the myriads filling the grocery store freezer. Just looking at it reminded her of Tyson's confidence in her and her store's acceptance in Brookview.

She snatched the treat out of her friend's hand. "You don't like it, you don't have to eat it. More for me."

"I didn't say that." Tessa snagged the carton back and grabbed a bowl from the cabinet. "It's just not your usual triple chocolate chunk or rocky road extreme."

"Change can be a good thing."

With ice cream balanced on the scoop halfway between carton and bowl, Tessa glanced at her. "Why do I feel like we aren't talking about ice cream?"

Charlotte plopped her own plastic bowl onto the counter. "Maybe because we're not. Tyson said—"

"Tyson said you should eat butter pecan instead of chocolate?" She passed the scoop to Charlotte. "I'm going to kill him. I need my chocolate fix."

"No. He said I didn't have to feel bad because my store is butter pecan instead of birthday cake with sprinkles."

"Come again?"

"You know, just because everyone likes birthday cake doesn't mean they don't like butter pecan too."

Tessa relished a bite of ice cream before sucking the spoon clean to shake in Charlotte's direction. "News flash. Charlie. You have it bad for the man. Otherwise, there's no way this conversation would make sense."

Charlotte rolled her eyes. "Of course, you'd think so. You're perpetually trying to pair me up, like romance is the only option. But think about it. Enjoying one flavor, or type of store, in this instance, doesn't mean you can't like another. Different flavors for different days. Soon, the town will realize it and love Living in the Past as much as I do."

"While I'm still confused about how your store suddenly turned into ice cream, I'm thrilled your talk with Tyson means you aren't wallowing in self-doubt anymore."

"I wasn't wallowing."

"Ah, but it *was* your talk with Tyson that made things look so rosy."

"Would you stop?"

"Are you seeing him again?"

"Ugh. I didn't see him this time."

"You kind of did."

"Did not."

"'Fraid so."

Charlotte stood, grabbed the empty bowl in front of Tessa, and crossed to the kitchen sink. "How do you figure?" She sprayed both bowls with dish cleaner and swiped a rag through them. "*Seeing* someone implies intentionally setting aside time to spend with them. I did no such thing. I didn't even invite Tyson to join me. He just plopped down in the space my friend had vacated. In traitorous fashion, I might add."

"It may not have been official, and it might have been impromptu, but don't think for a minute it didn't turn into a date."

"It wasn't a date. We talked business, and business does not a date make."

Charlotte's phone dinged with an incoming text. Tessa glanced at the screen. Her eyes widened. Charlotte dove for her phone, narrowly missing it as Tessa swung it out of reach and angled her body to create a blockade against retrieving it.

"Give me my phone!"

Tessa raised her arm in defense against Charlotte's onslaught. "What's this? *I really enjoyed getting to know you at the diner yesterday.*"

While Charlotte gave up trying to get the phone back, she refused to smile at the dumb boy voice Tessa employed to read the message.

"*Thanks for not kicking me to the curb. I'd like to see you again. Can I call you sometime?*" Tessa handed the phone back to Charlotte with a smirk. "I believe his exact words were, 'I'd like to see you *again.*' Again. Funny word. Correct me if I'm wrong, but it stands to reason if he wants to see you again, then he feels he's *seen* you before. And not for business."

Charlotte quickly scanned then swiped the message from the screen. Tyson wanted to see her. She tried to bite back a smile. Her happiness would add fuel to Tessa's fire. No one needed it to go from the current spark to an all-out blaze.

"Whatever."

Tessa cocked a hip to the side as she planted her hand on it in a no-nonsense pose. "Don't 'whatever' me. You think I don't know you? Girl, I can see how hard you're trying not to smile. Let it out."

Her friend's dramatics won the battle. Charlotte laughed, letting loose the smile she worked to control. Once she did, there was no taking it back.

Tessa grinned. "There it is."

"This is ridiculous." Charlotte shook her head, still laughing. "I'm an adult. I shouldn't be giddy about some guy wanting to go out with me."

"First, giddy? You just proved antiques are your life. No one's used 'giddy' in a million years." Tessa added her own laughter to the mix. "Old soul, young-ish body."

Charlotte slapped her shoulder. "Hey! I'm not old. I'm barely in my thirties."

"Older than me."

"Do you have a point?"

"An old soul, not old."

"Whatever." Charlotte rolled her eyes.

"The point is, age doesn't matter. A hot guy being interested in you is always reason to be a little—how did you put it?—giddy. It's especially true when he's the town sweetheart and a believer to boot." The last bit was thrown over her shoulder as Tessa moved from the kitchen to the living room.

"How do you know he's a Christian?" Charlotte followed and parked herself on the sofa beside Tessa. It was better to ask. Assuming only led to issues later. She'd not repeat the mistake of falling for a great guy only to find out he didn't share her faith.

"Brookview's a small town." Tessa shrugged. "Everybody knows everybody. He was a couple years ahead, but I went to school with Tyson throughout high school. He's gone to Brookview Chapel all his life, was baptized at summer camp, and can sometimes be found reading his Bible or praying in public settings. Oh, and *The Princess Bride* is his favorite movie."

"Really? *The Princess Bride*?"

Tessa shook her head. "All the info I gave you, and you're stuck on *The Princess Bride*? No, I don't know his favorite movie. I made it up because you're being a little over the top. You can figure out movies on your own. But yes, I know he's a

Christian, as well as anyone can know someone else's spiritual state."

Charlotte shoved her bangs out of her eyes. "You don't have to be snotty. It's my favorite movie and everything, but usually, guys are more into superhero movies and stuff."

"Again. Not. The. Point."

"Got it. He's a Christian. Fair game. I should doodle hearts on my notebook paper and test how my first name looks with his last. Giddiness approved."

"You are so extra."

"But you love me."

Tessa sighed. "I do. And before long, so will Tyson."

Charlotte flung a pillow, hitting Tessa. Direct hit, square in the face. Her giddiness erupted in laughter.

CHAPTER EIGHT

*T*yson glanced at his phone beside the cash register. Nothing from Charlotte. Had he misread the situation? He thought they'd hit it off. They'd stayed through several drink refills talking about everything. Her concerns about the town topped the list, but they'd also shared little bits about their personal lives.

"Doesn't seem right." Tim Kendrick tossed a packet of beef jerky on the counter next to the metal shelving kit he'd left there before searching for a snack.

Not having been in a conversation with him other than a greeting as he entered the store, Tyson had no idea what the man had taken issue with this time around. But it was as typical a small-town conversation starter as "Did you see the game?" or "The sky looks like snow today." It left Tyson little choice but to respond. Anything else would be rude.

"What's wrong, Tim?"

"That girl up and changing the candy store." He ripped the top off the jerky and shoved a piece in his mouth. "It would break Annie's heart to know all she worked for was down the drain, just like that." He snapped his fingers.

Despite having fought similar feelings prior to their talk, protectiveness for Charlotte welled up, leaving Tyson itching to tell Tim not to talk with his mouth full, and if he didn't have something nice to say, not to talk at all. Instead, he took the jerky from the man's hand, scanned it, and passed it back without a word.

"Antiques? Why do we need an antique store? The kids always loved the candy store. Now, what are they going to do?"

"Maybe avoid cavities." The snarky comment slipped out quietly as Tyson rang up the rest of the purchase. "Seventy-five forty-nine, please."

A slight narrowing of the man's eyes warned Tyson he'd crossed the line of the allowable in friendly small-town communication. Too bad Tyson didn't feel like backtracking. He accepted the debit card from Tim's outstretched hand and slid it through the reader.

"Have you been in there?" Tyson knew the answer without asking, but it was the closest he would come to acquiescing. "It's different, for sure."

"See." Tim snapped his fingers. "Right there."

"I said it was different. Not bad." Tyson handed the man's bags across the counter. "The place looks really good. And Charlotte's got some great stuff in there."

"She's gone and changed everything." The man grunted. "Annie would be appalled."

"I wasn't aware you and Annie were close."

"We weren't especially close. But it don't matter. Everyone works hard to establish their trade. No one wants to see their work tossed out like trash, especially by someone who isn't a part of things around here. Would you up and change your daddy's store?"

Tyson scanned the store he inherited from his dad. He loved the place and couldn't imagine giving it a complete overhaul. Not what Tim needed to hear. He shrugged. "The way I see it,

Annie knew Charlotte and gave her the storefront. She trusted her great-niece's judgment. She would've protected it if she felt strongly about it. As for Charlotte not being part of things, I have a feeling she wants to be. But have people given her a chance? It's sad, because I've always known the people in this town to be friendly and welcoming to everyone."

The man harrumphed and walked out without comment. Tyson wanted to call him back, argue his point. It would do no good. Until Tim was ready to listen, truth wasn't going to change his mind. It was the same with everyone else.

And while they clutched their dismay tighter than a dog clenches a marrow-filled bone, Charlotte was left walking the tight-rope of their approval without a net. Change was hard. But it didn't have to cause a rift.

If only he could figure out a way to smooth things over. The dark screen of his phone taunted him from the counter. Disappointment diluted his determination. Charlotte must not have been as interested as she'd seemed. Maybe she was merely being polite.

Still, even if she didn't need a relationship, Charlotte needed an ally. He'd be her friend. The only question left was how to win over the doubters.

"Wow." Tyson accepted the newspaper article with its black-and-white photo from Charlotte. "Is that Annie?"

Charlotte shook her head. "Nope. Wanda Matthews. She started the candy store. Annie bought it from her."

"Cool." He examined it closer before handing it back. "I wish the photo showed more of the place and not just Wanda. Would've been great seeing the store back then."

Charlotte glanced at the piles they'd already dug out. "Maybe there are more photos in this mess. I can't believe Annie didn't sort this stuff."

While she scrutinized the photo and article, Tyson continued emptying the filing cabinet contents onto the folding table Charlotte set up in the small office. His initial relief when she'd finally answered his text plummeted into disappointment when she'd said she couldn't get together in the near future. She still had too much to organize at the store that couldn't be accomplished during regular working hours. Offering to help her was inspired, allowing him to be a good neighbor and getting to know her at the same time.

Tyson didn't mind the work, and he was glad to spend time with Charlotte. Intent on the next haphazard pile of paperwork, he almost missed Charlotte's quiet gasp. His own breath hitched when he spied her excited smile.

He set his pile aside. "Want to share with the class?"

Her hazel eyes sparkled. "It's this article. It's the answer I've been searching for."

She turned the clipping his direction. He glanced at it, seeing exactly what he saw before.

"Still lost."

"Did you read the article?"

"No. Just took a look at the picture. Why?"

Looking at the article once more, her fingers brushed over it as if it were a precious treasure. She peered back at him. "This is my tie to the town. At least, a start. The store was news because it hosted a town-wide event, a scavenger hunt for the tourists."

Excitement radiated off Charlotte. Tyson grinned. He had an idea where she was headed, but with her exuberance making her eyes sparkle, he wouldn't have interrupted her thoughts for anything.

"In changing Auntie Annie's to reflect who I am, I've alienated everyone else. But this," she waved the paper, "this will show them I'm not out to destroy anything. Oh, for the love of chocolate, I run an antique store. I love history and tradition."

Tyson couldn't stop his laugh. "Did you just say, 'for the love of chocolate'?"

Her blush only accented the light in her eyes. "Sorry. I forget most people don't say weird things. I tried to say something else once. Annie forbade it because of its origins. But chocolate? We could all agree to love chocolate, and it had no ties to anything else."

"Your great aunt was something else."

The light dimmed as Charlotte looked around the one room that still held the essence of the aunt she loved and lost. The admiration she held for Annie was obvious. How could anyone think she'd taken Annie's gift lightly? And more importantly, how could he reignite her excitement from only moments ago?

"So ... what? You're going to post a copy of the article in the store?"

He silently congratulated himself when a smile replaced her contemplation.

"Don't be ridiculous. I'm going to host a scavenger hunt in honor of the original store and the town itself."

"How would it work?"

"The plan is right here." Charlotte tapped the article. "Each store chooses an item and writes a clue. In the original event, people had to have the owner sign some form showing they found the item. When you've finished finding them all, turn in your form. At the end of the hunt, I'll draw one winner from each correct entry. I'll donate something for the prize."

"You could ask the rest of the town owners if they'd like to donate too. Get them involved and increase the prize to get more people interested."

"Great idea." She glanced at the piles of the past surrounding them. "We've made headway. Why don't we take a break? We can go over to Soups and Subs for food and brainstorming. My treat."

Tyson stood and followed her out the door to the front of the store. "No."

"Oh. Okay."

"Dinner will be my treat."

"But ..."

Tyson shook his head. "My treat or no brainstorming. Sorry, Charlie."

"*Sorry, Charlie. Sorry, Charlie.*" Cracker Jack called his repetition from his place behind the counter.

Charlotte's shoulders dropped. "Great. Now, she's going to be saying that forever. Tessa thought it was so funny to teach her to say it. Took me weeks to get her onto something else."

Tyson tried to look repentant. It was difficult, considering he found it humorous. "Sorry."

"*Sorry, Charlie. Sorry, Charlie.*"

Tyson laughed.

Charlotte swatted his arm. "Would you please stop?"

"Okay. Okay." He held up his hands in surrender. "Honest, I didn't mean it. But I do have one question."

"Not until we're out of Cracker Jack's earshot." She opened the door and motioned him through so she could lock it behind them. "Go ahead."

"Tessa taught your bird to say, 'Sorry, Charlie.'"

"Not a question."

"No. I know." Tyson stepped between Charlotte and the road as they walked down the sidewalk. "But the first time I saw you together, I thought Tessa called you Charlie. I used the name, and you looked at me funny. I thought I'd misheard. But she did call you Charlie, didn't she?"

"I love my name. I think Charlotte fits me and my interests perfectly." She shrugged. "Tessa changed it to Charlie almost immediately. Never liked Charlotte. Said it sounded old and stuffy. I'm not sure what she thinks that means for me, but whatever. Anyway, after teaching Cracker Jack, I don't think it's going away anytime soon. Tessa is, however, the only one who gets by with it."

"She's wrong, you know. Charlie may fit, but so does Charlotte." Tyson sucked in a deep breath and kept his focus on the path in front of him. "And from what I've seen, you're a lot of things. Old and stuffy are furthest from the truth."

CHAPTER NINE

W armth exploded with a flurry in Charlotte's middle, and she tucked her bottom lip between her teeth to control the silly grin fighting to be seen. A quick glance at Tyson from her peripheral showed his attention on the pavement in front of them, but his inflection confirmed he meant every word.

"Thank you. I like it too."

How could she keep her voice so calm when all the girlish cells in her body wanted to relish the moment with a squeal of delight? It might have something to do with the quiet voice of caution whispering in her head. She'd been down this path before. Enamored with a man and ultimately allowing herself to love him, she'd lost herself in being the woman of his dreams. Doing so nearly cost Charlotte her own dreams, not to mention delivering a crippling shot to her self-confidence.

If Annie's gift hadn't come along, Charlotte didn't know if she would've had the strength to break away. The storefront provided an opportunity to show her competence as a businesswoman. The nest egg and small home Annie left gave her time to grow into this new venture. She wouldn't allow anyone to steal her dreams again.

While it didn't seem like Tyson took issue with her plans, they'd only just met. Maybe he questioned it at first, but not once he saw her store. The rest of the town would come around. God provided this opportunity in an unexpected way, and following His leading, she would succeed.

Could she accept the attention of a great-looking guy without losing who she was? If he wanted her to succeed as much as she wanted to, it couldn't hurt anything. Right? She wished the answer was a resolute *yes*. She'd matured a lot over the last ten months without Eric.

Enough of the past. They were part of the old Charlotte and had nothing to do with the here and now where she was strolling down Main Street with a cute guy who didn't mind her old-fashioned name or her antique store. It was beyond time to move her focus to him.

"Have you always wanted to own a hardware store?" Perfect. A casual question to peek behind the curtain of his life. A subject safe from the deep end of conversation, where inquiries into hopes and dreams dwelled. Way too early for those questions.

"It was my dad's store." Tyson looked over his shoulder toward the shop in question. "I've worked there since before I was old enough to legally earn a wage."

"And it passed to you when he retired?"

"No." His voice was weighted. "It passed to me when he died five years ago."

Charlotte swallowed the bitter aftertaste of her assumption. "I'm so sorry. I had no idea."

His smile was strained as he glanced at her. "You couldn't have known."

Charlotte's heart broke at the hurt still evident in his voice. "You must've been close."

"Dad was my best friend." Tyson stared ahead as he spoke.

"We always planned on me taking over the store, but not this way. We had a lot of dreams for the place."

Broken dreams? Charlotte understood those completely, though the situations causing them were entirely different. Should she continue the conversation or move on to happier things? She searched his profile for clues. Some found talking cathartic. Others, not so much. She'd never excelled at social cues.

Pain shot from her big toe straight up her shin.

What had she kicked? She lashed out to grasp something to steady her. But it was inevitable—she was destined to meet the ground.

Tyson must have seen whatever was in the path because, though they'd been walking shoulder to shoulder, his arm was just beyond her reach.

Flailing windmill-style, Charlotte tipped forward, making a quick descent to the brick-paved walk. Tyson tried and failed to catch her, scratching her hand in the attempt. Her mind captured her graceless collision with the ground in slow motion, though reason told her it was mere seconds. Seconds of klutziness to inflict days of humiliation, more if the sidewalks were crowded.

But she had her answer. No more talk of painful subjects. Couldn't God have simply told her in spirit rather than forcing the issue in such a pride-shattering way?

"Charlotte! Are you hurt?"

She shook her head, afraid to trust her voice.

"Let me help you."

His hands gripped her upper arms, steadying her and helping lift her from the ground in tandem with her own efforts. Why did his success have to happen a few seconds too late? Time returned to normal as she stood. A surreptitious glance around showed, mercifully, few people milling around the area.

While some didn't seem to notice her fall, others glanced in their direction with anxious expressions. She grimaced and waved. Content that all was in hand, they returned to their shopping or strolling or whatever they were doing prior to her embarrassment.

Eager to escape the incident, Charlotte stepped forward. Pain sliced up her leg from her ankle. Air fled her lungs with a hiss. Tyson's hand slid from her triceps to her elbow.

"Here." He turned her toward a nearby bench. "Let's sit a minute. Make sure you're okay."

Merely a few feet from the heavy planter she'd stumbled over, Charlotte offered a prayer of thanks she hadn't cracked her head against the wrought-iron bench—or anything else. Leaning her weight on Tyson helped lessen the ache in her leg enough to maneuver to the bench and sit.

"You're bleeding."

Charlotte stared at her hand nestled palm-up in Tyson's. While her winter coat kept her arms safe from the impact, her hands took the brunt of the fall. Pebble-dotted scrapes covered her palms, but only a small spot of the mild road rash bled.

"Wait here."

Tyson went into the shop behind them. Her body ached too much to turn and watch him go, but if Charlotte remembered correctly, there was a handmade beeswax candle shop by this bench. She hated to tell Tyson, but candles, even nicely scented ones, weren't going to make this go away, especially not the humiliation.

"Here." Tyson plopped onto the bench next to her and opened the small first aid kit he must have retrieved from the store owner. "Let me see your hand."

It didn't matter what the little box contained. Nothing could compare to the balm soothing her aching palm when he carefully cradled her hand in his. She couldn't stop the wince as the antiseptic spray hit the scratches any more than she could suppress the shiver that skittered through her when Tyson noticed her discomfort and softly blew on the area to ease the pain.

She closed her eyes. Enough, Charlotte. You aren't some twitterpated teenager. You're a grown woman, fully recognizing fairy tale romance is for books and movies. Real life is anything but *I*'s dotted with little hearts.

She opened her eyes. Her inner chastisement did little, if anything, to douse the flames of interest Tyson's gentle care fanned without intent. His complete attention was focused on her hand as he gingerly picked the last brick pebble from her palm and placed a bandage loosely over the area.

"Let me have a look at your legs."

"Tyson! Really?" Her giggle betrayed her mock horror at his suggestion.

A grimace distorted Tyson's expression as red crept up his neck. Charlotte laughed at the discomfort his awkward phrasing caused. Her *faux pas* may have been more damaging, but at least she wasn't the only one to do or say things she instantly regretted.

"That isn't … I meant ... you know exactly what I meant."

"True." Charlotte leaned down to grip the hem of her jeans. At least she'd worn bootcut jeans. They slid up past her knee without rubbing denim over scraped skin. "But it's so much more fun to spread the humiliation around."

Tyson's lips quirked to the side. "Thanks. I appreciate your generosity." He angled to see her leg. "It's not as bad as I figured. You're going to have a good bruise, though."

She glanced at the affected area. Red and already turning a beautiful shade of purple. But Tyson was correct. The denim was thick enough to provide protection from scrapes, for the most part. Nothing to clean or cover.

"It won't be my first." She pushed her pant leg back into place. "I think my toes probably took the brunt of the damage."

"Can you put weight on it since you've rested?"

Without standing, Charlotte lifted her heel and pressed her toes into the pavement. She sucked in a fortifying breath against the pain. Walking wouldn't be comfortable, but she doubted anything was broken. Whether it was or not, she would work under the premise of wholeness until her body told her differently.

"It hurts. I can walk, but probably can't race to the restaurant." She stood and slowly stretched each sore muscle. "No powerwalking for a while."

He glanced down and back up the length of her. One brow rose as his lips quirked in a smirk which sparked a flutter in Charlotte's chest.

"I'm not really getting the powerwalking vibe, even if you do drive a crunchy car."

"I resent that. Just because I don't want to kill the environment with toxic fumes or pay a month's mortgage at the pumps does not make me or my car crunchy."

"Whatever you say."

His playful grin, coupled with a dramatic roll of his eyes, assured Charlotte he was only joking. And while she'd never considered herself of the same mindset as those commonly thought of as crunchy, she could admit she shared an affinity for clean air.

"You think it doesn't fit?" She lightly limped next to him.

He quickly stepped forward and swung open the door to the restaurant, waving her inside with all the pomp of a servant motioning in a queen. Once seated and with their drink orders placed, Tyson considered her in silence. Was he still pondering her question? For reasons she didn't want to examine too closely, she was eager to know what Tyson thought of her and her crunchy car.

"Honestly?" He nodded thanks to the waitress, who placed their drinks on the table in front of them. "I didn't see it at first. Seemed odd. You loving antiques but driving a hybrid car. Thinking about it from a different direction, it makes sense."

"What do you mean?"

"Well, buying and selling antiques keeps perfectly good stuff out of the dump. Older stuff isn't cheaply made like a lot of products today. There's no reason to trash them. Reuse is good for the environment. And that fits with your windup car."

Charlotte reached across the table to shove his hand. Too late, she realized he was lifting his glass to take a drink. Her flirty chuckle died in her throat as the glass tipped, sending a tide of sweet tea into his lap.

Tyson jumped from his seat as the icy liquid filled his lap. Trying to set the glass back on the table and deal with his wet jeans, Tyson missed the solid surface. The clink of glass on the table edge barely preceded the shattering of it on the tile floor. Ice cubes danced between droplets of tea, creating a haphazard pattern worthy of a work of abstract art.

"Oh, honey." Emma Lou, the owner of the restaurant, rushed to the table. "What in the world happened?"

Tyson's finger itched to point in Charlotte's direction, but just in time, he realized Emma Lou's targeted gaze had already zeroed in on her. No way was he going to add fuel to the fire. Charlotte had enough issues trying to make inroads with the town. Destruction of property, albeit innocently, did not need added to the list of things to overcome. Especially since they were supposed to be discussing her plan to solidify her place in the residents' hearts.

Tyson shook his head. "Just being butterfingers today." It wasn't a lie. He didn't say who was clumsy. "I'm so sorry about the glass and the floor." Again, totally true. "Direct me to the mop and broom, and I'll clean it up in a flash."

With one last glance at Charlotte, who looked mortified with her bottom lip tucked between her teeth and sporting the color of a garden tomato in July, Emma Lou pasted her sweet smile back in place and waved off his suggestion. "Oh, posh. We have the Wilson boy for messes like this. Needs to earn his keep. Don't think nothing of it. But we do need to move you to another table."

Tyson glanced at Charlotte. He could be wrong, but her eyes seemed to silently beg for escape. Damp as he was, going out into the cold wasn't enticing, but he couldn't ignore Charlotte's discomfort either.

"Actually," he pointed to the counter, "we can wait over there. We just need two grilled cheese and tomato soup specials to go. And," he smiled his most endearing smile, "a couple of drinks to go?"

Emma Lou's face registered doubt, but one quick look at the floor and Charlotte brought acquiescence. "You go on over. I'll take your order to the kitchen and have it ready in a jiffy."

Tyson reached down to take Charlotte's hand to steady her as she rose from the booth. Once Emma Lou had made her way to the kitchen and the Wilson boy's attention was on the mess they'd made, Tyson leaned close to Charlotte's ear.

"I hope you like grilled cheese and tomato soup. I figured it was the quickest way for us to escape."

Was a tiny smile prodding the corners of her mouth upward? Good. Maybe she wasn't as traumatized as he feared.

"Thank you." Her whisper barely reached his ears. "And who doesn't love grilled cheese and tomato soup?"

Paper bags holding their order in hand, Tyson slid two twenties across the counter to cover the meal and the mess. Emma Lou wouldn't expect it, but she'd appreciate it and be less likely to hold it against him or Charlotte next time they visited.

"Where are we headed?" Charlotte waited until they were outside the restaurant before asking. "My office is a mess."

"I know the perfect place, but it's not on the main street. Feel like a short drive?"

"Anything to keep from facing Emma Lou's displeasure." Charlotte laughed. "I don't think you fooled her at all. Thank you for trying, though. Do you always play the knight in shining armor to the damsel in distress?"

"Hmm. I've never been compared with a knight before." He puffed out his chest and swaggered toward his truck. Unlocking the door, he opened it and slid the bag into the middle of the seat before stepping out of the way for Charlotte. "I know you may consider this gas-guzzler more dragon than noble steed, but my chariot awaits, fair damsel."

"Actually, I've always liked trucks."

Her saucy tone and the flip of her hair would have been much more effective if her leg didn't cause a grimace as she tried to get in. After the second try, she handed Tyson the cups she carried, pulled herself into the seat, and took back the drinks without a word. Looking straight ahead with her shoulders back and a "so there" look plastered on her face, Tyson could envision her as a feisty storybook princess.

"Mom's place is only three or four miles south of Main Street. Close enough for convenience, but far enough for space."

"We're going to your mom's house?"

Charlotte sounded like a child who'd been sent to the principal. Tyson should know—he'd ended up there his fair share. Usually sticking up for someone who couldn't or wouldn't stick up for themselves. Kind of like what he was doing with Charlotte. Hmm. Maybe there was something of the knight in him after all.

"Don't worry. Mom won't mind."

Charlotte didn't look convinced.

"Really. We don't even have to go in the house. It'll be fine."

Her brows dipped as deeply as her lips. "But it's cold. We could've sat outside in town. Or even crowded into my office. It's better than being outside."

Tyson chuckled. "Trust me. You're not going to be cold, and we don't have to disturb my mom."

His mother's face lit up like an indigo sky on the fourth of July when she saw Charlotte get out of the truck. He knew the look, and it settled like a rock in his gut. All he'd wanted was a warm place for him and Charlotte to eat and some dry clothes. Mom's house seemed the logical choice. His place was out of the question. Of course, he hadn't given his mom's reaction a thought. He didn't really date and hadn't even dated much in high school. Mom prayed for the day he'd bring home someone special. Now, he'd have to burst her bubble.

"Hey, Mom!" He lengthened his stride to reach her before Charlotte could make it to the porch. He kissed her cheek. "We had a bit of an accident at Emma Lou's. I need some dry clothes, and I think I left some here last weekend. Don't worry about entertaining us or anything, though. We're heading out to the shop."

Mom's smile deflated, but not enough that Charlotte would notice. "Oh, of course. Come on in and change. I'll show Charlotte to the shop."

CHAPTER TEN

harlotte circled the table in the middle of the shop, taking in every detail of the miniature grain mill carved into the tree stump. The windows flickered with light from a battery-operated tea light inside the hollowed-out space Tyson had transformed from a forgotten piece of wood to a tiny mill. Flat, wooden shingles were stained and added to the roof. Replacing the candle, when needed, would be easy, thanks to a working door. And the wheel on the side of the building lacked only water to make it turn.

Steps wound up the stump from bottom to top where the mill resided. Along the path, Tyson had taken time to carve evergreen trees into the edges of the path. There was even a miniature fox resting under one of the trees. No detail was inconsequential.

"This is beautiful." Charlotte pulled herself away from the mill to survey the various pieces throughout the shop. From tables created as boardgame tops and oversized games for outdoor parties to rolling pins and wooden canisters, each item showed the same care in its creation. "All of them. They're all beautiful."

As her gaze skimmed over the window, something outside

drew her attention. Moving closer, she figured out what the odd shape was. Tyson's workshop sat to the side and back of the house, but the yard was completely enclosed, blocking off the view from the path his mother had taken when leading her out. The window, however, gave a clear view of a beautifully manicured lawn with terraced gardens she knew would be a riot of color in the spring.

In the middle of the gardens and winding rock paths stood a gazebo unlike any Charlotte had ever seen. Rising from a circular base, the slatted walls of the structure were rounded, giving it an open orb shape with rounded windows in some of the sections and cushioned benches built into the walls. In the center was a beautiful stone firepit begging for a fire to compete with the canvas of sunset color in the background.

"It's amazing." Charlotte shook her head, still staring out the window. "I've never seen anything like it."

"Thank you. It's one of my favorites. Took the longest too."

Charlotte spun around, knowing her mouth hung slack in her surprise but unable to stop it. "Took longest? You made that?"

"It was the last piece my dad and I created together." He stood beside her, looking out. "A Mother's Day gift for Mom ..."

His voice trailed off. Charlotte glanced at him from her periphery. An invisible cord of memory tied him to the gazebo outside. Charlotte was unwilling to sever the connection. Loss was loss, and she understood the ache better than some. She slid her hand into his, allowing it to speak her understanding, despite the silence.

How could strength come from something as delicate as a slender hand woven with his? Tyson sighed. Charlotte standing beside him, letting him be in the hurt but not alone, lightened the haze. He didn't talk about it any further, but her touch told him it wasn't needed.

A gentle squeeze conveyed his thanks before Tyson dropped her hand and moved to the worktable in the middle of the room. He emptied the food from the takeout bags and pulled a stool up to the table adjacent to the one already there. Charlotte took the hint and sat.

"Looks like you stay busy when you're not at the hardware store." She slipped the lid from her foam soup container and began unwrapping her sandwich. "Why run the hardware store, when you could be doing this?"

Tyson shrugged as he chewed a bite of his grilled cheese. "I love the store, and the town needs it. Besides, this is for fun. Do it to pay the bills, and suddenly, it isn't fun anymore."

"Makes sense." Charlotte glanced around the room. "But you have talent to spare if you ever change your mind. You could make a go of it."

It didn't matter that he'd only known Charlotte a short while. Her praise of his work, even if it wasn't how he made his living, prompted a surge of pride. "Dad and I had a plan to incorporate woodcraft at the shop. There's not enough space now, but we wanted to expand the store and offer weekend classes. We'd do more complex project classes for locals, but we'd also offer quick, easy projects for kids to complete with their parents. Those classes would bring in some of the tourist trade. We rarely see anyone but locals as it is."

"It's a great idea." Charlotte dipped the corner of her sandwich into her tomato soup and took a bite before giving him a pointed look. "You know we make quite a pair."

Tyson put a rein on his suddenly racing pulse, mentally reminding himself that Charlotte wasn't calling them a couple. "What do you mean?"

"You're a store owner loved by locals, wanting to grow into

the tourist business. I'm a store perfectly fit to the visitors, but locals want nothing to do with me." A wry frown pulled her lips to one side. "I'm not sure they don't want to run me out of town, if we're being honest."

"They don't want you to leave." Tyson shrugged. "They just want you to give up antiques in favor of jellybeans and lollipops."

Charlotte rolled her eyes and huffed. Tyson fought a laugh until he caught sight of the grin she tried to hide. Freeing his laugh earned a tentative smile from her before she looked away. Staring down at the empty food containers, a pensive expression reminded Tyson they weren't on a date. They met with a purpose, bringing Charlotte and the town together.

He gathered up the wrappers and bowls to put in the trashcan. "If we're going to flesh out your grand plan and get you back to the shop in time to put Cracker Jack down for the night, we'd best get to it. After all, one of us really should be able to realize the dream, and you're in the best position to do it at this point."

Charlotte's lips parted and closed again. Whatever she'd thought to say, she'd changed her mind. Maybe she thought he was being defeatist. He wasn't. One day, his plan would take place. Possibly even sooner rather than later, if the loan he applied for that morning came through. Without a downpayment and only his store as collateral, Tyson had to wait. Charlotte's plan, on the other hand, had potential and needed only the specifics to make it work.

"This scavenger hunt of yours." Tyson grabbed the notebook he kept his design sketches in and flipped it open to a blank page. "Let's figure out the moving parts."

Charlotte's eyes looked deeper into him than Tyson would've guessed possible. He reassured her with an easy grin. After a moment more, her shoulders relaxed, and she began laying out the plan. Each detail drew more excitement from Charlotte.

When they finished over an hour later, Charlotte was practically jumping up and down beside him.

Tyson froze as Charlotte threw her arms around him and squeezed him.

"Thank you." An excited squeal accompanied a tightening of her arms. "It's going to be great. This town's not going to know what hit it."

With Charlotte's joyful expression of thanks leaving her in his arms, Tyson could relate.

CHAPTER ELEVEN

"*I* thought Tyson called this meeting?" Ellen Myers' gaze bounced between Charlotte and Tyson, standing together at the diner's counter.

Charlotte opened her mouth, but Tyson couldn't let her speak yet, not if she wanted the town on her side. He stepped forward, assuming control.

"We," Tyson wagged a finger between Charlotte and himself, "called this meeting to present an idea to benefit all our businesses. Credit for the plan belongs to Charlotte. But I know it's going to be a great success for every Brookview business."

Charlotte moved beside him. "Actually, the idea is from an article written about the town years ago, back before my great-aunt owned the candy store."

Ellen's doubt was plastered on her face. "So, you've got an idea used ages ago? Obviously it didn't make much of an impact since we don't still do it. Yet, you want us to resurrect it?"

Grumbles and murmurs filled the diner tables. Thankfully, they'd waited until after hours to host the town meeting, and no tourists were present. They had to get control, but it was difficult with Ellen in the mix. As owner of the town's most popular bed and breakfast, she held a lot of sway. They needed her on board to garner support from the rest of the town.

"I don't know why the town didn't keep up the practice." Tyson shrugged. "The article said it was a huge success. Everyone had fun, businesses saw sales increase, and it fostered town spirit."

"Well, get to it." Peter Riley huffed from his booth. "You've talked all around this great idea but have yet to tell us what it is."

Charlotte pulled copies of the article from her folder and passed them around. "We'd like to host a town-wide scavenger hunt for Valentine's Day." She lifted one hand to stave off dissent. "Now, I know it's only three weeks away. But if we get it up on the town website now and start pushing it in media in the surrounding towns, I believe we can get semi-local visitors for this year's event. Then, next year, we can concentrate on promoting it in advance to draw in those who come from farther away."

Ellen frowned. "Let me get this straight. I'm supposed to support this thing, even though it's not going to help my business until we reach out to the actual tourists?"

"Not at all." Charlotte smiled. "Even the semi-locals planning day trips can be enticed to stay overnight if we hold special evening activities in addition to the scavenger hunt. Maybe a coffee tasting at The Bean Counter. Perhaps one of the restaurants could have live music."

Tyson could tell Ellen wasn't budging. Not unusual, but this time it grated. Charlotte had worked hard on this plan, and he wanted it to succeed. It would help her standing in the town, but it would also benefit the businesses. Couldn't Ellen see the potential?

"Hmm." Charlotte considered the naysayer. "Your B-and-B could even have a staycation special for locals or semi-locals choosing to stay and participate in the scavenger hunt. More business for you without the wait."

Pride welled up as Tyson watched Charlotte gracefully handle the negative comments. Ellen wasn't completely on board, but the other business owners' expressions were open. With the ease of a professional negotiator, Charlotte segued from individual concerns to the running of the hunt. Openness shifted to interest before excitement sparked in the business owners' faces.

"I'll donate a twenty-dollar gift certificate to the grand prize and a love-themed journal and pen set for the winner." Amy, the bookstore owner, was the first to commit. "Can I use my blind-date-with-a-book display for the clue?"

"Of course. Your clue could tie in to having them find the perfect date for Valentine's Day."

With the first commitment, ideas started pouring like sweet tea from a pitcher on a hot summer day. Tyson grinned as Charlotte invited each one into the process and had them working together to write the clues to guide visitors through their town. Laughter and good-natured ribbing dominated until the work was complete and store owners went their separate ways with Charlotte's promise of promotional graphics posted on the town's website and social media the next day.

"Can you get everything ready by tomorrow? It's a lot."

After dealing with Ellen, the naysayer, Charlotte was tempted to take Tyson's comment as a criticism. But he believed in her, in the plan.

"I know you're busy. If you need help, let me know." He slipped his hand around hers as they walked down the sidewalk. "It's not your weight to carry alone."

Charlotte couldn't tell if it was his concern or the way his thumb grazed over the back of her hand, fanning the spark inside and warming her more than her coat ever could. She kept her smile content and nothing more. Tyson didn't need to know how far gone she was, especially since she didn't know his mind on the matter.

He nudged her with his shoulder. "Well?"

"Well, what?"

"Are you going to let me help?"

She shrugged. "How good are you with words? I've got a design app I know will create eye-catching graphics. It's the accompanying copy I have trouble with. I've never been proficient at using my words to draw people in."

A pull on her arm stopped Charlotte short as Tyson planted himself in place. Seeing his crinkled brows and a frown, Charlotte rewound the conversation. What offended him? Nothing sprang to mind.

"Are you serious?" His soft voice was tinged with disbelief.

"About what?"

Tyson took her other hand in his and stepped in close, his eyes begging for her complete attention. Charlotte was more than willing to comply. Those pale blue eyes drew a person in and didn't let them go.

"Charlotte, I don't think you realize what you accomplished tonight." He captured her gaze and held it. "You were amazing. It started off rough, but it wasn't your fault. By the end, you had this town working together in ways I haven't seen in ages. I'm not sure why you doubt it, but you won them over with your words."

Charlotte couldn't hold back her smile any more than an umbrella could hold back a flood. Contentment held her in place, allowing Tyson to search her face the way she did his.

Amazing. Was it a deliberate word choice or an empty platitude? Something akin to a person stating their love of tacos or their great-aunt Gertrude's homemade potato salad.

The admiration in his eyes argued otherwise. Tyson believed in this idea. No. He believed in *her*. Gratitude welled up, threatening to spill over her lashes and down her cheeks. It was a gift to have someone's unwavering confidence when there was nothing in it for them and no history of friendship to demand loyalty. Even more so in the face of the town's doubt.

"You're a good man, Tyson Abbott." Charlotte loosed one of her hands from his and brushed a strand of hair from his face before resting her palm on his cheek. "A very good man."

The billows of their cold breath merged as the space between them lessened. Tyson placed his hand over hers on his cheek and breathed deeply.

"As are you, Charlotte."

As his intensity increased, Charlotte giggled. The invisible current pulling them together tensed and then evaporated completely with Charlotte's soft snort.

Tyson's confused frown danced on the line of perturbed. Pulling her hand from his cheek, Charlotte used it to cover her smile. It would only make matters worse. She cleared her throat, forced her face to conform to the picture of piety, and dropped the guard from her mouth.

"Sorry." A tiny giggle bubbled out.

"Which is funnier? The fact I find you amazing or that I thought we were sharing something real?"

"Neither."

He blinked. His face remained a blank slate.

Charlotte tried again. "I'm so sorry." She touched his arm. "When I said you were a good man, you said I was too. Not being a man, it struck me as funny. But I know what you meant. I shouldn't have laughed."

"No." His lips twitched before flattening once more. "You're definitely not a man."

Charlotte tilted her head to one side and batted her eyelashes. "Am I forgiven for my social *faux pas*?"

"My error started this debacle." He sighed. "I forgive you." His eyes took on a devious twinkle. "On one condition."

"What?"

Tyson smirked. "You won't kill the mood next time I'm about to kiss you."

Charlotte gaped as he dropped his bomb and swaggered away without another word. Tyson wanted to kiss her! Of course, she'd botched up the attempt in true Charlotte fashion, but she'd not thought about it in the moment. She'd missed her chance to find out if his lips were as soft and warm as they looked. Her mood plummeted to the earth.

Wait. Wild energy shot through every limb. Charlotte developed a new kinship with those women in romantic movies who danced and squealed with abandon after catching the eyes of their princes. If she didn't already have a shaky reputation in this town, she would have joined their ranks. She would have another chance.

He said *next time*.

CHAPTER TWELVE

"The scavenger hunt's going well." Tessa lifted the completed entry forms from the decorated box in Charlotte's store. She flipped through the papers. "No one left any blanks, and from first glance, the store names and items appear to be in the correct places."

Charlotte turned the sign on her front door to *Closed*. "I'm impressed with the extra traffic. At least, I think it's extra. I may not be the best judge of usual Valentine's traffic."

"This." Tessa held up the stack, "is definitely not the norm. And Ellen over at the B-and-B? Said she's full this week. Every day. A lot of the guests are from the next towns over. Your staycation idea paid off."

"It's not enough, though."

"What do you mean?"

"The town barely got on board. And I'm glad it's a success." Charlotte tidied up the counter displays. "But what about when the event is over?"

"What about it?"

"The town will go right back to their dislike of me and my

store. Single events are fine, and at least this one blends the past and future. But I need my store to do the same."

Tessa leaned against the counter. "Two questions. One. What do you have in mind? And two. Have you prayed about it?"

Charlotte rolled her eyes. "I haven't stopped praying since I got here. Even before, I guess. Auntie Annie set me up perfectly. I own this space outright, and I have a place to live. I'm not going to waste this chance. This store can't fail. I can't. Not like last time."

"Let it go, Charlie." Tessa shook her head. "*You* didn't fail. Ending things with Eric was the right choice. He used you for success in what he wanted, and you two achieved everything you set out to do. But at what cost? You lost everything that made you Charlie." She swung her arm wide to encompass the room. "This is you getting back to yourself."

"But if the town doesn't accept me—"

"Stop." Tessa sliced her hand across her throat, eyes wide. "You've got to give people time. They're a close-knit group. While there are pluses to everyone knowing everyone, there's also a big downside. You're seeing it first-hand."

"There's got to be something I can do."

"No. There isn't. Even if there is, you can't run your business to make everyone else happy. If you do, it's Eric all over again. Make changes if you want. But make them because *Charlie* thinks they're important, not everyone else."

Charlotte stared out the front window while Tessa patiently allowed her time to absorb what she'd said. The scavenger hunt was a great way to honor the past and allow everyone to reap benefits in the present. With the hunt ending at her store, it was a great way to introduce the shop to the semi-locals who may not have otherwise made the trip.

Tessa was right, though. She'd betrayed herself when she allowed her relationship with Eric sway her business decisions. She couldn't do that again. Not even to win the heart of the town.

Their feelings were understandable. Nostalgia was powerful. If it wasn't, her store would never succeed.

The shop catered to people's desires for times gone by, no matter their reasons for their sentimental attachment. Every item purchased was the customer's link to a memory.

"Wait." Charlotte ducked down to rummage through the shelf under the counter. "I know it's here somewhere."

"What?"

As Charlotte popped back up, Tessa, who'd stretched herself over the counter, barely moved in time to avoid smacking their heads together. Charlotte lifted the lid off the box she'd retrieved and flipped through the contents. Excitement built with each item until she finally found the one she wanted.

"Look." She held out the photo for Tessa to take. "I discovered it when Tyson and I found the scavenger hunt article."

Tessa glanced at the photo and then back to Charlotte. "Is this the candy store?"

"Yep. When it first opened. Great shot, right?"

"Sure."

Tessa failed to find the vision. Of course, her lack of understanding could have something to do with Charlotte's own oversight in explaining her idea. She took the photo back and laid it on the counter, tapping it with one finger.

"This would make a great wall mural." She splayed both hands and fanned them across the space toward the front of the store. "Can't you see it as the backdrop of an area dedicated to vintage toys? And to fully incorporate the store's beginnings, I can even add a selection of old-fashioned candies. My dream blended with the dreams of those who came before."

"Sounds perfect." Tessa turned and leaned back on the counter, taking in the space. "But where? You're already filled to capacity."

Excitement melted like a popsicle in mid-July. Space was an

issue. She needed each one of the vendors and couldn't encroach on their booths.

She came off the counter and spun in Tessa's direction. "Next door."

Tessa frowned.

"No. It's perfect, and it's for sale. I can put up the house or the shop as collateral to get the loan. I think the sign even said the upper floor is set up as a studio apartment. If I needed to, I could sell the house and buy it."

"Do you need another full store?"

"Well, no. But I could add more booths." Charlotte gasped as another idea formed. "Or I could even set aside space to host events. Classes on antiquing. Upcycling furniture. Even fashion shows depicting different eras. It would add an interactive element to what I offer."

"Oh, that would be fun." Tessa plucked the picture from the counter, smiling as she examined it. The excitement in her eyes mirrored Charlotte's. "You've got to do it. Do you think the bank will work with you?"

Charlotte shrugged. "I don't see why not. I've got the collateral. I'll work on the plan tonight and talk to the loan officer tomorrow. In a day or two, I should know what kind of offer I can make."

Having a direction lifted a weight from Charlotte's shoulders. It might not pan out, but God was in control. She'd cover it in prayer. If it was God's will, He would make the way. Right now, she would enjoy what she believed was God's answer for her store.

"This is so exciting." Tessa squealed and grasped Charlotte's arms.

Drawn into her friend's energy, Charlotte laughed as the two joyfully jumped up and down like children at play.

Tyson stopped with his hand on the door to Charlotte's shop. The glass provided the perfect view of Charlotte and Tessa doing a happy dance. He pushed open the door.

"What are we celebrating?"

Pleasure and peace were present in Charlotte's sparkling eyes. Her bright smile enticed his own. Though he still had zero clue as to the cause, he'd enjoy it all the same. The woman stole his breath on a normal day. Now, she was practically radiant.

The joyous jumping ended, but excitement exploded from them. Turning from him to each other, a silent conversation passed between the girls. Tyson watched in amazement as subtle expressions flitted over their faces. They must have reached their conclusions, though, because they turned back to him, still grinning.

"I know what I'm going to do with the store. It's perfect. Past and present together and interactive." Words tumbled from Charlotte as quickly as river rapids over rocks. "The town is going to love it. And I can't tell you about it yet, because I've not worked out the details. But it is so good. I can't believe I didn't think of it sooner."

Her enthusiasm was contagious. Tyson had zero details, but it didn't matter. A desire to see her plan move from idea to reality filled him.

"I can't wait to hear about it." Tyson raised his palms in front of him. "No rush. I won't push for details. When you're ready to share, I'm ready to listen." He eyed the stack of papers on the counter and nodded toward them. "Looks like the scavenger hunt is going well."

Tessa scooped up the entries. "We've received more than I

imagined we would this early in the event. And if I'm going to weed out the incomplete and incorrect tonight, I'd better head out." She nodded to Tyson, then Charlotte. "Call me after you iron everything out tomorrow and let me know how it went."

With Tessa vacating the premises, Charlotte turned her attention on Tyson. A look of apology siphoned some of the gas from her joy of only moments ago.

"What's wrong?"

Charlotte moved behind the counter and began shutting down the register. "I know we were supposed get together tonight, but can we reschedule?"

His confidence faltered, though he hid it behind a shrug. "Sure. Something wrong?"

"No. I just need to get stuff done this evening."

Stuff? Sounded like a brush-off. Maybe the almost-kiss had been a fluke. Charlotte hadn't acted like it, but maybe hindsight convinced her she dodged a bullet. Maybe she wasn't as into him as she was into having his help. Had her epiphany regarding the store rendered him useless?

"Okay. Anything I can help with?" It never hurt to test the waters and draw out more information. Then, he might have a clue where she stood.

Charlotte shook her head. "Not this time. Like I said, I don't want to voice my idea out loud yet. I need to flesh it out, see if the details fall into place. And pray."

"Prayer's always good." Tyson's relief convinced him he might need a little more time praying and trusting as well. Her hesitance had nothing to do with him. Charlotte was brainstorming. "And I may even follow your lead tonight. Remember how I told you Dad and I had a plan to expand?"

"Yeah."

"I didn't say I'd been working toward it recently. Things look good, and it wouldn't hurt me to give the details some attention."

"That's great, Tyson." Charlotte covered Cracker Jack's cage for the night before grabbing her purse from under the counter. "Sounds like we both need to dream and plan tonight."

"I can get on board with that ... if," Tyson paused and raised his brow as Charlotte glanced his way.

"If ... what?"

"If you'll come with me tomorrow after work. I want to show you something I think is going to be a big deal for my shop." Tyson smirked. "And don't worry. It's not a real date, so, I won't even collect what you owe."

"What do I owe you?"

"I believe I'm due a kiss."

"Due a kiss. Due a kiss."

Tyson laughed as Cracker Jack called from under his covering. "See? Jack agrees."

Charlotte glared at the covered cage. "Don't know why I ever thought a parrot would be the perfect pet. Turns out he's nothing but trouble."

"I don't know." Tyson draped an arm over her shoulders and aimed for the door. "I like him a little more every day."

CHAPTER THIRTEEN

Charlotte's whistled tune swirled into the cold air as she
made her way from the realtor's office. Finally, she
enjoyed the perks of small-town life instead of the downsides.
With her business plan complete, the deed to the home Great-
auntie Annie had left her, and a good downpayment from her nest
egg, securing the promise of a loan from the local bank hadn't
taken the days she expected. The loan approval was done in-house,
and she could sign papers to finalize everything the next day.

Though it meant calling in a favor with Tessa to cover the
antique shop, Charlotte was able to meet with the realtor shortly
after for a tour of the shop space next to hers. The narrow spot
would make a perfect addition.

And the rumors were true. There was the most adorable
apartment above the space. The whole floor was open, except the
three-quarter bath, which would work well even if she decided to
make it additional store or storage space.

"But why would I? It's the perfect place for one."

Charlotte nodded at two strangers who stared at her talking to
herself as they passed. Hopefully, if they came into her store

later, they wouldn't recognize the crazy lady they'd seen without her puffy coat and scarf.

It didn't matter. Nothing could dampen her spirits. Though the realtor informed Charlotte there was time to think about whether she wanted to make an offer or not, she hadn't needed it. The space was exactly what her plan called for. She'd already priced having a mural of the photo made and stocking old-fashioned candy. Some of the candy store's containers in storage would work perfectly for her displays.

Time to hurry up and wait—see if her bid was accepted. The realtor mentioned another bidder, but according to the bank, Charlotte could go higher. Besides, she sensed God's leading in this. If true, she didn't need to worry at all.

Her phone buzzed, and she pulled it from her pocket. A reminder from Tyson about their non-date. One more piece of perfection to add to her day. Her plans were falling into place, and she had something to distract her while she waited for her answers.

The *something* rather *someone* she was really beginning to care about didn't hurt either.

"Thank you, God." Charlotte's praise slipped out in a whisper as she tugged open the door to her shop. "My dreams are coming true without sacrificing myself, and You've allowed me to get to know a great guy too."

"How'd it go?" Tessa didn't even wait for Charlotte to slip out of her coat before pouncing on her for answers.

Charlotte ignored the question until she'd unwound her scarf and hung it on the coat rack behind the counter. "Absolutely amazing."

"*Amazing. Amazing.*"

Tessa turned toward the bird. "No one asked you, Jack. Be still."

"*Be still. Be still.*"

Tessa pointed one finger at Cracker Jack and opened her mouth to respond before Charlotte's laugh cut her off.

"You do realize you're about to get in an argument with a bird, right?"

Tessa still looked unconvinced it was a faulty path.

Charlotte gave her a pointed look. "And arguing with a bird is just plain crazy?"

"*Plain crazy. Plain crazy.*"

Tessa grimaced.

Charlotte laughed. "You're not helping yourself, Cracker Jack."

Charlotte grabbed a treat from under the counter and shoved it through the birdcage wire. Cracker Jack dutifully grasped it with his sharp claws and went to work munching it with his beak. The offering would earn them a moment's peace to talk.

"The bank gave me the loan. I sign tomorrow. The property is perfect. And I've put in an offer."

"When will you know if they accept it?"

Charlotte shrugged. "I'm not sure. Apparently, someone else is bidding too. It could take some back and forth before it's decided. How have things been here?"

"Business is steady. The final scavenger hunt forms have been turned in. I'll work on those tonight. Want to help?"

"I can't. I'm meeting Tyson."

"Oooo. Meeting Tyson. Another date so soon." Tessa batted her eyes and made kissy lips.

Charlotte swatted her arm. "Stop it. What are you, twelve? First off, not a date. He's done something for his business he's excited about and wants to share it with me."

"Will there be smooching on this outing?"

"It's not really your business, but we've not kissed yet."

One brow rose impossibly high while Tessa's hip kicked out to the side as she used it to plant her hand on. "Girl, what are you waiting for? That man is so kissable. Plus, he's totally into you."

"We almost kissed the other night. It was a movie-worthy setup." Charlotte bit her bottom lip to keep from grinning like a lovestruck teenager. "And after I destroyed the mood with a fit of giggles, he did promise we'd revisit kissing."

"You did what?"

"I laughed right before our lips met."

"You did not!"

Charlotte didn't answer. The heat filling her cheeks filled in the blank.

Tessa sighed. "You're a mess. I can't believe you'd waste a cinematically worthy kiss moment by laughing at the man who wanted to kiss you. What's wrong with you?"

"I didn't mean to."

"Promise me you'll control yourself in the future?" Tessa huffed as if she'd been the one to miss out on the kiss. "Next time, you better be ready for a kiss."

"Why do I need a blindfold?" Charlotte scrutinized the bandana with the intensity of someone trying to ferret out a bomb's hiding place.

"Seriously." Tyson shook his head. "It's not going to attack you. I need your completely unguarded, first reaction. Do you trust me?"

She eyed the cloth, then him. Tyson sensed her refusal dancing dangerously close to being spoken into existence. While he could still get her reaction to his plan without the blindfold, swaying her to a *yes* was suddenly of utmost importance.

A slight tilt of his head, eyes widened imploringly. "Please."

Her shoulders rose and fell. "Fine."

Her acceptance wasn't as sweet as he imagined. Even teasing, he shouldn't have pushed.

"You don't have to." He shrugged. "I don't want to make you uncomfortable."

A breath passed between them before she slid the blindfold from his hand and raised it to her eyes.

"Here." She turned her back to him with an end of the blindfold in each hand. "Help me tie it."

The bright scent of oranges and vanilla met him as he stepped closer. He breathed it in, committing it to memory, as he tied the bandana. Before tightening the knot, Tyson smoothed her hair out of the way. Her orange-scented shampoo did more than make her hair smell great. The strands under his fingers were silky and soft. The combination tempted him to linger longer than necessary, maybe move even closer.

His imagination filled with the image of Charlotte cradled against his chest. The soft strands brushed his cheek as he rested it against her hair. One day. Maybe.

He stepped back. But not today. They'd only just started dating. And Charlotte was currently wearing a blindfold and trusting him completely. He'd never do anything to destroy her trust.

"Okay." He took her hand and swiveled her toward the door. "Just let me lead, and we'll be there in no time."

Cold air hit Charlotte's cheeks as Tyson swung the door open.

"One small step down."

Warmth shot up her arms as he took her hands in his to guide her safely across the threshold. With his touch bolstering her confidence, she stepped, unseeing, out of the store.

"Wait here."

The cold rushed in where his touch had been. The jingle of her keys on their ring assured Charlotte her guide was locking up behind them as he'd promised. She held her palm up. Freezing metal landed in the middle of her hand seconds later. With barely a fumble, Charlotte deposited them in her coat pocket and zipped it closed.

"Ready?"

She nodded.

"Don't worry." He took her hands in his once more. "I'm walking in front of you the whole time."

Charlotte hoped no one was milling around them. What a pair they'd make. Her blindfolded, and Tyson walking backward, holding her hands in his to guide her. Crazy. That's what everyone would think. At least she couldn't see which neighbors she needed to avoid in the near future.

Uncluttered pavement became littered with pebbles and felt less smooth under her feet. A coolness fell over her left shoulder. Something blocked the last rays of the evening sun.

"Where are we going?" It didn't seem like they'd been walking very long, but Charlotte couldn't picture their location.

"You'll see. Be patient."

How was she supposed to be patient when she was completely disoriented? Time spent told her they'd not gone far, but her senses also created the feeling they turned and headed back in the direction they'd come. She had to be wrong. Tyson wouldn't lead them back to her store.

"We're here. Just a minute."

He dropped her hands. Charlotte stood still, helpless to go anywhere with the silly blindfold on. The jingle of keys in a lock confirmed *here* was a building, but anything more was only a guess.

Charlotte hid a start as he took her hands again.

"There's a little step up."

Charlotte shuffled her feet forward until she felt the step with her toes and stepped up. Each footfall held the hollow echo of walking on a wood floor. The sound bounced from the walls. An empty building, then.

They stopped. Charlotte sensed Tyson behind her, felt his hands messing with the knot in the blindfold.

"Ready?"

Charlotte growled playfully. "Just take it off already. I want to see the place enabling your grand plan."

Fabric fell from her face. Charlotte opened her eyes to a blurry room. A few quick blinks cleared the cobwebs from her sight. The empty space was familiar—very familiar.

She breathed in deeply. "The storefront between our shops." Her voice barely entered the room, as her eyes slid shut.

"Isn't it great?" Tyson came around her, gesturing as he spoke. "Over there I can shift my regular stock a bit to make more room for the items appealing to tourists. And right there is where I'll set up workbenches to host the workshops Dad and I always talked about. It's finally happening."

Tyson faced her. The moment he realized all was not right was evident. His exuberant smile faded. His brows crinkled with a frown. He took a single, tentative step toward her.

"What's wrong? You don't like it?"

Charlotte swallowed. "This is the space between our stores, correct?"

"Yes?" He cocked his head to the side, face full of confusion. "Which makes it even better. It made putting in an offer a no-brainer."

Disappointment choked Charlotte, and she swallowed the sudden nausea. This couldn't be happening. "You put in an offer?"

"Yes?"

"On the space between our stores?" Her brain seemed incapable of grasping this simple information.

"What's going on?" Tyson shoved his hand through his hair and stared at her. His expression bounced between concern and confusion. "Why aren't you excited for me? This." He waved his upturned hand to indicate the entire room. "This is my dream with my dad coming true. I thought you wanted it to happen."

"I do." Charlotte fought tears. His dreams realized meant her plan fell apart. "Really. I do. It's just ..." She shrugged.

"It's just what?" Frustration crept in where confusion was only moments before. "You don't think it'll work? You were humoring me?"

"Not at all." Charlotte laid a hand on his arm. "I know you'll succeed."

Tyson's jaw tightened. "Then what's the problem?"

Charlotte gazed around the room. "It's my chance too."

"What?"

Charlotte walked to the front window and stared out. If she faced Tyson, there was no way she'd be able to explain without breaking down. The warmth of her sigh fogged the cold glass pane.

"I put in an offer too."

"You what? Why?"

"The plan Tessa and I were excited about? The one without all the pieces in place?" She looked over her shoulder long enough to see Tyson nod. "This is the final piece."

"I don't understand."

"My store is about the past, but it doesn't have a space for its past. I planned to open up this room to my shop and let the old candy store have its place to shine. Not to win the approval of the town, but for me. I need to honor the gift given to me."

Tyson shifted behind her. Though she couldn't see him, she felt him draw closer.

"How does expanding accomplish your goal? Can't you use the space you have?"

"No. It's too small and full. Plus, I want to put a mural over there." She gestured to the far wall. "It's a great black and white photo of the candy shop when it first opened. The whole room will be antique and vintage toys, puzzles, children's books, and old-fashioned candy displays. Full of fun, just like the candy store. I'll even have a space for interactive events like vintage fashion shows or classes on antiquing."

"Those changes mean a lot of updates. Your store is new. Sure you want to burden yourself with such a big expense right out of the gate?"

She shrugged. "Annie gave me what I need. I'm going to sell her house and live in the apartment upstairs. I don't need the extra space."

"Sounds like you've got it all figured out."

Charlotte turned to face Tyson. His eyes registered disappointment. An invisible fist tightened around her heart. She needed this in ways he couldn't understand. But he'd wanted this for so long, and she couldn't dash his hopes completely.

"They've not accepted my offer yet. Yours could be accepted and mine not."

"I don't have a chance, and we both know it. I've got my store to put up as collateral, but I only qualify for a limited loan amount. Sounds like you've got more to pull from." Tyson's shoulders dropped. With one hand, he massaged the back of his neck. "The only way I realize my dream is if you bow out of yours."

He wasn't asking.

But he was. His pale blue eyes translated what he felt with more clarity than an anime character's. Hope sparked in their depths. Charlotte knew he'd never come out and ask, but he wanted her to step away.

While she couldn't blame his desire to realize the dream he shared with his dad, she'd promised herself her store would be successful. It had to be. She'd never be free of Eric's shadow otherwise. He'd stolen her dreams and shaken her confidence.

Expanding held the key to success both for herself and in being accepted in town. She *needed* this win.

"I can't back out."

"I didn't ask."

She lifted her chin. "Maybe not, but you wanted to. I see it in your face."

"I can't help my frustration." The tightness in his tone suggested he couldn't control it either. "You know what this means to me. You encouraged this."

"I did not." Charlotte's voice didn't hide her feeling any better than his. "I encouraged you to offer the classes. I never said anything about buying this place. Why would I have, when I need the space?"

"Until a couple days ago, you didn't even have a plan. Now this place is key to your success?" His expression questioned her sanity. "Have you even considered other options? I mean, I've had this plan in the works since before your store even opened."

Charlotte huffed. "New doesn't mean less valid. And what happened to you wanting to see me succeed?"

"Good grief. Would you listen to yourself? You're being ridiculous." Tyson jammed his hand through his hair and dropped it with a slap to his thigh. "Of course I want you to succeed. Haven't I shown that enough over the last few weeks?"

"Oh, please." Charlotte rolled her eyes. "You hung around because you wanted a date. Backing my plans earned brownie points."

"Brownie points?" He shook his head. "Are you even listening to the words coming out of your mouth? I liked you, Charlotte, and I got behind the scavenger hunt because I knew it would help you and the town at the same time."

Liked. Tyson said he *liked* her. As in past tense. Apparently since she wasn't supporting his dream over hers, his feelings had changed. It was Eric all over again. Every act of support, every touch and flirtation was calculated to win her over and ask her to surrender herself to his wants.

Charlotte clamped her mouth shut. Anything she said while frustration rampaged through her would not be nice. Talking was getting them nowhere. They stared at each other, the anger between them heating the room better than a furnace ever could. Charlotte sucked in a deep breath.

"I can't give this up. Neither can you. I don't think there's anything left for us to say." She refused to look back as she walked toward the door. "Goodbye, Tyson."

CHAPTER FOURTEEN

*T*yson banged the truck door shut and stalked toward his workshop. All his plans quickly flowed down the drain in two days. After the disaster with Charlotte, he'd returned to the bank. Outbidding her couldn't happen without additional funding.

As much as she'd cried foul when dealing with the town, Charlotte had what it took to secure the larger loan. His standing as a Brookview multi-generational family didn't count for much in terms of dollars and cents.

His dad's dream, their dream, was dead.

Tyson glanced around the shop. At the sight of tools not in their place and sawdust coating the floor, irrational irritation swept over him and into the environment.

Toss the hammer in the toolbox. Slam it shut.

Cram leftover wood into the bin.

Snatch up the broom. Take out his frustration on the dusty floor.

"Ahem."

His mother's throat clearing from the door did nothing to arrest his attention. When her hand covered his on the broom, he nearly yanked it away before realizing what he was doing. His mom deserved no disrespect. Even if she did, he wouldn't be the one to give it.

He sighed.

"What's wrong, Tyson?" Mom moved away from him to sit on the stool by the worktable. "You looked like a man on a mission when you got out of the truck. Now, you're throwing around your tools and sweeping the floor like your life depends on it."

He leaned his weight on the broom in his hands. "What's wrong? Everything."

The faintest turn of a smile curved her lips. Mom didn't argue. She sat. Waiting. She'd always excelled at drawing information from someone with her silent prompting.

"Fine. Not everything. I'm just tired of losing what's important all the time."

"Is this about your dad's things?"

"What?" He scrambled to catch up with the train of her thoughts. "No. It has nothing to do with selling Dad's things."

She remained silent.

"Okay. Maybe that's one more thing to add to the list, but I get it. Really, I do."

"What else did you lose?"

"The storefront."

Mom stiffened. "What?"

"No. Not the shop." The broom clattered to the floor in Tyson's rush to put his hands up in surrender. "Don't freak out. The storefront next to ours. The one I planned to use as a hands-on area for the store like Dad and I always talked about."

"I thought you got the loan and put in a bid?"

Tyson nodded. "I did. So did Charlotte."

"Charlotte? Why?"

"She wants to expand the antique store. Include old-

fashioned candy and kids' toys and stuff. Paint some mural on
the wall of the store when it opened."

"Does she need it?"

"Thinks she does. Believes it will help the town accept the
changes and allow her to host special classes and events."

"Will it?"

"That's not the point, Mom." Tyson rolled his eyes.

Mom ignored his annoyance. "Isn't it? You know how hard
she's worked to fit in. And it sounds like her plans for her store
are very similar to your plans for the hardware shop."

"So I should just let her have it and forget Dad's dream?" If it
was anyone other than his mother challenging him.

"No." Mom shook her head. "I'm asking you to take a
minute. Look at it from her perspective." She placed her hand
over his.

Only his love for his mother kept him from yanking his
away.

"You're both trying to accomplish the same thing for your
stores. Don't allow it to make you enemies."

"Too late. She hates me." He leaned against the counter and
jammed his fingers through his hair. "Says I only helped her to
get dates. My unwillingness to step aside and let her steal my
dream proves it."

"Did you?"

"Of course not." The insult crept into Tyson's answer.
"Charlotte is an amazing woman. Smart. Fun." He smiled even
as his shoulders sagged. "A little bit clumsy. Maybe a lot, but in
an adorable way. She and her store are worth the town's time. I
worked with her because I want them to see Charlotte the way
I do."

"It's sad."

"You mean how the town won't get behind her?"

Mom smiled. "No. I meant you obviously care about
Charlotte. But you've let this get in the way of something with

potential to be great for both of you. I've seen you two together. The interest was reciprocated."

Tyson didn't know what to say. Wasn't sure there was anything. When Mom continued to sit in silence, he grasped at the only thing he could.

"So, what? I'm supposed to toss my dream out the window and be happy about it?"

"Can you change the situation? Outbid her?"

"No."

"Then reworking your dream seems inevitable." She stood and drew him in for a hug. Stepping back, she laid a hand on his cheek. "I know this makes it hard, but your dream can happen another way. God will open a door when the time's right. But losing something that could be more life-changing than a business opportunity? That's the real shame."

Charlotte hung up the phone.

"Well?" Tessa leaned in, barely containing her curiosity. "What happened?"

"I got it." Charlotte didn't turn, instead staring at nothing in front of her.

"The storefront? You won the bid?"

"Yeah."

Tessa's fingers closed around Charlotte's upper arms seconds before the shaking began. It took a moment for Charlotte to register it wasn't her body's doing but Tessa shaking her.

"Earth to Charlie." Tessa shook her again. "What is the matter with you? You got the store. You should be elated. Dancing. Screaming. Running around and whooping."

A slow smile stretched Charlotte's lips. Her shoulders

relaxed. Focusing on Tessa, she giggled. "You're right. It doesn't seem real, but I got it."

The initial numbness gave way to a buzzing energy.

"I got the store."

"You got it."

Charlotte pumped her raised fists in triumph. "I got it! Look out Brookview. Here comes Charlotte Herring."

"Told you Eric was wrong." Tessa punctuated the statement with a forceful point in Charlotte's direction. "You don't need him or any other person to succeed. Your dreams are just as valid and achievable."

"Thanks for believing and sticking by me."

"I wasn't the only one." Tessa waved away the praise. "Tyson was right beside you too."

A bucket of ice water wouldn't have chilled the celebration as quickly.

"I don't want to talk about him." Charlotte strengthened her warning with a glare. "He's just like Eric, leading me on with false encouragement only to ask me to give up my dream for his when both became impossible."

"No. Eric asked you to. Tyson didn't."

Tessa's calm worked like dryer lint in a fireplace to light a flame inside Charlotte. Her jaw clenched as she narrowed her eyes. Tessa was not intimidated into backing down. Simply raised one brow. Daring Charlotte to honestly counter her statement.

"He wanted me to." The words rumbled from her lips.

Tessa shrugged. "And you wanted him to."

"He was using me."

"That's a lie, and you know it."

"Is not."

"Please." Tessa smirked. "Keep telling yourself that to keep the guilt away. You know he's into you. The whole town knows he's into you. I'm pretty sure even the tourists know."

Charlotte looked everywhere but at Tessa. "Doesn't matter. It's over now. Especially since I won the bid. He's not going to forgive me for this."

"You walked out, not him." Tessa placed her hands over Charlotte's on the counter.

Charlotte glanced from their hands to Tessa. She swallowed against the lump formed as she recognized the disappointment in her friend's eyes.

"Charlie, I know you're trying not to repeat the mistakes you made with Eric. I'm glad to see you regaining your confidence. But nothing says you've got to swing from one extreme to the other. You can enjoy success *and* a relationship."

Charlotte turned her head away from the intensity. Tessa's silence hooked Charlotte's attention and reeled it in. The earnestness in Tessa's expression wouldn't let go.

"Eric was a self-centered user. Tyson is nothing like him. And if you believe he is, you've got to ask yourself why you're settling on a lie instead of admitting the truth." Tessa squeezed her hands. "The shop closes in an hour. I'll watch the store. Why don't you take a walk and think about what I said?"

Charlotte nodded and stepped from behind the counter. With the yo-yo of emotions jerking her back and forth, she needed time to sort it out and pray. Grabbing her coat from the hook, she walked through the store and out the back door. No need for an audience. She sucked in a deep breath, allowing the frigid air to create an ache in her lungs, all while clearing her mind.

In the cold, the gazebo at the park should be empty. Charlotte headed toward it, praying as she went. God's will seemed obvious. The path to buying the neighboring store was cleared. God must want her to take it.

"Except ... maybe, Tessa's right." She half-spoke to herself, half to God. "Did I hold onto this so hard and push Tyson away because I'm afraid of the past? Am I so terrified of losing myself that I put this between us? Do I have to let go of one to have the other?" She stared up at the sky like a window to heaven rested in the clouds above. "God, I don't want to be afraid. I want to be everything You want me to be."

She plopped on the bench in the gazebo. Plain and simple. Nothing like the beautiful structure Tyson and his dad built for Mrs. Abbott. It was a combination of practicality and beauty. Form and function. In perfect balance.

It doesn't have to be one or the other. Those were Tessa's words. She was right. Charlotte had swung from one extreme to the other. Maybe balance was needed in her perspective.

"Father God, please, show me what balance looks like in this mess I've made."

CHAPTER FIFTEEN

Charlotte's eyes wandered to the clock on the far wall as she rang up her final customer of the day. Five till six, and Tyson hadn't shown up yet. Of course, he had to close his own store before he could.

"Thank you." Charlotte managed a smile for the woman, though her customer must have felt her distraction. Probably thought it was the end-of-the-day jitters. If she only knew.

She tapped her phone again. The blank lock screen lit up. No message alerts. Maybe Tyson wouldn't come after all. When she'd texted him at noon asking him to stop by, she'd expected an answer at least. But as the hours crept by at a glacial pace, the only thing Charlotte received was a near panic attack as her nerves amped up.

She closed her eyes and breathed out slow and controlled. "If he doesn't come, I'll have my answer."

"If who doesn't come?"

Her eyes popped open as she turned toward his voice. "You." Her smile came instantaneously despite her nervousness about the discussion to come. Man, did he look good. "You came."

"You asked me to."

The matter-of-fact tone may have been there to build a wall, but Charlotte saw through the cracks. Tyson was wary but open to hearing her out.

"I'm sorry." She'd said it in text, but this deserved a personal delivery.

Tyson nodded. "Me too."

This wasn't going as well as she'd hoped. But he was here. The door was open.

Charlotte rushed from behind the counter with the realization that the literal door was open too. His confused frown tempted a laugh as she came toward him, but she couldn't risk running him off with her humor. She reached around him and twisted the lock before flipping the sign to *Closed*.

"We don't want interruptions."

He raised a brow. "We don't?"

"No." She straightened her shoulders and shook her head. Confidence. That's what this situation needed. "I've got some papers to show you, and I don't want customers barging in."

Charlotte slipped a manilla envelope off the counter and slid out the papers inside. She held them out. Tyson stared at them like they were a snake poised to strike.

"Those about the storefront?"

"Yep."

He shifted weight from one foot to the other. "I don't think I want to see them."

Charlotte started to speak, but he cut her off.

"I can't, Charlotte. I admit I was wrong in my reaction before. I never meant to make you feel like you should give up your dream so I could have mine. It wasn't intentional, but I didn't correct you either. I'm sorry." An unmistakable ache filled his eyes. He nodded to the papers. "But I also can't look at those. They're a hurdle in the path to my dreams, and I'm not ready to deal with them yet."

Charlotte laid the papers aside and stepped toward him. She

took his hands in hers. His throat worked as he swallowed. So much disappointment and hurt. And she had a part in creating it.

"I'm sorry too. I was afraid. I've given up my dreams for someone else before—I lost myself completely. This time I was determined to succeed." She sniffed as her emotions threatened to overtake her. "I was wrong to accuse you. You're the knight in shining armor to my damsel in distress."

He looked away before returning to her gaze. "But this damsel didn't need saving. She already had everything she needed waiting to save the day."

"Maybe." Charlotte raised one shoulder. "But that didn't mean there wasn't a place for a knight in her life. And maybe … maybe she shouldn't have acted so much like the fire-breathing dragon. For that she's—no, *I'm* sorry."

"Where does this leave us?"

"Partners, I hope." She grinned.

"What?"

"Those papers you don't want to look at. They aren't the sales papers. They're a rental contract between you and me."

Tyson straightened and dropped both her hands. "Rental of what?"

"I need the storefront for my plans. That's why I bought the place."

"Yeah?"

"Yes. But there's an apartment with a completely open floorplan right above it, which I don't need."

Tyson slacked one hip and watched her with a frown. "But you're moving in there. Selling your house to pay for the store."

Charlotte's grin grew. "Nope. I put up the house as collateral with my downpayment instead of buying it outright."

"Why?"

"Because I can think of nothing I'd love more than seeing both our dreams come true."

Understanding began to dawn. Tyson's shoulders relaxed. While he wasn't smiling, the tightness in his expression lessened.

"How would this work?"

She swiped up the papers and jammed them toward him. He took them this time, quickly perusing them, though she doubted he read anything.

"You rent the top floor from me." She bounced on her toes. "You can host your workshops there. I only ask you to keep power saws to a minimum during work hours. We both get the space we need, and the town gets two businesses with additional activities for the tourists."

Tyson continued to flip through the papers. Every page loosened his smile even more. Finally, he glanced up. "How did you come up with this?"

"I prayed for balance." She shrugged.

He laughed. She joined him, the last vestiges of anxiety slipping away. Their relationship may not be revived, but their friendship was. And they were both going to realize their dreams. She couldn't ask for more.

"I'll agree." He flashed his pirate smirk. "On one condition."

She bit her lip and stepped toward him. "Really? What condition?"

"We sign these papers." He leaned closer.

"Yeah." She lifted her chin ever so slightly.

He brushed her cheek with his thumb. "But first, we seal the deal."

"Uh-huh?"

"With a kiss."

Charlotte closed her eyes and leaned in. His breath warmed her cheek. His hand slid from her jaw to cradle the back of her head. Anticipation burned through her as time seemed to stop. A fraction of an inch more and …

"With a kiss. With a kiss. With a kiss."

Charlotte's eyes flew open.

Her head dropped back as she groaned. She kept her promise to Tessa and didn't giggle even a little. Tyson, however, dropped his hand from her hair and went straight past a chuckle into a full-blown laugh.

Charlotte growled as she marched over to the bird. "Hush, Cracker Jack." She threw the cover over his cage.

Then, she strode back to Tyson.

"As for you." She cupped her hand behind his neck and pulled him in, stopping mere inches from his mouth. "We've got a deal to seal."

Charlotte could still feel his smile as her lips met his. It melted away as he enclosed her in his arms. His fingers played in her hair. She returned the favor. Their kiss deepened until Tyson pulled away, both breathless.

Taking his hand, Charlotte moved to the counter and found a pen. While Tyson signed the papers, Charlotte silently thanked God for realized dreams, a hardware store selling peg boards, and a mouthy parrot spouting pickup lines.

ABOUT HEATHER GREER

Heather Greer is a preacher's kid and pastor's wife who loves using her passion for reading and writing to encourage others in their faith. She has been a finalist for the Selah Awards twice. In addition to all things book-related, Heather loves baking. Christmas baking is her favorite, and each year, she makes dozens of treats to pass on to her family and friends in southern Illinois. And while it isn't her favorite, she's even been known to add gingerbread people to her cookie trays.

Snowflakes
and
Puppy Love

A Novella
by
Beth E. Westcott

CHAPTER ONE

S leigh bells jingled as the door at Archer Books opened. From the front counter, Brianna Kinney stopped hanging bookmarks on the display rack and turned her head.

An attractive man, probably in his late twenties to early thirties, nodded a greeting. His lips curved up, and sapphire blue eyes framed by dark lashes momentarily connected with hers.

Wow!

He removed a blue cap and ran his hand over short blond hair. Blue jeans encased slim hips and long legs, and the blue plaid flannel shirt under his open leather jacket complemented his eyes.

Brianna's stomach dipped, and she brushed a wisp of hair off her cheek. She faced him. "Good afternoon." Her usual greeting for customers, but this time her voice squeaked. She cleared her throat. "May I help you?"

"Is Robin here?" His eyes roamed the Christmas decorations hanging from the ceiling then shifted to the shelves of books.

Robin Archer, the store owner, knew nearly everyone who came in.

"Yes, she's in back."

"Cooper." Robin's voice came from the nonfiction section, and she appeared at the end of the aisle. "I thought it was you. What can I do for you?"

The customer sauntered toward Robin. Disappointed he didn't ask for her help, Brianna returned to the bookmarks. She'd probably misread his interest in the momentary look that passed between them.

Why did it matter? She shook her head at her schoolgirl reaction to a good-looking guy. Yet, she couldn't deny her interest in him.

The two stood close enough for Brianna to hear what they said.

"Tessa asked me to get some books for the kids." Cooper's baritone voice resonated inside her.

Of course he's married, and he has children. Lucky Tessa. Heat crept into Brianna's face. What was wrong with her? At least no one heard her thoughts.

"We have some great ones right over here." Robin used her best salesperson voice, and Cooper's leather-clad shoulders disappeared down a row of bookshelves. Their murmurs reached Brianna as they moved to the children's book section, her favorite part of the store.

She added the last bookmark to the rack as the sleighbells jingled again. An older woman with gray hair entered. Brianna didn't know her name but recognized her. The customer smiled, nodded at Brianna, and wandered to the table displaying Christmas items Brianna had helped Robin arrange that morning.

"Good afternoon. Please let me know if I can help you with anything."

"Thank you. I will." The customer continued browsing.

Cooper returned carrying two picture books. He placed them on the counter by the cash register and pulled out his wallet. "I think I've found what they'd like. Dogs for Lexie and big machines for Noah."

Brianna smiled. "How old are they?" She rang up the books and told him the price, then she slid the books into a bag while he inserted his debit card into the card reader.

"Three and four."

He had muscular, work-roughened hands. Like Luke's. Her chest tightened.

"You have your hands full then." She gave him his receipt. Tingles shot through her when her fingers grazed his palm.

"You're right about that. They keep me on my toes. But they're good kids." He pocketed the receipt and slid the card back into his wallet.

No ring on his left hand.

"I think they'll like the books you chose." She dared to meet his riveting eyes. His long lashes must be the envy of many women.

"Thanks. I hope so." He lifted the bag from the counter. "Tessa usually buys their books."

Huh, why didn't Tessa buy the books today? Brianna hadn't met Tessa in the three months she'd worked here.

His eyes crinkled in the corners as his face lit with a thousand-kilowatt smile. "Thank you. See you around."

Wow! A chill passed down her spine. "Bye." She bit her lip as he exited to the jingle of the sleigh bells.

Should she ask Robin about him? No, it was too soon. She wasn't sure she was ready for another relationship. But this was the first time she'd had such a response to a man since Luke. And this man was apparently married anyway.

"Can you tell me the price of this?"

Brianna stepped from behind the counter to help the customer at the Christmas display. "I'll look it up for you."

Cooper Stiles glanced in the bookstore window on the way to his truck parked along the street. Good, Robin had already posted the flyer about the Snowflake Festival. The festival wouldn't be held until the end of January, but it was important to get the word out now, before Christmas.

The clerk inside was talking to another customer. He'd never seen her before. She must be new. Who was she? He should have introduced himself and learned her name.

Her brown hair that fell in waves to her shoulders and light brown eyes the color of honey distracted him the moment he entered the store. The dark green pullover sweater she wore reminded him of the Juniper trees up by the falls. Just in time he'd remembered why he was there—the books for Noah and Lexie.

Was she married? He didn't see a ring. He could've asked Robin, but that was too obvious and might start rumors. He fell victim to too many match-making schemes on the part of well-meaning but interfering women. Robin wasn't one of them. However, he didn't want to put temptation before her.

Cooper preferred to purchase books online, but his sister-in-law would rather support the local businesses, especially this bookstore owned by her best friend. Work slowed for him during the winter, although he had a couple of indoor jobs lined up next week. He had time today to find books for his nephew and niece.

He liked to read. Robin had a good book selection in her store, or she could order one for him. He'd have to come back. Soon. He'd introduce himself to the clerk and learn her name.

He shook his head and strode to his truck. He didn't have time for dating or romantic involvement. Noah and Lexie were his priority. He'd promised Tessa. And he was committed for six more months.

Before she left, Tessa had arranged for Noah and Lexie to be in daycare during the week. Kylie Ott, the Little Lambs Pre-school and Daycare owner, was a fellow member of Grace Church, and Cooper knew they were safe and happy there. He had a few more errands to complete before picking them up.

"Business has been good this season." Robin switched the positions of two ceramic figurines on the table.

The display table, covered by a red cloth and with a small Christmas tree in the center, held a few children's picture books, a couple of books about decorating and traditions, several Christmas romance novels, packages of Christmas cards, and a few ornaments and decorations. Other Christmas items were arranged throughout the store.

"I think your decorations brought customers in." Robin gestured with her hand in a sweeping motion.

Snowflakes and colorful red balls hung from the ceiling. Strands of white Christmas lights intertwined with green garland lined the edges of the ceiling. A decorated Christmas tree in the front window with suggested gift items invited customers into the store. Robin had supplied a beautiful ceramic nativity set for the window display, denoting the true meaning of Christmas.

Brianna ran her hand over the cover of a romance novel then glanced at the store window. That man Cooper had paused to look at the window display after he left the store.

"Thank you for letting me do it. I always enjoyed helping my third-grade students decorate the classroom for Christmas." Brianna hadn't decorated much at home in the last two years.

"Do you miss teaching?"

Brianna shrugged. "I miss the kids. But when the school district downsized last year, I decided I needed a change. I've always loved books and reading, so here I am."

"I'm glad you're here." Robin's words warmed Brianna. "With Martin Luther King, Jr. Day in January and Black History Month coming in February, we'll set out books in the biography and history sections right after Christmas. Will you make a list of what we have available and send it to me? I'll be in my office. I have a book shipment to check in before we close."

"Certainly."

When Robin walked away, Brianna stepped behind the counter and clicked on the computer inventory screen.

"Oh, by the way."

Brianna swiveled her head, surprised that Robin stood nearby.

"Looking ahead for Valentine's Day, I want to feature romances and books on dating, marriage, and wedding planning. And maybe you'd like to decorate." Robin grinned and headed for her office. She peered over her shoulder. "My husband calls me a hopeless romantic."

Romance. Brianna sighed. She'd met her true love, Luke Kinney, ten years ago, in high school. They didn't fall in love right away, but their friendship eventually blossomed into love. They'd been married only two years when Luke died in an auto accident on a slippery, snow-covered road. Brianna's shattered heart took a long time to begin mending, although she finally moved forward with her life. She hadn't personally celebrated Valentine's Day since then, although she'd let her students decorate the classroom and have a party.

She could make the store festive with decorations and maybe set up a table with a simple craft for kids. Valentine's Day didn't have to be just about romance.

CHAPTER TWO

he Friday following Christmas, Brianna parked her
car under the carport beside her apartment. Work had
been busy, waiting on bargain shoppers looking for sale items
and customers buying books with gift cards during the first few
days after Christmas. Brianna anticipated some downtime over
the weekend.

Virginia Moore, her landlady, opened her car trunk in the
driveway on the opposite side of the house. Several shopping
bags protruded from the opening.

Brianna stepped out of her car and followed the stone walk in
front of the house to Virginia's vehicle. "May I help you?"

"I guess I could use a little help, thank you."

Virginia was her mother's age, about Brianna's height, thin
with an angular face, prominent cheekbones, and an aquiline
nose. Robin had directed Brianna to the widow when Brianna
moved to Juniper Falls. Located in a pleasant neighborhood of
modest homes, it had a small backyard and a flower bed along
the front, both presently snow-covered.

A blue pickup truck passed by and honked. Brianna couldn't
see the driver, but Virginia waved.

"That's Cooper." Virginia hefted several bags from the trunk.

Bookstore Cooper with the kids? How many Coopers would there be in a small town like Juniper Falls?

The truck turned into the park entrance across the street.

Brianna lifted four bags and followed her landlady to the side door. She deposited the bags on the kitchen table where Virginia indicated. She hadn't been farther into her landlady's domain than this sparkling clean room. A locked door along a shared kitchen wall separated her landlady's living space from the apartment.

"Hello."

The voice came from another room, and Brianna twisted her head in that direction. Did her landlady have a visitor?

"That's just my cockatiel." Virginia chuckled. "Hello, Samson."

"Oh." Brianna had never met Virginia's pet. She laughed and stepped toward the door.

"Thank you for your help, Brianna."

"You're welcome." She turned back. "I'm planning to adopt a dog from the animal shelter this weekend. We talked about it when I signed the lease."

"Yes. A small dog is allowed." Virginia lifted a milk carton from one of the bags. "But I hope it won't bark a lot and or shed much."

"I'll do my best." Brianna had read about different dog breeds and watched dog training videos on YouTube.

Virginia opened the refrigerator door. "Don't forget you're responsible to clean up after your dog."

"Yes, of course." Was she trying to discourage Brianna from getting a dog?

Virginia placed the milk in the refrigerator and stepped back to the table. A smile softened the severe lines of her face. "A dog will be good company for you. Samson is for me."

The cockatiel whistled.

"Well, good luck." Virginia folded a grocery bag.

"Thank you." Brianna stepped outside and closed the door behind her.

She and Luke had planned to wait until they bought a house before getting a dog or having children. Hopefully a dog would provide company in her apartment on the long winter nights without Luke.

Brianna filled out some preliminary dog adoption information on the county animal shelter website and decided that a small, mixed breed would suit her best.

All dogs barked. How much barking would Virginia tolerate?

Her cell rang as she pulled into the animal shelter parking lot early Saturday afternoon.

"Hi, Mom. Is something wrong? I only left your house a few days ago."

"No, everything's fine. How are you?"

"I'm okay." She didn't have much to say. They'd caught up when she went home for Christmas. "We've been busy at the bookstore. Robin says it will slow down then pick up again in a couple of weeks."

"Your father has been talking to our local school board president, and they have an emergency opening for a first-grade teacher after Christmas break. He told the president you might be interested."

Her mother spoke so quickly Brianna struggled to absorb what she said.

Brianna shook her head. "I'm just settling into my new home. It's too sudden and too soon to move again. I like Juniper Falls, and I like working at the bookstore."

"But we know how much you love teaching. And if you come here, you'll be closer to your family. You can stay with us until you find a place."

"I'm good here." Her mother worried about her, but, at twenty-seven, she could take care of herself. "You and Dad will have to come visit me soon."

"Well, Dad gave the board president your number, so you'll probably get a call."

Did Mom even hear my invitation?

Brianna twisted a lock of hair around her index finger, irritated that her father gave her phone number to anyone without her permission. At least her mother warned her. "I'm pretty sure the answer will be no. Most likely the school district has substitutes available."

Mom sighed. "All right. Well, your father will be disappointed."

You too. Brianna's brother had moved away after college graduation, and her sister, a senior in college, only came home during school vacations. Mom must miss fussing over the three of them.

"I'm sorry, but Dad should have asked me first. I'm sure they'll find someone local to take the position. Please tell Dad I'm fine, and I love him. I love you too. I have to go now."

"All right. I love you."

Ending the call, she returned her phone to her purse and got out of her car. She still had days when memories of Luke crashed in on her, but her parents had to accept that she was fine.

When she opened the animal shelter door, the muffled sound of barking dogs greeted her. She breathed in a faint scent of animals and disinfectant, but the clean and bright office welcomed her, its tile floor in multiple shades of brown and its beige walls decorated with multi-colored cat and dog silhouettes.

A middle-aged woman greeted her from the front desk. "Hello, may I help you."

"Yes, I'm Brianna Kinney. I called you about adopting a dog."

"Of course, I've been expecting you. I'm Sadie." She stood and Brianna shook her outstretched hand. "We're so glad you want to adopt. If you follow me, I'll introduce you to our present residents. Do you know yet whether you want an adult dog or a puppy?"

After eliminating several larger dogs whose eyes begged her to give them a home, Brianna crouched in front of a cage holding three puppies. They appeared to fit the small dog category.

Was she crazy to attempt to housebreak a puppy in the middle of winter? Nights could get very cold.

Sadie squatted beside her. "We got them yesterday. The person who brought them in said she managed to find a home for one puppy in the litter. A family emergency has made it necessary for her family to move, and they can't take care of them."

"How old are they?"

"She said four months. They've had good care. They're up to date on their shots. They eat puppy food and are housebroken. We should be able to adopt them out quickly."

Housebroken. That's good.

One of the puppies, with wavy, blond fur and four white feet, brown eyes, and short ears that flopped over at the tips, sat in the middle of the pen watching the two women as the other two pups, both brown and white, tumbled over each other in play. The blonde one resembled the puppy on the cover of the book the customer Cooper bought his little girl before Christmas.

The puppy wagged its tail and tipped its head—and captured Brianna's heart.

"That one." She pointed.

Sadie stood and opened the pen, pushing back the two active puppies as she reached for the third. The blondie wiggled and licked Sadie's face as she cuddled it to her chest. Stepping out, she closed and latched the door before turning to Brianna. "This little girl's a sweetheart. All three are. I'd adopt them if I didn't already have two at home."

In Brianna's arms, the trembling puppy laid her muzzle on Brianna's shoulder, then, with one quick, moist swipe, licked her cheek.

"I'll take her." She stroked the soft, silky fur, and the pup settled into her arms with a sigh.

What will I call her? Not Blondie. "Cricket. I'll call her Cricket." She'd seen the name in a list of girls' names and liked it.

"A good name for a sweet dog." Sadie rubbed between Cricket's ears with her fingertips. "We've checked your references, but there are some other papers for you to fill out and the fee to pay. Let's go to the office."

As she followed Sadie through the doorway, Brianna glanced over her shoulder. The two other puppies had stopped wrestling and watched them from their cage.

Please let someone adopt them soon.

"Are you staying for the meeting?" Alix Lin followed Brianna into the church aisle.

Alix taught fourth grade at the local school, and the two women became friends when they met on Brianna's first visit to Juniper Falls Chapel. Alix came to the bookstore once or twice a week to talk to Brianna about school and books and Alix's engagement.

Brianna faced her friend. "The Snowflake Festival sounds fun, and I want to help, but I can't stay today." She checked the time on her phone.

"Oh, why not?"

"I have to get home. I have a puppy—" She yawned. "I didn't get much sleep last night."

"Ooh! You have a puppy? When did you get it? What does it look like?" Alix's brown eyes sparkled.

"Her name's Cricket." Brianna showed Alix a photo on her phone. "I got her from the animal shelter yesterday. She's so sweet."

"Aw, she's cute." Alix pressed her hands to her chest.

Brianna moved to the side to allow a couple to pass them. "Why don't you stop by about three and meet her, and we can have hot cocoa and cookies." Although she'd been invited to the homes of two or three church families and the Archers, this was the first time she'd invited someone to her apartment.

"I'd love to. And I'll tell you more about the festival. Shall I add your name to the list of volunteers and tell Doug and Esther you're in?"

"Yes, please do that." Brianna hugged her friend and greeted other people on her way out. She usually stayed after church and talked for a while, but she didn't dare make Cricket wait any longer today.

Brianna opened the door into the kitchen. "I'm here, Cricket."

Whines greeted her from the crate, crowding a corner of the kitchen. Hopefully, Cricket hadn't barked while Brianna was at church. She'd wrapped a hot water bottle and ticking clock in a blanket and left them in the crate with the puppy to comfort her.

Cricket wiggled and licked her face when Brianna lifted the puppy out of the crate. She turned her face out of the line of fire and grabbed the leash from a hook by the door. "Hold still, you silly thing! I can't get this snapped to your collar."

After their visit outdoors, Brianna measured out puppy food. Then she heated leftover spaghetti in the microwave and put together a tossed salad for herself. "I invited Alix over to meet you. You'll like her. But I promised her cookies, so it's cookie-baking time. What do you think—chocolate chip?"

Cricket ignored her, intent on her own food.

Brianna chuckled. At least she couldn't be accused of talking to herself.

Brianna baked cookies while her puppy took a nap in her crate. The apartment filled with the scent of freshly baked cookies and warmth from the oven.

Dishes washed and cookies baked, Brianna cuddled with Cricket in her recliner, reading a romantic suspense novel. Promptly at three, the front doorbell rang.

Brianna opened the door with Cricket in her arms.

"Mm, it smells good in here." Alix stepped in.

"Chocolate chip cookies. I hope you like them."

"Who doesn't?" She reached out and stroked the puppy's head.

Shrugging out of her coat, she handed it to Brianna in exchange for Cricket. Alix held Cricket in front of her and stared into the puppy's eyes. "You are so adorable."

Cricket licked Alix's nose. Alix laughed. "I guess that's a 'thank you' for my compliment." She rubbed her nose with the back of her hand and drew the puppy against her chest.

"She has two siblings still at the shelter who need a loving home." Alix had never said she wanted to adopt a dog, but Brianna wished she could find homes for Cricket's siblings.

Alix shook her head. "As tempting as that is, I don't have time right now to take care of a puppy. Maybe after the wedding, when Mateo and I are settled."

"Will he be here for the festival?"

"Yes." A smile stretched Alix's lips, and she gave a little bounce. "He'll be here for the whole weekend. I haven't seen him since Christmas."

Christmas had been less than a week ago.

"Oh, before I forget, will you be one of my bridesmaids? My sister will be matron of honor. I've asked my best good since elementary school to be a bridesmaid, and I'd like you to be one too."

"A bridesmaid?" Brianna smiled. "I'd love to. Thank you for asking me."

"Okay, good. We haven't set an exact date, but it will probably be in July or August." Alix's face glowed when she talked about her fiancé and her wedding.

A warm memory flowed through Brianna. Planning her wedding with Luke had been exciting. "I'm so happy for you." Brianna hugged her friend, being careful not to crush Cricket.

"I'll put Cricket in her crate," Brianna held out her hands, "and we'll have our cookies and hot cocoa. You can tell me all about the festival."

"Why don't I put Cricket in her crate while you make the hot cocoa. The festival schedule is on the Juniper Falls webpage."

"I'll get my laptop." She poured milk into a pan, set it on the stove, and turned on the burner. She then scooted into her bedroom. Returning with her computer, she set it on the kitchen table and booted it up.

Steam rose from the mugs of hot chocolate she set on the table along with a bag of marshmallows and a plate of cookies. She positioned the laptop so they both could see the screen.

Brianna typed in the link. "The town has been buzzing about the Juniper Falls Snowflake Festival since before Christmas. There are flyers in shop windows and on bulletin boards announcing it. Customers at the bookstore talk about it, and I've seen the advertisement on the Juniper Falls website."

"It's a tradition everyone loves, a family event." Alix shifted her chair closer to the table. "We raise money for the county food pantries. The money comes strictly from donations, and people are generous. Doug and Esther know you want to help. I signed us both up to supply cookies, and you can choose a time to work at the church booth."

"Robin said she's closing the store on that Saturday so she can enjoy the day with her family. I'll be able to take a shift at the booth."

Alix pointed to the schedule on the screen. "The firemen make an ice-skating rink in the park. That will be available Friday night, maybe sooner, along with sledding. The festival officially begins on Saturday morning." She slid a marshmallow from the bag and dropped it on top of her hot cocoa.

"I haven't skated for a while." Not without Luke. "I'll have to find my skates."

A note on the schedule indicated that Grace Church, the big church in town, sponsored a teen snow night on Friday at the park, although it was not an official festival activity.

"Different organizations, like our church, set up booths with refreshments along with a donation box. Also, crafters have booths to sell their creations. The deli has a food tent, and food trucks come in."

Brianna sipped her drink as she read through the schedule. "I see there are crafts scheduled for the kids at town hall on Saturday. Do you think they're looking for people to teach a craft?"

Alix pointed to the screen. "There's a contact number if you're interested."

"Want to do one together?"

Alix's eyes widened. "I think that will be fun. Do you have any ideas?"

Brianna went into the living room and returned with a snowman. She plopped it in front of Alix. "It's made with socks and rice. My third graders loved making these."

"Oh, I adore this. And it fits the festival theme." Alix examined the snowman, front and back. "Let's do it."

"I'll call the contact phone number and sign up. And I'll make a list of what we'll need. Maybe they can give us an idea of how many kids to plan for."

"I'll ask Mateo if he wants to help us." Alix pointed to the screen. "The snow sculpture contest is always fun. They give out prizes. I might convince Mateo to do this with me. Of course, there has to be snow."

"There's snow now." Brianna reached for a cookie. "We'll pray for snow. What's a snowflake festival without snow?"

"If there's no snow, there will be outdoor games for the kids, and if the weather is rainy or too cold, the booths will be moved indoors. The volunteer firemen work with the festival committee. Unless there's a storm that closes roads and businesses down, the festival happens."

Alix pointed to the schedule. "We always look forward to the Farmers' Country Band performance on Saturday evening. Make sure you get your ticket early. The concert is held in the school auditorium because so many people attend. Then the potluck community dinner is held Sunday after church at the town hall. And that's followed by a talent show."

"They pack a lot into the weekend. But it sounds like fun."

Some friends had told Luke about the festival, and they had planned a get-away weekend in Juniper Falls to attend the festival. Juniper Falls remained in her mind, so when she started looking for a new job, she checked their website and found the ad for Robin's store.

She'd attend this year. But without Luke.

CHAPTER THREE

Cooper pulled in front of Little Lambs Pre-school and Daycare.

The last Friday in January brought clouds and light snow. Nothing like snow to get the people of Juniper Falls excited about their annual Snowflake Festival. Several inches of white covered the ground now, with a couple more predicted overnight. Perfect for the festival.

"Can we go ice skating tonight, Uncle Coop?" Noah unfastened his booster seat harness.

Warmer than usual temperatures and a couple of fire calls earlier in the week had forced the volunteer firemen to wait until yesterday to fill the ice-skating rink in the park. At least the weatherman promised snow and cold for the weekend.

"It's Friday. You have to talk to your mom tonight." Too bad the kids would miss out on the outdoor fun, but they needed this connection to Tessa.

Cole and Tessa had named him the kids' guardian in their wills. He didn't understand Tessa's decision to fulfill her contract after Cole's death. But when she asked him to care for Noah and Lexie while she went overseas for twelve months, he said yes.

SNOWFLAKES AND PUPPY LOVE

Both sets of grandparents lived out of state now, and Tessa wanted her children to live in Juniper Falls, the town where she and Cole grew up.

Lexie clapped her hands. "I talk to Mama."

"Oh, I forgot." Noah bit his lip. "When can we go skating?"

"We'll make a day of it tomorrow, okay? We'll go skating and sledding, and we'll build the best snowman in town." He wanted his brother's kids to love the festival as much as he and Cole did when they were kids.

"And make candy with maple syrup on the snow?"

"Yes, jack wax. We'll eat lunch at the big deli tent, and you can do a craft in the town hall." Cooper opened his door.

"And me and Lexie will sing in the talent show."

"Yes, I signed you up."

Cooper got out and came around the truck. His nephew opened his door and hopped out onto the sidewalk.

"Hold on. Let me get Lexie." Cooper leaned over to help his niece, who was already halfway out of her seat. When had she learned to unbuckle herself?

Cooper pulled open the daycare door and let the kids walk in before him.

"Good morning." Kylie Ott greeted the children with a hug.

"Morning." They hung their coats on the hooks opposite the door and removed their boots, lining them up under their coats.

Cooper handed Kylie the bag with their snowpants and sneakers and gave Noah and Lexie each a hug. "Be good and have fun."

Animated children's voices filtered in from the next room.

"Put your sneakers on and ask Lila to help you tie them." Kylie gave them their shoes, and they padded in to join their fellow students and the two assistants.

"They're all excited about the festival." Kylie turned to Cooper. "Any news from Tessa?"

"The kids will video chat with her tonight."

"They talk about her a lot, and they miss her. But they seem to be happy with you. You're doing a good job with them, Cooper."

"Thanks. I try my best. Some days are better than others." A bachelor uncle couldn't entirely fill the void left by their absent mother.

He turned toward the door.

"Are you going to the sweetheart banquet this year?"

"What?" He whipped his head to look over his shoulder at Kylie. Why did she ask that? "I'm not planning to. Why would I go?" If he invited a woman to go to a sweetheart banquet with him, he wouldn't ask just anyone. She'd have to be really special, and there was no woman like that in his life. Not now, anyway.

"You're not getting younger, Cooper. There are some nice single women at church, and you'd make a great husband and dad."

He faced her, his hands on his hips. "Now you sound like my mother." Why were the women trying to marry him off?

"Your friends care about you too." She directed her gaze at him.

"I know. And thanks." He relaxed and dropped his hands. "Noah and Lexi are my main concern right now. I have to take care of them until Tessa comes home. I'll make their Valentine's Day special." He moved to the door and grasped the handle. "I have some things to do for the festival today. I'll pick the kids up at four."

Kylie hung Noah and Lexie's snowpants under their coats. "Have a good day."

"You too." He closed the door behind him and strode to his truck.

Before he spent two years on the mission field helping build schools, churches, and clinics, he thought he'd marry his college girlfriend. But by the time he returned, she'd married someone else.

Until Tessa came home, he had enough to do looking after his brother's family.

He hadn't been in the bookstore since before Christmas. There was a book by a new author he wanted to read. Next week, after the festival, he'd stop in and see if Robin had it in stock. Maybe he'd meet her clerk this time.

Parking his blue Silverado beside Ethan Archer's red F-150 in the parking lot at Juniper Community Park, Cooper walked over to the skating rink.

"How does it look?"

He fell into step with Ethan as they circled the rink.

"It looks good." Ethan gestured toward the ice. "The surface is smooth and hard, ready for any skaters who come tonight."

"You coming?"

"No. Our kids have outgrown their skates from last year. Robin's been occupied at the store, and I've had several jobs to do, so we'll have to go to the mall tonight to get new ones. Besides, the rink will be busy for Grace Church's teen snow and bonfire night. We'll skate tomorrow. You?"

Cooper shook his head. "No, Tessa video chats with Noah and Lexie on Friday nights. I promised them we'd make a day of it tomorrow."

"The festival won't officially start until tomorrow morning anyway." Ethan turned and gestured with his hand. "I see the areas for the snow sculpture contest have been roped off already."

The snow sculpture contest, with first, second and third

places for best in show and most original in different age categories, created a lot of excitement every year. Families, friends, and co-workers joined together for this favorite event.

"Mom, Dad, Cole, and I participated every year until Cole and I went to college. We even won the occasional prizes. Noah and Lexie want to make a snowman. Well, if Lexie has her way, we'll be making a snow puppy."

"Zoe and Adam are convinced they'll win first prize. I hope they aren't disappointed. They're old enough to do it on their own this year, but Robin and I will be there to encourage and advise." Ethan pulled a key on a lanyard from his coat pocket. "Let's get the benches out of the storage shed. Then we'll go over to town hall and set up for the indoor events."

The men headed for the shed that stood between the skating rink and the sledding hill.

"I signed up Noah and Lexie to sing "Jingle Bells" for the talent show. They wanted to do it."

"I remember how Cole used to play his guitar and sing." Ethan unlocked the door.

"Yeah, I don't think the kids ever heard him perform, but music is in their blood." Cooper missed his brother.

As they placed the benches around the rink, Cooper caught sight of a person walking a dog on the other side of the park. He couldn't tell who it was, probably a woman based on the lavender coat. She crossed the street and entered Virginia Moore's apartment. Must be Virginia's tenant.

He'd seen her from his truck, getting out of her car or talking to Virginia. She was the new clerk at the bookstore.

Alix met Brianna at her apartment a few minutes after four o'clock on Friday to wrap cookies for the church festival booth. Brianna would take them over to the booth in the morning.

"What time will Mateo be here?" Brianna held the door, letting Alix go in first.

Cricket welcomed them from her crate with a bark.

Brianna glanced at Alix. "Uh-oh. That's the first time I've heard her bark."

"Well, dogs do bark."

"Yes, but my landlady wants me to keep the barking to a minimum."

Alix giggled. "Can you train a dog not to bark?"

"We'll see." Brianna smiled and shrugged. "There's a video on the Internet."

Brianna took Cricket's leash from a hook by the door while Alix placed her containers of cookies on the table.

"Mateo said he'll be at our house about eight." Alix lived with her parents several miles outside Juniper Falls.

"After we finish the cookies, I'm going to the deli for a sub. Want to join me?"

Alix glanced at her phone. "I'd love to."

"We can eat at the deli or …" Brianna let the wiggly puppy out of the crate and snapped the leash to her collar. "If it's all right with you, we could come back here? Cricket needs our company."

"Certainly. I'd never say no to a visit with Cricket."

When Brianna and Cricket returned indoors, Alix rolled a ball across the floor, and Cricket pounced on it while Brianna prepared the puppy's food.

Brianna and Alix individually wrapped twelve dozen cookies and set them carefully in nine-by-thirteen-inch aluminum pans. Alix said the almond cookies, butter cookies, and cookies with a fudge center were traditional for her family celebrations. Brianna made chocolate chip cookies, snowball cookies, and sugar cookies shaped like snowmen and snowflakes.

Despite the line at the deli, it didn't take them long to get their subs and return to Brianna's apartment.

"Do you have time to inventory our supplies for the craft we're doing tomorrow? I think we have everything we need, but it won't hurt to check." Brianna's list lay on the table.

"Yes." Alix read the list while Brianna washed her hands. "Always best to be prepared."

After eating, they went into the living room. Brianna pulled two blue plastic containers to the middle of the floor.

Cricket eyed them, her ears pricked forward.

"We really don't need your help with this." Brianna offered the puppy a chewy bone. Cricket settled on her stomach and began to chew.

"My mother loves the snowman I made." Alix picked up Brianna's snowman from the end table. "I think adults will want to make them too."

"We probably don't have enough supplies for adults to make them this time. They're cute, though, and seasonal. I take mine out every winter."

They checked their supplies against Brianna's list and agreed they had enough of everything they needed. After closing the containers, Brianna pushed them to the side.

"I'll drop these off at town hall in the morning."

"Okay. Thanks for letting me eat with you." Alix slipped on her coat. "I'd better go home. I want to be there when Mateo arrives. Are you doing anything tonight?"

"I think I'll try out that new skating rink in the park. I dug out my skates last night."

"That should be fun. Perhaps we'll try it tomorrow."

Would anyone else be there tonight? It was always more fun to skate with a friend.

She closed the door behind Alix, and the silence pressed in

on her. She turned. Oops! She nearly stepped on Cricket, who sat watching the door with her head cocked.

She lifted the puppy and tipped her face away in time to avoid a sloppy kiss. Brianna laughed. "You sweet thing. You're good for me." Cricket had become the perfect canine companion.

As she dug her skates out of the bedroom closet, sadness pierced Brianna's heart. Luke would have been right in the center of everything this weekend. He loved the outdoors and being with people. Although the pain had lessened, she still missed him. And she'd be skating alone.

CHAPTER FOUR

aturday morning, Brianna stepped outside her
apartment wrapped in her coat, hat, gloves, and boots.
She breathed in the crisp, invigorating air. The sun peeked over
the horizon. A couple of inches of fresh snow blanketed the
ground, but someone had cleared the sidewalks. The local
weatherman had promised a perfect day for the festival.

She loaded her car trunk with the containers of craft supplies
and cookies and drove to the town hall. Carrying a plastic tub,
she approached the front door of the large, two-story building.
The door opened. Ethan Archer, Robin's husband, reached for
the container.

"Hey, Brianna. Here, let me take that." Ethan wore an
unzipped navy winter jacket, his brown hair short, and his face
displaying an attractive five o'clock shadow. He came into the
store from time to time to help with new shipments or to
rearrange shelves for Robin.

"Okay, thanks." She followed him to a table labeled for the
snowman craft.

"Is it possible for us to have two tables? We need room to set
out supplies and to give the kids workspace."

"I think that can be arranged." He pulled a second table end-to-end with the first. "Is this all right?"

"Perfect. Thank you."

Someone had taken a lot of time and effort to set up the hall. Tables for crafts were arranged in half the large room. At one end of the room, a man helped two women decorate the stage with lights and snowflakes in front of a painted snow scene background. An artificial evergreen tree stood at one side, artificial snow lining its branches. Three microphones stood across the front edge of the stage. Folding chairs were lined up in rows facing the stage, with more propped against the walls, probably for tomorrow afternoon's dinner and talent show.

"Do you have more? I'll get them for you."

She swiveled in Ethan's direction. "Oh, yes. In the car." The container wasn't heavy, just a little awkward. She could carry it herself, but she appreciated Ethan's thoughtfulness.

"Robin and the kids are at the skating rink. The kids were early birds this morning and helped me clear the snow off so they could skate."

"Do you skate?"

Ethan lifted the container out, and Brianna closed the trunk.

"I do, but the volunteer firemen help with the festival. The skating rink will be left up for the remainder of the winter, weather permitting, so I'll go another time."

"I went last night. It's really nice."

"Were many there?"

"Just the whole youth group from Grace Church."

Etha chuckled. "You didn't know about the snow night for teens?"

"I saw it on the schedule, but I'd forgotten. I enjoyed their company, and some of the teens there attend Juniper Falls Chapel." This time, Brianna opened the door for Ethan.

"Every year, Grace Church has a teen night as outreach, inviting kids from town and from area churches. So far, the festival committee allows it. I think it's been an unofficial part of the festival for years." He set the second container on top of the first.

"I enjoyed skating with them, but I only stayed a half hour. The muscles in my legs reminded me I hadn't skated for a long time." Brianna looked around once more. "Thanks so much for your help. Alix and I will be back later to take care of these."

"You're welcome. Have a good day."

As the town hall door closed behind her, Brianna's growling stomach reminded her she hadn't eaten breakfast. The aroma of food and coffee wafted in the air, and her mouth watered for a cinnamon roll from Village Bakery. But she had one more stop.

She lifted the pans of cookies from the trunk of her car. Balancing the cookies on one arm, she closed the trunk and turned toward the town center.

The banner across Main Street announced the Juniper Falls Snowflake Festival. Tents and booths lined the street in front of the shops along Main Street. A sign in front of one of the booths read *Snow Sculpture Registration*. In the town's large park on the other side of the street, a fence-enclosed playground stood at one side. A hand-painted sign marked a section of the park for the Snow Sculpture Contest. Beyond that lay the skating rink and the sledding hill.

Farther on were hiking trails, the woods, and the beautiful waterfall that gave the town its name. She had walked there with Alix once.

Along the sidewalk outside the park, a printed, laminated sign hung from the front edge of a wooden booth, reminding people that donated money went to the county food pantries. The light blue vinyl banner with snowflakes stretched across the front of the serving counter indicated that the booth belonged to Juniper Falls Chapel.

Brianna didn't know Doug and Esther Camp well, but she

was happy to help a good cause. She set her pans of cookies on the serving counter. "Do you need help?"

Esther taped signs to the two large urns Doug placed on a sturdy table inside the booth. One read *Hot Chocolate* and the other *Coffee*.

"No thanks. We've got this." Esther paused at the counter. "A couple of teens will be here soon to help us. Thanks for the cookies."

"You're welcome. I'll be back later for my shift."

No Parking signs lined Main Street, which would soon be closed to traffic. The parking lots at town hall, the school, the park, and spaces along the side streets would fill fast. Robin said the festival attracted people from neighboring towns and farther away. Even at seven-thirty in the morning, Main Street was busy.

Before the festival opened, she'd take her car home and leave it there. She lived close enough to walk by cutting across the park.

Munching her cinnamon roll and sipping her coffee, she perused several craft booths and talked with the crafters setting up their wares. She'd return later to purchase what she wanted.

On her way back to her car parked at the town hall, she discovered a local maple syrup producer setting up a display and making jack wax.

"You pour hot maple syrup over clean snow," he told her. "We use a candy thermometer to make sure the syrup is the right temperature." He gave her a sample. She licked her fingers and lips to capture all the yummy maple sweetness of the taffy-like confection.

She drove her car home. Cricket gave a couple of barks when she opened the kitchen door.

"Shh, Cricket. I know you're glad to see me, but we can't disturb Virginia."

After taking the puppy outside, Brianna spent a few minutes

playing with her and cuddling her before returning to the festival.

If she had time, she'd take Cricket for a walk in the park around noon. Cricket needed the exercise, and it would get her used to being around people.

"Thank you," Brianna said to a couple who dropped money into the donation box at the end of the counter.

She lost count of how many cups of coffee, tea, and hot cocoa she filled and how many cookies, muffins, and pastries she handed out. Two teen volunteers helped her, for which she was grateful. From what she could tell, people donated generously to the food pantry fund. Even children dropped their coins into the locked box on the counter.

She waved to the Archer family, who strolled along the sidewalk in front of the shops across the street. They stopped to talk to a man in a leather jacket and brown knit hat accompanied by two small children, one in blue and one in pink. Cooper, and his kids with him.

The little girl in pink waved toward the Juniper Falls Chapel booth. Brianna glanced around. Was the girl waving at her or someone else? She shrugged and waved back.

Cricket pulled on her leash and sniffed the snow beside the sidewalk in the park. Her body wriggled, and she tried to lick all her admirers who stopped to pet her and talk to Brianna.

"A puppy!" A little girl, probably three or four, bundled in a pink snowsuit, stood up from making a snow angel—the little girl who'd waved to her from across the street.

She waded through the snow toward Brianna and reached for Cricket. Jerking her hand back, she turned her face up to Brianna. "Can I pet your puppy?" Her fingers wiggled inside her mittens as though feeling fur.

Probably she'd been told not to touch dogs without the owner's permission.

Cricket's body squirmed, and her tail wagged. She pulled on the leash to get to the girl. Brianna lifted her puppy from the ground.

"Sure. Cricket loves to be petted." She crouched down to the child's level. "Let her sniff your hand first so she knows you don't want to hurt her."

Cricket licked the snowy, pink mitten, and the girl giggled. "Hi, Cricket."

Snow-encased, brown work boots and small, blue snow boots moved into Brianna's line of vision. Her upward gaze met familiar blue eyes.

"Cooper?"

She blurted out his name even though they hadn't been officially introduced. He didn't know her name—at least she hadn't told him.

"Hello, bookstore lady."

If he wasn't a married man, she'd say his eyes and voice invited her to flirt. Heat rushed to her face despite the cold outdoor air.

"Oh, I'm sorry." She stood. "I should have asked if it was all right for your little girl to pet my puppy."

"No problem. Lexie likes dogs, and this one sure is cute." He stepped closer and scratched Cricket under her chin.

Brianna's insides wobbled like a dish of gelatin.

"There were two more like her at the shelter." They'd probably been adopted by now.

"Unca Coop, I want a puppy." Lexie clung to Cooper's hand, and her eyes begged him to say yes.

Uh-oh, have I opened a package of trouble? Wait. Uncle *Coop?*

"I want a dog, only bigger." The boy's hand came up to the level of his chin.

I think the boy's name is Noah.

"Wow, you want a big dog." As a child, Brianna had wanted a dog, but her family had cats. She loved the cats.

"Uh-huh. I want a big, black one."

Cooper shook his head. "That's something you both will have to work out with your mother when she returns home."

Lexie's lower lip protruded, and the boy shrugged.

Brianna's phone alarm dinged. "Oh, I have to take Cricket home and get to town hall. It was nice meeting you." She turned away.

"Wait." Cooper's command stopped her.

She spun around.

His eyes crinkled at the corners when he smiled at her. "You know my name, but I don't know yours. You have an unfair advantage."

"Oh, uh, Brianna Kinney." She peered into his eyes, and a shiver ran down her spine.

"It's nice to know you, Brianna Kinney." He held out his hand. "I'm Cooper Stiles."

After a moment's hesitation, she placed her gloved hand in his. He grinned. Did he know the effect his smile had on her? He squeezed her hand and let it go.

She wanted to stay but had other obligations.

Lexie waved. "'Bye, Cricket."

As Brianna walked away with her puppy in her arms, Lexie's

pleading voice reached her. "Please, Unca Coop, I want a puppy." She heard only the rumble of Cooper's voice when he responded.

So, Cooper is their uncle. Who is Tessa to him? And where is their father?

oe and Adam Archer entered the town hall and headed straight for Brianna's table, with Robin, their mother, trailing behind.

"I want to make a snowman, Miss Brianna, and so does Adam."

"Okay, Zoe. There are two spots open right here for you and your brother."

"I'll take your coats." Robin held out her hands. They slipped them off and gave them to her. "I'll hang them up over there." She nodded toward the two long coat racks that stood against the wall by the door.

Brianna gave the Archer children their craft supplies and helped them get started, then she walked back and forth along her side of the table, helping where needed. Alix worked on the other side, and Mateo assisted whoever asked for help. The snowmen were a big hit with the kids six-to-twelve years old, and there was seldom an empty spot around the table.

"I'm not sure we could have done this without you, Mateo. Thank you for staying to help us."

"I don't mind, Brianna. I didn't want to wander around without Alix, and this sounded like fun."

A child's sobs drew Brianna's attention. Just inside the door, Cooper talked with Robin as he held a crying Lexie. Noah gazed up at the adults and held Lexie's hand.

"I bet Lexie's sad because her mom's not here." Zoe hot glued an orange pom-pom nose to her snowman's face. She held her handiwork up for Brianna's approval.

"Good job." Brianna smiled and nodded. "Where is her mother?"

"She's helping the Army."

"Oh." How was the mother helping the Army? Was she in the Army?

The absence of Lexie's sobs caught Brianna's attention. Cooper set down his niece and helped her take off her coat. He hung hers and Noah's coats on the coat rack, and Robin took each child by the hand.

Cooper said something to Robin before opening the door. He rotated his head, catching Brianna's gaze in his for a moment. His frown chilled her.

Was he mad at her?

Brianna took a deep breath and turned her attention to a boy who asked for her help. She glanced up to find Alix watching her from the other side of the table. She turned her attention back to the boy and his snowman.

Robin led Noah and Lexie to the snowman craft table and admired her children's snowmen. Leaning toward Brianna, she spoke softly. "Lexie's put out because she can't call her mother for her permission to get a puppy."

Had their meeting in the park earlier prompted Lexie's tears?

"Cooper asked me to look after these two. He and Ethan have an emergency. One of the snow sculpture contest judges canceled at the last minute. They have to find a replacement."

Had that and not her caused Cooper's frown?

Brianna opened her mouth to volunteer to be a judge when a small hand tugged at her sleeve.

"Where's your puppy?" Lexie sniffled.

Brianna crouched down and stared into Lexie's red-rimmed eyes. "Cricket's at home. She doesn't know how to do crafts." She pulled a clean tissue from her jeans pocket and offered it to the little girl.

"She doesn't have fingers." Lexie held up her hands and wiggled her fingers. Then she accepted the tissue and wiped her nose.

Noah watched Adam glue buttons on his snowman. "Can I make a snowman?"

Brianna bit her lip. She didn't want to say no, yet making the snowman would be too hard for the preschooler.

"They're making pinecone owls over there, Noah, and paper plate penguins at the other table." Robin grasped Lexie's hand and held out her other one to Noah. "I think you and Lexie will like making one of them."

Glancing once more at Adam's creation, Noah took Robin's hand. "Okay."

Brianna stood and mouthed 'Thank you.' The children went along with Robin, Lexie skipping, her puppy woe evidently forgotten.

Brianna, Alix, and Mateo remained busy, helping kids craft their snowmen. What fun. Brianna missed teaching. Did she want to teach school again? Maybe.

As the time for the snow sculpture contest drew closer, parents collected their children, and the room emptied.

"There's hardly anything left to pack up, Bri. We figured our supplies about right." Alix lifted two pairs of socks, a bag of rice, and a few other items from the tables.

"We did." Brianna gathered two handfuls of scraps and threw them in the large trashcan nearby.

When Mateo went to get his and Alix's coats, Alix nudged

Brianna with her shoulder. "What was up with Cooper Stiles? Is there something going on there?"

Brianna's face heated, and she pushed wisps of hair back from her face. "We met in the park earlier when I took Cricket for a walk. Lexi liked Cricket."

"Is that all?"

What could she say? She didn't know Cooper well enough to respond to Alix's question. She could only think that he resented her ownership of the puppy that made his niece cry.

Mateo returned with his and Alix's coats.

Whew, rescued!

Brianna brushed grains of rice into her cupped hand and threw them in the trashcan.

"Want to come with us, Bri?"

"No, you two go ahead. I know you want to build your snowman. I can finish here."

"Are you sure?" Alix placed the last of the leftover supplies in one of the plastic containers and closed the lid. "What about these? Want Mateo to carry them out?"

Brianna bit her lip. "No, the containers will have to wait until tomorrow. I left my car at home." She'd forgotten she'd need her car.

"Let me put them in my SUV now." Mateo touched her arm. "We'll drop them off at your place this evening."

"That will be helpful. Thank you. If I'm not there, please leave them under the carport."

While Mateo held Alix's coat for her to put it on, Brianna checked the two tables and the floor beneath for snowman debris. She shrugged into her coat and zipped it. She lifted one container, and Mateo the other, and Alix held the door. They were the last to leave.

Shouts and laughter echoed from the park and Main Street.

"We'd better get going." Mateo closed his SUV's tailgate.

"There's a snowman waiting to be built, and we don't have much time." He grabbed Alix's hand. "Come on."

Alix turned to Brianna. "Come with us, Bri."

"I'm fine, Alix," she said, touched by her friend's concern that she not be left alone. She'd be in their way for sure, an intrusion on their fun together. "You and Mateo go on. I'll be right along."

Their laughter, as they jogged toward the town center, blended with the other sounds. They'd have to hurry to get their snowman done.

Although she didn't have anyone to partner with to make a snow sculpture, she could still enjoy others' creations. Had they found another judge for the contest?

Cloaked in loneliness, she slid her gloved hands into her pockets and sauntered toward the park. Twice now, she'd mistakenly interpreted Cooper's friendliness for interest. He wasn't looking for a relationship. Perhaps she wasn't ready yet, either.

"Brianna!"

She squinted. Someone was waving at her. *Virginia.*

"Brianna, there you are." Breathless, Virginia hurried up to her.

"Is something wrong?" Brianna grasped the older woman's arms.

"No." Virginia held on to Brianna while catching her breath. "Are you busy? The high school librarian had a family emergency, so we need another judge for the snow sculpture contest. Are you willing?"

"I'm finished with the craft, so I'd be glad to help. Is it all right that I know some of the participants?" She'd met many of them today.

Virginia waved her hand. "Everyone knows everyone in this town. That's not a problem, so long as you can be unbiased."

She wanted to hug Virginia. "I'll do my best. Thank you for

considering me." She fell into step beside her landlady. "Who else is judging?"

"The mayor and me. It's a tough job because the participants put in a lot of effort, and we don't want anyone to be disappointed. Of course, we consider the age of the participants. It's fun, though. Mayor Dart is waiting by the registration booth. He'll explain everything to you."

Virginia introduced her to the mayor, who gave her clear instructions. Clipboard in hand, Brianna followed the other two judges to the park. Throughout the designated area, snow sculptures, from dragons to rabbits to trucks and snowmen of many sizes, covered the ground. Brianna gave a score of one to ten for each of the ten categories on the score sheet and added up the total points for each entry.

Zoe and Adam stood proudly beside their snow rocket ship, their parents watching from behind them.

"This looks ready to launch," Mayor Dart said. "Is it going to the moon?"

"Mars." Adam rested his hand against it.

The mayor chuckled, and Brianna and Virginia smiled.

"You did a good job," Virginia said to each group.

"Thank you." Zoe shared a glance with her brother, hope shining in her eyes.

Brianna finished filling in the scoresheet, waved to the Archers, and followed the other two judges to the next snow creation.

A few minutes later they came upon Cooper with Lexie in his arms, sleeping against his shoulder. Noah knelt on the ground, piling snowballs behind a dog-shaped mound of snow.

"It looks like the princess has had enough, Cooper." The mayor began to mark his scoresheet.

"Yes, she has been going non-stop all day."

Noah stood. "We let her have a snow dog because she can't have a real one."

"What did you want to make, Noah?" Virginia apparently knew everyone on a first-name basis.

"I wanted a motorcycle, but Uncle Coop said it would be too hard. He wanted to build just a snowman."

"So, we compromised and built a snow dog." Cooper grinned. Brianna's gaze met his, and her heart jumped before she lowered her eyes to the scoresheet.

The dog's ears were different sizes, and the muzzle was a little to the side of the face, but it looked like a dog. Brianna took into consideration the pre-school age of two of the sculptors. Their uncle had let them do much of the work, for which she silently congratulated him. Her admiration for him notched up.

"That was nice of you to let Lexie have her way, Noah. You did a good job." This time, Brianna gave the encouragement.

When Cooper nudged him, the little boy smiled shyly. "Thank you."

"You're welcome."

Cooper grinned, and the corners of his eyes crinkled. He winked at her. Better than a frown. Butterflies danced in her stomach.

"I like the Farmers' music. They're good." Brianna stood and stretched, reaching for her coat on the back of her chair.

"I agree. I think everyone looks forward to their concert." Alix slid her arms into her coat that Mateo held for her. "Mateo and I are going ice skating now. Do you want to come?"

"Miss Bri, Miss Bri!" Lexie, in her pink coat, ran up to her and threw her arms around Brianna's legs.

People standing nearby chuckled.

She leaned over the little girl. "Hi, Lexie. Did you enjoy the concert?"

Lexie, with blue eyes framed by dark lashes like her uncle's, peered up at her and nodded. "I like music."

"So do I."

Cooper ambled toward her in his leather jacket, one hand in his pocket, the other holding Noah's.

She inhaled a shaky breath.

He smiled. "Hello, bookstore lady."

"Uncle Coop," Noah tugged on his hand, "why do you call her bookstore lady? Her name is Miss Brianna."

"Well, I met her in the bookstore. But I will call her Miss Brianna if you think that's better."

Noah nodded. "Yes."

"Hello, Miss Brianna." He gazed directly into her eyes, and his voice lost its playful tone.

Her heart rate increased, and she shivered. "Hello, Cooper." She couldn't deny her attraction to this man, but would he frown at her the next time they met?

She slid her arms into her coat and buttoned it. Then she moved toward the door with Lexie's hand in hers.

"Me and Lexie are singing "Jingle Bells" tomorrow." Noah grasped her other hand.

"I signed them up for the talent show." Cooper's low voice close behind her sent shivers down her spine. "They wanted to sing, and they're pretty good."

Cooper stepped around her and held the door open. The cold air hit her face when she walked out with a child clinging to each hand.

Alix and Mateo stood arm-in-arm a short distance from the school entrance. She hadn't answered Alix's question about skating.

"I'm sorry, you guys. You asked me a question. I …"

"Brianna Kinney, I finally caught up with you."

She whirled around, releasing the small hands she held. "David?" Why was her former co-worker in Juniper Falls?

"Hi, I'm David Jones." Not waiting for Brianna to introduce him, he shook hands with Mateo, Alix, and Cooper, and they each said their names. "Brianna and I taught school together."

"He teaches fifth grade at Mount Avon." Why is he here?

"We're going to say good night." Cooper stepped back. "I have to get these two to bed if we're going to make it to church in the morning." He nodded toward Noah and Lexie, who stood beside Brianna.

Brianna's eyes went to Cooper's face then to the children looking up at her. She wanted them to stay. Would Cooper have stayed if David hadn't appeared? Did he think she and David were a couple?

Bad timing.

She gave the boy and girl each a hug. "Sleep tight. I'll see you tomorrow."

Cooper held out his hands, and the children went to him. His eyes held hers for a moment before he turned and walked away into the shadows.

Brianna watched them as they made their way through the crowd. Had Cooper's expression telegraphed disappointment? She was super chagrined.

"I went to the bookstore earlier, but it was closed." David touched her arm, and she faced him. "Can we talk, maybe get a cup of coffee?"

"Um." She tried to think of an excuse. Alix and Mateo still waited.

"It's business."

"Business?" What kind of business did he mean? Well, he was a friend, not an ogre. "Oh, all right." She turned to Alix. "Thank you for asking me. You two have fun at the skating rink. I'll go with you another time."

Alix hugged her and Mateo nodded. They glanced at David before they ambled away, leaving her alone with him.

"I'm sorry to take you from your friends. It looks like you've settled here quite well."

"Yes, I like Juniper Falls. It's a nice town." Brianna stuffed her hands in her pockets. "I think there are still a couple of places open for us to get coffee." She didn't really want coffee, but she did want warmed up.

They strolled toward the center of town. Brianna tried to relax her tense body. She liked David as a co-worker and friend, but he tried to push her too far on their one date, her only date since Luke. David wanted to hold hands and kiss, and she wasn't ready. Would he try that again tonight? She kept her hands in her coat pockets.

David broke the silence between them. "You judged the snow sculpture contest."

"Yes, I substituted at the last minute. I enjoyed it."

"And you taught that snowman craft you used to do with your third graders."

"Yes." Had he kept track of her all day, even though she never saw him?

They lined up behind several others at a booth and soon walked away with steaming cups of coffee.

Talking and laughter filled the still, cold air around them. Brianna didn't feel like talking to or laughing with David.

"Have you been here all day? I didn't see you." There'd been a lot of people, and she'd been occupied since the festival opened.

"I came around noon. I saw an advertisement about the festival online. I knew you'd moved to Juniper Falls and thought I'd drop by. I found your snowflake cookies at one of the church booths, so I knew you had to be around."

She had occasionally treated the teaching staff with her sugar cookies.

Cooper probably had the kids tucked in bed by now. She'd never know if he wanted to invite her for coffee or hot cocoa after the concert or to take a walk with him and the kids.

"You said you have some business with me?"

David sipped his coffee. "Do you like your job?"

She searched the crowd for familiar faces, avoiding his. "Very much."

"Do you miss teaching?"

"Sometimes." If the district hadn't downsized, she'd have stayed. "I mostly miss the students." Today, while helping the kids with the craft, she realized how much.

"There are a couple of openings at Mount Avon School, or will be next school year, and I thought you might be interested."

He was the second person since Christmas to find teaching opportunities for her. "I've lived here less than a year. I'm not ready to move again so soon."

"But what if you could have your old job back?"

Would she? The opportunity to teach again tempted her.

She shook her head. "I like living in Juniper Falls and working at the bookstore. If I decide to teach again, I'll apply to schools near here."

Alix had suggested Brianna apply to take her fourth-grade position in the Juniper Falls school district. To be honest, she wanted to see how things worked out with Cooper. She couldn't leave now.

"A lot of the other teachers say how much they miss you. I've missed you. If you came back, I thought maybe you and I could date again, see where our relationship ..."

What!

"You and I, David?" She stopped and faced him. "I told you I don't want to date you again. I thought you understood there's no *us*."

Could they even count their only dinner at an area restaurant with a fellow teacher, a friend, as a date? She knew that night she could never have a relationship with him and even told him so. "I'm not interested in more than friendship with you, remember?"

Her rebuke came out sharper than she'd intended. She averted her eyes and bit her lip.

He stared at her, then he replaced his stunned expression with a weak grin. "Can you blame a guy for trying?"

She could. He didn't believe her no meant no.

"Thank you for telling me about the teaching opportunities, but I'm not planning to go anywhere. I have a job, a nice place to live, and friends. I'm not interested in moving again right now."

She pivoted and walked away from him. She sipped her coffee and wrinkled her nose. *Ugh! I've had enough of David and the coffee.*

"That guy, Cooper, with the two kids. You're dating him aren't you?" David caught up with her. "Is he the reason you want to stay?"

The tempest brewing within her broke. She whirled to face him again. "What business is that of yours?" Her stomach rolled with anger.

Several people glanced their way, and she bit her lip and dropped her gaze to the ground.

"I'm sorry." David held up his hand. "I guess that was a bad question."

"Yes, it was. I'm tired. It's been a long day." She threw her cup in a trash can a little harder than necessary. "I'll say goodnight."

"So early?" He took a last sip of his coffee and tossed his cup in the trash. "May I take you home?"

Perhaps he was just being polite, but she didn't care to let him know where she lived.

"No, thanks, I don't have far to go."

"I'm staying at the B-and-B outside of town tonight."

"I've heard it's a nice place." She should invite him to

church. And before she could stop herself she blurted out. "I go to Juniper Falls Chapel on Sundays. You're welcome to come if you're interested. There's another church, Grace, right in town. And there's a talent show tomorrow afternoon." If he stayed, she'd probably see him, but she wouldn't seek him out.

"Yes, the dinner and talent show are on the schedule." He stuffed his hands into his coat pockets. "I'll see you tomorrow at church." He turned in the direction of town hall, probably to get his car from the parking lot.

She wasn't sorry to see him go. She wouldn't change her mind about him. Although pushy, he wasn't a bad person. Just not for her.

Did he really think she'd want to move back to Mount Avon? She'd left because, without Luke, she had nothing to hold her there.

The day had been nearly perfect until David showed up and spoiled what she hoped would be an opportunity to spend time with Cooper and the kids, Cooper especially.

CHAPTER SIX

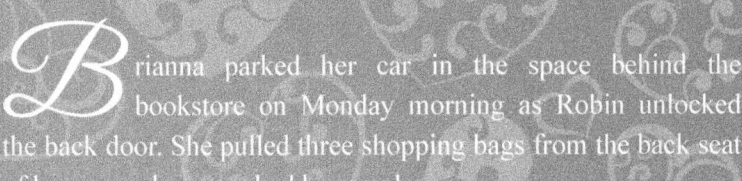

*B*rianna parked her car in the space behind the bookstore on Monday morning as Robin unlocked the back door. She pulled three shopping bags from the back seat of her car and approached her employer.

"Good morning, Robin. I thought I might have to open this morning after the weekend festivities."

Robin pushed the door open and allowed Brianna to go in first.

"It was a struggle getting the kids up and out the door for school, that's for sure. But we had a wonderful weekend. What did you think of the festival?"

"I had a great time. I like family events, and I look forward to next year's festival."

With David sticking to her side like glue yesterday, Brianna didn't talk to Cooper at either the dinner or the talent show. He seemed to be avoiding her. She had smiled and waved to him across the room, but he merely nodded without returning her smile. Lexie and Noah pointed to her, and he shook his head.

Robin flipped the light switch in the entryway, and they hung up their coats.

"My kids were so excited to win first place for most original for their rocket sculpture."

"They did a good job and deserved it. Did you see Noah and Lexie's expressions when the emcee announced they'd won third place in the talent show?"

"Cooper was so proud of them."

"And I could hardly believe how much money we raised for the food pantries." Brianna followed Robin into the office. "Do you want me to put up the Valentine's decorations today?" She held up the bags she carried.

"That will be great, unless we get busy." Robin turned on her desk computer and shuffled some papers around. The blinking red light on the answering machine begged for attention. "Ethan brought over a table for you to use for the kids' craft, and you can decorate to your heart's content."

Brianna stepped toward the doorway.

"The couples' sweetheart banquet for Grace Church is coming up in two weeks. Ethan and I made our reservations. We always go to a nice restaurant and have a special speaker. Might you be interested in attending?"

A sweetheart banquet? She swiveled back. "Not really. Who would I go with? It's for couples, like you and Ethan."

"Just asking. I thought maybe you'd met someone."

Brianna had met someone she'd like to get to know better, but it was too early for them to attend a sweetheart banquet.

"No." Brianna shook her head. "I'm not really interested in dating." And yet, if the right person asked, like a blue-eyed uncle, maybe she would be.

Robin folded her hands and rested them on her desk. "Who was that man talking to you after the concert Saturday night? Then again on Sunday."

Great, the Archers had seen her with David. "Just a fellow teacher from Mount Avon. He came for the festival."

"We had a lot of visitors from out of town." Robin appeared

satisfied with her answer. "Do you ever think about dating or even marrying again?"

Brianna shrugged. Robin wasn't the first to ask this question. "Sometimes."

"I know someone …"

"No, thank you." Brianna shook her head. She refused to allow her employer to become her matchmaker. And she wouldn't attend a sweetheart banquet with a stranger.

Robin typed something into her computer. "Well, will you babysit? I have two adorable children who will need a responsible caregiver for the evening."

She could hug Robin redirecting their conversation. "I'd love to. You and Ethan can enjoy yourselves." And she'd have the opportunity for a kid fix.

"Good. Zoe and Adam will love spending time with you. They're your adamant fans since the Snowflake Festival. We'll probably need you about five o'clock, but I'll let you know for sure when it's closer to the time."

"Do you think they'd like to go out to eat? And maybe come back to my apartment to decorate cookies and watch a movie?" She'd have an excuse to make sugar cookies again.

"I'm sure they would."

"Good. I'll plan on doing that. I'm going to decorate the store now."

"All right. I'll be out to help you in a bit."

Grace Church scheduled its sweetheart banquet for the Friday night before Valentine's Day. Robin closed the store early to get ready for her special date with her husband. Brianna had only a few more things to do to be ready for her party with the kids.

"We're going to have company tonight, Cricket, so I want you to be on your best behavior." Cricket cocked her head as Brianna measured food into the puppy's dish.

Sugar cookies in the shape of hearts, flowers, and snowflakes sat on the counter in a plastic container. Frosting divided by color in several covered plastic bowls lined the back of the counter.

She checked the TV listings for a movie Zoe and Adam might enjoy, and she pulled several DVDs from the shelf, just in case.

To leave more space in the kitchen, she moved Cricket's crate into the bedroom. She took Cricket outside one last time before closing her in her crate.

Brianna had everything ready. She'd invited Virginia to join them when they returned from eating out.

Robin had said five o'clock, and Brianna didn't want to be late picking up the kids.

Cooper collected Noah and Lexie from daycare after work on Friday and took them out to eat. Tessa had switched her video call to Saturdays because of a change in her schedule.

He didn't mind cooking, and he thought he did well preparing healthy meals for them. However, tonight was Grace Church's sweetheart banquet, and Cooper wanted to be sure he could give anyone who asked a good reason why he wasn't there. His nephew and niece needed him.

"Cricket!"

As soon as Cooper opened the door to Jean and Jake's Family Diner, Lexie bolted toward the woman with her hands full of glasses of drinks. Brianna Kinney's pink turtleneck layered with a pink plaid flannel shirt matched the color of the roses in his mother's garden.

Somehow, Brianna managed to keep the liquid from spilling as Lexie grabbed her legs and held on tight. "Hi, Lexie. Cricket isn't here, but Zoe and Adam are."

"Miss Brianna, can Noah and Lexie sit with us?" Zoe asked, and Adam patted the seat beside him.

The request wasn't surprising, as they attended the same church, and their mothers were best friends.

Accepting the invitation, his niece and nephew slid into the booth, Noah beside Adam and Lexie beside Zoe. Brianna, still balancing the drinks, her eyes brimming with laughter, turned her gaze to Cooper. Her lips twitched.

His heart thumped, and heat crept into his face as he stood rooted inside the door. He hadn't seen Brianna since the Snowflake Festival when the sudden appearance of her boyfriend quickly erased his plan to ask her to go for coffee after the concert. He'd avoided the sweetheart banquet, but he couldn't avoid this awkward situation.

He found his tongue. "Where is Miss Brianna going to sit? And we haven't ordered yet." He took off his cap and tucked it into his back pocket.

"Why don't we pull that little table over here next to the booth, and you and I can sit at that." Brianna had a knack for smoothing over a situation.

He rubbed his hand through his hair. Did he have a choice? The problem was, they'd be sitting across from each other. Not a problem, really. A pleasure. But she already has a boyfriend. He nodded and did as she suggested.

She set Adam and Zoe's drinks on the table in front of them and sat in the chair next to Lexie. "I'll wait with the children while you order your food."

"Thanks."

Noah and Lexie had already told him what they wanted, so

with one more glance at the cozy table scene, he went up to the counter where Jean waited for him.

"No date tonight, Cooper?" Jean asked as she entered his order into the cash register screen. Jean and his mother were good friends, although his parents had moved south.

"My nephew and niece." He smirked when he gave what he thought was a smart answer.

"Isn't it nice you can join Ms. Kinney and the Archer children? Their parents went to—"

"The sweetheart banquet. I know." He didn't have to be reminded.

He glanced over his shoulder. Brianna's brown hair was gathered into a ponytail, and her attention was focused on the children sitting with her. Lexie leaned against her arm.

She'd be a wonderful mother and someone with whom he'd like to have a family. His stomach somersaulted. Where had that thought come from?

"She's single, a widow." Jean leaned forward and whispered. "She used to be a schoolteacher."

He groaned inwardly as he imagined the next telephone conversation between Jean and his mother. He shook his head and opened his mouth. He had to say something to halt the matchmaking before it got out of hand.

"I'll bring your order to your table when it's ready." Jean grinned at him." Let me get your drinks."

She turned away, and he twisted his neck and relaxed his shoulders. He could handle this. None of the other diners who occupied the booths looked his way. Noah waved to him, and he waved back.

"Here you go, Cooper." Jean set the drinks on the counter. "Your food will be out shortly."

He lifted the glass and two plastic cups with lids. "Thanks, Jean."

When he got back to their table, Brianna's description of

Cricket playing in the snow had the children giggling. *That puppy again.* He held his breath, waiting for Lexie's outburst. Huh? Lexie didn't whine for a puppy this time.

He set their drinks down and leaned toward Brianna, inhaling the sweet, floral scent of her hair. "Do you want me to sit beside my niece? She can be a little messy when she eats."

"I think I can handle it." Brianna smiled. "But it's your call."

Zoe heard him. "Mr. Cooper, this is the girls' side. You have to sit over there."

Brianna's lips twitched, and she covered them with her fingers.

He barely contained his laughter. Point well-taken, Zoe. "You're right, Zoe." He sat beside Noah on the boys' side.

"We waited for you, Mr. Cooper," Noah said. "Miss Brianna says it's polite to wait until everyone has their drinks before we drink ours."

"Thank you. How about we pray and thank God for our food now." He glanced at Brianna, and she nodded. "Miss Jean told me our food will be ready soon. And let's not drink so much now that we can't eat our food later, okay, Lexie?"

Lexie nodded.

"Okay, Noah?"

"Yes, Uncle Coop."

Raising his head after praying, he peered into the honey-brown eyes of the woman seated across from him. Her cheeks turned a lovely shade of pink that matched her shirt, and she lowered her eyes to her glass of iced tea and sipped it. Like moths against a screen door, his stomach fluttered. Tongue-tied, he checked on Noah and Lexie. They chatted with the Archer kids, who helped them tear the paper off their straws and poke them into their cups.

He didn't have anything to occupy his hands. He clasped them in his lap to stop their trembling.

"You didn't go to the banquet tonight?"

Brianna's voice drew his eyes back to the pretty woman across from him. She stirred the ice cubes in her tea with her straw.

"Ah, no. I don't date. The kids are my priority." *That excuse is beginning to sound old. I can get a babysitter if I want to take her out.* And he did.

"Oh." Was disappointment expressed in her one word? She peered over her shoulder toward the counter. "Our food should be ready soon."

Resting his arms on the table, he leaned forward. "Why didn't you go?"

She frowned. "Go where?"

"To the sweetheart banquet. Robin probably told you about it."

"Yes, she did." She shook her head. "I don't … I'm taking care of Zoe and Adam, so Robin and Ethan could go."

What happened to the boyfriend?

Just then, Jake and Jean brought their meals, each carrying three.

"We thought you'd all like your food at the same time since you're eating together." Jean winked at Cooper as she placed his meal in front of him.

He might as well resign himself. By tomorrow, he'd get a call from his mother, and by Sunday, the matchmakers at church would be abuzz.

His conversation with Brianna was further delayed as he and Brianna made sure the four children had everything they needed. He picked up his double cheeseburger and took a bite.

'I don't date.' Cooper's words chilled Brianna now as his frowns had at other times. He'd put up a one-way road sign, pointing away from him. Could that change? Should she even try?

She laid her napkin on her lap and took another sip of tea. Her grilled chicken sandwich had mayonnaise, lettuce, and tomato but no onions. The curly fries lay golden and hot on her plate. Just what she'd ordered.

Here was the opportunity to become better acquainted with the handsome man seated within arm's reach across from her, but for that to happen, they had to have an intelligent conversation, right? Food appeared to be the only thing on his mind right now.

The children chatted among themselves as they ate, paying little attention to the adults.

Brianna cleared her throat. "What do you do for a living?"

He swallowed the food in his mouth and finally looked at her. "I'm a carpenter, and I build houses."

"Is that a seasonal job?" She knew the answer to her question. Luke had worked for a home improvement store that sold lumber and supplies to builders. But it was a safe subject to begin with.

"Well, most of the outside construction is completed in spring, summer, and fall. During the winter, I do inside work and repairs. Right now, I try not to overbook so I have enough time for Noah and Lexie."

She tore open a packet of ketchup. "If you don't mind my asking, where are their parents?" Zoe's comment about their mother helping the Army increased her curiosity.

He clenched his jaw and swallowed. Lowering his eyes, he twisted his drink glass.

I shouldn't have asked. "You don't have to answer. I'm sorry."

"No, it's all right." He glanced at the children, then bent slightly toward her. "Their father, my brother Cole, died."

With another quick look at the children, he leaned back, his lips pressed together.

"I'm sorry." She could relate to his grief. She reached across the table and touched his hand. A shock passed through her fingers up to her shoulder, and he flinched. She pulled her hand into her lap.

"My sister-in-law Tessa is fulfilling a commitment to a contractor overseas. She's a language translator in an area rebuilding in a former war zone. She's cautious about saying where she is or exactly what she does."

How is her work more important than her own children?

"She knows several languages, and she trained for the work while she was still in the Army, before Noah was born. Cole died during overseas deployment. I think it's her way of grieving and honoring his memory."

If Brianna had children, wouldn't they be her first responsibility? Yet, each person handled grief differently, and Tessa had left Noah and Lexie in the care of a person who loved them, their uncle Cooper. *Forgive me for judging, Lord.*

She bit into her grilled chicken sandwich, and, as she chewed, she dipped a curly fry in catsup. Lexie grinned at her and picked up the last chicken nugget on her plate. The four children were almost finished with their food, but Brianna had just started eating hers.

"Why are you working at the bookstore if you're a schoolteacher?" Only a couple of fries remained on Cooper's plate.

She stared at him for a moment. How did he know this? Had he asked someone because he was interested in her, or had the information been passed around through the town grapevine? "The school where I worked downsized, and I found Robin's ad for the bookstore online."

"I gotta go potty," Lexie whispered.

There goes our conversation.

Brianna stood and held out her hand to the little girl, but Zoe said, "I'll take her."

Cooper nodded.

Brianna returned to her seat and took another bite of her sandwich. Before she could restart their conversation, Adam tapped Cooper's shoulder and spoke softly to him behind Noah's back. Brianna couldn't hear what he said.

"Me too," Noah said.

"Okay, guys, we'll all go." Cooper stood and waited for the boys to slide out, then glanced at Brianna. "We're going to the restroom."

"All right."

During their absence, she finished her meal while an idea swirled around in her mind. *I need your help here, Lord. Should I, or shouldn't I?*

Ten minutes later, Brianna stepped outside the warm restaurant into the cold air with Cooper and the children. When she unlocked her car doors, Adam and Zoe got into the back seat. Brianna shivered, but not entirely from the cold.

CHAPTER SEVEN

I'll do it. Brianna took a deep breath and approached Cooper's truck, parked two spaces away from her car. He buckled his nephew and niece into their car seats and closed the door.

"Cooper, I'm taking Adam and Zoe to my place to decorate Valentine's cookies and watch a movie. I think Noah and Lexie would enjoy it. Do you want to come?"

They'd be crowded in her small apartment space, but it would give her more time with Cooper, and he'd have another adult to talk to. Well, two adults, because she'd invited Virginia to join them.

He turned to her and tugged on the visor of his cap. She couldn't see his face clearly.

Please say yes. She clasped and unclasped her hands. "I told Cricket we're having visitors tonight. She'll be happy to see Lexie." *Oops! Probably not the best way to get his consent, seeing that Lexie starts crying for a puppy every time she sees Cricket. Well, it's said, and the damage is done.* Her heart racing, she held her breath.

"I don't know." He folded his arms and leaned against the

truck. "It's like this. If Lexie sees that puppy of yours, she'll either beg to stay with you tonight or try to take Cricket home with her."

"If you don't want to, I understand." Her shoulders sagged, and disappointment washed over her. She turned away.

He grabbed her arm, sending a shock wave through her.

"Wait a minute. I didn't say no." He straightened and dropped his arm to his side. "I was teasing when I said that. You didn't see my smile." He shifted his cap back on his head. "We'll come unless the kids don't want to. But I expect they will."

Yes, thank you, Lord.

She caught herself before she threw her arms around him, embarrassing them both and giving any spectators cause to gossip. You'd think she'd won the grand prize on a game show.

"Good. I live in Virginia Moore's apartment."

"Virginia told me. And I saw you in the yard with her."

"Okay, then, I guess we should go."

"I'll follow you."

She slid into the driver's seat of her car and turned to Zoe and Adam. "Cooper, Noah, and Lexie are coming to our party."

Zoe clapped her hands, and Adam said, "Miss Brianna, do you like Mr. Cooper?"

Um. She buckled her seatbelt. "Of course. He's a nice man."

"But do you really, really like him?" Zoe this time. "Because I think he likes you."

Kids notice things, even when you don't think they're paying attention.

How could she know for sure? Cooper had been giving mixed signals. She might know more after tonight.

"I don't know him very well yet, but he's a friend." She started the car.

Several dozen decorated sugar cookies sat on the kitchen counter on paper plates wrapped in cellophane, ready for her guests to take home with them. *Workers are worthy of their hire, the Bible says.*

Brianna shut an exhausted Cricket in her crate in the bedroom. The excitement of having company and playing hard tired the puppy out. Getting Lexie to stop playing with Cricket long enough to decorate a couple of cookies had been difficult.

While she took care of Cricket, Cooper washed up the cookie-decorating equipment without being asked and set up the living room. Virginia made the hot cocoa and laid out the snacks Brianna had prepared.

Brianna entered the living room last with a paper plate of food and her mug of cocoa. The four children sat on the floor in front of the TV. Her cutting board for sewing, covered with four plastic placemats, created a make-shift table for their plates and drinks. Virginia had chosen to sit in the recliner, which left space for her beside Cooper on the sofa.

Her stomach fluttered as she sat beside him. She set her mug of cocoa on the end table and picked up the TV remote.

"You're a good party planner, Miss Brianna. You make crafts, entertain children, train dogs, work in a bookstore, teach school, and make delicious sugar cookies. Have you any other talents I should know about?" Cooper grinned and took a bite of a snowflake cookie.

Warmth filled her. "Well …"

"She judges snow sculptures," Virginia said.

"Miss Brianna, this is like a picnic," Noah said. "It's fun."

"I'm glad you like it, Noah. I'm going to start the movie

now." It was already after seven and the movie ran for ninety minutes. Cooper probably didn't want to keep his niece and nephew out too late.

Lexie got up and leaned against her knees. "Can Cricket come in with us? Please."

"Cricket is tired, Lexie, and she needs to sleep. She can do that best in her crate. And if she came in here, she'd gobble up all our food." Brianna tickled the little girl.

Lexie giggled and squirmed. "Okay." She resumed her seat on the floor and bit into a cheese cracker from her plate.

The TV screen came alive with the movie Brianna had chosen with the kids' approval. The four youngsters appeared totally absorbed in the story of a grandfather who teaches his grandchildren about conservation and wild animals. Brianna liked the movie, but she enjoyed watching the children even more.

She was also aware of every move the man beside her made.

His arm lay casually across the back of the sofa and his legs stretched out in her direction, his feet nearly touching hers. She glanced at her landlady, whose attention was on the TV, then back at Cooper, whose eyes studied her. A smile played at the corners of his mouth. His expression telegraphed interest, and a current zinged through her.

The whole scenario took on a family feel. Hers and Cooper's.

The movie came to an exciting conclusion, and Zoe said, "Where's Lexie?"

Brianna hadn't seen her leave, and neither had anyone else, but Lexie's place on the floor was vacant.

Cooper stood and strode into the kitchen. "Lexie!"

"I'm sure she's all right, Cooper. We'll find her. There aren't many hiding places in my apartment." Surely, Lexie wouldn't have gone outdoors by herself. At least, Brianna hoped not.

Lexi wasn't in the kitchen or the bathroom.

"Wait a minute. I think I know where she is." Brianna

entered her bedroom. Lexie lay curled up with Cricket in the puppy's crate, sound asleep. *How cute.*

"She's in here, Cooper. She's okay." If she had her cell phone with her, she'd take a picture so Cooper could send it to Tessa.

In the doorway, Cooper puffed out his breath. "I think it's time for us to go home. Get your coat, Noah." His lips pressed together, he grabbed his own coat from the pile of coats on the bed and put it on.

With Lexie safe and well, why was he so grumpy? Brianna shook her head.

Kneeling down, he opened the crate. Cricket lifted her head and yawned. He handed the puppy to Brianna, then pulled his niece out and into his arms. Lexie never awakened, even when Brianna helped Cooper slip her arms into the sleeves of her coat and zipped it up. Standing only inches from Brianna, he never looked at her.

With a sleeping child on his shoulder, Cooper pulled his key fob from his jeans pocket and started his truck from inside the apartment.

"Oh, don't forget your cookies." Adam handed the plate of cookies to Noah, who held them carefully in his mittened hands.

Brianna opened the door. Cooper went out, followed by Noah. Brianna watched from the doorway as Cooper placed Lexi in her car seat. He took the cookies from Noah, who clambered into his booster seat and fastened his safety harness. Cooper handed the plate back to Noah and shut the door. Without another word, he went around to the driver's side.

She'd call this a crash ending to a lovely evening. Was he mad at her because Cricket attracted Lexie like a magnet?

Brianna started to close her door.

"The kids had a good time tonight."

She looked out.

"Thanks." Cooper waved to her and ducked into his truck.

Well, that was a half-hearted thank you. She closed the door and sagged with her back against it.

Time to clean up from the party.

Virginia stood by the kitchen table. "Zoe, Adam, and I picked up the living room, and I washed up the mugs and cocoa pan. I'll say goodnight now."

"Thank you for your help." Brianna pasted on a smile to camouflage her disappointment. "And thank you so much for coming over."

"The pleasure was mine." Virginia's hug surprised her. "It was nice to spend the evening with friends."

Brianna leaned into her, absorbing a momentary comfort from her usually undemonstrative landlady.

"Don't forget your cookies." Brianna lifted a plate of cookies from the counter and handed it to Virginia.

Leaning close, the older woman whispered. "Don't give up on Cooper yet. He's a great guy."

Brianna stared at Virginia's back as her landlady left the apartment through the connecting door. The lock clicked behind her. The evening had held several surprises, including Virginia's interest in her love life.

She'd been with Cooper only during the Snowflake Festival and tonight since they first met in the bookstore. Like the fine print on an over-the-counter medicine bottle, he was hard to read. She shook her head. Perhaps she should heed the warnings.

Cricket's growl and the children's laughter from the living room reminded Brianna she still had company. In the time left before their parents picked up Zoe and Adam, maybe they'd like to play a board game.

Cooper's phone rang while he was mixing pancake batter the next morning.

Mom. Jean must have been in touch with her already.

He put the phone on speaker. "Hi, Mom."

"Good morning, Cooper. How are you?"

"I'm well. Making pancakes for breakfast." He spooned batter for four pancakes on the hot griddle. They sizzled.

"I'll bet the kids will like that. How are Lexi and Noah?"

"They're fine. I'll let you talk to them in a few minutes." Thumping above his head warned him they were up.

"I'd like to talk to them. But first I want to talk to you."

Here it comes.

"Jean called and said you took the kids out to eat last night."

"I did. Tessa changed her video chat time to Saturday, so I thought they'd like to go out."

"It gives you a break too."

"True, although I don't mind cooking."

"And the Archers' children were there with their sitter. Jean said Grace Church held its annual sweetheart banquet last night."

"Yes." He flipped the pancakes. He knew exactly what she'd say next.

"And you didn't go?"

He counted internally to ten. "No, Mom. You know I have to take care of Lexie and Noah."

"I know. Jean likes the Archers' sitter. She works for Robin at Archer Books."

"Yes, Brianna's a nice person and works for Robin. Lexie adores her puppy. And we unintentionally met at Jean and Jake's last night and ate together." *Mom didn't have to know about the party afterward.*

"Yikes!" He nearly dropped the pancakes on the floor when he transferred them to the waiting platter. *That's what happens when I get irritated.*

"Is everything okay?" His mother's worried voice reminded him that she was on the phone.

"Yeah. I nearly dropped the pancakes, is all." Not all, but enough for her to know.

Footsteps on the stairs warned him he'd have company in the kitchen soon." I hear the kids coming down now. I'll let them talk to you while I finish getting breakfast."

Noah and Lexie entered the kitchen dressed in their pajamas and with frowns on their faces.

Lexie peered up at him. "Unca Coop, can I have a cookie for brefas?"

"No, Lexie, we're having pancakes."

"Told you!" Noah glared at his sister.

Cooper sighed and shook his head. Not a stellar start to the day.

"Grandma's on the phone and wants to talk to both of you." He waved the pancake turner. "My phone is on the table. It's on speaker, so you don't have to touch it."

Noah leaned against the table. "Hi, Gramma."

"Hello, Noah."

Lexie climbed into a chair. "Hi, Gramma."

"Hello, Lexie."

Cooper continued making the pancakes as he listened to the conversation. He turned off the burner and transferred the last pancakes to the platter and heard "puppy," "Miss Brianna," and "party."

Oh, no.

"We went to Miss Brianna's and decorated Valentine's cookies and watched a movie. We brought some cookies home." Noah eyed the plate of cookies on the counter.

"And I felled asleep with Cricket." Lexie giggled.

"So, you had a party too. Did you have fun?"

"Breakfast is ready, kids. Say goodbye to Grandma." If he

didn't intervene now, this conversation might snowball into an abominable snowman.

"Bye, Grandma," they chorused.

"Have to go now, Mom. Thanks for calling. We'll talk again soon."

"Oh, all right, Cooper. I know you're busy. Your dad and I pray for you every day."

"Thanks, Mom. Prayer is always appreciated. Say hi to Dad. Love you."

"Love you too."

At least his mother hadn't pressed him for more details about the party. He ended the call before she could say more. He'd enjoyed last night, and he really liked Brianna, but he wasn't prepared to tell his mother that. He didn't want to be trapped in another matchmaking scheme.

Brianna may not even want to see him again after he left the way he did. Yes, he remembered at the last minute to say thank you, but he hadn't been very gracious when they discovered Lexie asleep in Cricket's crate. The idea of family—he and Brianna and kids—had bubbled up in him during the movie and scared him. Perhaps he'd been a bachelor too long. He hardly knew her, he had his niece and nephew to care for, and there was work.

He didn't have time for dating and falling in love. Did he?

CHAPTER EIGHT

"*Y*ou look like a man with a lot on his mind." Ethan clapped Cooper on the back as they walked out of the men's Sunday School classroom together and headed toward the auditorium for the worship service.

"Yeah, well, I do." Truthfully, he couldn't get Brianna Kinney out of his mind this morning.

"Robin and I had a great time at the sweetheart banquet Friday night. You missed a fabulous dinner," Ethan patted his stomach, "and an inspiring speaker."

"I'm glad you had a good time." *Where are you going with this, my friend?*

"Zoe and Adam said you ate with them at Jean and Jake's, then you all went to Brianna's for a cookie-decorating party."

He could brush off Ethan with a simple yes or no, but an explanation might allay the chance of more questions. He gave a brief rundown of their evening, not including the current of attraction that zipped between Brianna and him all evening. "Did your kids tell you that Lexie fell asleep with the puppy in her crate?"

"Yes, they thought it was hilarious."

Instrumental music from the church sanctuary warned them that the service would begin soon.

Saved by the music. "We'd better get in there if we don't want to be late for morning worship. Robin will be looking for you. Talk to you later."

It wasn't that Cooper was opposed to getting married. In fact, he thought he'd have a family of his own, like Ethan, by this time in his life, and not just practicing fatherhood by caring for his brother's children. But he wasn't going to be pushed into a relationship until he was ready, and he'd choose his own wife.

He thought he'd found her at last, but he'd messed up.

Holding Noah and Lexie each by a hand, their Sunday School and Kinder Church papers folded and stuffed in his sports jacket pockets, Cooper stepped out into the hallway.

"Hi, Cooper." Robin strolled toward him, her two kids following her.

Is she going to say something about Friday night? He cringed inwardly, although Robin didn't usually pressure him about relationships. Not one of the matchmaking women in church had said a word to him about Friday night.

The four children formed a tight circle and began talking with each other.

"Did Ethan remember to invite you over for dinner this afternoon?"

"No, he didn't."

"Well, consider yourself invited, you and the kids. Will you come? We have plenty."

"Thank you, we will." The Archers often invited them for a meal. "The usual time?"

"Yes, but…" She bit her lip. "Will it be all right with you if I invite Brianna? She's alone, and the kids all like her."

He gazed at the kids, needing time to think. He'd really like to see Brianna again. He needed to apologize. Lexie and Noah liked her. And he didn't want her to have to eat Sunday dinner alone. It was a family-and-friends time, and she was the Archers' friend. His too.

"Robin, it's your home. You have the right to ask whoever you want to come."

"I know. It's just …" She stepped closer and lowered her voice, "Zoe and Adam told us all about what happened on Friday night. How you ate together and then went to Brianna's for a Valentine's cookie decorating party and movie. And I thought—"

He nodded. "Uh-huh. And you thought you'd do a little matchmaking on the sly." He didn't mind her interference this time, but that David what's his name might. "Isn't she seeing someone?" Robin would know.

"Brianna?" She frowned and shook her head. "No, not that I know of."

"A guy came to the festival. He said his name is David, and he acted like they belonged together."

"Oh, I think I know who you mean. She said he's a schoolteacher from Mount Avon, and he came for the festival."

"He said they taught at the same school. So, they're not together?"

"I'm pretty sure they're not."

No boyfriend. That's good.

Robin touched his arm. "Look, Cooper, I don't mean to push you into anything, but I think you and Brianna would make a great match. She's a wonderful person. And there's no harm in spending time together as friends, to get to know each other."

He raised his eyebrows. "I'll allow you to get away with it this time." He grinned as excitement bubbled up inside him. He ran his fingers through his hair. He'd see Brianna again this afternoon.

Robin smiled and pulled her cell phone from her purse. "I'll call her right now. Her church service should be over." She walked a few steps away and stood with her back toward him.

The children surrounded him.

"We ate up all the cookies already, Mr. Cooper." Adam licked his lips. "Noah said you did too."

They must have been discussing Friday night.

"And they were so good. Daddy said she should go into the cookie-making business," Zoe said.

He assumed they were talking about Brianna and her cookies.

He chuckled. "The cookies were good, but I'm not sure she wants to start a cookie business. She likes working for your mom."

Robin joined them. "I caught her just in time. She said she'd love to come over."

"Okay. Great." His insides vibrated with excitement.

"Is Miss Brianna coming over for dinner?" Zoe asked.

Zoe doesn't miss much, does she?

The girl sidled up to Cooper, stood on her toes, and he leaned down to catch her words as she whispered in his ear. "You really do like her. I can tell."

Cooper wasn't sure how she could tell unless she could read his mind. He didn't deny it, but he shrugged and smiled.

Robin looked at Cooper, her eyebrows raised. He just smiled. Zoe and her mother had probably already talked about what Zoe whispered to him.

"Yes, she's coming for dinner." Robin strode down the hallway. "We'd better find your dad and get home. See you in a few minutes, Cooper."

Zoe and Adam trotted after their mom. Zoe glanced over her

shoulder at him with a knowing smirk. He nearly laughed out loud.

Robin opened the back door. Brianna entered the kitchen with Cricket on a leash. The scent of roast beef and other good things made Brianna's mouth water and her stomach growl. Cricket sniffed the air.

"Hi, Robin. It sure smells yummy in here." If she'd been invited sooner, Brianna would have made a dessert or a salad to bring. She welcomed the last-minute dinner invitation, however, and she looked forward to a meal with Robin's sweet family.

"Thanks. I'm getting a bit hungry myself." Robin bent over and scratched the puppy under her chin.

"Thanks for letting me bring Cricket. She spends a lot of time alone, and I want to give her more opportunities to socialize so she knows how to behave wherever she goes."

"No problem. We have plenty of space, and the kids will enjoy playing with her."

Brianna pulled a bag of M&Ms from her purse. "I had these left from decorating cookies. I wanted to bring something."

"I didn't expect you to bring anything. It was a last-minute invitation." Robin took the bag from her and set it on the back of the counter. "Thank you. We'll have them for a treat later."

Laugher erupted from the living room, followed by two male voices talking. *Ethan and ... Cooper?* She didn't know he'd be here. Of course, the families were friends and attended church together. But was Robin trying to set her up with Cooper?

"I'll hang up my coat and be back to help you." Brianna had to pass through the living room and past Cooper to get to the coat closet by the front door.

"Okay. Everything's about ready," Robin said. "The men put the extra leaf in the table and made sure there were enough chairs for everyone. The kids set the table."

Brianna took a deep breath, determined to appear cool and calm. She wasn't about to risk her heart if Cooper wasn't interested.

Ethan and Cooper sat in recliners, chatting. The kids, seated on the floor, watched a kids' program on the TV.

"Hello, Brianna," Ethan said.

When Cooper's eyes met hers, her heart thudded, and a rush of heat rose up her neck into her face. His smile engulfed her like an ocean wave, washing over her and leaving her breathless.

She and Luke had never discussed remarriage should the unbelievable happen. Luke, her first love, would always have a place in her heart. But she believed he wouldn't want her to be alone for the rest of her life if she found another man to love and marry.

Did Cooper's eyes and smile mean any more than a friendly hello?

Before Brianna found her voice to respond to Ethan's greeting, Lexie dashed over and dropped to her knees. "Cricket." Cricket crawled into her lap and licked her face. Lexie giggled.

"Hi, Miss Brianna," chorused the three other children.

"Hi, kids."

If Cooper greeted her, she didn't hear him.

Brianna handed Lexie the leash. With four young people to occupy her, Cricket didn't need her. Brianna hung up her coat and scurried back into the kitchen.

"Are you all right?" Robin turned off the electric knife she used to cut the roast.

"What do you mean?" Brianna looked around for something to do. She couldn't meet Robin's gaze.

"Your face is flushed, and you look like, well, like you've had some shocking news or something."

Ah, the vegetables. Brianna scooped mashed potatoes into a large serving bowl on the kitchen table. "Did you have an ulterior motive for inviting both Cooper and me today?"

"Well, maybe." Robin turned on the knife and resumed cutting the meat. "I've tried not to play matchmaker with Cooper. He doesn't like it. But I've known him for years, and he'd make a great family man. And there's you, my friend and employee, who'd be a perfect match for him. Zoe told me she's sure you like each other, and I thought so at the festival."

Brianna set the potato pan in the sink and ran water into it. "Thank you for your honesty." Beans and carrots fit into two smaller bowls.

"Are you mad at me?" Robin set down the knife and bit her lip as she waited for Brianna's response.

"I don't think so." She shook her head. "No." She poured gravy from the pan on the stove into the tureen Robin had set on the counter. "Cooper said he doesn't date, and the kids are his first priority."

"That doesn't mean you and Cooper can't spend time together and get to know each other, at least as friends."

Cooper's baritone voice and laughter from the living room pulled Brianna's gaze in that direction. Being friends with Cooper wouldn't be a bad thing, and today presented an opportunity to learn more about him.

"I like him. He loves those kids." She chuckled. "And I think he likes my dog."

Friday had been fun. Electrical attraction zipped between them from the moment he stepped into the restaurant. Yet, he ended the evening abruptly, getting out of her apartment as fast as he could, his *thank you* a reluctant afterthought. Sleep eluded her for a long time on Friday night, her mind full of Cooper. Should she open herself to a man like him and face possible rejection and heartbreak?

Robin rinsed the cutting board off in the sink. She gave

Brianna a hug. "Okay, everything's ready. Will you start setting the food out while I call everyone to the table?"

"Sure." Brianna inhaled deeply and exhaled slowly, trying to calm the fluttering inside before she had to deal again with those incredible eyes and the man they belonged to.

He'd have to be first to signal his interest in making their relationship move forward.

"I know Noah and Lexie are your priority, but that doesn't mean you can't spend time with Brianna, get to know her. Include her in some of the things you do with them, like ice skating or going to a movie. You might even consider taking her out on a date." Ethan placed the last dish in the dishwasher and closed the door.

Cooper didn't mind helping Ethan clean up after dinner. It gave him time for man talk with his friend.

"I don't know how she'd feel about a date with two kids in tow."

"Robin and I will be glad to have them over if you want to go out. We'd do the same for Tessa."

Cooper finished wiping down the counters with the dishcloth. "I'll consider it."

Brianna had been quiet during dinner, only responding when spoken to. She hadn't talked to him. The few times he caught her looking at him, she didn't smile, and she lowered her eyes quickly.

I hurt her feelings on Friday.

Ethan added soap to the dishwasher and turned it on. "Well, you think about it." He looked around. "We're done in here. Let's see what the others are up to."

Cooper followed Ethan into the living room. Robin and

Brianna sat on the floor at the coffee table putting together a jigsaw puzzle. Giggling from upstairs indicated the children's whereabouts.

Cricket, lying beside Brianna, lifted her head and wagged her tail. Brianna, however, kept her eyes on the puzzle.

Cooper crouched down and stroked the puppy's back. "Hello there, pretty girl." Cricket moaned and rolled over so he could rub her tummy.

Brianna glanced at him, but quickly returned her eyes to the puzzle. If he raised his hand, he could touch the smooth softness of her cheek or brush the errant lock of hair away from her face. How would he get her to talk to him? Of course, he still needed to apologize. His inability to find the right words to say to her frustrated him.

If he could have only a moment alone with her.

"Thank you, guys, for cleaning up," Robin said.

Ethan leaned over his wife and kissed her on the lips. "For my beautiful wife, anything."

Cooper averted his eyes and stood. The display of affection between the Archers didn't surprise him. Ethan loved his wife and wasn't afraid to show it.

What would it be like to kiss Brianna? He stuffed his hands in his pockets and licked his lips. From the corner of his eye, he stole a glance at her in time to catch her looking at him before lowering her eyes to the puzzle in front of her. Did her pink cheeks mean she was thinking about kissing him? He hoped so.

Footsteps clunked on the stairs. Adam tramped into the living room first, followed by the other three children. "We want to go outside and play."

"I think that's a great idea." Robin stood. "Is it all right with you, Cooper?"

"Of course. I brought Noah's and Lexie's snowpants and boots. They're in the truck."

"Let's all go out," Ethan said.

The kids cheered and rushed to retrieve their outerwear for playing in the snow.

Returning from his truck with boots and snowpants, Cooper nearly collided with Brianna when he opened the kitchen door. She had her coat on and held Cricket in her arms. She stepped back.

"Thank you for dinner, Robin. I have to go now. Alix is coming to my apartment to talk with me about her wedding, and we have church tonight."

She has to leave now? Cooper handed Noah his snowpants and boots, then he knelt in front of Lexie to help her put hers on. *What can I say to keep her here?*

Robin hugged Brianna. "I'm sorry you have to leave so soon. Thank you for coming. Next time maybe you can stay longer."

He tipped his head up and caught Brianna's gaze. "I was looking forward to a snowball fight." He winked and grinned, hoping to convince her to stay.

The corners of her mouth curved up, and she pressed her free hand against her hip. "I have a pretty good aim. I'll take up that challenge another time."

Before he could utter a comeback, Lexie's hand against his cheek pushed his face toward her.

"I want to make a snowman, Unca Coop."

He pulled her knit hat down over her ears. "We'll do that, Lex."

"Miss Bri, can you and Cricket play in the snow with us?" She hugged Brianna's legs. "Please?"

"Not today, Lexie. Another time, perhaps."

If Lexie couldn't convince her, anything more he might say wouldn't do it either.

Cooper zipped Lexie's coat and held her mittens while she pushed her hands into them. He opened the door, and Lexie scooted out to join Ethan and the other three kids rolling snowballs. Brianna walked out with her dog, and Robin followed. He pulled the door closed behind him.

First fastening Cricket to her dog seatbelt in the back seat, Brianna got into her car and drove away with a wave of her hand.

Cooper scooped up a handful of snow and formed a snowball. Brianna's playful response about a snowball fight gave him hope. Maybe he should accept Ethan and Robin's offer to babysit for the kids.

"Come on, Uncle Coop," Noah called.

"We've reserved the Juniper Falls Chapel for August fourth, the first Saturday in August." Alix brought up her calendar app on her phone. "The wedding ceremony will be at one o'clock. And my parents will set up a tent in their backyard for the reception. There's plenty of room there for the number of guests we'll invite. Will you help with decorating? You're so good with that."

Brianna rested her cheek against the palm of her hand, her elbow propped on the table. She plucked at the corner of the paper in front of her. She didn't have to leave the Archers' house when she did this afternoon. Yes, she had to meet with Alix and later go to church. But she could have stayed a little longer. Although she didn't have her boots with her, she could have watched the others. The shift to the outdoors gave her the opportunity to leave gracefully.

"Brianna?"

"What?" *Oh, Alix asked me a question.* "I'll be glad to help. Do you have any ideas yet?"

Alix set down her phone. "You seem to be a little distracted,

Bri. Is something the matter?" Worry lines creased the space between Alix's eyebrows.

"Not really." She shrugged. "Maybe."

"Want to talk about it?" Alix laid her hand on Brianna's arm.

Brianna heaved a sigh. "I'm sorry. We came here to talk about your wedding, not about me and my problems." She glanced down at Cricket lying on the floor beside her, chewing on a ball.

"That's okay. It sometimes helps to talk to a friend. I want to help if I can."

Perhaps she could use a friend's objective input. Robin was too close to the situation, and Virginia wasn't someone she'd confide in. She didn't want to involve family members. Although a little younger, Alix was a good friend.

"How well do you know Cooper Stiles?"

Alix pulled her hand back and leaned her arms on the table. "He built my parents garage, and I've seen him at school with the Archers when Adam and Zoe are in a program. He's a native of Juniper Falls and a volunteer fireman. I've spoken with him a few times."

"I had dinner with the Archers today. Robin invited Cooper as well."

"Is that bad?"

Brianna shook her head. "I don't think so. The two families are close friends. Cooper and the kids eat there often."

"You really like him, don't you? I'm glad for you."

"Yes, I do. But I'm not going to risk my heart on a one-sided relationship."

"Why do you say that?"

Brianna told Alix about Friday night at Jean and Jake's and later at her apartment. "When he left the way he did, I decided he'd have to make the next move. With so many people at Robin's house this afternoon, it was easy to avoid talking to him. He didn't say anything to me either until the end when he looked at me and issued a snowball fight challenge." She smiled at the memory. She'd almost accepted his dare. "I could have stayed a little longer, but I left."

"You've had more experience in the romance department than I've had. However, I don't think you should give up. When he looks at you or talks to you, I think his interest is obvious. Mateo agrees."

If Cooper's interest had been that obvious to Alix and Mateo, and to Robin and Zoe, and to who knows who else, perhaps she should hope.

"So, what are you going to do?" Alix leaned back in her chair.

Brianna folded then smoothed out the corner of the paper. "I'm not sure, except I'll wait for him to indicate what he wants. He told me he didn't date because of Noah and Lexie. They're his priority, and I respect that. It's when he turns into a grump, especially when it comes to Lexie and Cricket, that makes me wonder."

Cricket looked up when Brianna said her name.

"He does have a big responsibility with the kids." Alix picked up her phone. "If I were you, I wouldn't give up yet. Pray about it. God knows what's best."

"You're right. Thanks for the reminder." Maybe it wasn't yet God's time. She picked up her pen. "Now, what do you want for decorations for your reception?"

CHAPTER NINE

ooper parked his truck along the street in front of Archer Books on Monday afternoon. He had fifteen minutes before he had to pick up Noah and Lexie from Little Lambs Daycare, so this would be a good time to get the book he wanted.

Who was he kidding? Brianna was the real reason he stopped by today. Yesterday at the Archers, he'd missed his opportunity to apologize and convince her to go on a date.

He didn't remember asking a girl for a date being this hard in high school and college. Maybe it had been too long, and he was out of practice. Or maybe he fumbled because this was so important to him.

Taking a deep breath, he opened the door to the jingle of sleighbells and entered. Valentine decorations had replaced the Christmas ones. Brianna wasn't at the cash register, and she wasn't in sight. Several customers browsed the shelves, and he heard voices, one of them Brianna's. He raised himself on his toes and peered over the shelves.

"Hello, Cooper. What can I do for you?" Robin popped up from behind the counter.

"Oh!" He dropped to his feet and swiveled toward her. "Hi, Robin. I, uh, thank you for dinner yesterday. The kids and I had fun." His face heated, like a kid caught with his hand in a cookie jar.

"You're welcome. It was our pleasure." She waved her hand in the direction of Brianna's voice. "She's with a customer. She knows a lot about children's books, so I let her help people find what they're looking for."

Did Robin read his mind, or had she seen him peering over the shelves?

"There's a book I'd like to read, and I thought you might have it." He handed her a paper with the name of the book and its author. At least he had a cover-up reason for being there.

"I don't think so. I'll check the inventory and see if we do. If not, I can order it." She typed into her computer.

"Thanks." Cooper leaned against the counter as he waited, tapping his fingers on the countertop. *Maybe she'll finish with her customer and come up here.* He stopped tapping and checked his phone for the time. Ten minutes left to get to the daycare.

"No, I'm sorry, we don't have it. It will be here in a few days if I order it now." Robin glanced at him. "Or you can check the library to see if they have it."

"I'd like to have my own copy, so you can go ahead and order it for me."

She told him the price, he paid for it, and she handed him the receipt.

"I have to get the kids." He couldn't wait any longer.

"I'll tell Brianna you were here."

It wouldn't do him any good to protest her assumption that he came to see Brianna. This was Robin, after all.

He nodded. "Thanks."

The sleighbells jingled as he went out. He'd have to come up with plan B. Maybe he could surprise her for Valentine's Day tomorrow. *If it's not too late.*

"Are you doing anything special tonight to celebrate Valentine's Day?" Brianna cleared craft sticks and construction paper off the craft table and placed them in a cloth tote bag. She folded the table for Robin to take home from the bookstore. They'd have no need for a Valentine's craft tomorrow, the day after Valentine's Day.

"No, Ethan and I attended the sweetheart banquet Friday night. I made a special dessert for the family, and we're going to stay home with the kids tonight. They had a party at school today, and they have school tomorrow. How about you?"

"It will be just Cricket and me tonight. I thought I'd watch a Valentine's movie on TV."

"I saw a couple of good ones listed." Robin waved her hand in a sweeping motion. "Let's leave the decorations up for a few more days. People have commented on how much they like them."

"All right. I'll see you tomorrow." Brianna headed toward the back to get her coat.

"Have fun tonight."

"Okay. You too."

Maybe watching a movie with my dog will be fun. At least it will be relaxing.

After taking Cricket out, Brianna considered her choices for something to eat. Fixing her own food or eating a TV dinner from her freezer didn't interest her. She could order pizza and have it delivered or get a sub from the deli. Jean and Jake's wasn't an option so soon after what happened there Friday night.

"Robin told me Cooper came into the bookstore yesterday afternoon. I didn't see him or know he was there." She closed the refrigerator door and lowered her eyes to Cricket sitting on the floor.

Cricket cocked her head at Brianna and whined.

"I know, Cricket. I like him a lot." She sighed. "I thought maybe God had given me another man to love."

"Arf!"

"Shh, Cricket, Virginia doesn't want you to bark."

Someone knocked on her front door, and Cricket scooted to the door, barking wildly.

"Cricket, stop that racket." Brianna followed her dog. Her landlady would be sure to speak to her about this. "Who can that be?" With her foot, she blocked Cricket from the door and opened it.

"Cooper," she breathed, her knees weak.

Cooper, in his leather jacket, held out a small bouquet of mixed flowers. "Miss Brianna, will you please go out to dinner with me?"

She clung to the door so she wouldn't collapse.

Cricket escaped Brianna's foot and jumped against Cooper's jean-clad legs.

When Brianna reached out to accept the flowers, her fingers touched his, sending a shock wave down to her toes.

He stooped and lifted the puppy.

A whoosh of cold air hit her, releasing her from her daze. "Please, come in, Cooper. I'm sorry about Cricket. I'm trying to teach her not to jump up on people."

He stepped in and shut the door. "She's my welcoming committee, aren't you, sweet girl." After hugging Cricket and scratching her under her chin, he put her down.

Cricket lay on her stomach on the living room floor, her ears perked up, her tail sweeping the carpet.

Cooper's fresh air and aftershave scent wafted to Brianna when he spoke to her. "You haven't eaten yet, have you? I'd like to take you out."

"B-but I'm not dressed to go out. This is unexpected." She enjoyed surprises, but the shock of having Cooper standing in front of her, looking so wonderful, clouded her thinking.

"Brianna." He grasped her hands, wrapping his fingers around the flower bouquet as well. "I've been trying to find the opportunity to apologize for Friday night. I left without thanking you properly. Thank you. I had a good time. I'm sorry. Please forgive me."

She nodded, her eyes glued to his. His touch left her speechless and engulfed by another current.

"I've also been trying to work up the courage to ask you to go out with me. Will you?"

"I ... yes." *He said he didn't date.* "But where are Noah and Lexie?"

"They're with the Archers."

"Oh." She remembered her earlier conversation with Robin. "This is what Robin meant when she told me to have fun tonight."

"I suppose so. Will you go?" His face expressed the eagerness of a boy waiting to open his Christmas presents.

"Yes, of course." She stepped back, and he released her hands. "Let me get ready." She had to put the flowers in water, change her clothes, and shut Cricket in her crate.

"What you're wearing is fine. Your sweater is pretty and very seasonal."

She'd chosen the sweater this morning because it was appropriate to be worn for work today, creamy white with red hearts. It looked nice with her black slacks and clogs. And it was sweet that he noticed it.

"Thank you. I'll be only a few minutes." She spun away to find a vase for the flowers. Butterflies still fluttered in her stomach, but she had calmed enough to think again.

Instead of watching an actress find her true love in a romantic movie, she'd be living her own romantic Valentine's plot line tonight.

Brianna sauntered through the almost deserted, snow-covered park with Cooper, her hand clasped in his.

They met two other dog owners walking their pets and an older couple out for a stroll.

"I've had a good time with you tonight." Cooper squeezed Brianna's gloved hand.

Brianna had agreed to his suggestion of a walk in the park, extending their date a little longer. It wasn't late, but he had to get the kids from the Archers and put them to bed. Cricket, excited to be released from her crate for a walk, trotted beside her. Fluffy snowflakes falling through the cold, quiet night air, and the lights scattered along the sidewalk and throughout the park, created an enchanting ambiance.

"And I with you." Every time her eyes met his, a wave of warmth rolled through her. "Thank you for taking me out."

Over dinner, they'd talked about their families and their jobs. Although they worshiped in different churches, he shared her faith in Christ. And the more Brianna learned about Cooper Stiles, the more he captivated her. *Is it too early to call it love?*

"I don't think of burgers and fries as a romantic Valentine dinner. I would have made a reservation for a nice restaurant, but I wasn't sure you'd accept my last-minute invitation."

"It was fine, Cooper. I like burgers and fries. Being with you made dinner special." And it was their first time alone together.

"But if I had planned ahead and hadn't resisted my better judgment ..."

She shook her head. "I didn't think you'd ever ask me to go out. I never knew if you'd smile or frown at me. Besides, you said you didn't date."

"I'm sorry." He gazed down at her. "That day before Christmas, when I first saw you in the bookstore, I wanted to know your name and was afraid to ask." He shook his head. "I've been the victim of several matchmaking schemes by my friends. Especially the women, my mom included, think I should be married with a family by now. I've tried to avoid getting trapped in a relationship not of my choosing. Noah and Lexie gave me an excuse not to get involved."

That explained a lot. "You're doing a good job as a surrogate parent, Cooper." She squeezed his hand. "When I taught school, I saw how single parents struggled to balance parenting responsibilities with work and other things that demanded their attention. Noah and Lexie need you, especially with their mother away."

"Thank you for the encouragement. Sometimes I wonder." He sighed "When I look at them, I see my brother. I'd never want to let him down. He and Tessa named me in their wills as the kids' guardian, so when Tessa said she wanted them to live with me, I agreed. I'm not sorry I took on the job, but it's hard at times."

He stopped and turned her to face him. He brushed her cheek with his gloved hand. "My niece and nephew will be my priority until their mother comes home. But when I'm away from you, I want to be with you. I'm falling in love with you, Brianna Kinney." His gaze darted from her eyes to her lips. "Do you think it's too early in our relationship for me to say I love you?"

Her breath caught as he lowered his face toward hers. She

didn't turn away but closed her eyes. His lips were soft and cold and gentle as he pressed them against hers. She responded, placing one hand on his back. It was just the two of them, she in the circle of his arms.

Cricket whined and jumped against her leg.

Cooper pulled away from Brianna's lips and looked down at Cricket. "You don't think she's jealous, do you?"

Brianna shrugged and laughed. "Could be. Or maybe she's getting cold."

He lifted the puppy and held her against his chest. "Sorry, sweet girl, I forgot about you. I like you too."

Cricket's body wiggled, and she licked his cheek.

With a chuckle, Brianna took Cricket from Cooper, and Cricket snuggled in her arms. Cooper fell into step with Brianna, his arm around her shoulders, holding her close.

She rested her head against him. "Friday night you upset me when you left so abruptly like you did. I thought you were mad because Lexie fell asleep with Cricket. And even before that, I thought you were mad at me for causing the trouble about Lexie wanting a puppy."

"I'm sorry. I didn't like Lexie's fussing for a puppy, but I didn't blame you. And I wasn't mad at you Friday night. The pull of my attraction to you was so strong, I panicked and escaped. I know I behaved badly. On Sunday, I couldn't think of the words to say to make amends." He squeezed her shoulder. "Yesterday, I came up with plan B, which included leaving the kids with Robin and Ethan and asking you out."

"I guess plan B was a success." She gazed up at him. "And you chose me."

Although receiving a little nudge from the Archers, their date hadn't been the result of a matchmaking scheme. A strong current of attraction already existed between them.

He pulled her closer. "You know, we might call Cricket a

matchmaker of sorts. Lexie's love for your dog brought us together."

Cricket's head snapped up when she heard her name.

"That's true. She's a treasure for sure."

Stopping at the park entrance, Cooper looked down at Brianna. "Lexie wanted to come tonight when she learned I had a date with you. I said no, that Cricket would be staying home, and she and Noah would go to the Archers. However, my better judgment now urges me to ask you to go ice skating with Noah, Lexie, and me on Saturday."

"I'd love to go skating with you. I have to work in the morning, but I'll be free for the rest of the day." She adored Noah and Lexie, so it was little sacrifice to include them in her dates with Cooper. Or maybe for her to be included in their outings. For now.

If she could be with Cooper, it didn't matter. When Tessa returned, there would be more times like tonight for just Cooper and her.

"Great. I'm sure they'll like having you join us. I know I will."

A car passed by them on the street, then they crossed. Virginia's living room lights reflected on the snow beneath her window. Brianna's outside light created a pool of brightness around her back door. She paused at the bottom of her steps.

Cooper tugged her into the shadow of the carport. He leaned against her car and pulled her into his arms, Cricket wedged between them.

Cricket sighed and shifted but didn't struggle to get away.

Cooper lifted Brianna's chin, and her heart skittered. His eyes caressed her face. "I'll call you tomorrow."

"I'll be waiting for your call, Cooper Stiles."

He brushed his hand across her cheek and kissed her again.

Brianna wouldn't trade her own Valentine's script for any romance movie on TV.

ABOUT BETH E. WESTCOTT

Beth began her writing career in second grade when her poem about her lamb appeared in the school newspaper. With an early love for books and reading, writing for children was her first passion. She writes stories for her grandchildren for their birthdays.

Beth has written articles for church newsletters, ventriloquist routines for her husband, church programs, devotions, puppet scripts, short stories and articles for children, Bible studies for women, and Bible lessons for children.

She earned a B.A. in English from Hartwick College, an ETTA certificate from Practical Bible Training School, a diploma from the Child Evangelism Fellowship Training Institute, obtained training with a crisis pregnancy ministry, and took a course in biblical counseling through a local church. Completing the basic course with the Institute of Children's Literature in 1992, set her on a path to learn to write well and seek publication. She attends Montrose Christian Writers Conference and is presently a member of a local writing/critique group.

A home missionary with Child Evangelism Fellowship from 1979 to 1984, she. assisted her husband as a Good News Club teacher and teacher trainer. As a pastor's wife for 33 years, she taught children, teens, and adult women and has been involved in music ministry. She became a 4-H leader for eight years, when her children belonged to 4-H, and homeschooled her three children for 12 years.

Some of Beth's holiday manuscripts appeared in Lillenas Drama's *Program Builders,* several devotions in *Penned from the Heart,* and one in *The Secret Place.* "Sadie and the Princess," a short story for preteens, is included in *Heart-warming Horse Stories.* Four contemporary Christian romance novels, *Meadow Song, Heart's Desire, A Heart's Journey,* and *Her Heart's Longing,* have been published by Scrivenings Press.

OTHER ROMANCE NOVELLA COLLECTIONS

Much Ado about Romance

A novella collection

The Marry Wives of Sweetheart by Shannon Sue Dunlap—Mrs. Augusta Page knows best—for her daughter, Anne, and the whole town of Sweetheart, Texas. When Anne's former boyfriend, Connor Fenton, returns after many years of absence, it's a rocky road to reconciliation. Joshua attempts to rekindle their romance, but Anne's wounded heart never forgave him when he left her behind for the big city.

Augusta enlists the help of her longtime buddy Veronica "Ronnie" Ford to do a little matchmaking, but obstacles abound. Her husband is against the romance, and foolish friend-of-the-family John Falstaff has taken a shine to Anne and asked for assistance. But the biggest obstacle is her daughter's stubborn heart. Mrs. Page and Mrs. Ford have their work cut out to inspire Anne Page to join the ranks of the "marry" wives of Sweetheart.

The Tempest in the Bay by Susan Page Davis—A famous writer has retreated to an island home with only his daughter. For ten years, he's hidden away and not sent his publisher any new manuscripts. His daughter Violet is now 20 and wondering if it's time for her to see more of the world since her contact with the mainland is only through Darrell, a rather sluggish man from the shore community who brings out supplies once a month.

Paul's brother Barney and the CEO of his publisher's company set out on a yacht to track him down. But a storm intervenes, and when the sailing party lands on his island, Paul isn't sure he wants to go back.

Much Ado about Matrimony by Linda Fulkerson—Tricia Waters has resigned herself to the fact she'll never have a happily ever after, so she focuses on making her cousin's upcoming wedding a memorable one. But when she discovers her ex-fiancé is the best man, she vows to evade him. That is, until the two must work together to prevent the happy couple from breaking up.

Reeling from a personal tragedy, Dr. Ben McIntyre travels to serve as his buddy's best man only to discover the maid of honor is the love of his life. Or she was, until she ended their engagement six years earlier. He plans to keep his distance from Tricia. When circumstances keep pushing them to work together, Ben learns that avoidance is futile.

Get your copy here:

https://scrivenings.link/muchadoaboutromance

Love Delivered

A novella collection

***Romance at Register Five* (by Amy R Anguish)**—Mack McDonald
isn't happy about the Grocerease app coming to his grocery store. But
he's committed to the sixty-day trial period, and braces himself to lose
money. Kaitlyn Daniels loves how the Grocerease app helps her make
ends meet so she can assist her mom, the reason she moved to small
Sassafras, AR. Mack and Kaitlyn struggle to overcome differing
opinions on the perks of the app. But if they don't, it could keep them
from something even better.

***Where Love is Planted* (by Sarah Anne Crouch)**—Ivy Aaronson is
surrounded by family at their flower shop in West Texas—just the way
she likes it. But she's given up hope on ever finding a man who
understands her choices. When attorney Grant Keller orders flowers for
his mother, Ivy wonders if maybe there are indeed some considerate
men left in the world…until she finds out Grant's relationship with his
parents is less than ideal. How can Ivy ever find love when every man
she meets puts career over family?

***Sweet Delivery* (by Heather Greer)**—After winning Cake That, Will
Forrester thinks his Pastry Perfect Baking Dreams have come true. The
sweetness fades when a chain bakery moves to town, and Will must

adjust his plans to keep his customers. Hiring Erica Gerard is one of those changes. As they work together, Erica challenges Will and offers new ideas to improve the bakery. Soon, Erica and Will start bringing out the best in each other. But Erica harbors a secret, and if it's discovered, Will might never be the same.

***The Mermaids, the Ex, and USSS* (by Rachel Herod)**—Braig Sanborn is the most loyal employee the United States Shipping Service has ever seen, which is why he agreed to transfer across the country with only a few weeks' notice. Bailey Bivens is so busy planning a friend's wedding, she didn't expect to fall for the carrier who delivers packages to her house. When they both find themselves in too deep, will they agree the relationship was doomed from the start?

Get your copy here:

https://scrivenings.link/lovedelivered

Love in Any Season

A novella collection

Spring Has Sprung—by Regina Rudd Merrick

Laurel Pascal, Assistant City Manager of Spring, Kentucky, is tasked with organizing the town's beloved Daffodil Festival, and she's not happy. An allergy sufferer all her life, she dreads the season from the first Daffodil bloom in the yard to the last coat of pollen on her car. Newcomer Dr. Owen Roswell volunteers to help, and soon finds that not only does Laurel need his expertise as an allergist, but help in appreciating the season she's obligated to celebrate.

What does he want more—for Laurel to fall in love with his favorite season? Or him?

The Missing Piece—by Amy R. Anguish

Beth Norton and Tommy England grew up together with best-friend moms who had a love of quilting and a business celebrating the craft. When high school ended, though, so did Beth and Tommy's friendship.

When Tommy moves back after seven years and his mother's death, he can't understand why Beth is so angry with him. Helping Beth and her mother stabilize the finances of the business, they're forced to work together. As Tommy sorts through his mother's things, he finds an unfinished quilt, and it turns into a joint project.

With each stitch taken, they work toward more than just a completed blanket.

A Sweet Dream Come True—by Sarah Anne Crouch

Isaac Campbell is living his dream of running an ice cream shop but fears he won't last past the first difficult year. Mel Wilson is a busy single mother who longs to be a chocolatier but is too afraid to turn her dreams into reality.

When Mel and Isaac meet at Bestwood, Tennessee's fall festival, it seems like divine providence. But once Mel agrees to help Isaac bring in customers by selling her chocolates at his shop, she realizes how challenging running a business can be.

Can Mel and Isaac trust in God's provision and make a leap of faith? Will their partnership end in disaster, or will it be a sweet dream come true?

Sugar and Spice—by Heather Greer

Emeline Becker, owner of Sugar and Spice Bakery, loves New Kuchenbrünn, except for the gingerbread. As the only bakery, she supplies the annual Gingerbread Festival with the one treat she can't stand. It's gingerbread everywhere.

Things get worse when Ryker Lehmann is hired as the festival photographer. He was her secret teen crush, her sister's boyfriend, and witness to her worst humiliation. Plus, he broke her sister's heart and bruised hers when he left town after graduation. Now, he's back in town, determined to fix their friendship before the festival ends.

With gingerbread and Ryker together, can Emmie make it through the festival with her mind and heart intact?

Get your copy here:
https://scrivenings.link/loveinanyseason

Candy Cane Wishes and Saltwater Dreams

A collection of Christmas beach romances

***Mistletoe Make-believe* by Amy Anguish**—Charlie Hill's family thinks his daughter Hailey needs a mom–to the point they won't get off his back until he finds her one. Desperate to be free from their nagging, he asks a stranger to pretend she's his girlfriend during the holidays. When romance author Samantha Arwine takes a working vacation to St. Simon's Island over Christmas, she never dreamed she'd be involved in a real-life romance. Are the sparks between her and Charlie real? Or is her imagination over-acting … again?

***A Hatteras Surprise* by Hope Toler Dougherty**—Ginny Stowe spent years tending a childhood hurt that dictated her college study and work. Can time with an island visitor with ties to her past heal lingering wounds and lead her toward a happy Christmas … and more? Ben Daniels intends to hire a new branch manager for a Hatteras Island bank, then hurry back to his promotion and Christmas in Charlotte. Spending time with a beautiful local, however, might force him to adjust his sails.

***A Pennie for Your Thoughts* by Linda Fulkerson**—When the Lakeshore Homeowner's Association threatens to condemn the cabin Pennie Vaughn inherited from her foster mother, her only hope of funding the needed repairs lies in winning a travel blog contest. Trouble is, Pennie never goes anywhere. Should she use the all-expenses paid Hawaiian vacation offered to her by her ex-fiancé? The trip that would have been their honeymoon?

Mr. Sandman by **Regina Rudd Merrick**—Events manager Taylor Fordham's happily-ever-after was snatched from her, and she's saying no to romance and Christmas. When she meets two new friends—the cute new chef at Pilot Oaks and a contributor on a sci-fi fan fiction website who enjoys debate—her resolve begins to waver. Just when she thinks she can loosen her grip on thoughts of love, a crisis pulls her back. There's no way she's going to risk her heart again.

Coastal Christmas by **Shannon Taylor Vannatter**—Lark Pendleton is banking on a high-society wedding to make her grandparent's inn at Surfside Beach, Texas the venue to attract buyers. Tasked with sprucing up the inn, she hires Jace Wilder, whose heart she once broke. When the bride and groom turn out to be Lark's high school nemesis and ex-boyfriend, she and Jace embark on a pretend romance to save the wedding. But when real feelings emerge, can they overcome past hurts?

Stay up-to-date on your favorite books and authors with our free e-newsletters.

ScriveningsPress.com

www.ingramcontent.com/pod-product-compliance
Lightning Source LLC
Chambersburg PA
CBHW060618100726
47907CB00006B/1667